NMU/ExP

We hope you enjoy this book. Please return or renew it by the due date.

You can renew it at www.norfolk.gov.uk/libraries or by using our free library app.

Otherwise you can phone 0344 800 8020 - please have your library card and PIN ready.

You can sign up for email reminders too.

NORFOLK ITEM

30129 086 176 840

NORFOLK COUNTY COUNCIL
LIBRARY AND INFORMATION SERVICE

D1142784

Legend Press Ltd, 51 Gower Street, London, WC1E 6HJ
info@legend-paperbooks.co.uk | www.legendpress.co.uk

Contents © Sarah Burton 2020
The right of the above author to be identified as the author of this work has
been asserted in accordance with the Copyright, Designs and Patents Act
1988. British Library Cataloguing in Publication Data available.

Print ISBN 978-1-78955-1-266
Ebook ISBN 978-1-78955-1-273
Set in Times. Printing managed by Jellyfish Solutions Ltd
Cover design by Sarah Whittaker | www.whittakerbookdesign.com

Sarah Burton was the Course Director of Cambridge University's MSt in Creative Writing. She has published non-fiction, children's fiction, short stories and reviews for *The Times*, *The Spectator*, *The Guardian* and *The Independent*. *The Strange Adventures of H* is her debut novel for adults.

As love is the most noble and divine passion of the soul, so it is to that which we may justly attribute all the real satisfactions of life; and without it, man is unfinish'd and unhappy.

Aphra Behn, *The Fair Jilt*

Though love, all soft and flattering, promises nothing but pleasures; yet its consequences are often sad and fatal. It is not enough to be in love to be happy; since Fortune, who is capricious, and takes delight to trouble the repose of the most elevated and virtuous, has very little respect for passionate and tender hearts, when she designs to produce strange adventures.

Aphra Behn, *The History of St Agnes de Castro*

PROLOGUE

f you have ever wondered why hangings always take place on a Monday, it is so that the chaplain of the gaol may dedicate all of Sunday to readying his charge to meet his maker. On this Sunday the usual sermon is set aside and in its stead the condemned sermon is preached to the condemned man, who is standing in the condemned pew, in front of which is placed his coffin, lest there is any chance he may for a moment forget that he is indeed to be launched into eternity on the morrow. (I do not pretend to know if this is universally the case, but it is certainly so at Newgate.)

For weeks before, all prisoners will have been required to pray daily at chapel "for those now awaiting the awful execution of the law", and while the condemned pew may have held ten or twenty following the last Old Bailey sessions, this figure will have dwindled – by disease, by suicide and by reprieve – until perhaps only three or four condemned men remain. On the occasion I relate, there was left only one.

On the day of the condemned sermon, the congregation in the prison chapel is swelled by visitors: curious ladies and gentlemen, who have paid for their seats, the best in the house, from which to view the proceedings. They have come for the next part of the ceremony: the service for the dead. This the chaplain directs at the man who is to be hanged.

He speaks at length in awful tones of vice and retribution, sin and suffering, shame and sorrow, grief and wretchedness, hellfire and brimstone; and of those orphaned and widowed by the crime and – worst for the condemned man – those to be orphaned and widowed on the morrow. The condemned man generally collapses, fainting under the weight of his fate, or he may turn white and clammy and become as still as a statue. Some go into a frenzy, spasm, fit, scream, and rave. This is allowed to go on for several minutes before the man is restrained, in order that those guilty of less serious crimes may be suitably impressed with the terror of his case, and so that the curious ladies and gentlemen may get their money's worth.

The service over, the wretch will be returned to the condemned cell, a stone box perhaps 6' by 8', furnished with a rope mat, a stable rug and a vigorous population of vermin of all kinds. His feast is bread, water and gruel. A small barred hole in the wall admits little air and less light, and he is allowed a candle at night. At first, he shared this cell with two or three others, but they have gone on, one way or another, and now he is alone.

I cannot tell you how Praisegod Fricker spent his last night on Earth, as I was not there, and the particulars I have given here I have found out by general enquiry. I know only that the chaplain will surely have exerted himself to break the condemned man's spirit, if it be not already broken, and to urge him to confess and repent, accept his fate with humility and, above all, not struggle with the hangman.

Fricker made no confession and remained unrepentant and by the time he was given the sacrament early the next morning, he was already drunk. Pinioned and shackled, with the hangman's noose ready round his neck, he was placed on a cart, facing the rear. He was then driven backwards through the city, through the crowds which lined the route at Holborn and St Giles, until he arrived at Tyburn, to a crowd of several thousand who had come to see him hang. The next part I may relate with greater certainty as to the facts, for I was there.

We had arrived two hours before the hanging, to get a good place, and indeed we were about ten heads in front of the Irish women selling fruit under the gallows. Their bawling, at such close range, with the cries of the piemen and gingerbread sellers and children blowing on their tin trumpets combining with the cacophony of the crowd, made it difficult for Kat and me to talk as we waited, and, being of low stature, I could see nothing past my immediate neighbours. But Kat was taller, and was telling me by signs that the cart bearing Fricker was arriving when a low rumble swept through the crowd. A hanging is like the theatre, but the condemned man must take his bow before the performance. This Fricker did now, as he was driven through the crowd who cheered and jeered in equal measure.

This, as you know, is unusual, as the vast majority of the spectators are generally united for or against the condemned man. They will always barrack and hoot at the executioner, and often throw stones at him, but depending on his crime and his demeanour, the condemned man often elicits some pity from the crowd, especially if his victim is seen as somehow bearing some guilt for their fate. Fricker's case divided the crowd after this fashion: his convictions were for arson and murder, each on its own a capital offence, but the house he had set ablaze was a brothel, and the woman who had burned within it was one of the most infamous bawds in London. So while his crime was heinous, there were many who sympathised with the intention to rid the city of such vermin, and consequently some cheered him as a hero, while others cried, "For shame," and "Pity on the poor whores."

A mixed cheer went up as the cart drew level with the gallows and silence fell as the crowd waited to see what, if anything, would be his final words. Would he beg forgiveness and make a good death, or would he scorn justice and die game? I had once been to a hanging where a famous highwayman had taken the constables, the chaplain and even the hangman warmly by the hand, smiling and thanking them, and then sung 'The Miller's Cock' for the crowd, many of whom shed tears at such a display of courage and defiance. I do not know whether this was worse than seeing the condemned man weeping, fainting, pissing himself and having to be half-carried to the appointed mark.

Fricker was visibly trembling, but though he staggered slightly, he seemed to resolve to gather himself, and then cried out: "God damn all whores!"

At this, a deafening cheer went up.

"And fuck you all!" he added, to an even greater wave of something between a mighty groan of opprobrium and a roar of admiration.

The hangman now had to act quickly. He covered Fricker's face, ran up the steps and attached the rope to the crossbeam. He came down, took away the ladder, and lashed the horse, who flew forward, pulling the cart behind him, leaving my gentleman swinging, kicking the air.

The onlookers were silent as he kicked and choked and shat himself. It was going on too long. People began to murmur disapproval. And then, to a universal gasp, the gauze slipped from his face, revealing his livid features, his swollen lips and ears, blood issuing from both, his eyes red and protruding from their sockets looking, as it seemed, directly at me. And still he kicked and kicked. I turned my face away.

"You must look," Kat said, forcing me, taking my chin in her hand. "You must see that it is done, or you will have no peace."

As he continued to struggle, the rope twisted, and to my relief his head turned away from me. The spectators were becoming increasingly dismayed. At this point, of course, friends or family of the condemned man would not be prevented if they chose to hang on his legs and end his agony. But it seemed Fricker had no friends or family. Voices appealed to the hangman to do the job himself. He hesitated, and as he did so those close enough became aware of a new horror. The rope had stretched so much as Fricker struggled that the tips of his toes now touched the rung of the ladder leaning against the upright. His feet scrabbled desperately for purchase. In one professional lunge, the hangman kicked away the ladder and jumped on Fricker's legs. This must have broken his neck, for after a few convulsive twitches, he was still.

There was a great sigh, as I suppose everyone had been holding their breath.

"There. It is done," said Kat finally.

And it is true that I did find peace of a kind. In the first place Fricker could now do me no harm. And in the second place it drew a line under the whorehouse murder. For though he had indeed set the fire which burned the house and the old bawd in it, neither Fricker nor anyone else knew that she was already as good as dead.

But Kat and I knew, for I had tied her up and Kat had beat her with the poker.

PART ONE

'H'

1

 was always H. As a child I never wondered whether I was once a Hannah, a Henrietta, a Hephzibah or anything else – H was my proper name as far as I was concerned and in any case I was not encouraged to ask questions. I was born in 1650, the youngest of eight children all told. The first two children, like our mother, survived only in family prayers; the six living were all girls.

As soon as my oldest sisters were of an age, Father was anxious to see them off his hands, and they were equally anxious to escape the parsonage. Generally, Father devoted all his energies to writing his sermons, but a frenzy would descend on the household whenever a bachelor – of any age or disposition – had the ill luck to cross his path. Clarissa and Diana were engaged and married with such dispatch that Diana's husband always claimed he knocked on the door only to borrow a book and came away with a wife.

So that left four: Evelyn, the twins, Grace and Frances, and me. I now see that Evelyn was spared marriage because we three were too young to be left with our father only. And Evelyn had always been a little mother to me. It was Evelyn I shared a bed with and who sat beside me through all the illnesses which beset childhood. She was, as you shall learn, the best of sisters.

I could never know enough about my mother. Evelyn would hold me on her lap and stroke my hair and feed me the scraps I hungered for: how good and kind she was, and how she would have loved me, had she lived. I clung to these thoughts as my father and grown-up sisters had a particular coldness reserved only for me, which I understood arose from a sense that my arrival into the world was a very poor trade for Mother's death.

Indeed, I was a naughty child. One of my earliest memories was of when I was very small and our cat, Tibbs, had kittens. Being left to my own devices, I decided to bathe the newborns as I had seen neighbours in their cottages bathing their babies. Our cook had a great ladle, which I fetched from the kitchen, and filling a basin with water (with great difficulty – I remember little of the incident but the trouble I had carrying the basin once it was full), I put each kitten in the ladle and dunked it in the water until, as I thought, it was clean enough; but actually, as one of my sisters observed, until it was dead enough.

I was upset that the pretty kittens had become still and cold, and Tibbs was howling her head off, but my father, when he was summoned, only kicked Tibbs out of the way and scolded me for spilling water on the carpet, swept up the kittens and cast them on the dung heap. He called me "a wicked, unnatural child", and sent me to my room. But Tibbs slept on my bed that night and purred. I could not understand it at all.

Another event I clearly recall, as though it were yesterday, because of its awful consequence, is my first sight of plays and playing, and it is by this detail that I know it was after the year 1660 and the return of the King. I had learned that a fair was coming to Harlow and I asked and asked and asked Evelyn to take me. She said no, I should stay at home with my twin sisters as she had things to manage as Father was away from home. But I had no mind to this and kept on. When Grace added her voice to mine Evelyn capitulated and we three left Frances climbing trees and set off for Harlow Fair.

I had never seen anything like a fair, I think, in my life. I straightway felt I was not dressed finely enough (though I had nothing fine, had I thought of it) as everyone seemed to be putting their best foot forward: bonnets fluttered with new ribbons, and Sunday bests were given a weekday outing. I saw some Morris dancers and some bell-ringers and we pushed our way through a crowd to discover they were all watching a cockfight, which I did not think nice entertainment, but which Grace affirmed was "better than Morris dancing, and more humane".

Then there was a tent of curiosities, in which, a man outside cried, there were "abundance of strange and fearfully deformed creatures", including a dwarf, a mermaid and a human pincushion. I was not suffered to see these wonders, as Evelyn said she did not want to be up all night with me having nightmares. I contented myself with watching the people go in and out, hoping to catch a glimpse of a monster through the curtain.

Evelyn showed me the men standing in line advertising for work.

"See, he carries a crook," she said. "He does that so everyone may know he is a shepherd, and if they want someone to look after sheep, they may find him. See, he carries a trowel; if someone wants a wall built, they can find him to do it. And he is a carter, for he carries a whip." And so on she went down the row of men, now making me guess each man's business by his sign, and as usual I admired her for her great learning in these matters, for Evelyn was not only kind but clever.

At the fair I noticed some young ladies in very fine clothes, but something in their demeanour caused me to look twice. They were *wearing* fine clothes but did not seem as I had seen fine ladies to behave. They were laughing and talking and looking quite boldly into the faces of the men who walked by, and sometimes called out to them, while some of the men talked back to them as they would not to fine ladies.

"And who are those women?" I asked. "What do they sell?" I could not make out any sign like a crook or a trowel. Evelyn grabbed hold of me more roughly than I was used to and pulled me away.

I think she would have pulled me all the way home except that we came to a troupe of players. I begged to be allowed to stay and watch what was occurring, but Grace wanted to look at some silks a pedlar was selling. Evelyn said Father would not approve of us watching a play, and Grace said Father would not approve of us being at a fair, so in for a penny, in for a pound, and why shouldn't H have a little liberty now and then? So I was allowed to watch. And my sisters soon forgot the pedlar and the silks and they watched too.

The players were telling an old story called *The Taming of the Shrew* by William Shakespeare. It was about a maid called Katharina who was proud and strong-willed, shouting and carrying on that she would not marry this man called Petruchio who was also proud and strong-willed and shouting. It was most amusing and we all laughed a good deal, but when it was over Evelyn noticed we had lost Grace and was looking about for her. During the play, Grace had had eyes only for Petruchio, as if she thought he were a real person. "He is so fine! So manly!" she exclaimed. "*I* would have him for a husband!" Grace had never had much wit about her and I had heard my father say she was gormless, and I remember wondering what gorm was, and why Grace had none. And now she had disappeared.

Evelyn went looking for her among the people watching, but I thought she might have gone to look at Petruchio again, so went behind the stage. You may imagine my surprise when I saw Katharina standing by a tree, her skirts lifted up, passing water like any man. Indeed, she was a man, of course. When he turned and saw me, he noted my amazement and laughed. I said I was looking for my sister and he helped me find Grace, who was indeed talking to Petruchio. Before they saw me, I noticed the tips of their fingers were twined together, as I had seen Diana and her husband do before they were married. My sister looked very happy and her face was all red, also like Diana.

Then Evelyn came and said we should go home and she and Grace argued somewhat. While that was happening, Petruchio was putting black paint on his face for the next play and the player dressed as Katharina asked me my name and said it was a funny one, and I said everyone said that, and then he showed me the properties they used in the plays. Up close they did not seem nearly so fine. Then he feigned to stab himself with a knife and I was frighted and cried out as I saw blood spurting out, but then he showed me it was only red ribbons. It was all most fascinating and I asked him if he liked to play ladies and he said not so much as he used to because only boys should play ladies, on account of them being smaller and having high voices, but that because the theatres had been shut for so long by old Oliver all the boy players had grown up, as he had. Besides, he said, there are now women on the stage in London, so there will soon be no more boy players anyway. Perhaps he could tell I was thinking what it would be like to be a player and dress up and make-believe rather than have to be married, as he said: "Perhaps one day you will be a fine actress in a playhouse in London, and I shall come and see you playing Katharina, and I will say to all the fine people: 'I knew Mistress H when she was but a girl.'" And instead of bowing, remembering he was in a gown, he curtseyed low to me, which made us both laugh.

At that moment Evelyn came and snatched my hand and marched me away so I could not even say goodbye to Katharina. She looked furious.

"Will Grace not come with us?" I asked.

"No," she snapped. "The little fool will get us all in a deal of trouble."

And indeed she did. Grace did not come home before our father's return, but was not missed until supper, when the whole story came out. Evelyn, Frances and I were sent to our room with no supper and no light, where we lay awake, listening for the latch on the garden gate. It never came.

In the morning, we went down as usual for prayers, which were unusually full of hellfire and damnation, and when we had finished our father detained us before we sat down to breakfast. I remember that he did not look at us while he spoke, but kept his eyes turned steadily towards the window.

"Children, I have very bad news to impart to you, concerning your sister. It is the worst sort of news."

At this, I burst into tears, as I knew poor Grace must be dead. I had worried all night that she may have fallen down a hole, or into a river, or been attacked by murderers on her way home in the dark. Now I knew it was true, and it was all my fault, because I had caused my sisters to stop and watch the players.

"Your sister, whose name my lips refuse to speak, has left this house and will never return. Her infamous behaviour has disgraced us all. It will be a most wonderful thing if our family ever recovers from the shame she has brought upon our house. No respectable man will wish to attach his name to that of a family bemired in vice of the most reprehensible and evil kind. Your sister has ruined us." He paused for a moment and seemed to hold his breath. Still looking out of the window, he said: "Her name is not to be mentioned again. She is dead to us."

We sat down to breakfast, but my sisters and I could not eat. My father ate in silence. It was as though the world had ended.

2

ne evening, many months later, Frances and I were sitting in the bedchamber I shared with Evelyn hemming handkerchiefs, which was our usual occupation when our father decided we had been reading too much, when Evelyn came in, her face as white as the cotton in my hand.

"Whatever's the matter?" I asked.

"I've seen Grace," Evelyn said and burst into tears.

When she could speak again Evelyn told us Grace's tale. That day at the fair the player (Petruchio) had given Grace strong waters and "ill-used" her and she had been too ashamed to come home and face Father. She thought she loved the player and determined to stay with him – they had been to London and he was kind at first but abandoned her when she announced she was with child. "Of course," Evelyn added. Now she was ill and starving and begging Evelyn to intercede with our father on her behalf. "On her way here, even… to eat," Evelyn broke down, sobbing into Frances's shoulder, "she had to… with men… just to eat."

I didn't then understand what this meant, let alone how Grace could be having a baby, for Evelyn had not mentioned her being married.

"Where is Grace now?" I asked.

"I left her at the crossroads. She will not come until I have spoken to Father."

At this Frances jumped up and snatched up her shawl.

"I will go to her," she said, and ran out.

"He will be kind, will he not, Evelyn?"

Evelyn looked at me.

"I'm sure when he knows she carries his grandchild his heart will soften towards her," she said and kissed me on the forehead before telling me to stay in our room and disappearing downstairs. I lay down on our bed to await the outcome of the interview but almost immediately heard raised voices. I ran out onto the landing and saw Father emerge from his study, followed by Evelyn, who was hanging onto his sleeve.

"Please, Father, I beg of you, if you won't have her back at least let her come in and eat something. Grace is—"

Sometimes something happens that changes everything. My father struck Evelyn, hard, across the face.

"I forbid you to mention her name again!" he said. "Ever!"

Evelyn stood absolutely still, her hand to her cheek, staring at him. Something had shifted in her.

"I'm going to bring her back," she declared, and moved towards the door. My father sprang forward and snatched her by the arm.

"If you leave this house now, you may never return." His voice sounded strangled. His face was purple. "You are as wicked as she is."

"It is not me that is wicked!" cried Evelyn, struggling to free herself.

"Don't go, Evelyn!" I cried, running down the stairs. But she went to the door and was gone.

I stood before my father, trembling.

"Punish *me*, Father!" I cried. "I was the one who made them watch the play! It's all my fault! Beat me, lock me up, do what you will, but please don't send my sisters away!"

He said nothing, but looked at me in a strange new way.

"Evelyn!" I cried, and ran to the door. As I grabbed hold of the latch a sound made me turn back. Father had fallen to his knees, gasping, and was clutching his chest. I knew I should do something. Should I run for the doctor? Or should I stay and help Father? He collapsed sideways and lay on the floor. I hopped from foot to foot, afraid to approach him, afraid to leave him. I snatched his coat from its hook, wrapped it into a bundle and endeavoured to make a pillow for his head. I knelt beside my father, watching him, his deep scooping breaths becoming more laboured, then shallower. Then he was quiet for a few moments and with a great moan he was still.

Now I had killed Father as well as Mother.

Straight after the funeral the whole family gathered at our house, to decide what was to be done with me, Evelyn and Frances, now that we were orphans. That is to say, the whole family except Grace, who was not at the crossroads when my sisters had gone to find her that night. We learned from Clarissa's husband that she had been taken up by the watch and conveyed to the House of Correction. He was not without influence in the town, being himself a clergyman, and had contrived matters so that her connection with our family was not made public. Clarissa beamed round the table at this great achievement, although we knew that this meant Grace's baby would be taken from her as soon as it was born. It didn't seem anything to smile about to my childish mind.

The Reverend Grimwade then talked about finding homes for me, Evelyn and Frances, as though we were so many puppies. He looked expectantly at Diana and her husband.

"I only came to borrow a book!" said Mr Pincher, but no one laughed. He cleared his throat and shifted in his seat.

"In that case," Reverend Grimwade said, "Clarissa and I propose to take in Frances. She can help with the children."

Frances looked as if she were going to be sick. Of all of us she was the least suited to domestic life, being something of a tomboy and always happiest roving about the fields. To keep her indoors – moreover under Clarissa's chilly eye – would be like tying a bottle to a dog's tail.

"We will ask Aunt Madge to take in Evelyn," said Clarissa.

To be parted from Evelyn was a horror I had not thought of. I felt the room and everything in it roll about.

"What about H?" I heard Evelyn saying.

I looked at the grown-ups and they all looked somewhere else. What were they not saying? Where was I going?

Then I saw Evelyn's chin was trembling and Frances's face was red. Evelyn was upset and Frances was angry. What did it mean? Then it struck me. *Nobody wanted me*.

"Let's see what Aunt Madge says about Evelyn first," said Reverend Grimwade. "She will earn her keep of course. We seek no charity."

Now I must fill you in on a piece of family history. Aunt Madge was the widow of a Royalist soldier, killed at Stow-on-the-Wold in the very last battle of the First Civil War. Under the Commonwealth, all his assets had been sequestered. Aunt Madge had married again and the recent death of her second husband and his legacy, added to the recovery of her fortune from her first husband after the Restoration, had left her more than comfortably situated. The highlight of our year had always been our trip to London to visit her. Her two sons, who were away at school during our visits, like Grace and Frances, were twins, and identical in appearance but vastly different in their natures. Frederick was quiet and studious, but Roger, the elder, was reputedly a most tearing spark, and a source of great anxiety to her. Perhaps because she had only boys, Aunt Madge was very fond of us girls.

"I won't go," Evelyn said, as we lay in bed that night.

"You will," I said. "You must."

We were turning the matter over in our minds, when Frances crept in.

"I must tell you something," she whispered, and we made room for her in our bed. "I'm not going to Clarissa's," she said. "I'm going to run away."

I instantly guessed this had something to do with her soldier-boy. Evelyn and I spent all our idle moments together, but Frances preferred to spend her rare hours of freedom thinking about this boy, for whom she had conceived – it seemed to me – an odd sort of affection. One time I came upon them together in the woods while I was collecting sticks for the fire. I drew back as soon as I saw them, not exactly to spy, rather so as not to be observed while I indulged my curiosity – though Evelyn later pointed out that this was precisely what spying was. I mean to say that I had not set out to spy on them, but now that I was there, I was interested to see what they were doing. It was not at all what I had expected.

Frances appeared to be marching up and down and going through a kind of drill while her soldier-boy shouted orders. She had a stick for a musket and on his command appeared to go through a routine which I supposed involved loading it. After she had done this several times, he caught her by the arm and tried to kiss her, but she pushed him away and said "Again!" and they repeated the whole performance. I did not stay to see more, and after I had told Evelyn about it, did not think of it again until much later, and did not understand it until later still.

"But Clarissa is taking you in, Frankie. That is kind, is it not?" I ventured, as although I had never cared much for Clarissa, this had seemed well-intentioned in my eyes.

Evelyn sighed.

"Not as a sister," she said. "As a servant. Frances will be a living sign of Clarissa's charity to the world. And full cheaper than a nursemaid."

"So, in fine, I am not going to Clarissa," said Frances.

To my surprise, Evelyn did not argue with Frances's rebellion, as she usually would, being so good and wise.

"The garrison leaves next week for Cheltenham. I am going with it," she said. "We'll speak tomorrow." She kissed us both quickly, scampered off to her own room and left us full of confusing thoughts as to what was to become of us all. Any security I had believed in in this world was vanishing and I held fast to Evelyn that night as I knew she too might disappear, along with every certainty I had hitherto clung to.

3

e awoke the next morning to a knock at the door. It was a messenger boy with a letter. I took it quickly and gave him a penny. I ran up to give it to Evelyn.

"It's too soon to be from Aunt Madge," she said. "And look, it is addressed to us both."

Dear sisters,
Do not worry, I will be quite all right. The boy who delivered this should be proof enough of that.
Love from
Frankie xxx.

I ran to Frances's room. She was not there but her clothes were. This made no sense. I ran down to the front door to call the boy back, but he was gone. I ran back up to our bedroom window, to see down into the lane. There was the boy. I struggled to open the creaking window and called out "Hie! You! Boy!" and the boy heard me, and turned, and still walking, but backwards, waved to me and smiled, and I saw to my astonishment that the boy was Frances. With her hair cut off and dressed in man's apparel, she did indeed look just like a boy.

"Come back!" I shouted.

"No fear!" she called back, and was gone.

Most amazed, I ran to Evelyn and told her. She did not look as surprised as I had expected.

"Why?" I cried. "She has cut off all her pretty hair! I don't understand."

"She has not just gone *away* with the garrison," explained Evelyn, "she will *join* the garrison."

"To be a soldier?" I asked, incredulous. "Did you know?"

"Yes," said Evelyn. "I guessed. That is to say, I suspected."

"Will she… will she pass for a boy?" I asked.

"What do you think? You answered the door."

And I had to confess that if I did not recognise my own sister, there was nothing in her appearance to betray her to strangers. Almost flat-chested and with a gait that Clarissa had described as "like a carthorse", Frances might look more herself as a boy than as a girl. It was all most strange.

"Should we not stop her?" I asked.

Seeing my worried face, Evelyn took my hands and said, "Listen, H. It is what she wants. She has more chance of surviving the army than surviving Clarissa's nursery. She is free and we can do nothing but wish her well."

When Clarissa and Diana learned what had happened they quickly gave our neighbours to understand that Frances had joined Grace with distant relations in Scotland. Even in their minds they had put them as far away as possible.

"Another one gone to her ruin," said Reverend Grimwade. "Thanks be to God your poor parents are not here to suffer this further humiliation," he added to Clarissa.

"This would appear to be the end of a most distressing episode for us all," she announced, "and I earnestly hope we will now be able to forget these most undeserving of sisters."

Even when people died, you remembered them, I reflected. On the tombstones of our parents and Belinda and Abraham, our sister and brother who had died before I was born, it said 'In loving memory'. To deliberately choose to forget someone seemed to me harsh indeed, especially when they were your own family, and still alive as well.

"H, let this be a lesson of where disobedience ends," Clarissa added.

"Yes, let this be a lesson," added Diana, who always liked to remind everyone she was just as respectable as Clarissa.

"However," Reverend Grimwade said, "I have had a reply from Aunt Madge. She says that she feels it would be impossible to take Evelyn on the terms we suggest." My selfish little heart sang. She was to be spared to me at least a little longer. "She says H is too young to be parted from her sister and therefore suggests that both Evelyn and H go to live with her."

And then I don't know what my heart did – it skipped, it hollered, it turned somersaults. I jumped up and ran to Evelyn and hugged her and we both cried for pure joy and relief.

"You see, it is this unchecked show of emotion the child is subject to which concerns me," I heard Reverend Grimwade say to Diana's husband.

"Indeed," said Mr Pincher, "but she's not our problem now."

4

Getting into a stagecoach as a child had a thrilling sensation to it that I have never forgot. Quite apart from the novelty of the scenery, the other passengers who got in and out were always entertaining, even if they said nothing, for Evelyn and I would make up stories about them in our heads which we would compare when we were alone.

I must have slept a good deal of the way for when I woke up it was to the sights and sounds of London, where there is everywhere something to look at, and often to wonder at. The sheer number of citizens always struck me forcibly – how so many people lived and worked in one place, how they did not use up all the air just by breathing seemed incredible. The first time I went to London I did not sleep all night, for there were sounds, be it watchmen, linkboys, carriages, chaises, carts, drunks, dogs, church bells near and far, and other unidentifiable cries and crashes. But by the end of my first visit I was in love with the endless noise and the never-ending parade of trade and transport; here you could see the most beautiful people in the world – and the most pitiful wretches – all in the same minute, and, if you had the money, buy anything you could think of. When I went home I could not sleep again, so unused was I to silence, yet the teeming throng of humanity stayed in my head, circling my brains, peopling my dreams for a long time afterwards. Though it was two years since I had been in London, the old sensations quickly came flooding back the moment we were within its great walls.

At home if a coach stopped anywhere everyone looked up to see who would emerge and I felt mightily important if I were one of those people. However, the road to London little by little diminished both the coach and the significance of its occupants, and of course no one looked twice when we got out near Aunt Madge's house. Everyone was far too busy being Londoners to notice two little girls from the country. Evelyn knew the way to take, and although I was now a great girl of thirteen or thereabouts, I am ashamed to say I still held tight to my sister's hand in case I should get lost. I sometimes think it is the curse – or blessing – of youngest children that they never quite grow up.

The first to greet us as we arrived at Aunt Madge's house was a little terrier who barked and barked and would not let us move from the hall until our aunt appeared. She seemed older and more tired than when we had last seen her, but still retained her essential sweetness which made her pretty, and she seemed touchingly pleased to see us, and kissed and embraced us and said how we had grown and we were now quite young ladies and so on. The little dog sniffed us and our shoes and our baggage suspiciously but finally seemed satisfied that we would do and contented himself with following our aunt about.

"I got him when your uncle fell ill," explained Aunt Madge. "He kept him company when he was confined to his bed. And now he keeps me company."

"What's his name?" asked Evelyn.

"Your uncle named him Puss," replied our aunt, raising her eyebrows.

Our uncle had indeed been a merry man and though we saw little of him as he worked long hours, he would sometimes play with us, which our own father never did, and let us ride on his back like a donkey, and also make us laugh by playing jokes and tricks, mostly on poor Aunt Madge, which he would then blame on us.

Uncle Harry was a spicer and they had this great house in Cheapside with his shop underneath – all the merchants' houses in that district having shops below, and being often split into several apartments above. After my uncle's death, my aunt had considered removing to the country (where she had a house and lands I had never seen, left to her by her first husband), and disposing of the whole Cheapside property, or letting it as divided dwellings. However, in the event she had only let the shop to a bookseller and kept the kitchen at the back on the ground floor and all the four floors above. She was too old to face the rigours of country life, she said (though I believe she was not above fifty years of age), London having spoiled and made her unfit for it. She also said the London house would always be worth a deal of money because of where it was situated, at the heart of the city's trade and commerce, and she could sell it at any time and live comfortably elsewhere.

As it was a great house with ever so many rooms, Aunt Madge had given us each our own bedchamber but Evelyn saw my face, I think, and quickly said, "We should like to share if it is all the same to you, Aunt, and then you will have an extra room for visitors." Then when we had seen the bedchambers, which were most comfortable, Aunt Madge took us down to the kitchen, which I had never been in before, where there was a stout red-faced woman making pastry, and two brown children, who were filling up a great cauldron with water.

The red-faced woman did not drop so much as a cursory bob to my aunt when we came in, which I thought mighty strange, and was introduced as Cook. The children were Sal, who was about eight years old, and her brother Joe who was a year or two older. Sal looked after the hearths and Joe fetched water, ran errands, carried messages and was a general dogsbody. I wondered how Aunt Madge came to have two little Indians in the house, but held my tongue as I had one question more pressing.

When we came out of the kitchen, I asked my aunt why Cook had not curtsied, or even nodded, as lame servants may, to her mistress. My aunt simply said, "Cook is a Quaker," and seeing that this did not convey any meaning to me, added, "she believes we are all equal in the sight of God."

I thought about this reasonable belief for a moment before asking my aunt if she minded. She said no, she didn't mind, but you couldn't have a servant like that upstairs as people of quality wouldn't understand. Emboldened by my aunt's answers I asked about the brown children and she said it was a long story she would tell us someday. I thought she started to sound tired and resolved to ask no more questions if I could help it. Later on we were to meet the footmen, who were to be addressed by their Christian names, Reg and Ted, as they were brothers, and Potter and Potter would have led to too much confusion, and the maids, Fanny, Sarah and Alice were also introduced to us. They were all very pleasant, but it seemed to me a great number of people to look after just one lady.

Aunt Madge showed us the rest of the house, as she had had some rooms done over after our uncle died. In the main room, where Aunt Madge and we girls were to spend many happy times together, a new picture hung over the fireplace, showing Aunt Madge seated at a table and her twin sons standing either side of her. She said that it was in fact a painting of herself and two Fredericks, as Roger had invariably missed the appointments to sit for the painter, which she seemed a little sad about. We had not seen the painting before as Aunt had commissioned it for her husband and had hung it in our uncle's office.

"You will recall your uncle was a very busy man, and always in and out and missing meals. The painting was sort of a jest from me, to remind him of what his family looked like. Now I wish I'd had one done of him."

Lastly, we came to the largest chamber in the house,

immediately above the shop, which had been our uncle's office, and which hitherto I had only glimpsed through the door, it being out of bounds. Here sacks and barrels of goods were stored, and two or three boys had assisted my uncle with inventories, bills of sale, calculations and so on, and used to run up and down the stairs continually between the office and the shop with messages and queries. I was looking forward to having a closer view of this room as Madge unlatched the great door and stood back to enjoy the effect on us. For it was entirely changed. This vast space was now lined entirely with books. We gasped.

"I did not know what to do with this room," she said, "so I brought the library up from Frocester. We never had space for it in town before." She could see at once that we approved of the transformation she had effected.

We had had few books at home, and reading, apart from the Bible, had never been encouraged. None of us had been to school. Mother had taught our elder sisters perhaps hoping it would in a manner filter down through the family, which it did tolerably. I could read and write with great facility from an early age, but my general knowledge was lamentable. I was also, as I think Evelyn was, still quite innocent of the ways of the world. Grace's fate had formed a horrible lesson which seemed to teach that the less we knew the better.

This was like opening the gates of paradise.

"Here, my dears," she announced, "is your university. Read widely and without prejudice. The whole world is within these walls. It is at your disposal in your leisure hours."

Evelyn and I looked at each other with open mouths before giggling uncontrollably. We would spend many happy hours in this haven, earnestly bent on improving our minds and attempting to build on the shamefully small stock of our knowledge of this world. However, you should by no means picture two serious little scholars, for we derived much nearer pleasure from reading poetry, and read and re-read one we thought very rude, which was only two lines long and was called 'Her Legs'. It ran:

Fain would I kiss my Julia's dainty leg,
Which is as white and hairless as an egg.

We also delighted in horrifying each other with pictures from books of medicine, and making each other shriek with laughter by reading from plays and acting out the parts, especially the great manly parts, huffing at the gods and so on.

Grace's fate had confirmed in us a healthy respect for the dangers of theatre-going but we did not believe (as our father had) that just *reading* plays was a vicious pastime. Father had more than once delivered sermons on this subject.

"Nothing is more disappointing than to come upon a young person, in the attitude of study, to discover they are reading..." here he would pause dramatically, "a *play-book*. For if a young man comes to be in love with plays, the next step will be to love playhouses, and if he does not take great care, the next advance might be perhaps to a bawdy house. For plays make a jest of adultery, a joke of fornication, in short, a mock of sin. Thereby the playhouse is the Whore's Exchange; the Devil's Church."

Aunt Madge and her husbands had also collected a vast array of what my father would certainly have called seditious literature. Amongst these, those we liked the best dealt with women's lot. Until we came to Aunt Madge's library, we had no idea that there even were pamphlets and books about women, excepting those that likened us to goddesses and other nonsense or those that taught us housewifery. Here there were writings about things I had never thought to question, but only wondered at, like why a boy should be better than a girl; why a husband should have control of all his wife's money and property; and a hundred other intriguing matters. It was as if someone had said "there is no God". These books and pamphlets turned everything upside down and looked at it anew, without being afraid or thinking it was sinful.

We would read and re-read phrases from these until we knew them by heart and could summon them like incantations at will. After receiving a letter from our sister Clarissa, full of her solemn admonishments to live cleanly and find husbands, we would intone Margaret Cavendish, who was our favourite. I can still remember some of this magic: "We are kept like birds in cages to hop up and down in our houses. We are shut out of all power and authority, by reason that we are never employed either in civil or martial affairs. Our counsels are despised and laughed at, the best of our actions are trodden down with scorn, by the overweening conceit men have of themselves and a thorough despisement of us." I am not sure I understood it all, but it made me feel stronger and better.

This was all, of course, our secret. We did not venture these opinions at table or in company. We hugged these secret comforters close to ourselves. When I think of that library now I realise I have omitted a most important aspect of the pleasure of being in it, which was the smell, which I can summon even after all these years. The scent of cloves, cinnamon, nutmeg, and all manner of other spices which used to be stored there still clung to the walls and floors, scenting even the books. It added a wholesome sweetness and pungency to our reading.

5

t was an odd sort of a life we led with Aunt Madge. When the Reverend Grimwade had written to her he had offered us as a sort of upper servants in return for our board. We were used to hard work and knew all the domestic arts, as our father had kept no servants but Annie Foster, the cook. The first day Aunt Madge would not let us work; it was a holiday, she said, and we explored the streets roundabout the house which were like rivers of activity and noise. I was most shocked by the fishwives who carried their wares in baskets on their heads with great expertise and let loose torrents of the most foul abuse to one another, including many words I had never heard before. Still, they did not seem to be really angry at each other but only, in a sort, to be prating in their own language. We walked all the way to the real river, and though Evelyn said I had seen it before I must have been little as I did not remember seeing such a marvel.

Londoners perhaps cannot imagine how the Thames seems to a stranger and take for granted this watery thoroughfare, busier, even, than the greater streets, and as full of hazard, with the great boats going up and down its length while the hundreds of smaller boats criss-cross from side to side as well. And the bridge, I think my favourite part in all of London, stretching across, packed tight with shops and houses. I used to dream of living in one of the houses, and wonder what it would be like to look out of the window and see the river flowing underneath you. And I wondered at how it had never been finished, until Evelyn laughed and told me it had been finished, but there had been a fire and the buildings at the end were lost. Still I did not understand how they had not built it up again, as I thought there must be great demand for such houses, and it was not as if there were other bridges. I earnestly wished to have a waterman take us across the river so I could walk back across the bridge, but Evelyn said another day, and besides we had no money, and perhaps I had better learn to swim before gadding in boats and such.

The next day after we had had our breakfast, Aunt Madge said: "Now I know you girls are anxious to be about your business," and took us into a large upper room where she opened a cupboard containing a deal of plain linen. Then she opened a pretty box (though in truth everything in her house was pretty) which for a moment to my fevered brain appeared to be full of jewels, but it was coloured silks, and they were of every colour of the rainbow and every shade in between – there must have been six or seven greens alone.

"Embroidery!" I said, ravished by their richness and the thought of handling them.

"I need, let me see, twelve, say fourteen napkins."

"What design?" asked Evelyn.

"Oh, you may choose," said Aunt Madge.

"What colours?" asked Evelyn.

"You decide, my chick," said Aunt Madge.

I had only ever used cheap wools and cotton threads before, and all we had been allowed to make were kneelers for the church or samplers with improving mottoes. It fell to our father to choose these and he never chose anything beautiful or uplifting, but always admonishments, such as 'Lying lips are an abomination to the Lord', or 'Out of thine own mouth will I judge thee', or 'Thou art weighed in the balances, and art found wanting.' (One day Evelyn had made me laugh so hard I was sent to our room, as she pointed out a quotation from the Bible to me, whispering that if father or the Reverend Grimwade wanted a kneeler, she had found a motto for them. It was from Ecclesiastes and ran: 'Be not righteous overmuch.') The endless handkerchiefs we also made we had not been allowed to decorate at all as Father thought it would encourage vanity, but in any case, while I stitched, I imagined I was sewing flowers and things anyway.

"Aunt Madge," said Evelyn, in a tone that made me feel she was going to give voice to a difficulty. "This is not work. You are very kind and I see what you intend, but this is not work. This is what ladies do to pass their leisure time. It is not what women are paid to do – not, of course, Aunt, that we want to be paid. When our brother-in-law wrote to you, he asked that you might give us board and lodging in exchange for real work, as servants do, until we may find our feet in this great city and gain independent employment."

Aunt Madge sighed and sank into a chair. And then she said that she had all the servants she needed. If she were to give us their work she would have to send them away and they depended on her. This was their home as well as their employment. Some of them, like Sal who looked after the hearths, and her little brother Joe, had no other home and no family. Here Evelyn and I looked and felt very sorry, as we had not thought of any of this.

"Then why, Aunt, why did you agree to have us come to you?"

Again, Aunt Madge sighed.

"You and your sisters came to me for a visit each time there was another baby to give your mother a rest, and then when she died," here she smiled sadly at me, "I asked you to come every year anyway. I have always been very fond of you girls, and I have only my boys," and here she stopped and seemed to hold her breath, and we guessed why for we knew Roger was nothing but a source of sorrow to her. "Anyway," she said, looking kindly at us, "I was never able to do anything for all of you, you being such a numerous family, but when I learned of your father's death and received Reverend Grimwade's letter I was pleased to invite you two. To keep me company is employment enough, is it not?"

"This is all very kind, Aunt," said Evelyn, "but we cannot accept your charity."

Oh but we can! I thought. I had never thought Evelyn to be so proud. This was becoming a most unhappy interview.

"Well," said she, standing up. "Let us reconvene this evening. In the meantime I beg you to consider how you may remain here. I should be very sorry to let you go." And after I dropped my curtsey my head smacked her on the chin as I came up, as she had moved to kiss me. As she rubbed her chin and I apologised she smiled ruefully at us. "Yes, we must indeed come to an understanding," she said, and swept out.

We immediately set about finding employment. First we went down to the kitchen and asked Cook if there was anything we could do to help her. Having established that "the missus" had authorised this initiative she produced a great greasy book. Laying it on the table and opening it before us upside down we at once understood the nature of the service we could do her.

"My mother gave me this girt book," she said. "She's long gone now and it's all I have of her. She couldn't read it no more than I can and I should like to know what's in it." She looked at us as if she were sizing whether we were equal to this task. "You do read, I suppose?" she said.

We said we did and told her it was a book of recipes which greatly pleased her and agreed to read some of it to her each day, so she could choose those she fancied the sound of and perhaps make them. As a result of this interview we learned that none of the three maids nor Joe and Sal could read, and we offered to teach any of those that wanted it. Cook was doubtful that the maids would bother with it, though Sarah, she said, had a beau who wrote her letters she puzzled over, and she had asked the Potter brothers, who did read a little, to read one to her once, but they had teased her so unmercifully she had never asked again. And she thought Sal and Joe were young enough to learn and it did make life easier after all, especially in these days when everyone seemed to read. I was about to offer to read the Bible to her if she liked, but then remembered she was a Quaker and, as I had no idea what this entailed apart from us all being equal, thought I had better not in case I offended her.

We spent the rest of the day going over the house making a list of all the things we could do, our criteria being that they were useful, but did not encroach on the employment of anyone else. We discovered that the library was in no order, with all kinds of books mixed together, and that we could arrange them more conveniently. We found that apart from the maids' rooms and our room, no one had gone into the other attic rooms for years, which were full of things useful and useless intermingled. Here was another task. And while the maids did the day-to-day mending of clothes and linen, we found no one was responsible for a frayed cushion here, a curtain with a falling hem there, and so on, and that such items were usually replaced when they got too disreputable rather than repaired before this was necessary. By the time we sat down with our aunt after dinner we had a long list of ways in which we could make ourselves useful. She listened with some amusement as Evelyn explained our plan, and when she had finished asked, "Are either of you clever with figures?"

"I used to do Father's household accounts," said Evelyn. "He said they were always very tidy."

"Excellent," said Aunt Madge and opened a drawer stuffed with papers. "I am at a loss to comprehend all that – your uncle used to take care of everything, and I have no head for it. Could you assist?"

"I'll do my best!" said Evelyn.

Aunt Madge seemed very pleased.

"Well, girls, are you satisfied now? I seem to have lost two nieces and gained a secretary and a housekeeper. May I assume you will do me the honour of remaining a little longer as it now seems to me that this household could not have managed a moment longer without you?"

We knew our aunt was teasing us, but were as happy as she was that we had settled a way to live together, at least for the time being.

We met ever so many interesting people at this time, as Aunt Madge was a woman with many friends. She had a dinner party on the first Friday of every month for her two favourites, an old bachelor and an old widower, as she did not seem over-fond of female company. Respectable women were, she believed, too careful of their own reputations to unbend and be entertaining, and the presence of unrespectable women, who might be better company, cast too doubtful a shadow on her own virtue, as she lived without a man in the house who might otherwise be expected to govern her. It was all too delicate, so she stuck in the main to gentlemen, and gentlemen, at that, too elderly "to be a nuisance".

"For you know of course," she told us, "a woman who has lost her good name is dead while she lives," and she looked at us wistfully, as if she wondered whether we understood how narrow were the gates and how straight the road we had to pass through. "London is not like the country, my dears," she said. "You must always have an eye to your backs, especially where ladies of quality are concerned. Here there are women aplenty who will gladly murder another's good name, if it serves to reflect agreeably on their own character. The world has cast us on hard ground indeed, where men do as they please and care nothing for reputation, so fling it to the women to fight over."

6

espite what had happened to Grace I was mad to see a play and the longer I lived in London, the more I felt sure that I had a good stock of the gorm she had lacked. I knew the London playhouses were nothing like the travelling players we had seen and the footmen, who loved to see the plays, told me such tales of how the playhouses were vastly improved since before the late troubles. In the old days, Reg said, the playhouses had no roof so if it rained everyone got wet but now they were indoors and had lights and scenes that moved and music and people of all quality went and even the King, he swore, he had seen there once (though I thought in this he must be mistaken), and instead of boys being the women there were real women (just as Katharina had said) and *such beauties*, he said and *so bold*. And most of all, Ted said, the plays were not all about kings and queens and huffing at the gods (though there were these still) and ending with everybody dead, but plays about *these* days, with people in them like they are today, dressed as we dress now, doing things that people really do and talking about things that really are, and ending with weddings mostly.

Early in our stay, Aunt Madge had offered to take us to the playhouse but Evelyn declined and she never asked again. In the first place Father had made it a condition of our earlier visits to London that we were never to be suffered to go to a bear-baiting, an execution or a playhouse. In the second place Evelyn would not allow Aunt Madge to be put to any unnecessary expense on our account. Again, I thought she was too proud, but I always deferred to Evelyn as she was so wise.

In any event, I had an opportunity to see inside a playhouse, if not see a play, because the Potters, one of whom Aunt Madge always sent ahead to get her a place, were employed repairing the coach and my aunt asked me if I would go instead and keep places for her and her friend Mrs Macready. I was about fourteen years of age at this time, but felt older, London having grown me up a good deal. It happened that Evelyn was abroad that day on an errand for our aunt so I readily agreed.

The playhouse, it has been said, is an enchanted island, where nothing appears in reality what it is nor what it should be. But please do not think this refers to the spectacle on the stage, for as I learned that afternoon the auditorium is its own stage and has its own play. I took my place in the pit, which Aunt Madge always maintained was the best place in the house, and looked about me. Of course, I was most excited but was already wise enough to learn that in society one never acknowledged surprise nor any sense of not belonging. A true Londoner could come upon a singing turnip or a squirrel dancing a jig and not disclose their amazement, if another Londoner were present. And if the other person were *not* a Londoner he would airily remark that this was an everyday occurrence. Londoners, it is a point of pride, take everything in their stride, however remarkable. It is a sign of their *sang-froid*, their urbanity. Your true Londoner gives you a superior sense that whatever you have seen they have either seen already or is not worth their notice. This at least I had observed and consequently wore on my face a blank mask which said I knew and was unimpressed.

Everyone about me appeared to become larger than life, as if the playhouse gave them license to show their shapes. Next to me a pair of rural gentleman, animated beyond measure, spoke loudly of their conquests of buck and doe, designed to impress, as it would in the country, which now I, a hardened Londoner, inwardly smirked at; there a languid beau, primped and pinked within an inch of his life, dared barely move a muscle for fear of displacing his frizzed wig or unruffling his cravat, both so carefully arranged to look as if he had just risen from his bed. Painted ladies in masks took in the scene while preserving their anonymity; others announced their presence with dazzling smiles, shining eyes and elegant gestures which drew attention as surely as if they were upon the stage itself.

However, even with the London ice in my veins, I jumped nearly out of my skin as a bully came roaring into the pit with the cry: "Damn me, Jack, 'tis a confounded play! Let's to a whore and spend our time better!" and this was greeted with so many jackals cackling loudly, yet without true mirth. Then a boy raised a bottle and cried back, "Damn me, Tom, I am not in a condition. Here's my turpentine for my third clap," which, uttered shrilly through his unbroken pipes, sent a ripple of derisory laughter round the playhouse. Then another came drunk and screaming and stood upon the benches and tossed his periwig in the air, speaking powerful nonsense very loud. There was something about this character that I thought I recognised, though I could not place him. Sprawling over several benches they had not paid for, these sparks commenced quarrelling with other men, talking scurrilous stuff with the ladies in masks, and mussing the orange maids.

But the ladies most of all threatened to discompose my cool expression, which was now quite paining the muscles of my face. At first I had tried not to appear to stare but it was clear that it was the business of all present to see and be seen, and once I saw the gentleman next to me snatch off his wig and hastily comb it, I decided to abandon my knowing air, to my great relief. After all, I was not here on my own account and merely keeping seats for my aunt. So I cast aside my urbane mask and gawped like a village idiot. So many great beauties under one roof I had not seen since I had once been in the picture gallery at Hunsdon House. Ranged and framed, just like the paintings there, in boxes, they fleered about with softest looks and gave encouragement to all the pit. A lady would cast a smile below and some overjoyed creature would stand and bow to the very benches, and rising, look about him to see who had seen, who had taken notice how much he was in favour with the charming goddess. On the entrance of another lady the whole pit turned as though moved by an engine to see her, as if she were the most entertaining scene in the house. The man I thought familiar bowed elaborately to one of the ladies above, before taking an orange, kissing it, and throwing it up to her. This I thought a very pretty gesture and was observing what she would do when there was a general commotion and people's attention turned towards one of the boxes where a very fine couple were taking their seats. The gentleman, who had a mighty handsome long dark wig, seemed to acknowledge them with a little gesture of his hand, and the lady inclined her head slightly.

"What d'you make of the Duke's new whore then, Tom?" Jack piped up, a little too loudly, I thought.

"'Tis not his whore, 'tis his wife, you shit-head!" roared Tom, and then retailed the exchange to the other cullies sitting round about them, and the one I thought I knew from somewhere laughed loudest and most mirthlessly of all and I noted that though his behaviour was ugly he was a most handsome-looking young man.

"Well then, a wife's but a whore with a priest for a pandar!" Jack squeaked back, but no one was paying him any heed now.

I gathered from others whispering about me that this fine couple were the Duke and Duchess of York, and though I did not like to stare I took an opportunity once or twice to look at them, and was a little shocked to see how they kissed each others' hands and leant on each other most familiarly in front of all the company.

I continued to cast anxious looks towards the door but still my aunt did not appear. And then the play commenced.

Against her coming late, I kept my seat, and turned my eyes to the stage. I do not think they left it for the next two hours.

I straightway understood why the playhouse was thought a wicked place. Although the playbills outside had said the play was called *Thomaso* the story was more about Angellica, who I now know was a courtesan. There is the first deception, I thought, and resolved to be on my guard. First of all it presented marriage in a very wicked light. A man told a lady (who, you may be sure, was no lady) that marriage was no better than a kind of sale, and in marriage a man wanted only the woman's portion and wanted her only as a chattel he takes to stock his family, as other cattle to stock his land. This seemed harsh and very likely against God, as God invented marriage. But then there were parts that made a deal of sense and reminded me of Margaret Cavendish, our friend in the library, as another man said "I do believe women may do most of their own business upon Earth themselves, if they would but leave their spinning and try." And I began again to wonder uncomfortably whether Margaret Cavendish might be sinful as well.

And again Angellica berated Thomaso, asking him why when a man and a woman sin together, the woman loses honour by the crime, while the man gains honour by it. I confess this puzzled me, as it made a deal of sense. It set me thinking on my poor sister Grace and how her life was ruined by a single act, yet her lover most likely gave it not a second thought. And then Thomaso objected because Angellica sold her love, being a mercenary prostitute creature, and then she said "Well, would you marry a woman without a dowry?" meaning he expected to be paid too. And he had no answer to that. And this set me wondering again.

When the play ended I clapped and clapped but could not see the players so well on account of the bullies in front of me getting up to go.

"'Tis excellent apt casting, eh Tom?" shouted one to the other. "Mistress Gwyn plays the whore as true to life!"

"Ah, but she has an unfair advantage – she and Hart, eh?"

and he made a circle with his left finger and thumb and thrust his right finger through it. I had never seen this gesture before, but immediately knew what it signified – after all, I was bred in the country. I thought I was like to vomit, it so powerfully affected me. I felt hot and wanted to get out and made my way blindly to the exit, but in all the confusion found I had mistaken my way and found myself behind the scenes. Casting about for a way out I saw behind a half-curtain the beautiful girl who had played the courtesan. She was getting undressed.

"Moll, are you there?" she called. "For God's sake don't suffer any of those pricks from the pit to come back here. Moll?" I scurried away, back the way I had come and finding the auditorium nearly empty followed the last of the spectators out.

I did not know what to make of my initiation to the theatre. It had been both a wonderful and a terrible experience. I ran all the way home, thinking it had not been at all like *The Taming of the Shrew*.

When I got home I went straightway to find my aunt. Evelyn had returned and they were playing a hand of cards with Puss at their feet.

I dropped a curtsey and then went to kiss my aunt.

"Did you enjoy the play?" she asked.

"Oh yes, Aunt, vastly," I said, and began to pour out the evening's adventures. But then I stopped and asked, "But why did you not come?"

"A head-ache, my dear," she said. "Happily it soon went. Put the cards away, Evelyn," she said and while Evelyn's back was turned she winked at me and I realised that she had never intended to come to the playhouse and I loved her the more for that kindness. "Did you see anyone we know?" she asked.

"No, Aunt, but I believe I saw the Duke and Duchess of York."

"Anyone else?"

"No," I said. And then my eyes fell on the painting of Aunt Madge and her sons, and I suddenly realised who I had recognised in the playhouse. "Oh!" I exclaimed and explained to my aunt that I had thought I had seen one of my cousins.

Aunt Madge seemed grimly satisfied.

"Who was he with? Did you notice?"

"Jack and Tom, I think they called each other," I said. "They were very – " and then I stopped as I did not want to tell tales, or bring trouble on my cousin. "High-spirited," I chose, thinking that safer and not a lie.

"I don't doubt it," said Aunt Madge. "In any event, your cousin is coming home on Saturday and you will be able to see whether this was the same person."

"Yes, Aunt," I said, hoping it would not be the same person, as though he was mighty handsome he was a very loud rough fellow and I did not like what I had seen of him.

7

was coming down the stairs on Friday morning with clean linen for the table for the dinner party that evening when I heard someone coming in at the door, and looking down I spied the man I had seen in the playhouse; evidently he *was* my cousin. He threw his coat and hat to the Potters before bounding up the stairs two at a time. He stopped when he saw me.

"Who the devil are you?" he said.

"H, sir," I said, dropping a curtsey. "I am your cousin from the country."

He smiled.

"Then welcome, coz," he said, and gave me a great smack on the bottom as he ran past, causing me to squeal and drop my linen. I had not been smacked so before and it took me some time to recover my composure. I picked up the linen and took it through to the dining room and then noticing a flower had fallen from the vase on the mantelpiece I replaced it, and happening to catch myself in the glass above the fireplace was surprised to see I was both grinning and blushing like a great country booby.

There was plenty to do that day, as we had to ready not only Roger's but also his brother Frederick's chamber, as he too was expected back from the university at Oxford for Easter. Their chambers were aired, the beds turned over, fires lit and fresh herbs hung about and I was hastening past Aunt Madge's room with a new quilt when I heard raised voices.

"You have been in town a week and not come home, Roger!" Aunt Madge cried, sounding most vexed.

"Mother, how many times must I tell you, I arrived only this morning and came here straight from the Oxford stage," answered Roger.

"That is a lie, to my certain knowledge," said Aunt Madge.

"How so?" asked Roger.

Aunt Madge sighed. Her voice dropped lower.

"You were seen at the King's Playhouse last week."

"There must be some mistake. Perhaps it was my brother."

"It was *not* your brother – that is an old song and will not serve."

"Who says I was there?" asked Roger angrily.

"That is none of your business," Aunt Madge said, to my great relief. "Suffice it to say I sent someone expressly to satisfy my suspicion."

This was a blow to me. I went on my way, hugging my disappointment to the quilt. Aunt Madge had not sent me to the playhouse for a treat, but to be her spy. I went to Evelyn and spilled it all.

"Do not be angry at our aunt," she said. "We came here to be of service to her, did we not? And you were of service. And I'm sure she thought you would like to see the play. I am not so blind as you think," she said, and winked at me, so I knew she knew.

I was fearfully excited about the evening ahead and looking forward to getting to know my cousins. There was also to be other company: Aunt Madge's old gentlemen that we knew – Dr Rookham, her physician, and Mr Fluke, her lawyer – and two young ladies that would be new to us. I had the impression Aunt Madge was not overjoyed about the ladies, whom Roger had invited, but he had said, "Zounds, Mother, do you want an old bachelor party? Besides, my cousins will want some female company. Sylvia and Melissa can teach them something of the town – civilise them a little."

One of the services we had found we could do our aunt was reviving her wardrobe; in an old chest we found many clothes we discovered she had cast aside not because they were worn through but because they were no longer the fashion. Evelyn and I had always made our own clothes and had restyled a number of her old gowns for her to her great satisfaction, but she had also given us some that she proposed to cast off, thinking them no longer suited to her years. (And indeed some were too small and would not admit enlargement to our aunt's now generous proportions.) "My day is past," she had sighed, giving us the pretty things. Evelyn and I had made ourselves three new gowns each out of this stuff, and new caps and kerchiefs, but two of the gowns were too fine to wear every day so this evening was to be their first outing. Evelyn's was pea green and mine a mustard, both in velvet, and we looked at each other rather abashed at how fine we seemed. We went in to Aunt Madge, who complimented us, and herself looked very grand, and we took a cup of sack with her. She and Evelyn began discussing what we were to eat, which did not interest me, as I could barely sit still, so I took the opportunity to slip out.

I ran downstairs to make sure everything had been made ready in the dining room, and found myself humming as I flitted about, but hearing a carriage draw up at the door ran back to the stairs in case it was the ladies as I did not want to face strangers without Evelyn at my side. On my way up the staircase I passed Roger sauntering down, and I don't know how it was – high spirits, I suppose, or possibly the sack as I was not used to strong waters – but before I knew what I had done I had smacked him on the bottom as he passed, saying "Two can play at that game, cousin!"

He stopped and looked utterly astonished and somewhat shocked, but I carried on up the stairs, and went back to Aunt Madge's chamber, where, to my consternation, I found Roger.

"And here is my other pretty cousin," he declared, bowing to me. "You have both brought the country freshness with you."

"I think," I whimpered, curtseying, "I just met Frederick."

"Good," said Aunt Madge. "Let's go down." She took Roger's proffered arm and led off, Evelyn and I following.

"What's the matter?" asked Evelyn. "You are all red."

"Nothing," said I, feeling hot and ashamed beyond measure.

8

immediately recognised Miss Sylvia and Miss Melissa as two of the gay ladies I had seen at the playhouse, Miss Sylvia being, I felt certain, the one to whom Roger had thrown the kissed orange. They were not painted (or perhaps only a little) as they had been when I saw them before, but both still wore patches on their faces. Sylvia's was round like a real beauty spot, but Melissa had two – one shaped like a crescent moon and another shaped like a star – which I thought extremely *à la mode*. (Oh, indeed I had a smattering of London French by this time.)

"These must be your poor cousins," Sylvia said, advancing towards Evelyn and myself as we curtseyed.

("Your *poor* cousins," Evelyn later repeated to me, as we undressed for bed.

"Perhaps she meant because our parents are dead," I suggested.

"Perhaps," said Evelyn, but neither of us was convinced.)

She looked us up and down before observing, "What original gowns. Is this the fashion in the country now?" Without waiting for an answer she and Miss Melissa swept past us and embraced our aunt without seeming to touch her which I thought most elegant and resolved to practise later.

Both young ladies were very finely dressed and I observed

that their gowns were vastly low at the front, but whereas their breasts had been almost bare at the theatre, now their charms were covered by transparent kerchiefs. As I tried not to stare at this, having not had such a near view before, Aunt Madge was evidently struck by the same thought as she said, "My dears, aren't you afraid you will catch a chill?"

"I'd sooner catch a husband!" said Melissa and they both laughed in a sort of twittering way which from my aunt's expression I guessed to be somewhat irritating to her. I began to suspect that my aunt may not, after all, have been the epitome of urbanity, for it was obvious that she did not share their cutting wit. This came as something of a shock, as often sudden revelations of one's betters' flaws – especially one's betters who are especially dear to one – constitute not only a surprise but tend to prompt a new valuation of their character. In short, I began to cease to view my aunt as an inviolable authority on the ways of the world. Melissa and Sylvia continued to laugh like this all the evening, flicking their fans before their faces in a way which, to tell truth, I found rather irritating too, but I repressed this sensation as, though their laugh seemed an affectation – as it were, to have no true happiness in it – this was evidently fashionable and therefore civilised. However I did not venture to copy them: I knew I yet lacked the refinement to carry it off.

Frederick and Roger saluted the young ladies, who, like everyone on first seeing the twins together, marvelled at their almost identical appearance. They really were as like as two peas in a pod, as the saying goes. Both twins were uncommonly handsome, but Frederick was slightly smaller in stature, and was the younger by only two minutes. Roger was fond of saying that those two critical minutes had made his fortune, otherwise Frederick should have been the heir and he the spare. Frederick always looked slightly pained on these occasions and indeed it seemed to me most unfair that twins should not inherit equally. Aunt Madge had often told us that when she was with child she had no idea she was carrying two babies, and Frederick's arrival had been an utter surprise to both her and the midwife.

"'Twas the last time Fred ever surprised anyone!" Roger quipped whenever she told this story, and it was easy to see that Frederick was the quieter, more sensible of the two. At first I thought him of a rather retiring, even bashful temperament, but soon saw that he rarely had an opportunity to shine, as Roger blazed away like a firework, dazzling everyone, and putting Frederick in the shade by comparison. Just before we went into dinner, when the other guests were being welcomed, I tried to gain an opportunity to speak with Frederick, but then realised that saying that I had mistaken him for his brother would still not excuse the familiarity I had shown. I hoped he did not think I was a forward young thing and bitterly regretted my moment of madness.

However, I could not escape him at the table as Sylvia and Melissa monopolised Roger's attentions, while Aunt Madge conversed with the senior gentlemen, leaving Evelyn and me to Frederick to entertain.

"How do you like the university, cousin?" Evelyn asked politely.

"Oh, very well," said Frederick.

"It must be pleasant to be there together with your brother," she added.

Frederick picked up a napkin and wiped his mouth before answering.

"To tell truth, we don't see much of one another in Oxford."

"But you share rooms, do you not?" I asked, as I had remembered Aunt Madge telling me this.

Frederick chuckled.

"We do, but I still don't see him much."

"But—" I began, but Evelyn gave me a warning look and I shut my mouth.

"Let's say – how can I put it? – we keep different hours… and different company."

Evelyn's look suggested this had better make an end on

the subject. I began to think Frederick rather a dry old stick and wished I were nearer my other cousin who seemed vastly more entertaining, as Sylvia and Melissa had been fairly twittering their heads off.

"So how did you find London?" Sylvia asked me and Evelyn, seeing to her obvious chagrin that Melissa had gained all Roger's attention.

"We just got out of the coach and here it was!" I said. Evelyn gave me a somewhat alarmed look but everybody else laughed. Sylvia seemed a little put out, but then joined in the laughter, again without mirth.

"I see you are a wit, Miss," she said icily.

"My niece is a very clever girl," said Aunt Madge. "They both are."

"I believe a clever woman will discover it a very difficult thing to find a husband who is not a fool," announced Sylvia, in a manner that ensured she received everyone's – in especial, Roger's – full attention. "For myself, I think it safer to conceal my intelligence."

"And, my dear girl, that you do most admirably!" interjected Roger and everyone laughed but Sylvia gave me a look as would kill, seeing I laughed hardest of all. From that moment on, I believe, she had me in her sights.

"In this depraved age," old Dr Rookham opined, "most think a wife learned enough if she can distinguish her husband's bed from another's."

"Dr Rookham!" exclaimed Aunt Madge. "Well! This is not the woman's age, is all I can say. Lewdness seems to be the business now. Love was the business in my time."

"To love!" Roger cried, holding his glass aloft.

"To love!" We all pledged our support, none so enthusiastically as Sylvia and Melissa, both of whom seemed to look on Roger as a shining god.

"Still, some things are better these days. When I was a maid, young ladies would never have gone to the playhouse without an escort – or even to dinner at a strange house without a chaperone."

"Those must have been terribly dull days," said Melissa.

"Indeed, now they affect a masculinity most deplorable," interjected Mr Fluke."They swagger and swear, game and drink like roaring boys."

"Come now, Mr Fluke," soothed our aunt, "you do not mean to insult the ladies present. There are some freedoms that are welcome. Now you are all able to gad about almost with the confidence of widows."

"I should love to be a widow!" exclaimed Evelyn so suddenly that the table fell silent. "I mean," she qualified, "of all women's states, that is the most enviable."

Still no one said anything, nor knew what to say.

"Their actions are less subject to... opprobrium," she explained.

I remember I wasn't sure what opprobrium meant but knew I had to run to my sister's assistance.

"I think Evelyn means," I ventured to suggest, "that of all women, widows are most free."

Still no one said anything.

"*Free* is perhaps the wrong word, my dear," Aunt Madge said, frowning. "It suggests... inappropriate liberties... a lack of modesty."

"Independent, then," Evelyn hastily supplied. "As a daughter, a woman must do as her father sees fit; as a wife she must do as her husband wishes; only as a widow is she mistress of her own destiny."

There was still an uncomfortable silence.

"Indeed, looked at in that light," Roger sighed, looking extremely serious, "it seems a shame that in order to be a widow, one must first be a wife!" Only then did we realise he was jesting and everyone burst out laughing. "To widows!" he proposed, and we all drank to widows.

"Ods bodikins!" exclaimed Dr Rookham. "Our English women have the most liberty in the world! A countess may marry her footman; married ladies may ramble, game and be lewd; a more incontinent generation of women has never been known."

"Indeed, our women are the happy women, sir," said Roger, raising his glass again to the ladies, though I noticed Frederick refrained from following him. What a sobersides Frederick seemed to me! And to think I had... I blushed to think of the incident on the stairs.

9

ater, when we had risen from table and had fallen into groups in Aunt Madge's withdrawing room, Melissa, who had been talking with my sister, moved to talk to me and I saw Evelyn raise her eyebrows at me as though in warning to watch what I said.

"Don't you think Sylvia is a great beauty?" Melissa said.

"She is very pretty," I replied, quickly adding, "but so are you," which, I am sorry to say, was an untruth.

"Ah, but I lack Sylvia's *je ne sais quoi*. She has a host of admirers, I assure you. But I believe your cousin has a special place in her heart." And she looked at me most meaningfully. I knew not what to say.

"She seemed to have many admirers at the playhouse," I said.

"Oh, you have been to the playhouse!" Melissa exclaimed, as though she had hitherto assumed I chewed cud in a field all day long. "Pray, what did you see?"

"*Thomaso*," said I.

"And what do you think of the actresses? They are bold trollops, or I'm no judge."

"I thought Mistress Gwyn very pretty," I ventured, "and a very good actress."

"All women are actresses, don't you know! At least, all ladies of quality," said Melissa. "Consider Sylvia." We looked across at Sylvia and Roger – Sylvia was affecting to be insulted at something Roger had said, but snickered all the while behind her fan.

Then Sylvia came over and, deliberately cutting me, drew Melissa aside to speak with her. Frederick began talking to me but I was distracted by Sylvia who, seeming to feel a pimple on her chin, reached across to Melissa's face, pulled the patch off her cheek, put it in her mouth and sucked it a moment to moisten it and then stuck it on her own chin. Unfortunately, Sylvia did not fail to notice the expression of disgust which my uncivilised face must have shown. Not for the first time, I cursed myself for my lack of refinement.

"Don't mind Sylvia," said Frederick. "She makes it her business to wound."

"I don't mind," I said. Perhaps emboldened by one humiliation, I took my opportunity to deal with another. "And cousin," I said, "I'm sorry about... on the stair... it was a foolish game I was playing – with your brother."

Frederick seemed to look at me a little sadly, and then said gently, "Take care with whom you play games, cousin." Then, having considered me a little longer, he seemed to brighten, and said "I suppose you are merely a child, H, and no harm done." Then he changed the subject, to my relief, as I felt very cast down to be called a child. "I see the party is disbanding. We must say our good-byes."

Roger and Frederick saw the young ladies home in the coach and Evelyn and I talked a while with our aunt. She always felt the cold most extremely. (She said this was why she could never be happy in the country, as English country houses, she said, seemed purposely designed to admit as much cold air, and their fireplaces to emit as little heat, as possible.) As a consequence, she had a habit, when there was no company, just we girls, of sitting in a chair by the fire with her feet on the mantelpiece, allowing the warmth to penetrate her usually heavily skirted nether regions. Either this, or she would stand with her back to the fire, with her skirts hitched up behind, her countenance betraying a state of the uttermost bliss.

Having adopted her unusual seated position, she enjoyed a few moments of elevation before asking us our opinions of Miss Sylvia.

"She is very pretty," I said, having discovered this was always an acceptable answer.

"Yes, but what say you to her character?" she asked.

It hadn't occurred to me that Sylvia had a character at all. She seemed, as I observed all fashionable people did, to exist mainly on the exterior.

"I don't think we know her well enough to tell," said Evelyn sensibly as always."But you have known her some time. What is your opinion, Aunt?"

Aunt Madge considered this.

"I fear she has a cold heart," she eventually decided.

"She seems fond of Roger," I ventured.

"I don't say she has no capacity for affection," my aunt explained. "I fear she may lack sympathy."

Evelyn and I kept respectfully quiet at this.

"Aunt," Evelyn eventually said in the tone I knew to presage something causing her some distress. "What I said at dinner about widows. I didn't think, I mean… I fear I seemed flippant."

"Don't trouble yourself, Evelyn," Aunt Madge said. "Your observation was quite correct. Widowhood has many consolations. I can keep the company and the hours I choose. I can mostly do as I please." She stretched her arms and yawned. "And just now I should like to go to bed. *Alone!*" she added, in mock tragedy and then smiled at us. "You are good girls. I confess to the sin of pride, as I felt very proud of you both this evening." She kissed us both and went up to bed, followed by Evelyn, while I remained to put out the lights.

I was tired but not ready to sleep so started clearing away the remaining dinner things as Aunt Madge had let the servants go to bed. I noticed that Sylvia had left her fan on the table and picked it up. It was very pretty, made of ivory or bone intricately worked, and green taffeta. I flicked it open experimentally. It had a smooth action and made a pleasing sound. I opened and closed it a number of times and then carried it to the looking glass above the fireplace and held it in front of my face. Then I had an idea and took a dab of soot from the chimney on my finger and improvised a beauty spot. Delighted with this effect, I practised a number of expressions: beguiling (fluttering my eye-lashes), disdain (chin up), amused (twittering); before I realised there was someone else in the room with me. In the glass I could see my cousin, though which one I could not tell. I turned round, holding the fan behind my back but could not tell whether it was too late – his expression did not tell me whether he had just come in or whether he had been there for some time, watching me.

"Roger?" I experimented.

"Fred," he said. "Roger's... gone on with some friends."

He came towards the fireplace and placed the guard in front of the embers, while I took the opportunity to slide the fan onto the table. Straightening himself, he considered me, then reached towards my face. For some reason I found myself trembling.

"Don't be afraid, coz," he said, cupping my chin and turning my face towards the light. He drew out his handkerchief and dabbed at my cheek. "You have got some soot, I think. There."

"Thank you," I heard myself squeak.

He stood back and looked at me again, with the same expression as when he had said I was a mere child.

"I should like to take you and your sister out tomorrow, if that would please you."

"Oh, yes!" I said. "I mean to say, I'll ask her."

He seemed to want to say something more, and then to change his mind.

"Up to bed, H," he said. "I'll lock up."

I said goodnight and just as I reached the door, he said,

"Have you not forgot something?" My mind misgave me I had committed some fault. I wondered what it could be. Had I neglected to say thank you for something? Should I have curtseyed? Seeing I was nonplussed, to my horror, he picked the fan up from the table and offered it to me.

"Oh, it's not mine," I said and turned and ran all the way up to our room.

10

he next morning, from my aunt's pursed lips whenever he was mentioned, I deduced that Roger had not yet come home. She agreed to join us for our little outing. We were to go over the river to the pleasure gardens at Vauxhall as the weather was so fine and then, in the afternoon, to see a play. I resolved to put behind me the humiliation of the night before and Frederick was very pleasant to us both and I soon felt at my ease again.

Evelyn and I were most cautious getting into the boat, as neither of us had been on the river before, but Aunt Madge jumped in with the carelessness of a true citizen. The river looked much bigger from here, and I hoped the boat would not sink as I could not swim. Frederick pointed out all the spires of the churches and our aunt supplied the names of those he did not know. It was windy, too, on the river, and smelt, as I thought, how the sea would smell. We had a good view of the bridge and the houses on it and Frederick told me that Nonesuch House (the great house in the middle) was brought in pieces from Flanders and reassembled on the bridge, and that due to the ingenuity of its construction, not one nail was used to hold it together. London was indeed full of such marvels. And Frederick said that the fire that had burned part of the bridge down was caused by a maid leaving a bucket of hot ashes under a staircase, which it ignited, and Aunt Madge said, "That's right! If in doubt, blame a woman!"

The New Spring Gardens were very pretty, though Aunt Madge said it was even better a little later in the summer, and there were all kinds of amusements, from a dancing bear to a marionette show. Frederick suddenly decided we should have some custard tarts, even though we had just had quince marmalades. Despite our protestations (and in truth my aunt never put up a convincing argument against tarts of any variety) he chivvied us into a booth and ordered us up some tarts and coffee before disappearing, as he said, to pay his respects to an acquaintance. While my aunt descanted on the relative merits of the tarts of the New and Old Gardens, my gaze followed Frederick and I saw that he had found Roger. I was just about to speak when I realised something was amiss and made an excuse to slip out to get a better view of what was occurring. Roger was with some ladies, who were very heavily painted and brightly dressed and they were all very drunk and noisy. I had never seen ladies drunk before and it was most alarming. One of them lifted up her skirts and showed her legs right up to her garters. Frederick turned away and seemed to be gesturing towards the booth, as if to encourage Roger to go away and not let his mother see him in this condition. Nevertheless, to my horror, Roger began to lurch towards the booth, surrounded by his exotic companions who seemed anxious not to let him out of their sight. As a last resort, Frederick put himself in Roger's way, and to my horror, almost before I had realised it, Roger threw a punch at Frederick, knocking him to the ground.

I immediately ran to Frederick, and on sight of me, Roger thought better of going further and staggered away with the painted ladies.

"Are you alright?" I asked Frederick, helping him up.

"Thank you," he said. "I tripped, merely."

We both knew this was not true, but it served to inform me that the incident was not to be discussed and we returned to the booth in silence. Though Evelyn and Aunt Madge did not detect anything amiss, the exchange had left me feeling most unhappy and I was glad when we got to the playhouse where my own thoughts would be put away for a while.

Yet even at the playhouse there were more confusing scenes, which began to make me wonder whether I had misapprehended Frederick's character. As we were filing into the auditorium, a stranger accosted him most angrily and Frederick gestured to us to take our aunt in and he would follow. When we had taken our seats, I saw him making his way towards us when another fellow stopped him and had, as my aunt would say, *words*. Both my cousins, it seemed, had an unnatural capacity for finding trouble. I looked across to see whether my aunt was aware of all this. She was.

"Do not judge your cousin," she said mildly. "Appearances can be deceptive. I'd wager he has been taken for Roger, and these gentlemen are Roger's creditors." She sighed. "Or he has done them some other wrong. Either way, dear Frederick thinks I do not know."

Having placated the gentleman, Frederick joined us, and I noticed his eye was puffing up somewhat from where Roger had struck him. Nevertheless, he smiled broadly at us all and sat down as though nothing was amiss. Yet I could not enjoy the play, and thought on the pain both he and my aunt must endure on Roger's account.

That night as we were in bed, I told Evelyn everything that I had seen at Vauxhall. She did not seem surprised.

"When we got home and you were helping Aunt I asked Frederick about his eye, and I thought tears welled up for a moment, and he said, with great feeling: 'I am no saint, but my brother is a devil.' And then he went to his room."

We both lay awake for some time. And finally Evelyn said,

"Other people's families are a mystery," and turned over and went to sleep.

The next day Roger was confined to his bed all day. Evelyn took him some tea and bread and butter on my aunt's instruction and I don't know what happened, but afterwards she came to me mightily distressed and said I was never to go into Roger's room alone. I asked her why, but she wouldn't say, only made me promise not to. Well, my readers will think I am a believing little fool, as I thought Evelyn meant I must not be alone in his room, but that if he were there it would be alright. (I had a habit of being blockheadedly dense on such matters. My aunt had once warned me, when we were going to a dance where there would be much to drink and little to eat, against what she called mixing drinks to avoid feeling ill the next day, and I assumed she meant not to mix them in the same glass, so drank freely of all kinds of things, but one at a time, and could not understand why I felt as though my brains had been baked in the morning.) Had I thought about it for even a second, I would have realised that I had never seen any of the maids go into Roger's room for Cook made an exception to not coming upstairs in his case and always brought him anything he needed herself.

Although I was extremely intrigued at what might be in Roger's chamber, I had no intention of disobeying my sister, and so forgot the matter. I could not help liking Roger when he was sober, thinking him vastly amusing and he told such tales of adventures at Oxford. It did not seem that going to the university entailed a great deal of work at all. He was training to go into the law, but said it was "dry old stuff" and he didn't care much for it. Evelyn seemed not to like Roger so much and when both brothers were there she usually talked with Frederick, of whom I also became increasingly fond, partly because he loved books, as we did. He was studying to go into the priesthood, though he was not like any clergyman I knew, and certainly not like Clarissa's husband. It was strange, but I barely thought of my family now. Evelyn and I would sometimes talk of our sisters, but we rarely heard from Clarissa or Diana, and we often wondered what had become of Grace and Frances and this always made us sad. The life we led with Aunt Madge seemed almost a different world to our first home, and it seemed strange to think of our sisters in other places living their lives.

Roger sometimes disappeared for days on end and it was plain to see why Aunt Madge despaired of him. When Frederick returned to Oxford, Roger found reasons to delay going, and then fell ill, which gave him an authentic excuse. I did not know precisely what was wrong with Roger and whenever Dr Rookham came to treat him, he would afterwards talk seriously with my aunt, but the door was always firmly shut on these interviews. I knew that whatever it was, the treatment was at least as unpleasant as the disease, for Roger dreaded the doctor coming and once, when he heard him announced, shouted out "Tell him he is not needed and that I am dead already!"

11

I had not seen Roger for about a week when I passed his room and heard him calling. Aunt Madge and Evelyn and the servants had all gone to church (except for Cook, who was a Nonconformist and had to get the dinner on) and I had stayed at home as we were expecting Mrs Macready, whom I was supposed to entertain until my aunt's return. Almost as soon as they had gone a message came to say that Mrs Macready was not coming, and while I briefly considered following the others to church, I decided instead to treat myself to a morning of leisurely reading. I was therefore not best pleased to be instead ministering to Roger, but there was no one else, and I did feel very sorry for him. I knocked before opening the door. The room was very gloomy, the curtains only partly open, and there was a most offensive smell. It crossed my mind that the smell might come from the thing I must not be alone with. Did Roger keep an animal of some kind here?

"What do you lack, Roger?" I asked. "Can I get you something?"

"Is that you, H?" his voice seemed thick. "Come here, I can't see you."

I approached the bed with some caution, as I was still wary of what might be in the room. Roger looked terrible, his skin seemed grey and he was shivering but also sweating.

"Please sit with me a moment," he said. "H, I feel absolutely done in."

"Oh, Roger!" I exclaimed, and felt tears pricking the backs of my eyes. I had not seen anyone close to me in such a desperate condition. I sat on the bed and took his hand in both of mine. "Can I do anything for you?"

"What would you do, H?" he asked.

"Anything," I said.

"Have you ever lain with a man, H?"

I thought I must have misheard him.

"I don't understand you, Roger. What do you mean?"

"I thought as much," he said, and laughed bitterly, so that I noticed his scabbed lips. I also realised, belatedly, that he was very drunk and that the empty bottles by his bed had not contained medicine. It was small wonder he was rambling in his talk.

I was feeling extremely uncomfortable now and began to withdraw my hands, but as soon as he felt them begin to slip away, he grasped them tighter.

"Cousin!" I exclaimed. "Tell me what you want and I'll get it."

"I want you, you little idiot," he said, grasping me by the shoulders and pushing me backwards onto the counterpane. As I opened my mouth to scream he put a pillow over my face so I could hardly breathe.

I need not fright my readers by recounting what then took place, and I do not recall it in detail and believe I may have fainted, for all that remained afterwards were disjointed senses of assault, both to my dignity and my person. I remember believing I might die, so unfamiliar and invasive was the pain, and that I might even have died already and be now in Hell, where they say torments are never-ending, as these seemed. Had a stranger attacked me in a dark alley, it would have been far preferable to this abuse at the hands of one whom I trusted and, in a sort, loved. It made no sense. I could not understand it. And compounding the dislocation of logic

71

were my cousin's repeated agonised cries, throughout, of "God forgive me! God forgive me!" And as, at times of peril, many disparate thoughts rush through one's head, suddenly I understood Evelyn's warning. There was no wild animal in the room. The beast was Roger himself.

I do not know how I found my way back to my own room, where I washed myself and wept and shivered and do not know whether I slept or not. I was shaking uncontrollably when Evelyn found me in bed and was unable to speak. She guessed I had caught a fever or an ague, and I did not disabuse her. Although my body suffered, my mind was strong, and even while the assault was happening I had been able to think clearly enough to resolve that no one should ever know of it. Mine was a private shame. I think even then I believed I could survive, but I doubted I could bear the humiliation of it being publicly known. I had seen what had happened to Grace. I had learnt that men walked away while women bore the consequences. I wanted above everything to tell all to Evelyn, but in my feverish state, fears ran round my head that Evelyn might actually kill Roger if I told my story, and then she would be hanged. And I also felt I had partly brought it on myself, as I had not heeded Frederick's warnings, nor understood Evelyn's, in fact had ignored the many signs that Roger was capable of great wickedness. It had simply never occurred to me that he might be wicked *to me*. Of all the many bad things I felt about myself, that which recurred most was that I had been, as Roger said, a little idiot.

Of course, little of this was clear at the time. Evelyn later told me that I lay in bed moaning and shivering and in a fever for three days and nights together and never spoke a word in that time. Then I began to rally. Dr Rookham had been sent for as soon as I fell ill and diagnosed a hysterical fever, prescribing only bed rest, but proposed to cup me if I showed no improvement. I later learnt I shrank so alarmingly from allowing him to examine my body that he was reluctant to force me, so the bruises and other hurts I had received disappeared in time, unknown to anyone else. As I gradually came back to the world, I began to be sensible of those around me, and though I still did not speak, could hear and understand them. One day I heard Dr Rookham and Evelyn talking in low voices in the room.

"Will you see my cousin while you are here?" asked Evelyn.

"Now there is a dog wants shooting," muttered Dr Rookham.

"He recovers, does he not?" asked Evelyn.

"He does," answered the doctor. "He'll soon be fit enough to go whoring again, and catch the pox again. This is his third blast in as many years, you know." Then he stopped, and in a most tender voice, added, "Oh, my deepest apologies, my dear. I have spoken out of turn. This is talk most unfit for modest ears. You are such an apt little nurse, I begin to forget you are a lady."

Horror gripped my heart. Roger had the foul disease. This made sense of my feelings of dirt and degradation that I found water could not wash away. I sank back into fever and insensibility. After another three days I rallied again, but this time continued steadily to improve. I had been only dimly aware of any human attentions, but had been touched by the almost constant presence of Puss, who had chosen to spend his hours of repose beside me. When I believed myself incapable of feeling, I was sensible to his friendly salute on entry, which was to sniff my face and lick my hand reassuringly before settling down beside my bed.

The morning I felt better, I sat up in bed and said "Hello Puss," and he cocked his head on one side, until I repeated the greeting, whereupon he jumped up on the counterpane and kissed my face with many affectionate licks, before jumping down and running barking through the house, as if to alert everyone to the change in me. As soon as Evelyn had satisfied herself of my well-being, she told me of the many kindnesses that had been shown during my illness. Cook had made tempting dishes every day for me, while little Joe and

Sal had been heard praying for my recovery every night. The footmen, whom I never considered even noticed me, had been very solemn and enquiring after Miss H and procured flowers for my room, and Frederick had twice asked after my progress by letter from Oxford. And dear Aunt Madge had been so concerned at Evelyn's fatigue – for she hardly ever left my side – that she had herself sat up one whole night watching over me when my fever was at its height. I had come to a decision, while what Aunt called Dr Sleep was doing his work, that just as I did not recollect much of my illness, I would choose to forget, as far as was possible, everything that had happened from the moment Roger had called me into his room until this moment when I spoke again. It had simply not occurred. It was the easiest path, and the most secure.

I quickly regained my strength, having always enjoyed rude health, and was soon back to my usual duties. This was rendered much easier by the circumstance that Roger had gone to stay with friends in the country to complete his convalescence. Still, I resolved not to dread seeing him again. After all, why should I? Nothing untoward had taken place between us. With each day I was able to swallow my necessary lie a little easier and was able to live again.

I had been completely well for above a week when Aunt Madge's monthly dinner party came round again. Roger was to be present, as were all the guests from the previous party excepting Frederick who was in Oxford. Evelyn expressed some doubt as to whether I should attend, but Aunt Madge said it would be good for me and that was that. I wanted to get it over with, and was ready to approach the coming encounter bravely, but then all threatened to be ruined by a stunning discovery I made the same day in the library.

While I had put away, with more or less success, the terrible events in Roger's room, I was sensible enough to realise I could not ignore the possible consequence: to wit, that I might have acquired the foul disease. I therefore waited for an opportunity to consult a certain medical book which

Evelyn and I had previously occasionally frighted ourselves with by looking at the pictures therein.

I sought to learn the symptoms of the disease I feared, so I would recognise them if they appeared. These I was relieved to find had not yet manifested themselves, but I memorised them as I feared to write anything down. The learned author told how the venereal fever was to be got from whores – a word at which I then trembled but which now does not give me the least unease – though gave no hint as to where the whores got it from. It said that the disease was most contagious when these women were "impelled to a satisfaction" which puzzled me, but I believed I had not been impelled to a satisfaction so far as I was aware and took some comfort from this. There was a deal of other sordid stuff about "foul scorbutic wombs" and then the author went on to deal in cures. These included various potions and compounds, the employment of turpentine and arsenic and the injection of mercury or solutions of metals such as gold and silver. This, the good doctor said, "inflicts the severest pain on the victim" and I almost felt sorry for Roger, which just proves what a little fool I was still. He then mentioned sweating tubs and other devices and the last cure the doctor suggested was "to lie with a sound woman", which I at first flipped past, as not applying to women, but then the horrible realisation crept over me that this was what Roger had done. I was his cure.

12

My plan was to avoid seeing Roger until dinner, when, in the company of others I would have no option but to behave in a way which would arouse no suspicion. This was easily accomplished, by reason that as soon as Roger arrived, he was summoned to my aunt's presence and there followed one of their customary noisy and emotional interviews. This one was much noisier and more emotional than usual and went on for nearly two hours and at one point Evelyn reported hearing my aunt sobbing. Evelyn observed that I looked pale and again asked me not to go down to dinner, but I insisted. Above anything I did not want to give Roger the satisfaction of thinking he had hurt me, or indeed was capable of having any effect on me whatsoever. I could not change what had been done to me, but I could choose the person that Roger perceived in me.

When Roger came down, Dr Rookham and Mr Fluke had already arrived and I made sure I was busying myself making them comfortable and appearing not to notice him come in. Mr Fluke asked me under his breath whether "those patched and painted little trollops" were expected with Roger, and I said I thought Miss Sylvia and Miss Melissa were indeed invited, and then talked to the elderly gentlemen of the weather, which was unseasonably hot for early May, and of how parts of the town stank abominably as a consequence, the street-rakers never seeming to keep up with the level of filth and rubbish. I kept on like this as I was determined that Roger should have to address me before I seemed to notice him. I was aware of him standing behind me and still did not turn. He coughed. I finally condescended to acknowledge his presence, and turned to face him, with a prepared and pleasant smile on my face.

"Cousin," he said, bowing.

I made sure I looked him full and steadily in the face before dropping a curtsey. I was delighted to note that he looked thoroughly uncomfortable and even afraid. I made sure he was aware that my gaze never dropped from his face as he saluted the senior gentlemen, who received his greeting with their usual courtesy, though it was clear to me now that neither of them had the slightest affection for him.

Evelyn also greeted him politely but as one who knew he was better kept at a distance, and Aunt Madge, who I saw had indeed been crying, seemed to behave towards him with unusual indifference. I realised, with some unbecoming elation, that Roger began to understand that *no one liked him*. I began to feel the hard glitter of revenge course through my veins: it was an unfamiliar and heady sensation to me to feel exalted because of another's pain.

Indeed it was pathetic to see him work so hard at being jovial, and I realised that two things were missing which usually oiled the wheels of his conversation. One was drink – Roger was, for once, and probably at my aunt's insistence, stone cold sober (this he remedied as soon as we sat at table) – and the other was Frederick, who I now understood tended to mitigate any unfortunate circumstance Roger got himself into. As well as being sensitive to his brother's failings, and willing to compensate for them or distract from them, he also supplied a foil to Roger and a butt for Roger's jokes. Also, as I guessed Sylvia carried Melissa around with her because she benefited by the comparison, so Roger shone brighter next to Frederick. On his own he began to cut quite a sorry figure.

Sylvia and Melissa then arrived and after greetings had

been exchanged, Sylvia immediately drew Roger aside and they whispered together. When Roger quit her side and approached his mother I made my move and presented Sylvia with the fan she had left behind last time. She looked at it as if it were a strange and foreign thing and then looked back at me.

"I understand you have been unwell," she said. "I trust you are quite recovered?"

"Oh, quite, thank you," I said.

"They say the plague is in town," she said.

"Oh?" I said. "I had not heard of it."

"Oh yes," said Sylvia. "Several people have died. Above forty I believe."

"Pish!" said Melissa. "There are plague cases every year. And in any case, it's only in St Giles. When you see how such people live it's no wonder."

"Yes," Sylvia agreed, looking at the fan again and then at me. "It mainly affects the poorer sort. Please keep it," she said.

I believe I succeeded in concealing the effect of Sylvia's insult upon me and politely insisted that she took the fan back.

"Indeed, no," she said. "I have above a dozen at home, and I doubt you have one." With a glacial smile, she turned away to indicate she had finished with me. I slipped the fan into my pocket thinking I should never like to use it now.

As usual, the conversation at the table became more voluble as each bottle was consumed. Roger was becoming increasingly loquacious with each brimmer, and I noticed my aunt place her hand on his arm when he reached for another decanter. "Zounds, Mother, it is a special occasion, is it not?" I heard him say.

In a low voice I heard my aunt say they had agreed not to mention it before the guests, but I could not catch the reason why, nor what it was. Roger seemed to pooh-pooh her and rose unsteadily to his feet. Raising his glass aloft he said, "Ladies and gentlemen, I should like to propose a toast to Sylvia, who has done me the honour to agree to become my wife."

I think everyone was shocked and surprised, but a quick

glance round the table told me that this was no surprise to either Aunt Madge or indeed to Melissa, who seemed ready to burst into tears at her friend's great good fortune. Sylvia smiled graciously. Seeing that everyone looked to her for their cue, my aunt composed her features, raised her glass and wished them great happiness, though I perceived tears in her eyes not of the happiest kind.

"May I enquire," said Dr Rookham, "when this happy event is to take place?"

"This morning!" volunteered Sylvia. "You see before you a bride of only some hours!"

Again this news was shocking and surprising to most of us and once more Aunt Madge had to lead in congratulations.

"Welcome to the family, my dear Sylvia," she said.

General conversation then broke out, and I observed Mr Fluke lean over to Roger and say with a grin, "Tonight's the night, then, my boy?"

"Indeed, sir," replied Roger, drinking deeply and setting down his glass rather heavily. "Tonight's the night."

He smacked his lips and the room vertiginously dropped under my feet; swimming before my eyes was Roger's face, huge, distorted and horrible. I am not sure I actually fainted as I was dimly aware of activity around me. Evelyn and Dr Rookham rushed to my side and pulled back my chair.

"The plague!" shrieked Sylvia, leaping to her feet. "I knew it!"

"Hold your tongue you foolish woman," snapped Roger. "It's not the plague, she has fainted merely." He pushed back his chair and stood up. "I will carry her up to her room."

"No!" said Evelyn sharply. "H, dear, can you stand?"

I found that I could.

"I think I need to lie down, only," I said, and Aunt Madge sent for Cook to make me some eggnog, while Dr Rookham held the door open for Evelyn and myself.

As everyone was occupied in helping me, I heard Roger say, "It is the shock, merely."

"What shock?" said Sylvia.

"That we are married, you halfwit," was his unguarded response.

"Why should that be a shock? To her?" She received no answer. "Roger?"

"I believe the child may have conceived an affection for me," he mumbled, confirming my suspicion that he would have attributed any claims I might have made against his behaviour to *my* own feelings for *him*. It was a most disgusting thing to hear pass his lips, as well as quite ill-advised on his part and made me feel sick again.

"An affection?" hissed Sylvia. "What kind of affection?"

"Oh, an infatuation, merely," Roger hissed back, digging his grave deeper and deeper.

Evelyn took me to our room and made me lie down though I assured her I was quite well. She blamed herself for letting me come to dinner when I had been so ill so recently. Once Cook had brought me my eggnog and Evelyn was satisfied I was comfortable, they both left me.

I lay there listening to my heart thudding until it slowed to a more regular beat and then must have fallen asleep. I woke to hear the bells of St Mary-le-Bow and knew it was eleven o'clock. I was hungry, as I had hardly eaten anything, and so began to make my way downstairs.

Crossing the landing on the next floor I could not fail to hear the rumpus going on in Roger's room. The tone was clearly that of people trying to argue quietly and as we passed I discerned only scraps, including "that little slut" and "in my condition" in Sylvia's voice, and "hold your tongue, madam, or I've something here will stop it," and then laughter, from Roger.

When I look back on that eventful night now, all this seems trivial. For even as we lived our little lives and fought our petty battles, death stalked the city, and soon would ride triumphant through the streets.

13

lmost daily noisy interviews took place between Aunt Madge and Roger behind closed doors over the next days, and it was a small matter, between what was audible and what Aunt Madge conveyed to us, to infer that Roger's marriage was unsatisfactory to her on almost every point. He had not consulted her on his choice of wife. He had thrown up his studies at Oxford. He had no plan as to how to keep himself. He had made no effort to find lodgings for himself and his new bride. Yet though Aunt Madge sustained all these objections to the match, she now took the philosophical view that it was done, and they had to make the best of a bad job. However, it soon became clear that, however much of a philosopher Aunt Madge might pretend to be, she was far from happy living under the same roof as her son and his new bride, who now took marital discontent to hitherto uncharted heights.

After a fortnight of living as a married couple at Cheapside, Sylvia announced she was confident she was with child, which seemed mighty fast work, and Evelyn and I looked at each other but said nothing. It was small wonder Roger had married in such a hurry. It was clear that if he ever liked Sylvia, he did not now, and would mope round the house (for she did not like him to frequent his old haunts) complaining to anyone who would listen, usually the footmen. I once caught sight through the kitchen doorway of the Potters entertaining the other servants with their clowning, playing Roger and Sylvia as if on the stage.

REG: *(A lace doily on his head as Sylvia)*: I curse the day I gained the vile, detested name of wife!

TED: *(A poker through his belt as Roger)*: And I curse the day I ever committed the hateful crime of matrimony! *(He pretends to drink from a bottle.)*

REG: Before we are wed you treat us like queens! But the hour of matrimony ends our reign! I was warned 'tis so and 'tis true! I have been such a fool!

TED: There, wife, you have truth. You have so little brains that a penn'orth of butter melted under 'em would set 'em afloat. *(He pretends to drink again.)* You took a knock in your cradle I warrant.

REG: Oh speak not to me of cradles! Oh, you beast, you sot! Brute, rogue, poultroon! Thou art a rogue, a hector and a shab! Oh scanderbag villain! *(Takes the bottle and drinks also.)*

I took care not to be seen witnessing this pantomime, as it would not have done to laugh at Roger and Sylvia before the servants.

A circumstance concerning problems with her estate in the country gave Aunt Madge what Evelyn and I thought an ideal opportunity to absent herself for a while, and at least gain some respite from the continual torment of living under the same roof as the happy couple. At first she protested she could not leave London, but finally we extracted a promise that she would at least consider whether, for her own health and ease, it would be better for her to go out of town for a period.

One morning she called us to her. She appeared to have had

little sleep and indeed we had all been aware at some point during the night of Sylvia screeching and Roger crashing about cursing.

"My dears, I am taking your advice and will go into Gloucestershire. I am most reluctant to leave you behind, but I will be frank with you and own that I do not wish to leave Roger and Sylvia in charge of the house. Roger will nominally be in charge of course, but I know you two will look after things and make sure the servants keep to the mark – for I fear they do not respect my daughter-in-law any more than they do my son – and also that they suffer no abuse. You can send to me at any time and I shall not be gone long. Perhaps no more than two weeks. Is this plan agreeable to you?"

We said that it was, and she should not trouble herself about us, as we could manage things perfectly well, and she should stay away as long as she wanted to. We eagerly agreed as to tell truth we were most concerned about our aunt's well-being, for she had not seemed truly herself since Roger's marriage.

"There are two further things," she said. "Firstly, if I am delayed, or any unforeseen circumstance occurs – should I be taken ill, for example, and unable to return for a time – I would like you to continue with the monthly dinner. I do not wish to abridge you two girls of any pleasure, and besides, Dr Rookham and Mr Fluke will prove true friends to you should you need to apply to them for assistance of any kind. I have corresponded with them both and they have readily agreed to watch over you in an avuncular capacity. You may depend on them." She stopped and looked earnestly at us and I could tell she was still debating whether she should leave us.

"Be perfectly easy, Aunt," Evelyn said. "We will do as you ask, of course."

"What is the other matter, Aunt?" I asked. "You said two things."

"Yes, I did." Aunt looked out of the window, took a deep breath, and then turned her attention back to us. "I want you to especially have an eye to Sal and Joe's well-being."

"Aunt," I ventured, "you are as kind-hearted a person as ever I knew, but there are thousands of children in London in the same condition as you found Sal and Joe. May I ask why you particularly took in two blackamoor children?"

"Blacks and tawnies as well as whites are descendants of Adam, H," said Evelyn primly.

Aunt Madge did not answer straightway, but indicated to Puss that he would be welcome on her lap and up he sprang. She pulled on his ears which I knew gave her, as much as him, much comfort.

"This is a delicate matter," she said at last, "and I have to trust you with a great secret." She sighed and beckoned us to sit close to her which we, much intrigued, did. She put her arms round our shoulders and went on in a low voice. "Though they do not know it, and even Frederick and Roger do not know it, those children are, in a manner, your cousins."

Our faces told her that we were none the wiser.

"Oh dear," she said, and reached for her glass of Canary and went on: "Your uncle you know was in spices and travelled halfway round the world in pursuit of his trade. It happened that he had another... another kind of wife... and these were his children. I did not know of their – or their mother's – existence until I came across some papers after his death... The other... kind of wife... died of a fever, and her people rejected the children, and they were like to starve, so your uncle brought them to England. He told me nothing of all this, of course, as he thought it would hurt me, as indeed it would have, as he and I had no children together." This was the only point at which her composure threatened to disintegrate, but she regained herself at once. "I discovered he had been paying a sailor's wife to look after them, but when he died and the money stopped, she turned them over to the poorhouse in Portsmouth. That is where I found them, and brought them here." She seemed to consider her empty glass, before adding, as an afterthought, "Only Cook knows."

Evelyn and I were speechless for some moments. Then

Evelyn, who always seemed to know the right thing to do, kissed our aunt and said she could rely on us both to protect our little cousins and to keep their history secret. We redoubled our assurances the next day as we waved our aunt off. As her coach went out of sight, we little guessed that the three of us would never be together again.

14

We had the household well organised by this time and had more leisure hours than hitherto, so went to confer with Cook about some special dishes from "the girt book" for the forthcoming dinner party. In the event, Sylvia made her excuses and remained in her room (she did indeed vomit most strenuously throughout the early months of her pregnancy) and Roger simply did not turn up.

By this time Roger and Sylvia had nothing more in common than their name and their misery. As soon as Aunt Madge had departed, Roger liberated himself from any pretence at husbandly dutifulness, and went out early and often. This meant we were left alone to entertain Sylvia, which did not discommode us too greatly in the mornings, as she rarely rose before noon, and after that she did not want our company any more than we wanted hers, though, because she looked for no employment, her time lay heavy on her hands, and she often sought us out if only to have someone to bear witness to her vexation.

As a result, we often took refuge in the kitchen, where we knew Sylvia would never deign to descend, and were treated to Cook's insights into life. Roger, she said, had always been a bad 'un. She showed not the slightest interest in Sylvia, although warned us about the terrific expenses of motherhood where a lady of quality was concerned; there would be cawdles, wines, sugar, soap, nurse, pot, pan, ladle and cradle needed, as well as fire and candle, a coral with bells for the child to rattle and twenty more odd knacks, whereas less fine children made do with tit, she said, and thrived just the same. She warned that, when the time came, our aunt could expect "an apothecary's bill more barbarous, even, than Roger's tailor's."

One night Roger came home just as Evelyn and I were locking up and told us some of his companions were joining him and we had best take ourselves to bed. He was already in his cups and knocked a candlestick over without seeming to notice, so Evelyn righted it and told me we had best stay awake until the revellers had gone, to be sure Roger did not set the house alight. Once Roger's guests had arrived, we settled ourselves on a couch on the first floor landing, where we could see into the hall and not be observed. The door to the dining room, where they assembled, being open, we could plainly hear most of what was said.

"So where's the lovely Sylvia?" asked one, who from his high voice I recognised to be Jack from the first night at the playhouse.

"A pox on Sylvia. I am tired of her already. Pox on it that a man can't drink without quenching his thirst," said Roger, to universal laughter.

"And is she tired of you?" asked another I presumed to be Tom, one of Roger's playhouse companions.

"I fully expect so," said Roger, and belched loudly. "Ours is a marriage of inconvenience." During the ensuing laughter one of the men rolled out of the door into the hall, vomited perfunctorily in a corner, and returned to the company. Evelyn and I looked at each other and said nothing.

"Still, there is Sophia... " said Jack.

"... and Lucy... " said Tom.

"... and Moll – there's one that swives like a stoat!" said Roger, to cackles from the company.

I looked at Evelyn as I didn't know what 'swive' meant and her expression told me she guessed, but did not care to say.

"If I had such a bitch I should spay her," piped Jack.

"Roger, dear heart," said Tom, "you've had more whores than Sodom's walls ever bounded – what, pray, has this Moll to make her so favoured of the sisterhood?"

"Ecod! Not just plain Moll, I prithee, give her her full title, *Posture* Moll. Egad, the slut's a veritable gymnast," asserted Roger.

I understood gymnast to be a very filthy word as at this Evelyn pulled me away and up to bed. Much later I heard her coming into the room again.

"They've gone," she whispered. "I've put out the lights and left Roger snoring on the floor. They've left a terrible mess of things." Indeed in the morning the dining room looked as though a carthorse had pulled his load through it.

Mr Fluke and Dr Rookham arrived as usual for the monthly dinner, though as I have said only Evelyn and I were present to receive them. They were very kind and I realised that however curmudgeonly they seemed they took very seriously the compact they had made with our aunt about keeping an eye on us. They were a good deal surprised at some of the dishes Cook had prepared for the event which she had got from her girt book, all of which featured, in some form, custard, which had been a great discovery to her. Still, we made merry, although the conversation took a more serious turn when Mr Fluke mentioned that he had seen his first shut-up house on the way to us, as he passed through Drury Lane.

I did not know the significance of this, so Evelyn explained that when there was the plague in a house, it was shut up by the authorities – the windows and doors nailed up – and a guard was set to watch it to make sure no one went out, and they put a red cross on the door and painted 'May God Have Mercy On Our Souls' on it to warn people how dangerous a matter it was to have ado them, and to resist bribery and so on. If, after such and such a time, others in the same house were hale, the red cross was changed to a white cross and if, after such and such a number of days (I forget now) everyone was still well, the quarantine was lifted. It was a safety measure to check the spread of the infection, Dr Rookham said. He had been called to a few cases, but as the disease was so infectious, he never went near the patient, but asked questions of their family and prescribed remedies from the door. He was confident there were more cases than were reported, as families naturally feared being shut up with a diseased person.

Seeing the expression on my face he told me not to worry, just to keep away from St Giles, which was the hotbed, and assured us that there had not yet been, to his knowledge, any cases within the city walls. Mr Fluke begged to differ with him on this point, saying that it had indeed spread to the city and also to Westminster, causing some nervous people of quality to remove into the country. Worse, he said, some men of the cloth, on whom the poor people depended in time of need, and even doctors, had taken fright and gone out of town. Still, he said, there were plague cases every year, and even in epidemic years it was always the poorer parishes that took the brunt and there was no cause for alarm. Dr Rookham told us to ensure we washed everything we bought, to see that the servants did the same, to avoid crowds and to breathe no noxious fumes; he reassured us that by these means we would escape infection. Given that Cheapside was a perpetual mobile throng this would prove difficult, but we were at least to implement his instruction to wash everything, especially food.

Yet when they left, Mr Fluke found reason to be the last to go, and told us that it was as well our aunt had gone out of town when she did, and that we would do well to follow her as soon as we could. Evelyn and I talked about this as we prepared for bed, and knew we could not leave because of the assurances we had given Aunt Madge, but we agreed Evelyn would write to her the next day urging her to remain in the country until the danger was past. We also decided to let the three maids go to their families if they wished. As we lay in bed Evelyn observed that Mr Fluke must indeed be concerned about the plague, as he had not mentioned the lamentable behaviour of the younger generation all evening.

15

he next day we let the maids go. Cook would not leave the children and the footmen were content to stay and try their luck with us. Evelyn told me she was going to pass on Mr Fluke's warning to Roger and Sylvia, as they had not just themselves but the baby to worry about now. As it transpired, Roger rolled home and went to bed just as Sylvia was rising, so after an argument which Sylvia was infinitely more willing to prosecute than was Roger, she came down to her dinner.

Sylvia would now have been a figure of pity – heedless of her appearance, unhappy in her marriage, sick in her pregnancy, unloved in an unfamiliar home – had it not been for her unrelieved nastiness. Venom and barb simply sprang more naturally from her than anything tending towards harmony. She could respond to no small act of kindness, no enquiry about her well-being, no suggestion for her greater comfort, without conveying her thorough despisement of us. She treated Evelyn and me as servants while resenting the fact that we were not. Our company was insufferable to her, while our absence rankled. In short, we could do no thing right by her, and though we understood this, we recognised that simply to ignore her existence would merely give her another cause to spite us. Bearing all this in mind, it took some courage for

Evelyn to bring up the subject of her removing from town at the dinner table.

Sylvia stopped with a fork mid-way between her plate and her mouth as if Evelyn had announced that London Bridge had finally fallen down.

"Leave town?" she repeated. "Leave town? Why on earth should I want to do that?"

"I do not suggest you want to, nor that it is convenient," said Evelyn patiently, "but it seems that this could be a serious outbreak. Mr Fluke thinks we should all leave as soon as possible."

"Oh, Fluke the Spook," said Sylvia, "that beastly antique!"

"Dear Sylvia," I interjected, not wishing to leave all the onus on Evelyn, "if not for yourself, for the child, please think of going into the country."

"Oh, the child, the child," Sylvia said, throwing down her fork. "It seems once you carry a child, that is all you are, a child-carrier, and that child must be all your care. I did not choose the child, I do not care for the child, and the sooner we are parted the better." She picked at her food angrily and neither of us had the heart to press her further. She threw her fork down again. "I am nineteen years of age!" she exclaimed, through a mouthful of dumpling. "I need company, plays, masked balls... I need Hyde Park! I need the Exchange and Covent Garden! I need fashion and quality about me to remind me that though I am married I am not yet dead! I cannot, will not, go into the shires and dwindle into a country wife! I would rather die!" And here she broke down and sobbed and Evelyn leapt up to put her arm round her, but Sylvia thrust her away, saying, "Don't touch me! Don't presume to pity me!"

Evelyn later tried to talk to Roger about it, but he was never in any kind of sensible mood and demonstrated, if possible, an even greater aversion to the country than had Sylvia, again principally for its lack of amusements and diversions. Evelyn could not argue with this, so, feeling she had done her duty to the best of her ability she desisted from further debate.

Roger increasingly peopled the house with his companions, and as Sylvia began to appear more often on these occasions and make herself agreeable to him by getting drunk with him, he occasionally took her out on his sorties. Again Evelyn made so bold as to suggest to Roger that with all the worries about the plague, it might be dangerous to be going out so much, especially to places of resort, where one might meet with many strangers. Roger merely laughed, called Evelyn an old woman, and added that if the quantity he drank didn't kill him, nothing else would.

As the days passed, one would have had to be actually blind or wilfully so not to see the signs that the situation was worsening. When the infection took hold in Westminster, those who had consoled themselves that this was 'the poor man's plague' suddenly woke up and took stock. Within days the streets became uncommonly busy in some places with the one-way traffic of the wealthy, who had somewhere to go and the means of getting there, leaving the city. A kind of panic had set in. We knew we had to act, for the sakes of little Sal and Joe, if not for our own.

Roger and Sylvia now existed in a kind of limbo between drunkenness and sleep, which bore no relation to the hour of the day or night. They had ceased to keep table at regular times and food was sent up to their room when they called for it. Evelyn and I kept out of their way as much as possible, as Roger had become indiscriminate in his lewdness (though, to be fair, he always let *me* alone), and Sylvia did not know what a civil tongue was. They reigned over the house like two overgrown tyrannical children, unreasonable and irrational, impossible either to please or tame.

Evelyn would not write to our aunt about this, for fear she would come back, which we now knew to be actually dangerous, but we were aware the life we were leading was hopeless and we began to plot a way to get ourselves and Sal and Joe out of the city and safe into our aunt's house in the country. Then we considered the other servants. In the absence of our aunt we were responsible for them too, Evelyn said. We would take them with us. One night when Roger and Sylvia were quiet in their room and presumably unconscious, we gathered Ned (the coachman), the Potters, Cook and the children in the kitchen and told them our plan.

Had we acted earlier, all would have been easier, but due to new regulations we now needed to acquire certificates of health, as the Lord Mayor had issued orders that no one was permitted to leave the city without them, to prevent Londoners carrying the infection into the country. Letters, we discovered, had some days ceased to be carried out of London for the same reason, so we now had no means of contacting our aunt or Frederick. We had also stopped sending Joe out with local messages as he was a child and would not understand what not to touch and who not to trust. So the next day I set off for Dr Rookham's house to see about the certificates, while Evelyn went to Mr Fluke to leave word of our going.

The world had changed since we had last ventured out. There was an air of quiet desperation everywhere. Everyone we met was fearful of everyone else, and above all it made our hearts heavy to observe how sad and serious they all were. Although we had both put on thick cloaks (which were most uncomfortable in the hot weather) and carried posies against the poisonous miasmas, we felt the danger everywhere.

I noticed some of the stalls along the streets had bowls of vinegar which coins were put into to disinfect them when a sale was made, and how empty the shops and stalls seemed, and many of them closed up, much of the trade having ceased, the town having been as good as quarantined. As I got further from home, and had to pass through areas worse affected than ours, I went down a road where it seemed every other house was shut up, and others had been vacated, and the streets, apart from the men standing watch, were almost empty. I closed my ears to the moans I fancied I heard within, the cries for mercy I hoped I imagined.

I sustained myself with my mission, to get to Dr Rookham,

yet when I got to his house, found him not at home, nor indeed anyone at home. Having knocked and waited, and gone down to the kitchen door and knocked and waited, and tried the door and found it locked, I peered in through the window and saw the place in some disorder and no fire in the grate, as if the inhabitants had left in a hurry and been gone some time. This threw me into some confusion, as I could not understand how Dr Rookham would have left without sending us word, and more urgently because I knew no other doctor, so wondered how we would procure the certificates we needed to get out of London.

I went straight to Mr Fluke's, thinking he must know some other doctor who would help us. The maid showed me straight into his closet, where Evelyn already was.

"Oh, Evelyn, Dr Rookham is gone!" I cried. "Whatever shall we do?"

"Now, now, young ladies," said Mr Fluke, "at times like these we must keep our heads. I promised your aunt I would stand for an uncle to you and I will. I would not now send you a strange doctor, as he may bring the infection to you, but I believe I can procure certificates for you. This is not legal, by any means, and will take time, and you must never say how you came by them, but we must get you out by hook or by crook. To avoid unnecessary journeys do not come back to me until I send for you, or I may come myself." Mr Fluke was serious but kindly and we began to feel a little reassured. "Now you must go home and make yourselves ready to leave the moment the papers arrive. There is some speculation that the city gates may soon be closed to all – certificate or no – but I have reason to believe we have at least a week's grace." He rootled in a drawer and drew out a purse. "Here is some money. Do not, on any account, buy food on the way, nor go into any inn, nor be persuaded to take any stranger into your coach. Take water too. Do not weigh yourselves down with possessions – your aunt will have everything necessary at her house. Now go, my dears." And he showed more tenderness as he kissed us goodbye than I think I ever saw in him. "And God speed and bless you."

16

may say that the days following seemed the longest of my life. During that time we discovered there was now barely a clergyman or a doctor to be found still in town and the people were left to shift for themselves as best they could. As news came that the court was quitting London the citizens understood that they were being truly abandoned, and it was only fear of congregations of people, I now believe, that prevented most unhappy scenes of violence and rebellion in the city. Everyone was afraid and angry and the King must have sensed this, for he made all the army withdraw from the city at the same time as the court, for fear they would lend their might to any revolt, it having been ordinary Londoners that turned against his father.

The only advantageous occurrence in that time was that Sylvia and Roger were frighted enough to cease their gadding out so much, though I was astonished at their continuing refusal to countenance leaving the city. I began to wonder whether it was a point of principle with Sylvia and that even if she wanted to leave, as I felt she must now, she could not alter her mind, for pride.

The playhouses had long been closed, and hardly anyone went to church anymore, but now even markets were cancelled and street stalls banned, inns and lodging houses closed. All this served to kill the last vestiges of trade in the city. The case was worsened by the fact that many wealthy families had turned out their servants before quitting town, leaving them not only jobless but homeless, unable to leave the city and ill-equipped to sit out the dark days ahead. The only employment remaining was of the most unsavoury kind but those left to wander the streets had no choice but to take it or starve.

As a consequence, the city was now run by a new and ragged regiment of watchers, scavengers and rakers, examiners, searchers and nurses, serving the usurper: King Plague. Frightening stories circulated daily; on the rare occasions when Cook ventured out to get milk or eggs to supplement our supplies, which, due to my aunt's habits of careful household economy and keeping in a good stock of pickled, cured and preserved victuals (habits, I supposed, learned during the civil wars, and hard to lose), stood us in good stead (though I ate a good deal more of her plum preserve in those weeks than I should ever like to see again), she invariably returned with new horror stories, of watchmen being killed by inmates trying to escape, of thieving nurses who abused and neglected their vulnerable charges while they drank their cellars dry and pillaged their belongings. Cook had heard a tale of a watchman hanged from a noose let down from an attic window, the inmates scaling down the same rope to freedom. While I secretly doubted this at the time, similar tales were to become commonplace. Others knocked down walls to get out or dug through cellars. It is hard, these days, to credit the extremities these poor souls were in, but if you lived through those times in the city you will well know the uncertain hazards people would run to save themselves from the certain danger within their own homes. I also later discovered as true the rumour she related that some refugees from London were herded into barns in the counties surrounding the capital, outside which stood men with guns ready to shoot them if they stirred, so afraid were the country people of Londoners carrying death in their train. The plague indeed engendered a kind of civil war, setting Englishmen against each other, neighbour against neighbour, brother against brother, as everyone scrambled over everyone else to save their own skin.

The whole texture and timbre of the city was changing and though we rarely went out we could feel it within the house. Even the quiet of our library, our favourite retreat, was usually tempered with an underlying roar of distant traffic, as well as local: of wheels rattling, horsehooves clattering, footsteps padding, the to and fro of buyers and sellers, the conversation of the citizens, and cutting through and over all, the street-cries and invocations to buy that, as a visiting country child, had seemed to me to be the motley song of London itself. Yet now Cheapside was so quiet, if we heard a noise we often ran to the window to see what it was. The calls of happier times, of "Round and sound, fivepence a pound, Duke cherries!" and "Here's your toys, for girls and boys!" and the song Evelyn loved best, "Ye maidens and men, come for what you lack, and buy the fair ballads I have in my pack!" not to mention the piercing professional cry of the boy "Sw-e-e-e-p!" – all these seemed buried and almost only to have existed in a dream. Now "Bring out your dead!" was all our night music, and bells tolled so continually for burials that when they on occasion ceased, you wondered whether the bell-ringer himself had been taken. In short, a phantom of the former city now reigned, a malign double of the town we knew had supplanted its original.

The plague seemed to encompass the city like a flood, impossible to stem. Unable to escape the rising tide, people's thoughts turned to how it had come about, what it signified, and who was to blame. Little Sal parroted what she had heard our visitors of quality say, that the poor, by self-neglect, had hastened their own destruction and now we all suffered. Cook at first averred it was a judgement from God to punish profanity, vanity and the sins of the dissolute court, though later decided it was a punishment for the Great Rebellion and the execution of Charles I (although, in truth, she had no personal sympathy for his case) and finally settled for it being a sign of God's wrath against a variety of religious enemies. Ted adhered to the prevailing medical authority, that miasma carried it, that it floated around, infecting those who inhaled it, while Reg was convinced it was much simpler, and that livestock, pigeons, cats and dogs, rats and mice, who had the freedom of the city, carried it everywhere they went.

And this last theorem brought a new fear, when we heard the crier declare that all cats and dogs found wandering in the city were to be killed, and offering a price per tail. This new source of income gave employment to any poor soul who had no skill, for anyone could kill a cat, and they prosecuted their cause with great vigour. This new battalion could be seen roaming the streets, easily finding hapless animals used to wandering around outside their homes, as well as those who never had homes, and bludgeoning them to death with hammers, axes, or any implement to hand, for there was no niceness anymore in such dealings. Everyone in our house had strict injunctions not to let Puss out beyond our private yard, and then only when one of us was present, but Sylvia and Roger often left doors open in their stupor, as they left many other things undone, and in the end I secured him in the old henhouse in the yard, and later bound his jaws so he did not betray his presence, for the dog-killers were paid by the animal, and were not above finding innocent secured dogs to make up their tally.

This was most cruel, as Puss could not understand why he was banished from the house and forbidden speech, of which he was most fond. He was unhappy and through whining, which I could not stop, threatened to betray himself, so in the end I carried him up to our room, which being at the top of the house, was private and safe, and there he remained except for the necessary times when I took him out. Sometimes I wondered if he might become the last dog in London, and if so might become famous one day, and then how we would regret his fanciful name. I entertained such wild fancies in this time that on occasion I would check myself and wonder if I had already contracted the plague, as in such strange countries my thoughts rambled. But then I decided it was merely the times that made us strange, and we must cling to our sanity, and accept there were fewer and fewer touchstones against which to check or measure it. It often felt as though it was a daily battle merely to stop ourselves running mad.

It was about this time, I think, for it all later became a jumble, that Evelyn suddenly said one day, "Are you quite well, H?"

Now it is to be understood that this was not a question which bore its everyday weight of kindly enquiry at this time. I suddenly felt that I was really quite ill, but said that no, I thought I was quite well and did she notice anything the matter?

"It is merely that I did not observe you to have had your flowers for some time," she said, evenly, as she occupied herself folding something, for Evelyn never liked to discuss matters below the waist.

I had not thought of it, being so occupied with present anxieties, but when I sat down and made my calculations, realised that I did not recall having my monthlies since before... since before – I suddenly realised in a rush of fear – the event I had chosen to forget. Indeed, I had so successfully alienated the memory of Roger's diabolical act upon my person from my daily thinking, once I had satisfied myself I had not caught the feared disease from him, that this was the one outcome I had not considered.

Such is the fate of women. I felt, in the first place, and Roger's words rang in my head again, a little idiot. When a man and a woman lie together, what may be the consequence? A child. How had I not thought of it? And what could I now do about it? I could not do the one thing, again, I wished for most, which was to tell all to Evelyn, for I still believed she could have killed Roger without a scruple. And then for a most wicked moment I entertained the possibility of allowing her to kill him, and tried to guess at the outcome, and even flirted with the notion of making it look as though Sylvia had done it, or even of killing Sylvia too, which demonstrates just how unbalanced my mind was in those days.

Then I pulled myself back from that madness and set my mind on a more practical course. I had so far only three examples in real life on which to base my idea of the choices I faced. For my sister Grace, pregnancy as an unmarried woman had led to exile and disgrace, and who knew what else – we did not. For Sylvia, it had led to a bad marriage, and again I had no high hopes for a happy ending. Lastly, and my most recent example, Aunt Madge's husband's kind of other wife had had her children and their father had taken care of them. I knew enough (from allusions Sylvia had made, and from reading the chapbooks in the library) that unborn children could be done away with before they were born, but also that this was a wicked thing. I also had no idea, had I harboured no objection to it, how this outcome was to be achieved. Much as I puzzled my small and confusing stock of knowledge on the subject, I could not see any of it helping me. So I decided to do as I had done before, concerning the event which had let to this disconcerting circumstance: to ignore it. Though in my heart I knew that this could not go on indefinitely, there seemed more pressing concerns.

17

By the first week of August it still continued very hot weather and we learnt from the Bills of Mortality that over 13,000 Londoners had died the month before. It was a measure of how removed Sylvia and Roger were from the true state of things that they decided they would revive the monthly dinner. Evelyn frankly begged them not to proceed with this plan, saying that they would expose the whole household to infection, but they were immoveable.

"This is precisely the time when we *should* have a party," said Sylvia, "when everything is so dismal. In any case, we have already told everyone." The guests were to be Roger's usual crowd, and Sylvia's friend Melissa was also to be present. Cook was mightily displeased about it, saying we should be being frugal with our reserves, not throwing it away on Master Roger's rabble, but we knew she would make a respectable show. Evelyn and I considered whether we could absent ourselves from the dinner, which we earnestly wished to, and sounded Sylvia about it – she was only too happy not to have us.

Sylvia came down at the appointed hour looking very fine, though it had taken her hours to dress herself and her hair, as she cursed the maids being gone and would not suffer either me or my sister to help her. Even Roger had put in some effort, though I observed he was now getting a little fat for his velvet coat, and his once-handsome features had a bloated character, and the unnatural glassiness of his eyes gave them the appearance of two black currants in an undercooked bun for a face. I realised he had now sunk so beneath my esteem I was incapable even of taking pleasure in this alteration.

We had already all eaten, so Cook could have the kitchen clear for the dinner preparations. Evelyn helped her while I took Sal and Joe up to the library for some reading practice. Sal and Joe were strange little creatures, who reserved all their affection for each other, but they were obedient and almost unnaturally quiet. Though younger, Sal seemed to have a natural appetite for books, but Joe had been more difficult to interest and whenever he was set to work, though quiet enough, we would usually find the fruit of his labours amounted to nothing more than a drawing of Puss on his slate. That was, until we discovered the poem 'Agincourt' which he loved us to read to him, as it was so stirring. He indeed began to know his letters by looking at the words that rhymed. He now began half-reading and half-reciting (for he had great parts of it by heart, being a forward child):

"Fair stood the wind for France
When we our sails advance,
Nor now to prove our chance,
Longer will tarry;
But putting to the main,
At Caux, the mouth of Seine,
With all his martial train,
Landed King Harry."

As I listened, I observed Sal looking down into the street, and followed her gaze to see a dead dog lying in the gutter, over which rats were already swarming. Now that cats and dogs had all but been erased from the city, the rats had no enemies and were having a field day; one saw them everywhere, and so numerous that they had no fear of humans and did not even scurry away when people came near to them. I was about to draw Sal into the room when I heard Sylvia calling up the stairs.

I ran down to her as she seemed in a great passion.

"Have there been any messages?" she asked.

"Not that I know," I said. "Have you asked the footmen?"

"Of course I've asked them, and now I'm asking you. Everyone's very late."

I looked at the clock in the hall and it was indeed a good hour past the appointed time of dinner.

"It's really most vexing," she cried, "when I have gone to so much trouble."

"Stop making such a damned row Sylvia!" Roger shouted from the dining room, where I could see he had been making a fair start on the wine. "People of fashion are always late."

Suddenly there was a knock at the door and Ted and Reg appeared, as they always did, as if by magic. Sylvia ran to the glass in the dining room, and after a short conference at the door, Ted and Reg returned, Ted carrying a letter on a tray. He headed for the kitchen.

"Where are you going?" asked Sylvia.

"I'll smoke the letter over the fire, madam," said Ted. "Miss Evelyn's orders." Seeing she looked blank, he added, "For safety, madam."

"Damn Miss Evelyn," said Sylvia, snatching the letter up and waving him away. It turned out not to be a note from a dinner guest, but a letter from her friend, Lady Enfield, at court. "Oh, it is long and wordy. Read it to me H." She held the letter out to me and while I debated taking it, Ted held out the tray again and she sighed and let it fall onto it. He went to the kitchen and returned a few moments later with the letter, a little sooty, in his hand, and gave it to me.

"You are all such sneaking timid things," Sylvia said scornfully. "You will die of fright long before the plague catches you."

I followed her into the dining room where Roger was reclining on a couch. She smacked his legs until he made space, then sat beside him and gestured to me to read.

"'My dear Sylvia,'" I began. "'You will see from the address that the court has removed again. It seems the plague in its impudence followed us to Hampton Court, and then to Salisbury, but nevertheless we are now settled fairly at Oxford, but might as well be on the Moon. There is no plague here but the infection of love, no anxiety but what to wear and with whom to dance, and no difficulty but deciding who is handsomest.'" This was wonderful news as it meant that Frederick was safe as long as he remained in Oxford. I was about to say as much, but Sylvia gestured her impatience for me to continue reading. "'In a word, there is nothing here but mirth, and there is talk that the King shall issue a proclamation that any melancholy man or woman coming into this town shall be taken up and put in the pillory, and there be whipped until he or she has learned the way to be merry *à la mode*…'"

"That's enough!" shrieked Sylvia. She snatched the letter from me and threw it into the fire. "Why has no one come? Or sent word?" she cried petulantly.

I saw fit to mention that hardly anyone sent messages now, and then only essential ones, and then but by word of mouth, so fearful were people of touching things of unknown provenance.

"Ridiculous!" said Sylvia. "How is life to go on if one can't send messages? How is one to arrange anything? Things have come to a pretty pass when a body cannot have friends to dinner!" She checked her rising hysteria and instead turned to whining, "There is no society anymore. No plays, no markets… "

"No taverns, no coffee-houses… " added Roger ruefully.

"Shall I have your dinner sent up?" I asked.

"I should have thought your mother's decrepit admirers would have come at least!" said Sylvia. "Rookham and The Spook are usually glad of a good dinner."

"Things have gone down a bit when you'd miss those old relics," observed Roger.

"Dr Rookham left town some days ago," I said.

"Really?" said Sylvia. "Why?"

I looked at her uncomprehendingly.

"Sylvia," I said gently, as I could feel anger and frustration rising within me, "we have tried time and time again to make you see that it is extremely dangerous to remain here. Thousands – not hundreds, not tens – thousands of people are dying every week. There are bodies carried through the streets all through the night. Do you not even hear the plague carts? The church bells for burials?"

Sylvia had, as usual, no answer, and turned her attention to berating her husband.

Evelyn and I had agreed that if we had not heard from Mr Fluke by the next morning I would go to him, which I did. I was surprised at the number of people that were about, yet nobody spoke to anyone else and even the rougher sort who would often jostle past you in a narrow alley would now stand aside until you passed, so that you did not touch them. And then I was waiting to cross a road, and a number of other people joined me, also waiting, but we all kept a safe distance apart, in an unspoken pact, and when there was a break in the traffic, we crossed and a person in front of me dropped like a stone to the ground in the middle of the road. It was as though a pebble had been dropped into a pond, as in a ripple everyone drew back, creating a circle around the body, but the strange thing was that everyone kept moving, and the circle around him remained, as everyone crossing the road in both directions gave the body a wide berth and not one person stopped to help him.

As I approached Mr Fluke's house my heart sank. No smoke issued from any of the chimneys. As I drew closer my worst fears were confirmed. A red cross and the fatal words had been painted on the door. Still I did not lose all hope. There was no watchman there. I looked up and down the street. The only watchman I could see was standing over the road, in front of another marked house. I knocked on the door. No one answered. I peered through the window, but it was too dark to see anything.

"What d'you lack, Miss?" a voice behind me made me nearly jump out of my skin. It was the watchman from across the road.

"Are they… are there people in there?" I asked.

"All dead and buried, Miss. Last one taken away last night." Seeing me sway under the shock, he moved to steady me, then remembered himself and drew back.

"When did Mr Fluke die?" I asked, not really knowing why, or what difference it made, now.

"The old gentleman? Oh, he left about a week since – just before the servants fell ill."

This was a stab to the heart. I could not help that my relief at his having escaped death was tempered by my chagrin at him having left without a thought to our plight. I thanked the watchman and began to walk blindly away, knowing we had now been utterly abandoned.

"Wait a minute, Miss!" called the watchman. He beckoned me back. "You wouldn't be Miss Haitch Evelyn by any chance?"

"Evelyn's my sister. I'm H," I said, still in a daze.

"Gentleman said to give her this, if she come." He withdrew a fold of papers in a wrapper from his pocket. "As I say, he left in a hurry, otherwise he'd have brung it himself."

"God bless him!" I cried, taking the papers, "And God bless you!" and though I would have flung my arms round him, I blew him a bouquet of kisses instead.

18

ran to the nearest brazier and held the packet over the smoke for as long as I could stand the heat before tearing the cover from the papers. A note had been hastily scribbled on the inside of the wrapper. It read:

Gold dust. Only four. God bless you. E.F.

The certificates were open, that is to say, the name of the person they certified was free from disease had been left blank, but they were numbered and had been signed by a doctor. Assuming Mr Fluke knew about our sort of cousins – he was Aunt Madge's lawyer, after all – he had got the certificates for Sal, Joe, Evelyn and myself. But what would we do with Cook? And would Ned the coachman need a certificate? Of course he would. I considered whether we could hide the children, in a trunk perhaps, and take Cook with us. Cook, Ned, Evelyn and myself was four. But what about the Potters, who had been so faithful? Should we forget the coach and the coachman, and send the Potters in the cart, which they could drive themselves, with the children? Or should we walk, in which case we were back to our original four? Or… And all these calculations were assuming Mr Fluke knew about our sort of cousins, and Aunt Madge had told us only

Cook knew. In which case he may have meant the certificates for ourselves, Roger and Sylvia. I walked and walked and thought and thought, turning the different combinations and possibilities over in my mind. Did it matter for whom Mr Fluke had intended the certificates? The children must be saved, but how did we choose who else should go, perhaps choosing who should live and who should die? Wasn't it a heinous selfishness to presume to number ourselves amongst the saved? But hadn't Roger and Sylvia refused to think of leaving, and didn't they therefore forfeit their chance of going? Yet Roger was our aunt's son, so perhaps we should, for her sake, save him, and her unborn grandchild, before ourselves?

I needed to go home with a plan, which we could immediately put into action, not go through all these tribulations of thought again with Evelyn, as I dreaded her offering to send me and stay herself, which I could not bear to think of. The certificates, which had at first represented liberty, now weighed me down and made me tired. To my astonishment I heard a clock strike four. I had been walking for hours, had had nothing to eat, and was exhausted both in mind and body. I stepped into a churchyard and sat down on a tombstone, meaning to rest for only a few moments, but awoke to the clock striking six.

I started to hurry towards Cheapside and had made at least part of a plan. As soon as I got home I would fill in the children's and Evelyn's name on three of the certificates, then no matter what Evelyn said I could be certain that she could not give up her place. I would worry about the fourth name later. Sometimes, I reasoned, one should act on half a solution, rather than wait for a whole solution and in waiting fail to act at all. My heart feeling a little lighter, I arrived home in about an hour and a half, and quietly let myself in through the kitchen so as to expedite my plan uninterrupted. Cook and the children were nowhere to be seen so I went upstairs to get pen and ink from the library. I got as far as completing the children's names when I heard footfalls on the stair, placed a piece of blotting paper over the certificates and went out to investigate.

The moment I saw Evelyn I knew something was terribly amiss. She was white as a sheet and her eyes were like saucers.

"Where have you been?" she asked, in a strange voice which frightened me.

"To Mr Fluke's. I have the certificates. We can get the children out, Evelyn." I moved towards her but she put out her hand quickly. I panicked. "Are you ill Evelyn? Please don't say you are ill?"

"No. I am perfectly well... but the children... " she looked like to cry, but stopped herself. "After you had gone, Cook went to get the children up, and Joe had a fever. She couldn't get a doctor, of course, so she sent Sal into her own room, so she should not catch it if it were the plague. She tried to make Joe comfortable, then when she went to see Sal, she had been taken ill too. Then she came to find me, as she didn't know what to do for the best. I gave the Potters some money and sent them away, but when Sylvia missed them she demanded to know the matter. And then... " and now Evelyn did break down, "she was all for having the children forcibly conveyed to the pest house by the authorities... but Roger said they would demand to know the address and the house would be shut up... and they plotted and planned and in the end ordered Cook to take them there, but made her swear to say she found them in the street, and knew not where they came from, and Cook... " She could not talk for a few moments for sobbing but would not let me touch or comfort her in any kind. "And Cook said she would not take them, and told Roger he could go to Hell before she would, and then Roger beat Cook and threw her into the street and screamed at the children to get out (for he would not touch them) and poked them out of their beds with a broom and frighted them so that they did run out to Cook, just in their shifts, and Roger shouted after Cook that if she said where they came from he would kill her. And Cook said 'May God have mercy on your soul, for this deed has damned you.' And then she told me to take you to Aunt Madge for we were not safe here. And then she took the children away." And here Evelyn sank to her knees and sobbed fit to break her heart.

I was stunned and could not believe all this had happened in the time I had been out. I knew the pest house was no hospital, and offered those brought thither little more than a makeshift filthy cot in which to die. Sal, Joe and probably Cook too had received a sentence of death and there was no remedy. When I came to my senses I went to comfort Evelyn but again she put her hand out and said she had nursed the children and she would stay in Sarah's room until we knew she was not infected.

Some moments of feeling are written in your heart for ever, and this unutterably painful scene, where my sister and I stood some distance apart, both brimming over with the deepest misery, yet unable to comfort each other, has never been erased in mine.

Evelyn was very tired and went up to bed, and though I was tired too I knew I could not sleep, and though I felt sick to the stomach knew I must eat, so I fetched Puss and went down to the kitchen, going quietly past the dining room where I heard Roger and Sylvia talking. As I waited in the yard for Puss to do his business, I wondered at how, only a few hours before, I had seriously thought of giving one of them, who I now considered as good as murderers, my chance of escaping the city.

The last thing I thought about before I went to sleep was that I had wasted two of the precious certificates. For all my fine reasoning half a solution had been worse than no solution, as now the children could not use them and neither could anyone else, and I resolved never to be tempted by half a solution again, and to think twice before doing things that could not be undone.

Still, there were two left, and that was all Evelyn and I needed.

19

s soon as I awoke next day, I went to Sarah's room to make plans with Evelyn. I was resolved we would not spend one more night in London. My heart skipped a beat as I saw Joe had left his little slate on the landing and with the sight of that familiar but now redundant object the horrors of the day before came flooding back with great force. But when I bent down to pick it up I saw on it, not his usual sketch of Puss, but writing in what I immediately recognised to be Evelyn's hand.

Don't touch
Keep out
Don't tell S & R
DO AS I SAY

In writing now, all these years later, I run short of words to describe my sensation on this latest and worst horror, and do not wish to overload the reader with so much feeling that it becomes devalued by repetition. Suffice it to say that Evelyn was not just my sister, but my parent, my friend, my conscience and my guide and life without her in it seemed an impossible thing.

I clung to her last injunction, DO AS I SAY, and tore myself away from the door and went to lie on my bed until

I had stopped trembling. Then I got up, washed, dressed and took Puss downstairs. It promised to be another hot day, and even as I opened the kitchen door for Puss this early in the morning the curdling smell of death and decay filtered in, as when you pass by a horse a few days dead. I got some victuals for Evelyn, and a jug of water, and as I went up, stopped in the library to find her a book and to put the certificates in a drawer.

When I got to Evelyn's room, Puss was already scratching at the door. I told him to stop, but he would not. I picked him up and put down the food. I knocked on the door. "Evelyn!" I called, hoping it was loud enough for her to hear but not sufficiently loud to disturb Roger and Sylvia. "I have left food. Please eat it. And get better." And then I turned to take myself away before my distress added to Evelyn's. And only then I saw a new message on the slate. It said simply:

Leave London now
Your loving sister

And again,

DO AS I SAY

I had already decided I would not do this. Evelyn would either get better or die. If she got better, we would leave together; if she died, only then would I go. But I could not move until I had seen which way the tide of fortune would turn, despite Evelyn's instructions. However, I could obey Evelyn in a manner by taking every precaution not to catch the disease. I would run no more risks.

As I went down the stairs I heard Sylvia calling my sister. I found her in the dining room pacing up and down. Roger was sitting at the table nursing his head.

"You'll do, H. There's no breakfast." She said this in a way that assumed I should do something about it.

"That will be because there is no Cook, I expect," I said.

Sylvia looked at me.

"None of your pertness, Miss. Roger did the right thing. It was for all our own good. Or would you rather be shut up with the little brats and die like a rat in a bottle? You can always leave, H. Try your luck on the streets."

"And then who will get your breakfast?" I asked. At this Roger looked up.

As I went down to the kitchen I realised what a relief it was to not have to be pleasant to Sylvia anymore. I also knew I was in no danger of being turned out of the house while they needed my services, and so in a manner I had the upper hand. Two long days passed, during which I slipped provisions up to Evelyn (although she now only took water and did not touch the food), listened for her increasingly laboured breathing, and covered her absence to Sylvia by various excuses. However, it was drink that undid us.

When Roger was drunk he became violent or amorous, and it was impossible to say which was worse. On the third night after Cook and the children had been turned out I heard him and Sylvia arguing in Roger's room. He staggered out on to the landing, raving like a madman, saying he could get it elsewhere and she would see. To my horror I heard him coming up the stairs and quickly locked my door and pushed a chest against it. He had not troubled me since the violation, and had instead menaced the maids to the point that they went about the house only in pairs. But now there were no maids. Perhaps in his drunken stupor he had forgot this, as he did not stop at my door but went on to Sarah's.

As soon as I realised this I pulled back the chest and flung open the door, ran out and shouted "No!" just too late to prevent him from going in. He stood absolutely still, and past him I saw what used to be Evelyn, almost naked on the bed, her body covered with great black bruises, her neck horribly swollen, her closed eyes sunken in their sockets and her breathing laboured and rasping through dry blackened lips.

Roger staggered backwards.

"Dear God," he said, and seemed to sober up immediately.

When he went downstairs and told Sylvia, all hell broke loose. Sylvia started screaming hysterically, then began to run up the stairs, then ran down again and did this several times before Roger slapped her and she ran into their room and threw herself on the bed howling. While they were thus incapacitated with shock, I had the presence of mind to run down to the hall and get Roger's sword, for I was fully prepared to do anything to prevent any attempt to get Evelyn out of the house.

When Roger came up the stairs again I said, "Don't come any further."

If he had looked alarmed before, he now looked terrified.

"I think she has gone mad," he said softly to Sylvia, who was on the landing below.

"Just get her out," Sylvia whined.

"She's got my sword," he whispered.

"Not mad, Roger," I said. "Not so mad as to allow my dying sister to be thrown into the street."

"Yes," Roger said finally. "I see that." He seemed to think a minute, "How long... how long do you think she's got?"

"Go away now, Roger," I said.

Evelyn died that night.

20

went down and told Roger and Sylvia as they were having what passed for breakfast. Sylvia was very pale and Roger was sober and seemed prepared to be reasonable.

"I'm sorry," he said. He gestured to me to sit down but I remained where I was. "The thing is, H, we don't want to be shut up, do we? So we can't let the searchers take her. We mustn't let anyone know there has been plague in the house. Must we?"

"I suppose not," I said. In truth I did not care if the house were shut up with them in it as I intended to leave as soon as I had seen Evelyn decently buried. However I, too, could not risk the authorities finding out before I had had the opportunity to take flight. I knew I would have to collaborate with Roger a little longer.

"We must leave her body outside—" began Roger.

"Not outside *our* house!" said Sylvia.

"– not outside anyone's house; but somewhere it will be quickly found by the burial-carts," he continued. "I will help you," he said.

"No you will not!" said Sylvia.

"Yes he will," I said.

I had already planned, in the long hours I stood vigil outside her door, how to prepare Evelyn for burial. I had seen how the plague-nurses wore gloves and long cloaks with hoods and muffled their faces, so that only their eyes were exposed to the air. It was easy to recognise them by the coloured staffs they, and everyone who had ado with the poor plague patients, were obliged to carry in the streets. I would adopt this dress in order to wrap Evelyn in a shroud, and burn it all afterwards, but had not thought further and now wondered how to carry her through the streets unobserved. I had seen bodies carried in all manner of contraptions and even in slings like hammocks on poles which two men carried on their shoulders and figured we could carry Evelyn in Ned's wheelbarrow without attracting undue attention as to the mode of transport, but we had no nurse or searcher whose presence would allow us to pass unhindered. And then thinking of the plague-nurses I reasoned that, could I make a coloured staff, I could walk before the barrow in my nurse's garb until we reached a church in a quiet spot, for if I were to leave my sister exposed in the street I was resolved at least to leave her by a holy place.

I told Roger my plan, which he accepted without question, and told him to equip himself with gloves and so on. I followed him into his room, where Sylvia was fiddling with her hair at the looking glass, and went into a great chest at the foot of the bed to fetch a sheet to make a shroud for my dear sister.

"Not one of the *best* ones!" Sylvia snapped, snatching the one I had chosen out of my hand.

"For God's sake, woman," Roger muttered, "have you no shame?"

"And while you're here," said Sylvia, who had no shame, "the piss pot wants emptying."

You may have wondered at my calmness or carelessness since Evelyn died, and divined an apparent want of feeling, but I now believe I was in a shocked state, and in this state, I took up the piss pot, which was almost overflowing, and went carefully across the room so as not to spill it, and tipped the entire contents over Sylvia's head.

"There," I said. "It is emptied."

Roger, I think, was in a manner unhinged for he looked at me and then at Sylvia and then laughed like a maniac, clutching his stomach as if he were fit to burst, and pointing at his wife, incapacitated by mirth. I picked up my chosen sheet and went out, to prepare my sweet sister for the grave.

That night, dressed in our protective clothing, Roger and I carried my poor sister's shrouded body down to the kitchen door, where we laid her in the barrow. I knew Evelyn was gone from the vessel we carried, but I still felt most tenderly about her remains, and wished heartily to touch or kiss her hand, and bid her body even farewell. But this was folly.

I took up my stick, which I had coloured by binding strips of a red apron about it and peered from the alley until I saw the street was empty. Then I struck out with the confidence I had seen in the plague-nurses, and Roger followed, pushing the barrow. I think if we had met with Aunt Madge that night, she would not have recognised us, so convincingly disguised and demeanoured were we. We walked past three churches ere we found one in a deserted street, and Roger was all for tipping up the barrow, but I stopped him and made him help me lift Evelyn's body out carefully and lay her gently on the ground by the church door. Then Roger said, "No time for weeping, coz. Let's be away." But I told him to go on and that I would come home later. I planned to wait in the shadows and follow Evelyn's body to wherever it was taken, and see her into the ground. Only then, I knew, would I be able to leave London and everything else behind.

I did not have to wait long before a cart came along and picked up Evelyn's body. They were businesslike but not as rough as I had prepared myself for them to be. They picked her up carefully enough, but then had to throw and let go of her to get her on top of the cart which was already quite full of poor souls. I did not mind this as much as I might, as in the moment they let go she seemed to fly upwards, and I imagined her soul flying up and up and away from all this life's misery.

And as I looked into the night sky, which was clear and full of stars, I saw, or thought I saw, a shooting star.

Now that the scavengers had decided the cart was full, it was no mean feat to keep up with it, and also to remain out of sight, for it was forbidden to follow the carts. I knew, from the route we took, that we were headed for no churchyard, and I had heard they were a long time already overstuffed; it was to the common pits we were going.

I was amazed at the degree of activity at the pits, the number of carts that came in and out, yet all was calm industry, and no confusion. I saw the bodies on my cart unloaded, and by this time lost sight of Evelyn, so in my heart blessed each sad package of humanity – and some were heart-breakingly small packages – as it was tossed into the pit. And the scale of the loss was made the more poignant, as there seemed above fifty bodies buried with Evelyn, and the pit was yet only half full, and there must have been ten more pits dug ready to receive more, and many more filled besides. A priest said a few words, but it was perfunctory and I was sorry for that, but then he went to another pit and repeated the same, and then another, and then another, and I could not blame him, for he had to bless them all. Then lime was thrown in on top of the bodies, and then more carts came, but I did not stay to see more packages cast into the pit on top of Evelyn and her fellows. I cast aside my plague stick and began my journey home.

I walked home so full of grief I could not even weep. Yet already the urge to self-preservation, I suppose, had me making plans. I had resolved to burn her clothes and the sheets and clean the room with vinegar, but now realised there was no time, and no need for this. While I pointlessly pictured in my mind where the vinegar was stored in the cellar I also thought of what I would pack to take with me. Ideas crowded into my mind, of practical tasks and of dreams of flight. For once I entertained no debates about the right thing to be done: I could leave Roger and Sylvia without a backward glance.

They had abandoned my sister and I could now with a clean conscience abandon them.

As I had followed Evelyn to her piteous grave I had been blind to anything else, but now I walked back alone in the dark, with nothing but my thoughts for company, I saw the city as it really was, as it really had become, and it seemed to me as a vision of Purgatory. Scenes of horror and desperation met me at every turn. Here a poor soul stood banging his head against a wall, slowly, deliberately, and blood ran down. Here a tiny figure wrapped in a sheet had been laid by the road, awaiting collection. Here someone lay moaning, vomiting, dying, his exposed arms showing the tokens of the plague. Here was a heap of dead cats and dogs, with newborn kittens sucking at their dead mother's teats and blindly mewling in frustration. Everywhere there was the stench of death and all was horribly illuminated by the fires that burned, now by order, day and night, tinting all in hellish colours.

I perpetually ran into poor souls, some hale, some sick, all desperate and all recoiling from me with the same fear and revulsion I felt towards them. I held my posy fast to my lips and nose, to admit no filthy miasma, but nothing could disguise the general stench of decay and disease. I passed whole streets where every house, it seemed, was shut up, and heard the moans and shrieks of the dying intermingled with the sobs and prayers of the living, entombed together in an awful muffled cacophony of despair.

This, I reflected, was all done for the greater good. How cruel the greater good now seemed. There seemed to me now no greater good than my own survival. I vowed that on my return home only that which was for my own good would be my guide. That night I had realised the plague did far worse things than kill people. Those it did not kill it made merciless, cruel as dogs to one another. We were all its victims.

Arriving at home, I realised how tired I was and thought I would go straight to bed and pack in the morning. I went to the kitchen door and found it locked and no light burned within.

I went to the front of the house and knocked at the great door. No one stirred. I threw a stone up to an upper window, where I saw a light, but to no effect. I called Sylvia, and Roger, and then both again, but there was still no sign of life. Then I heard an upper casement open. Sylvia put out her head. Her face glowed red from the flames below.

"There's no point trying to get in," she said. "The doors are all locked."

It took a moment for this to sink in to my reason.

"Let me in!" I cried.

"Save your breath," said Sylvia. "There's nothing for you here."

"How can you do this?" I cried. "Where am I to go?"

"You are a fool, child," sneered Sylvia. "Surely you did not think we would admit you when you have been with your sister? You are dead already, don't you see?"

"I have been careful! I can burn all this! I have been very careful!"

"Go away," said Sylvia, "before you attract the watch, you little idiot."

"At least throw down my things!" I implored, tears now coursing down my face. I heard a voice within – Roger's – but not what he said.

Sylvia turned and said, into the chamber, "I'm not touching her plaguey things. Are you mad?" Then she turned back to me. "Go away and don't come back. We will not own you if you say you are of this house. Now, go, before the watch comes." She leant out further and looked up the street. A burial party was advancing. "Go! Or I will say you run mad with the sickness and have you conveyed to the pest house!" She slammed the window shut.

I did not know what to do. Never mind my belongings, which were few, but my certificate, my passport to safety, was in the house. I thought of breaking in to get it and to liberate poor Puss, who was shut up in my room. I crept round to the kitchen and tried the window. I could not move it. I went back round the front. If I waited until the street was empty I could perhaps gain entry through the shop. I saw a party of searchers approaching with a constable, and concealed myself in a passage opposite the house and waited for them to pass.

But they did not pass. They stopped at the house and knocked at the door. Sylvia threw the window open again and shouted, "For the last time, go away! I shall not tell you again!"

"Open this door!" cried the constable.

Finally the door opened and the constable exchanged words with Roger which I could not hear, and then the searchers forced Roger back into the house and followed him in, leaving one man on the door. Within, it seemed, only moments, the men were out again and swarmed around the house with their tools, nailing down the casements, while the constable read something out to Roger, Sylvia all the while screaming at him. Another man took a brush from a pail and began deftly painting on the door, 'May God Have Mercy… ' The men worked swiftly and it was only when they were gone, leaving watchmen both at the front and the back of the house, that I fully took in what had happened.

The only explanation I could think of was that Cook had given our address on arrival at the pest house. But the fact which struck me most forcibly and strangely was that Roger and Sylvia, by their selfishness and cruelty, had probably saved my life.

PART TWO

'DOLL'

21

lthough I lost track of time during the weeks that followed I have since calculated that I lived for above two months on the streets of London, but nothing transcended the misery and terror of that first night, when I did not sleep, but wandered aimlessly, not knowing what I sought.

When dawn broke it revealed a ghost town; streets that had teemed with traffic were not merely deserted but had grass and weeds beginning to grow in them. In mockery of the city's desperate doomed state, buttercups and daisies bloomed in Fleet Street. Drawn to the river, I found that too unnaturally quiet, though thousands of people, it had been said, were living in boats on stretches of the river, to try to quarantine themselves. The smaller boats of the watermen bobbed at the quayside, with no one to row them and no one to be rowed across. It was as if everyone in the whole world had departed, leaving me alone in it, and I thought this must be what Hell is like. Not hot and full of pain and confusion, but cool and grey and empty, where you are shut out of everywhere, yet cannot leave.

Gradually life began to stir, though specimens of humanity were few and far between, and many of them seemed like myself, to have nowhere to go and nothing to do. I saw a girl climb out of the window of a house with something – food, I guessed – in her apron. While it was obvious she was stealing she did not look about her, but seemed to just go about it in a businesslike way. I soon learnt to do the same.

I do not choose to dwell on this period of my life, as I broke into empty houses, slept in other people's beds and ate other people's food. I took clothes, money and anything else I wanted. I learnt to hide from the watch and to bargain with desperate people, and get the better of them. I learnt to exploit any advantage I had, whether it was a basket of apples or a bundle of firewood. I hardened my heart against the suffering of others and thought only of myself and how to survive another day. And each day I became more aware of that other me, the life that grew within me, my child that was to be, and this strengthened my resolve to live, whatever the cost.

The news – on the rare occasion when one could hear a crier – continued very bad. Whitechapel and Stepney fell to King Plague. Fires were ordered now at every sixth door to burn for three days and three nights to drive away noxious fumes. The hours of darkness were no longer sufficient to shroud in decency the burial of the dead, and now the plague carts rolled through the streets by both day and night and funeral bells tolled with barely any interval. The few clergy who remained stood in the streets admonishing us all to weep, fast and pray, as if not enough of all this were going on already, without the advice of the church.

At some point the weather suddenly turned cold and at about the same time the tide of plague seemed to begin to turn. The weekly Bills of Mortality began to show a marked drop in the number of deaths. Quarantine measures were abandoned, though I think this was more to do with the impossibility of enforcing them once the population had dropped below a certain level, and, though nothing like normal life resumed, people began to come out of their houses and an improvised kind of business began.

You would think that when a general return to the city

commenced in October those of us remaining in London would have cause for celebration. But there were no bells and bonfires. Clergymen and doctors who had been among the first to leave were coldly received by those who had been left behind and I saw one priest jeered and pelted with rotten fruit as he reopened his church and another was actually spat on. Wealthy families who had fled and left their servants to shift for themselves expected everything to return to the way it had been, but these relationships were never to be quite the same. When the court returned, none lined the streets to welcome the King home. If it had been hoped that this collective near view of death had bound Londoners together, it proved to be far from so. The plague had widened, rather than contracted, the divisions between rich and poor. When the cards were on the table, the ordinary people knew, the rich would always save themselves first. Everyone in the city had been cast in the role either of abuser or abused in that terrible plague summer and it was to be a long time before Londoners felt at ease with each other again.

From my own point of view, and that of the many like me, the general return was a disaster. The number of empty properties, which had supported us, contracted, and the long-neglected law began to be rigorously enforced. I eventually found all my adopted homes were reoccupied, and I was soon as destitute and bereft as on the first night I was turned out of my aunt's house.

I had given little thought to what I should do after the plague, in part because I had been entirely concerned with merely surviving, and in part because, until the tide eventually turned, there had sometimes appeared to be no hope of an end to the plague, and it seemed quite possible that it would eventually kill us all. But now that a kind of normality was being established, I had to think of a legitimate means to support myself.

I had not been back to Cheapside but once, a few days after my exile, when, during my period of aimless wandering, I had found myself in the street my aunt's house was in. Afraid to be recognised as a member of the household, I did not stop, but walked past on the opposite side of the street, and merely looked up, to be transfixed by a still, white face at the window. Sylvia saw me, and stared at me, and I stared back at her, and she half-raised a hand but I turned and went on my way. Her face continued to haunt my dreams for a long time afterwards, and the hand went on to form many shapes – sometimes a weak wave, sometimes a gesture that implored pity, and sometimes, most horribly, she beckoned to me, smiling – but, as I had forced myself to become used to doing, by day I hardened my heart and thought on other matters.

I found a room with a hearth above a tavern and though I was willing to work in the shop, the landlord preferred the rent in coin, so I now had a roof over my head, but I could not keep it without employment, as I only had money for two weeks' rent and that was without eating. I calculated which clothes (all of which I had of course stolen) I could absolutely not do without given winter was well on its way and sold the excess. That bought me food in the short term, but I needed to buy more time.

I invested in a bunch of rosemary sprigs and got a pot of beer from the tavern and set about washing and shining my hair. I had heard that long fine hair, which mine was, could fetch up to three pounds an ounce, so when my hair was dry and combed I went to a wig-maker who had reopened his shop nearby. He said times were hard (which of course I knew) and although he said my hair was of a good quality, it was not fair so was cheaper and in short he would give me one pound for the lot. I had no option, and emerged from his shop feeling cold and strange, but I had argued him up to a guinea so that was something.

22

had already discovered that no one wanted to employ a pregnant girl with no letters of introduction and no one to vouch for her, and my condition was quite obvious by this time, so all I had done was purchase more time in which to consider my plight. I knew that once I had sold my clothes and my hair there was nothing left but my body itself. I had seen prostitutes beginning to return to their trade and observed how they attracted customers.

There was a code of sorts, both in their dress and their behaviour, so that they could immediately be known for what they were. They were heavily painted and often wore masks which were then the fashion, and wore much finer and brighter clothes than the majority of working women, though their gaudy apparel often had a bedraggled look. They stood about in certain known places, such as Long Acre and 'Change Alley, and whereas respectable women were always on their way somewhere, or engaged in some business, these indicated their profession by their entire want of employment. Again, unlike modest women, they did not avoid men's gaze but rather sought it, fixing likely customers with a bold stare which seemed to say 'I am at your service.'

In places which were known for the trade they openly approached men, and even called out from their windows and doorways, exposing their legs or breasts, as a shrewd merchant keeps his best goods on the counter. I entertained strong doubts about my fitness to play this part and the women's confidence was most intimidating. I also, of course, shuddered at letting a man do to me what Roger had done, and the thought of it brought back those memories which I had so successfully hidden from myself. For the last time I desperately ran over other possibilities, each time drawing only blanks.

I could go back to my aunt's house at Cheapside. She would have returned from the country, and Sylvia and Roger would either be alive or dead, but that did not matter. What would her reaction be to her niece, unmarried and now showing she was with child? Kind as my aunt was, she was too chary of her reputation to have ado with anything of that sort under her own roof, and she could not be blamed for that, for it was the way of the world. And she would want to know how it came about and I could not tell her what Roger had done, as, alive or dead, he was her son, and it would break her heart, and I loved her too much to give her a pain that time would probably never heal. It was better that she thought that Evelyn and I were both dead.

I considered the rest of my family. Frances, who had gone to be a soldier, could be anywhere, or nowhere, killed by now. Evelyn had kept up a dutiful if desultory correspondence with our other sisters, Clarissa and Diana, before the plague disrupted communications, but they had always disliked me and I knew they would think me in some sense culpable, as girls, like the poor, brought ruin on themselves. And I knew how they would deal with me and my child, for I knew how they had exiled Grace and allowed her child to be taken away. This was to me unthinkable, as my child was all I had, my only reason for going on, and I had resolved that, should we both live, we should never be parted. And that only left poor fallen Grace herself: I knew not what had become of her, nor whether she was alive or dead.

I had thought that however poor I might be, I would never sell myself. But as I considered my small stock of money, I knew that if I were to survive, I must eat. By hook or by crook I must get that shining dirt, gold. I considered thieving, which I had been able to justify to myself during the dog-eat-dog plague months, but now that things were getting back to normality it seemed wrong, and though prostitution was wrong, it was not theft. I would be paid for a service rendered; it was not getting something for nothing, but a business. Going over all this for the tenth time in my mind one morning I quickly threw on my cloak, snatched up my purse, and went out to spend the last of my coin purchasing items necessary to my chosen profession, before my resolve faltered yet again.

I returned home that afternoon with the paint and clothes I needed. In those days looking glasses, in especial the small portable kind, were most hard to come by and expensive and I confess this was the one item I had stolen from a house that I could not pretend was a necessity. I was not sure at the time why I had taken it, but perhaps fate had a hand as it now proved most needful. I put on my new habiliments: a deep scarlet gown with a front lower than I had ever worn before and a little green jacket with a peplum and a cap to match (to cover my absence of hair). Then I set to work with my paints. First I laid on a white cream (though most people's skin was unnaturally pale that winter, as people had feared to go abroad in the streets during the summer), then blackened my eyes, rubbed on Spanish paper to redden my cheeks and applied cochineal to my lips. I finished all with a black silk patch in the shape of a diamond and regarded the full effect. It was most successful: I looked a perfect whore.

I doubted that anyone who had known me would know me now in this guise, but I put on the mask also, and with the upper part of my face covered I felt braver, and began to think I could do this, if I became another person while I was doing it. It had struck me that I looked like a little painted doll, and so chose this for my name. I would be Doll the whore and H the person. Doll was a mask that would keep H safe.

I put on my cloak, which I had trimmed with an abundance of red ribbon, and tarried on the landing until I could hear no one on the stair and then slipped down and out of the side door (for The Rising Sun was on a corner) and then, while I considered where to go, walked round to the front of the shop. I had only seen my face in the little mirror, but now caught sight of my whole being in the window of the tavern. As I marvelled at the transformation, the landlord suddenly appeared.

"Can I help you Miss?" he asked, in a voice that suggested I should clear out if I had no business there.

"I doubt it," said Doll, who, I discovered, talked like a lifelong Londoner, and I walked away with what I considered to be a dignified air.

The fact that the landlord had not recognised me strengthened my resolve. It all now seemed possible. I struck out for Covent Garden.

23

vening was now drawing in, and I dawdled at the stalls, turning over the lace and nick-nacks on sale, and I was trying on some gloves and had almost forgot why I was there when a gentleman spoke to me.

"How much?" he said.

Did he mean the gloves? Or did he mean Doll? I suddenly realised, little fool that I was, that I had no idea how much to ask for.

"Two and six," I said. From his expression it seemed I had hit on just the right amount. Then I wondered if it was too little. Well, I thought, I would learn.

"Lead on," he said. He evidently expected me to take him home.

"I live on the other side of town, sir," said Doll.

"Very well," he said, "follow me." And though I knew it a foolish thing to go Lord knew where with Lord knows who, what did I expect? And he was young to middle-aged and well-dressed and reminded me a little of my uncle, whom I had liked, so I obeyed, and he led me to a coffee-house and after a brief interview with the landlord, we were shown up to a room. There was no fire, but a bed and a table and chair and it seemed quite clean. He called for wine and asked my name, and sat at the table and told me to sit on his lap, which I did.

"Are you not going to remove your cloak?" he said. I obeyed and I don't know whether he observed I was with child or just thought I was fat. He put his arms round me and kissed me, so I put my arms round him and kissed him. Then in one deft movement that spoke of years of practice he all of a sudden had one of my breasts out of the top of my dress and fell to kissing it. This rather shocked me, but did not hurt, and then he put his hand up my skirt and ran it all the way up to my most private part, and again though it was rather a surprise, it did not hurt. These were all new and extreme sensations and I did not know how to respond. Suddenly he stopped and said, "You're a queer one, Doll."

"How do you mean?" I asked.

"You're a cold fish, girl. Show a little passion, won't you? Give a man a little encouragement at least."

And then I knew I was failing and not carrying it off at all. I began crying.

"Oons!" he exclaimed, getting up so suddenly I nearly fell on the floor, "what a witch it is!" And he poured himself some wine and went to stand by the fireplace.

"I'm sorry, sir," I said. "The truth is," and as I started talking truth I checked myself and remembered I must be Doll, "I don't know what to do. I ain't done this before."

At this he first looked astounded and then burst out laughing.

"That is the prettiest play-acting I have seen outside Drury Lane," he said. "So you play the innocent do you? You are the first virgin with child I have ever known. Still, this game may have some relish in it." He poured me a glass of wine and I drank it down in two draughts. He continued to look at me with some amusement. "So, tell me your story." I began to think of a history for Doll, but before I could formulate a tale, he said, "No, no, let me see if I can guess. Let me see." And he began to stride around the room as he spoke. "You are a poor innocent country girl, a milkmaid, I daresay?" I inclined my head as though this might be correct. "Or a maid in a great house, perhaps. Yes, and you were ruined by… the son of the house?" I shook my head most definitely. The further from the truth the better. "The squire himself, then?" I nodded. "And when you found you were with child he turned you out?" I nodded. "And you came to London, the goodliest forest in the world to shelter a great belly?"

"You have it, sir," I said.

"And, check me if I have hit it wrong, but you only had ado with the squire just the one time, and have never looked at a man since?" He seemed to be enjoying this enormously.

"Yes, sir. He took me against my will and it was just the once."

"Marvellous!" he exclaimed. "This has spice in it! In fact this may take all evening!" And he called for a fire to be lit and ordered some dinner to be sent up and more wine, and seemed to be very pleased.

"In that case it will be five shillings, sir," said Doll, quite to my surprise.

"You are a cunning jade, Doll, but fair's fair, five shillings it is." And he gave me the money and there was no going back.

"Now, shall I be myself? Or shall I be the squire?"

"I did not like the squire, sir," I said.

"Well we can't have that," he said. "I shall be myself, then. The first man to show you what pleasure really is."

And then we had dinner and I drank more wine and with each mouthful I felt less uneasy about where I was and what I was doing, especially as Pinky, as he said his friends called him, seemed to be enjoying himself so heartily. When we had finished Pinky pushed back his chair and said, "Now Doll, it is time."

I stood up and he led me over to the bed and began kissing me and undressing me, but the first thing he did was to pull off my cap and I put up my hand to try and stop him, but he did anyway.

"You have cut off your hair," he said, as if I didn't know.

"Well sir," I said, "I needed the money."

"That squire," he sighed, continuing to undress me and to kiss each part that was newly exposed. "What bastards men are." When I was just in my shift he bade me lie on the bed and undid his breeches, and I was most surprised at what lay within. I had seen men's members before, of course, when bathing or pissing, but this had grown to a mighty size and he put my hand on it and it felt quite firm like a fresh-made black pudding.

Then he lay next to me and kissed my breasts again which I began to like a great deal, and then put his hand between my legs which I was less sure of, and then he said, "You must protest, Doll."

"What? I mean, I beg your pardon?" I said.

"You must protest. You have been ruined once, but you are yet a good girl. You must protest, and then, when I ravish you, only then must you like it."

"Yes, sir," I said. So I protested a good deal, but I do not think I was very convincing, as I did not convince myself, and found I did not mind being ravished nearly so much as I had thought I would, and though it was uncomfortable, it had its merits, and it was gratifying to see how much it pleased Pinky, and I seemed to know what to say then, but then Pinky cried out as if in pain and it all ended abruptly and I knew I must have done something wrong.

But I had done nothing wrong, Pinky said. I should go on the stage, he said. Which I took to be a compliment. We got dressed and finished off the wine and Pinky said he would recommend me to his friends and asked where I could be found. As I did not want to give H's address I said I would be in Covent Garden at about the same time most evenings. And then we parted.

24

he most significant consequence of the encounter with Pinky (apart from the five shillings of course) was that I was no longer afraid of having ado with a man. I had not realised that there would be quite so much playing involved and this made it much easier. It seemed that as well as H pretending to be Doll, Doll could also pretend, and this was all part of the service. It had all been most illuminating, and I slept better that night than I had for a very long time.

Over the following weeks I learned a great deal more about my new profession. Pinky and his friends proved a reliable source both of income and education and these evenings had the advantage of often being entertaining as well, as I enjoyed playing my part, and they enjoyed it too. I also discovered, thanks to Noddy (all Pinky's friends had odd names), the purpose of a part of the female body that I had seen in a picture in one of the books in Aunt Madge's library, which was labelled 'Clitoris' but which seemed to be called anything but that by real people. Noddy had shown it to me with my ever-useful mirror and demonstrated what could be achieved with it. I was most surprised and gratified and must confess to not minding Noddy's visits nearly so much as some of the others. He called it "the mount of pleasure", and said it was "near the well-spring", which itself was next "the valley of desire" so I supposed he had been to one of the universities.

However, the novelty of the ruined maid soon wore off on both sides and in any case I needed to make more money, more than was sufficient to live on, as when the baby came I would not be able to work and I would have to have money put by. So Doll engaged in street work, which was sheer drudgery and often disheartening as the men did not care about stories or playing parts but just used her in a doorway or an alley or some filthy room. Still, these had the advantage of being quick to accomplish, and Doll could do several a day, and all those shillings and sixpences added up.

And then I fell ill. To this day I do not know what was wrong with me, but I could not get out of bed for weeks together for fatigue. To cut a long and sorry episode short, though the landlord and landlady were very kind to me (I took care they never saw Doll), I had soon used up all my savings and by the time I was half-recovered I was worse off than I had ever been, and by this time I was great with child and even your citizen in search of a few moments of relief will baulk at a woman who looks likely to calve at any moment when there are plenty of skinny whores about. I had to face the fact that I was unable to earn the means to keep me alive, let alone a baby as well, and then I happened across something which fairly finished me off.

I had decided to take myself to the parish workhouse. Although these are not pleasant places at least one has somewhere to sleep and something to eat. It would give me a safe place to have the baby without incurring debts which I could not repay, which was the only other alternative, and would lead inexorably to the debtors' prison, which would not be so easy a matter to leave. All I needed was a space in which to get through my confinement, and then when I was set on my feet again I could go back to the game and keep myself and the baby tolerably well. I decided that I would say my husband was a sailor and overseas, and then they would not be able to take my baby away, which was my main concern. In short, it was a desperate but necessary measure. And winter was coming.

I happened to approach the workhouse just as a detachment of women was coming out, escorted by their superintendents, I supposed to work in the watercress beds I had passed down the lane. They were a sorry sight indeed, their skin, hair and clothes all seemed a uniform grey and there was not one smile to share between them. And then I got a hard shock, as I thought I recognised a woman among them. And as I looked harder, I saw that it was my sister Grace, most sadly aged, and dead-seeming in the eyes. She looked at me, but did not see me. I made to call out to her, but, as in a dream, could make no sound with my mouth. And what, after all, would be the point? I could do nothing for her, and the sight of me in my desperate condition could only add to her distress.

Who knows what trials she had endured since running away from the House of Correction in Ware? What had brought her to London and then abandoned her here? And how desperate must she have been to end up back in a workhouse? And what had happened to her poor baby? Well that changed my purpose. I would not go into the workhouse, as however you went in, you all ended up like these grey people, the walking dead, I decided. I would rather be truly dead. And that was the direction in which my thoughts now turned.

Three days later I was on London Bridge with nothing to my name but the clothes on my back and a shawl in which were wrapped my paints, patches, looking glass and comb. I had decided to see the bridge before I died, and to choose a house for myself, that I might have lived in one day, if things had gone differently. Even in my utterly cast down state I experienced a kind of satisfaction from being on the bridge at last. It was not at all as I had imagined. I had thought the thoroughfare running down the middle would be broad and bright, like a wide street, but it was both narrow and dark, carts passing each other with some difficulty, and over-reaching upper storeys of the houses almost touched across the street, so it had more the feeling of a tunnel than a bridge. You could not even properly see Nonesuch House, the buildings were so close together, but as it spanned the entire width of the bridge traffic passed under it through a great arch. And then further on there was a space between the houses, where some washing was hanging up to dry on one side and just a pile of rubbish on the other. Here you could go right to the parapet and see all the way up the river. I did this and then crossed to the other side and looked downriver, imagining I could see all the way to the sea, which was most exhilarating, and then down at the water, which flowed especially fast between the pillars. Here there were places where the parapet was fallen down and I could stand right on the edge.

I looked about for stones and began filling my pockets with them. The advantage I had was that I could not swim, but I knew that people could naturally float so people intent on drowning themselves were wise to weigh themselves down. And then I considered my bundle, and how it might be useful to some poor whore, might indeed make the difference between eating and going to bed hungry, so I went back into the street and soon saw a painted lady, who on closer inspection proved little more than a slip of a girl.

"Here," I said, holding out the bundle. "There are paints and things. You are welcome to them." She looked at me uncomprehendingly but took the bundle just the same, and I went away.

My pockets were dragging me down something terrible and that and the weight of the child made me unconscionably tired. Still, my journey was nearly at an end, and my babe and I should soon have blissful rest together for ever. All I looked forward to was the relief death would bring, and not one more morning of waking up dreading how I would get through the day. I placed myself right on the edge of the bridge and closed my eyes and said a prayer. I prayed for my sisters, my aunt and my cousins. Though I knew what I was doing was sinful and that I would not go to Heaven I made a special prayer to Evelyn to be ready to meet my innocent baby if it went there, and look after it as I imagined she looked after our sister Belinda and brother Abraham that had died young. And then I realised that I should never now meet my mother. That thought put a stop to all others and an end to caring. Just nothingness would be a relief, so weary was I of life.

I was so tired and had not eaten for so long I believe I was a little delirious, and I seemed to feel the river pulling me downwards. I readied myself to jump forwards and did jump, but had the sensation of flying backwards and then remembered no more.

25

thought I was back in my bed in my old room again at Cheapside, and Puss was licking my hand. It was a most pleasant sensation and I remember thinking that perhaps Heaven *was* my old room in Cheapside with Puss licking my hand, and the sensation of Evelyn being there, and me being ill and cared for and not having to do or say anything.

I awoke again, as I thought, and this time felt sure I was in Heaven, for out of the window I could see only open sky and the river and boats, so I must be in my dream house on the bridge. Yet Puss was still licking my hand and someone was moving about in the room and I had an impression of kindness. Perhaps Puss and Evelyn and everyone I loved could be in Heaven with me in my house on the bridge, I thought. And I drifted away again.

I seemed to be swimming in treacle, to be struggling to awaken, and each time I thought I had awoken, there seemed another pair of eyelids over mine, and I had to struggle to open those, and then there were more closed lids beyond, and it was a tremendous effort to open those, and yet it was still not light and all I knew was that Evelyn was dead and the sense of her being there had been a cruel fantasy.

Eventually the light came. It began as a dull square in the wall. Then it gradually brightened, and then I saw that it was a window and I really was in a bed in a room on the bridge. I looked about me. The room was small and sparsely furnished but tidy and clean, and there was a girl asleep on a chair under the window, and beside her was my bundle, and on the floor beside my bed lay Puss.

"Hello Puss!" I said, and he jumped up and licked my face to welcome me back and barked and barked so that the girl woke up.

"Hello there!" she said in a most kind and friendly but very loud way. "Back in the land of the living, are you? It was Toby what saved you. He went mad when I brought your bundle in, sniffing it and sniffing it, then he ran off after you and fairly pulled you away. He seems to have taken a shine to you, or I'm no judge."

"We're old friends," I said, fussing Puss. "And his name is Puss."

"Puss?" shrieked Janey, as I soon discovered her name to be. "I ain't having no dog called Puss. That's a *girl's* name!" she objected. And then she went off and returned with some broth for me and a bit of bread and as I was famished it was all gone in an instant.

"Blind me!" she said. "You'd better not have any more till that's gone down a bit. Don't want to make you sick." She considered me for a moment, and then tended the fire, and then returned her attention to me.

"Now then. Where d'you live?" she demanded.

"Nowhere," I said. "I left when I couldn't pay for my room."

"Alright. Who are your friends?"

"I have no friends."

"Come on now," chivvied Janey, "everyone's got friends." And when she saw that I did not, she said, "Family?" and I shook my head, and she said, "Really? No one at all?" and I shook my head again.

"Pfffff!" said Janey, which I was to learn was her regular expression of exasperation. "You're in a right pickle ain't you?"

I confessed that I was.

"Still, worse things happen at sea, eh?" and with a grin she took my bowl to fetch me more broth.

While she was gone, I stroked Puss's ears and wondered what journey had brought him here, and whether he had escaped the house before or after it had been shut up. Still, it mattered little now. The miracle was that he had found me again.

"Right, missy," said Janey, when she came in again. "While you was asleep I took the liberty of inviting a certain lady here who may be able to help you. I don't say she *will*, mind, I just say she *might*."

Then Janey asked me a lot of questions about my past, having correctly ascertained that we were of the same profession, but I was careful to mention nothing of my real past, and let Doll do the talking. It transpired that Janey was going to live with the lady she had invited, and thought I might go too. It all seemed most encouraging but I was so tired I went back to sleep again, with Puss at my side.

It seemed only moments later, but must have been some hours, that Janey woke me suddenly and said I must make the best of myself as the lady was here and I must put my best foot forward. As it turned out there were two ladies, and they made a mighty challenging and interesting pair. Mrs Fotherington was extremely tall and thin and Mrs Cresswell was exceedingly short and fat, so they were like an amusing picture in a child's chapbook and it required me in my half-fevered state to exert some control over myself not to see them as made-up characters, but as real people. As I soon found out, in Pris Fotherington and Mother Cresswell, I had the honour to be in the company of two of the most infamous bawds in London. However, by their fine but not over-fine dress and by their discreet and sparing use of paint, they looked almost as respectable as any lady my aunt would entertain, were it not for a rather alarming wig worn by Mother Creswell, which she must have chosen for its colour (orange) rather than its size (a little too small).

Janey introduced us and then went to make tea. Mrs Fotherington and Mrs Cresswell settled themselves on the only two chairs in the place, and considered me.

"She does indeed have a face," said Mrs Fotherington.

"Janey's a good girl," observed Mrs Cresswell, "she wouldn't send me on a wild goose chase." Then she addressed me. "How long have you got, dearie?" she asked.

"Not long. Not long at all I believe," I answered.

"Oh she speaks well!" exclaimed Mrs Fotherington.

I cursed myself for forgetting Doll.

"I can speak as well as you please when it is warranted," said H, "or as common as you like when it serves, missus," said Doll.

Mrs Fotherington clapped her hands in delight.

"Oh she is a rare one. She might do very well."

Mrs Cresswell looked at me earnestly.

"Have you worked for anyone before?" she asked.

"Only for the gentlemen," I said.

She smiled.

"I mean to say, did you look after your own money and live in your own place, or did you have a bully – a gallant – a gentleman to look after you?"

I shook my head.

"There's only me," I said.

"And… you haven't been managing?" she said gently.

"No," I said, and felt my chin begin to wamble, but held fast.

Something passed between the two ladies which seemed some kind of assent or agreement that I would do. Janey had come back in the room and was serving tea and I heard her tell Mrs Cresswell that I had no family and no friends and this strangely seemed to recommend me to her. There was more conferring between the two ladies and then Mrs Cresswell said:

"Well Doll, I have a proposition to put to you. I keep a nice house for girls like you. No more street-walking, no more back alleys, no more over-a-trunk-in-an-out-room. I keep a nice house for nice girls and nice gentlemen. I look after my girls when they are in a condition – as you are – and I look after 'em when they're sick. I'm like a mother to 'em, so I am. And in return I expect them to be good girls. I don't stand for no nonsense. Not for keeping any gifts and suchlike. I am a plain dealer and I expect the same from my girls. My house has a good name and that is the root, I say the very root, of my success."

"A bawdy house is like a school," chipped in Mrs Fotherington. "One child kills itself on a bit of bad meat and it takes years for it to recover its reputation. Ladies like ourselves cannot afford a bit of bad meat. For bad news has run a mile while truth is still putting his boots on."

"Indeed," said Mrs Cresswell. "Bad news spreads like wild flowers."

"Wildfire," said Mrs Fotherington.

"And wildfire," concurred Mrs Cresswell. "You only have to agree to stay long enough to recompense me for looking after you in your time of need, and then we can both reconsider terms. What do you say, Doll?"

26

he next day I was feeling much stronger and Janey and I set off for Mrs Cresswell's, whom we were now to call Mother. Fortunately, Tobypuss (as Janey and I had agreed he could be called) had ingratiated himself so well with Mother Cresswell that he also accompanied us. Her house was outside the city in Clerkenwell and had as many rooms as my aunt's house, though they were smaller in size. We had a room each and Mother Cresswell put me and Janey next to each other on the first floor, so I should not have too many stairs to climb. She was able to have such a fine house she said "on account of the stink" and indeed the industry round about the area was concerned with saddle-making and leather and suchlike and did indeed stink most abominably, which was why, Mother Cresswell said, leather-making was banned within the city walls. There were many things, she said, that went on outside the city walls, that were prohibited within.

"Are there no constables here?" Janey asked, as we both knew from our street-walking days that they were to be avoided, though if you were caught, they were not above taking a turn with a girl on the quiet and letting her go.

"Them rogues?" said Mother Cresswell. "Oh yes, but I have 'em in my pocket my dears. You need not vex yourselves on that score."

According to Mother Cresswell the plague had ruined her business, along with those more legitimate trades, and though now some of her old girls had come back, she was restocking her house, as some of her girls had "gone to a better place", which at first I thought might be Mrs Fotherington's, but was set right as she added, "God rest 'em." Janey and I now met some of the other girls, though Janey knew some of them already and they were a friendly and kindly collection of wenches, and did not have the sorry and bedraggled appearance of many of the whores I had seen in the city. Three of them were gathered in what Mother Cresswell termed her 'saloon'.

"Ladies, meet your new sister, Doll," said Mother Cresswell. "This is Bessie," she said, indicating a pretty girl who came from the North. "Tell 'em one of your poems Bessie," said Mother Cresswell, explaining to us, "she is a very pretty poetess, is our Bessie."

Bessie stood up and said:

"I know no man who's worth a fart;

So nowt but gold shall charm my heart."

Then she curtseyed and all the girls clapped.

"A powerful good maxim," said Mother Cresswell, "for what is a whore's worst enemy, daughters?"

"True love," they chorused.

"Just so," Mother Cresswell approved. She turned to a tall, slim and very elegant-seeming girl. "And this is Kat. She has a certain *je ne sais pas*." And then to a rosy-faced smiling girl, who was pleasingly plump. "And this is Winnie. She has *joy de vie*. You'll meet the others by and by. Now," she addressed us all, "Doll will be staying with us as a guest until she has passed her hard bargain and is recovered. Then she will be working here until she finds her feet again." Mother Cresswell seemed at pains to emphasise that my staying there was a temporary arrangement, to be renegotiated at some point.

"There ain't much chance of finding your feet when you're flat on your back," quipped Winnie and the other girls laughed.

"*Joy de vie*," smiled Mother Cresswell. "She has it in spades."

Then Mother Cresswell went out on some business and the girls made a great fuss of Tobypuss, and were very kind to me and solicitous about the baby, as it turned out Winnie was also expecting, though had only just discovered this. They were remarkably incurious about my past, which suited me, and in general it was very rare that anyone spoke of their life before joining the trade. It was as if I had entered another world that existed side by side with the ordinary world, but had different rules.

As it was a Sunday, it was the girls' day off, though they said if there was great demand Mother Cresswell relaxed this. We were all up quite late in the saloon that first evening, some of the girls playing cards, and I was beginning to feel quite at home, and helping Janey write a letter, when a terrific commotion set up in the street. Winnie ran to the window and looked out.

"It is the Viscount and his cronies," she said, "and in no fit state to call on ladies." At this the girls all laughed.

Then a hail of stones hit the window. Seeing my alarm Winnie said, "Don't mind 'em, Doll; the bullies often break the windows. 'Tis a way they may vent their frustration when their guts are full of ale and their pockets are empty."

Even Mother Cresswell, who was a little deaf, had been disturbed and bustled in. She opened the window and shouted down.

"What is your will, gentlemen, to be knocking up respectable women at this hour?"

"A whore! A whore! A whore!" came the chorus and more stones were thrown at the windows.

"And what will you give us?" asked Mother Cresswell. "Let me see your purses," she demanded.

Then there were some discouraged noises and cursing and presumably nothing was produced to persuade Mother Cresswell to open the door and admit the gentlemen, for she called down: "Do you see the sign of a banker here? Or a money-lending Jew? We give no credit! Come back on the morrow, when your purse matches your inclination!" and she slammed the casement shut. She sat down and employed herself feeding tidbits to Tobypuss, who had quickly become her favourite. She seemed quite unconcerned although there was still more shouting and more stones thrown at the windows, so that I feared they were like to break.

Then Mother Cresswell sighed, got up and threw the window up again.

"Do you hear me, you dogs? Will you make me call the constable? Hearken to my words, and if you are deaf, as you seem to be, read my lips: *no fee, no fuck*." And she slammed the window down and there was silence. "Come along, my dears," she said to us sweetly. "Come kiss your old mum goodnight. Time for bed."

27

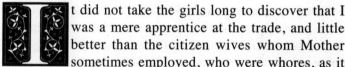t did not take the girls long to discover that I was a mere apprentice at the trade, and little better than the citizen wives whom Mother sometimes employed, who were whores, as it were, only part-time, and otherwise stood at their husbands' counters in inns or shops or coffee-houses, or pursued other trades, applying to Mother only when times were hard and they needed a little extra money. We were not encouraged to mix with these "amateurs" as Mother termed them, and indeed had little occasion to, Mother's role often consisting in arranging an assignation elsewhere and handling that delicate aspect: the money.

When the girls apprehended how green I was they gave me many hints on how to conduct myself in future, particularly regarding the avoidance or escape from nasty customers: that is to say, those that will hurt you. I am sorry to say that even in her delicate condition, Doll had encountered such men, and on one occasion had been beaten senseless and left in a gutter, where the watch had found her early the next morning. She also had some scars on her buttocks, indeed I still bear them faintly, from a devil who took a horsewhip to her, while assuring Doll it gave him, if not her, great pleasure. The girls were very kind in this and other things and said it was a marvel I had survived so long, given my remarkable ignorance of life on the streets.

As I was not working, I busied myself helping prepare meals and keeping the house clean and tidy, though in truth I was not much help to the maids as my back ached terribly and my stomach was so swollen I could barely turn round without knocking something over, which was a source of great amusement to Janey.

"Watch out! Mind your backs there and make room!" she would shout when I went down the corridor, "There's an elephant loose in the house!" (I was not terribly insulted at this until some years later, when I saw an elephant, and then felt very humiliated indeed.) I kept out of the way when there were gentlemen present in the saloon as Mother said that she didn't mean to seem unkind but the mere sight of me might put them off. On these occasions I stayed in my room and rested and read. Mother had given me a little pin money and the first thing I had bought was a book of plays, which I loved to read, and on other occasions the girls loved to have me read to them, and this used to remind me of the hours Evelyn and I spent in the library at Cheapside, causing me to reflect that that was in another lifetime, when I was someone else.

Mother of course was her own library of wisdom on the subject of the gentle craft, which she maintained did more to promote matrimonial harmony than any church vows.

"Married people ought to learn to love bawdy houses, as Englishmen love Flanders: it is better that war is maintained there than brought home to their own doors," she would say. She felt we girls offered a civic service, which, among other things, protected respectable women from the importunities of lustful men, who could not govern their appetites, Mother said, any more than a hen could govern a fox. She was quite clear that men, not women, were the weaker sex, and had to be indulged like spoiled children, and that women were harder and tougher, and God made us that way so we could bear children and bear hardship equally. "There are some women you may never get to the bottom of," she would say, "but you can size up any man in a twinkling." I did not think that Mother liked the male sex very much at all, but rather as my Aunt Madge had not liked to eat celery; it was not an aversion, she merely did not see the merit in it. And while she was kindly to me, she drove a hard bargain, and having heard how she had dealt with one girl who had kept back money from her, I should not have liked to get on her wrong side. I had a home now and would do nothing to risk losing it.

We were sitting in the saloon one afternoon, and my back was aching worse than ever and I had not been able to get comfortable all night and was all day shifting in my chair and getting up and sitting down and I noted the girls were looking at each other in a meaningful way and I began to realise the baby might be on its way.

"Lie down on the daybed if it will make you easier," suggested Janey, "and I will rub your feet." I struggled to stand up, which was by now quite comical to watch I imagine, and suddenly felt an alien sensation of pressure released, as when you let the cork out of a barrel, and suddenly realised I was all wet and stood in a puddle of water.

"I think I have pissed myself," I said, and all the girls, as one, suddenly leapt up and started running in all directions.

"The waters have broken!" exclaimed Winnie.

"I'll make ready her bed!" said Frenchie.

"I'll put the copper on!" said Kat.

"There, there, now," said Janey, putting her arms round me. "It's alright. Do you feel sick?"

And I vomited in response and considered the mess I had made of Mother's rug and felt most sorry for myself and commenced weeping.

"Fetch clean sheets from the great trunk on the landing!" Mother ordered Kat. "Not the best ones! And make up my bed, not Doll's. There's more room."

And suddenly I felt a great twinge in my back and had to hold on to Janey and not move for a moment. When it passed she had me sit down and between them those blessed girls managed to undress me and wash me and put me in a clean shift, and now I had stopped crying it was quite comical to see how, although they all tried not to show it, they were quite astonished to see, when I was naked, how absolutely enormous I had grown, for I am only of a low stature and a small frame, and my great belly must have made me seem like a very large fat pea in a very little pod. The girls were then anxious to get me to bed, but Mother and Janey (who, it turned out, had delivered no fewer than three of her own brothers and sisters and one of her sisters' babies) opposed this and said it was better that I could move about if I wanted to, and now nature must take its course, and we should permit me to do whatever made me easiest. And indeed I was glad of this as the twinges grew into great waves of pressure and when they were at their height I did not know what to do with myself and could not have lain still.

Because of all the kindness around me I was not afraid, and it was pretty to see how excited the girls were, especially Winnie as she was expecting too, and for the whole of that afternoon and night they were as good as real sisters to me, and although they were supposed to be available for work, in the end Mother got tired of keeping gentlemen waiting with various excuses and gave up and locked the front door and declared it a half-holiday.

Janey explained there would be a long time of hard twinges before the baby came, as first babies always took an age to arrive (and then she had the goodness to whisper in my ear and check it *was really* my first), and I was just to be as comfortable as I could be, and as soon as I felt any sort of urge to push, I must say so straightway, as I should by rights be in bed by then. I confess I do not know why I give these details as nearly every woman knows only too well what it is to give birth, but perhaps because it was the only time I ever did, and the outcome was so memorable, it all remains very vivid to me to this day.

I think I must have been among the lucky women as none of the labour was past endurance and it was all more hard work than agony. After one of the very powerful pains they got me into Mother's room and helped me onto the bed and she chivvied all the other girls out, but I begged that Janey stayed, which Mother seemed reluctant to permit, but seeing my distress, allowed. There was a little dressing room or closet attached where Mother had Janey put the hot water and clean linen ready to bathe and dress the infant, and in truth her room was much more convenient than mine and, between pushing when I was incapable of thought, I thought that very kind of her.

When the first urge to push came it was so irresistible I thought if God Himself ordered me not to push I could not have obeyed Him. After that I seemed to be pushing for hours and it was at the point where I began to wonder whether I had the strength to carry on that Janey cried out "The head's there! I can see the head! Look Mother!" And Mother looked and cried, "Push Doll! You're nearly there! Push!" And with these encouragements, I pushed with all my might, and when I thought I could push no more, still pushed, and to cries of delight the baby came out.

"It's a little boy!" cried Janey. "You've got a little boy Doll! Oh but he's a tiny little dear!"

"Let me see him," I said, but Mother thought it better to wash him and make him warm first. "Oh Janey!" I cried, clasping her hand, "I still want to push!"

"That's alright," Janey said, "the afterbirth has got to come out yet."

So I pushed again a few times and Janey called out "Blind me! There's another one! Blind me if it ain't twins! And blind me if it ain't another little lad! No wonder you was such a whopping size, Doll!"

Janey cut the cord and carried the child to the dressing room where Mother took him from her, while I was weeping with relief and surprise and of course joy. Janey seemed to be gone for a long time, though I may have been a little delirious. But when Janey came back to me to deal with the afterbirth her face was serious and her lip quivered. She took my hand.

"Doll, be brave darling but one of the little lads has gone."

"Gone?" I said. "Is he dead?"

"Yes Doll," said Janey, "I'm sorry," and I think the way her voice broke when she said it upset me as much as anything, for Janey never cried.

Then Mother came to the door and looked at Janey and shook her head.

"What?" asked Janey, and then, in disbelief, "Lost both of 'em?"

Though many years have since passed, of my grief that night my pen refuses to write.

28

fter Christmas, Doll was well enough to go back to work, though I still lacked colour and was thin after so many weeks of illness. I had got very sick after the twins died and the doctor was sent for several times and said I should probably not be able to have anymore children, which indeed proved to be the case. So that was that.

I think H died for a time when the twins did, or went away somewhere, but there was an emptiness where she used to be anyhow.

At the end of the first day I'd been back at work, as I kissed Mother goodnight, she hugged me and whispered, "In a way, though it won't seem it now, it all turned out for the best." And I tried to believe her. My body was recovered but every night I had bad dreams, often about little Joe and Sal, who I had failed to save in time, from which I would awake in a panic and with extreme sensations of grief and guilt.

Doll became rather wild and intemperate and took on more customers than anyone else and the ones that no one else wanted as I became entirely obsessed with earning enough money to get out of the game.

"Pfffffff! You know everyone says that," observed Janey. "Your oldest most decrepit whore in Dog and Bitch Yard maintains she's just working till she's got enough to stop. We all dream of building up a little fortune, of buying respectability where no one knows us, of setting ourselves up as widows with an independent income, maybe even of marrying a decent man and having a family. No one ever does though."

In fact, there were not many old tarts in those days. You sometimes came across them in taverns, as some were powerful drinkers and only earned enough to keep them from being thirsty, and Doll could drink well enough and sometimes a bit too much, and when they were in their cups and tending to the maudlin, those that had served the profession before the Commonwealth would tell you of how hard times were when the playhouses were first closed down. That was going back over twenty years so these were rough old birds. All the places, in fact, of assignation, dried up. Some of our sisters, Mother once told me, were even driven to church to find trade in the days of old Oliver, whom they hated as much as if they had been Cavaliers. Some of the poor wenches – and here she would affect to sniff and wipe at her eye at the memory – were even forced into honest occupations or – and here she would pretend to look about her as if she were going to say something slanderous – took husbands. When the second King Charles rode into London – it must have been May Day for there were maypoles up, taken by our trade to have significance – it was the poor whores, Mother averred, who were the first on their knees in the streets weeping for joy.

The restoration of the King and the restoration of the profession went, as you might say, hand in hand. There was even a new class of whore: the private whore, or Miss. Both Mother Cresswell and her friend Pris Fotherington would work themselves into a passion when they discussed this subject, saying these private correspondences and arrangements were destroying public trading, threatening to ruin the houses they kept, and there should be a law. I must confess I learnt a deal of history under Mother's roof, as before that I had no notion of the politics of the late troubles save what I had learned at my aunt's – namely that under the Commonwealth birth did not count for privilege, property was redistributed, women achieved more liberty, censorship ended, working boys were sent to school, and equality before the law began to be established, and that when Charles II came back mercifully everything went back to normal.

Mother Cresswell's house, I soon learnt, was known for its *types*, which is to say that the girls played speciality parts. Bessie did a line in virginity ravished which would have made the most hypocritical actress blush. We girls (egged on of course by Janey who was always full of mischief) used to sometimes tease her by calling her Oohsir, for Bessie knew what *protesting* was. We used to listen at her door for entertainment when custom was slack; it was all: "I hope you mean me no harm, sir! Ooh, sir! You do not mean to... ooh sir! You will not hurt me, sir!" and so forth, and "Surely it is too big, sir!" shortly followed by "I am undone! Ooh sir! Oooooooooh siiiiiiiir!"

Bessie usually wore a white frock but also had a milkmaid's costume. She had meant to play the milkmaid as another string to her wanton innocent part, but the first gentleman she tried it with made her milk him like a cow. After she told us this story we called her Moosir for a bit, but it did not stick as he never came back.

There was Frenchie, who was, as you might guess, from France, and she used to specialise in the gentlemen that liked to be tied up or whipped. Bessie and Winnie played sisters when required, while Kat played the lady to men who liked to be a footman ravishing their mistress, and she was also Cleopatra on special occasions. This kind of play-acting suited me no end as I chose to keep everything on the surface. And there was a kind of satisfaction in giving a man exactly what he sought, and thinking of new ways to add spice and surprise to it, so that he would come back and ask for you again. I had no particular speciality – like Janey I made it up as I went along.

And though I say I kept everything on the surface and kept Doll between me and everything else, I did have a soft spot for Janey, and was as fond of her as I think I ever was of anyone but Evelyn, for she did not appear to look at you without seeming to care about you and even when she teased, like saying I was an escaped elephant, there was affection in it. And she scolded me when I drank too much, which no one else did.

29

t had occurred to me that as no one in my Cheapside life had ever known of my pregnancy, and there was no child as proof of my shame, I might be able to pick up the pieces of my old life and maybe even return to my aunt's household, if I could come up with a convincing explanation of my long absence. But to do this I needed H, and H was not there. I seemed to lack the confidence to be able to put H together again, she had become such a complex thing, a broken thing, somehow scattered and escaping, whereas Doll was simple and robust and undemanding. H had always thought of others, but Doll thought only of herself, and this single-mindedness made her strong and safe.

It was Doll, in fact, who began to cheat Mother Cresswell. There were two rules the importance of which Mother impressed on us with great vigour: we were not to steal from the gentlemen, and if our gentlemen gave us extra money or other gifts we were to give these to her. (What happened to these gifts we had no idea, though we were all aware of a great key Mother kept tucked in her bodice on a grubby bit of ribbon and guessed that, as we never saw it used in the house, it was the guardian of our surrendered bounty.) The first rule was easy enough to obey, for the fact that whores are notorious thieves, and that a man knew he did not have to watch his pocket at our house, made it a popular resort. In any event, we would have been fools to steal from our gentlemen, as our house was not in one of the corners of town known for the trade (Mother Cresswell maintained this aided our reputation as a "house of quality") so a great part of our business depended on our regulars and on recommendations. The second rule, however, was less rigorously observed. While we would not steal, we felt entitled to keep gifts, and so only rendered to Mother sufficient so as not to invite her suspicions. Most of the girls laid out their extra money on clothes which, as well as being an ornament to their trade, they took pleasure in, not having a great deal else to do in their leisure time, while others sent it home to their families. I continued my habit of making my own clothes and instead stored up my little fortune as you never know what lies around the corner and I was determined never again to be poor. Also, I had had to work for two months for nothing but my bed and board to pay off my debt to Mother for keeping me when I first came and afterwards when I was sick, so I felt I had to make up for lost time. I do not in any sense mean to justify theft here, for I did not think this was a fair rule, and in any case Mother made quite enough out of our labours without the gifts as well. And there was something else, for there was a kindness in gifts that there was not in ordinary earnings. And most of us had little enough of that in our lives.

I became quite friendly with some of my regulars. There was Jasper, who was a youthful heir to a vast fortune, which he was borrowing against with great determination. He used to come with a flotilla of young sparks who used to roister in the saloon, peppering the nonsense they talked with curses of new invention (for they considered themselves as in the very vanguard of fashion) such as "Stap my vitals!" and "Damn my diaphragm!" and "Slit my windpipe!" and seemed to shout and laugh as much as they did anything. I am not sure that they came to the bawdy house for any other reason than that they could say they had been there, as they made a lot more noise than their spending warranted. The rest of the company (which altered in composition with each visit) seemed in a manner, hangers-on, but Jasper spent enough to justify the imposition, buying drink for them all, and of course paying for my company. He always hailed me as though it were a great surprise to find me there, such as greeting me, "Sink me ten thousand fathom deep, if it ain't Miss Dollie!" But he was easily satisfied and had the virtue of being quickly dealt with. Indeed there was something a little sad about these boys who had so much more money and leisure than sense, and they reminded me not a little of Roger and his playhouse bullies. They used generally not to mind who they got, but Jasper took a shine to me for some reason and as I said, he was easy enough to please and he had the advantage of being very generous with gifts, so he was a good one I could count on at least once a week.

Then there was a member of parliament, whom I only saw in term time, but who would come punctually twice a week and lecture me at length on the depravity of my ways before testing the depravity of my ways until he was satisfied I was quite as depraved as he had left me the last time. There was a clergyman who evidently battled with his conscience all week before giving in and bidding me enact a range of outlandish scenarios which beggared even my imagination; in the pursuit of these he too liked to dress up, and afterwards he made me pray with him for forgiveness. Another priest would only have ado with me through a hole in the sheet (I kept one specially for the purpose) and would not look on me nor speak to me before or afterwards except to recite the Lord's Prayer as he approached the point of no return. This, Doll jested to the other girls, was as good as going to church and full as inconvenient, which was as good an excuse for not going, as some of them did on a Sunday, as any. And besides, Doll had turned her face away from God.

There were those that came and went, such as a sea captain who was often away for long periods, but when he was on dry land would come and see me nearly every night, quietly intent on making up for lost time, and married men who would come when they had fallen out with their wives, or when they had not fallen out with their wives, but often seemed to feel sufficiently uneasy to give some explanation as to why they had come.

A wealthy merchant in the city told me I reminded him of a girl he had once loved very much and wanted to marry, but he had not the fortune at the time to match her dowry.

"Could you not have run away?" I asked. "Married without the money on either side?"

"Poverty and marriage don't suit," he said. "In any event, she would not entertain it. 'Marrying without an estate is like sailing in a ship without ballast,' she said. I had nothing to offer her, and in truth she was probably in the right. But I still think about her."

"Perhaps it would have turned out the same," I ventured. "They say every marriage is stale within a twelvemonth."

He was still for a moment, and then said quietly, "Ah, but what a twelvemonth it would have been."

Even my own Jasper had been feeling for some time the increasing weight of his obligation to his family to "commit matrimony", and when I asked him why he prevaricated so, he said darkly, "To have and to hold are dreadful words, Doll," as if that explanation should suffice. Jasper had an ability to get under my skin which irritated me, as I found myself worrying about him even though I did not particularly care for him very much. I think I sensed early on, and indeed it proved to be true, that Jasper was forging an attachment to me which might become troublesome, though he had too little confidence ever to declare this. Yet I felt it was there, but as I needed the money decided not to address it until such time as it became obvious, caused difficulties and required dealing with.

One of my married gentlemen, Sir Robert, as we lay on the bed one night after the business had been done (and this was a time when my gentlemen most freely expressed their thoughts), said, "The thing about you, Doll, is I can just come and take my pleasure with you. My dear wife, bless her, wants hugs and kisses and endearments, and in a manner to be courted all over again before she will give herself up. Why can she not be like you?" And I am ashamed to say I turned my face to the wall so he should not see the tears that welled up, for H put in an unexpected appearance, as she sometimes did at the least convenient moment, and H would dearly love to be hugged and kissed and told sweet things, but I pressed all this down and Doll said, in a light voice, "Well, perhaps you should try giving her a sovereign." And he laughed, but I divined discomfort in his laugh and regretted what I had said as none of my gentlemen liked to be reminded that they paid for their pleasure.

I believe things are in a manner today better in this regard, or at least that men are kinder to their wives than they then had license to be, or than was then the fashion. The incivility of husbands to their spouses was so proverbial that whenever voices were raised under her roof, Mother Cresswell would calm the situation by crying, "Forsooth, gentlemen, show a little courtesy – these are not your wives, after all!"

I have since found that many people assume that men frequent whores merely for physical relief, and while it is true that many do, I found that others wanted an impression of real affection which they so lacked at home. In weaker moments I pitied them and pitied their wives that they were locked together in a loveless marriage until one of them should die. I think it made me a cynic on the subject of marriage, which as a girl I had hoped could be a love-match, but I saw few enough examples of this in reality. Yet, I reasoned, due to my occupation I would be likely only to see the rough end of the institution. Still, so many unhappy people bound unwillingly together seemed a terrible waste of lives which could otherwise have been quite tolerable.

Lord A was my favourite. (Of course that was not his name but I do not like to invent one in case there is a lord of that name.) The minute I laid eyes on him I knew what was required. This one didn't want a chopping loose-talking daughter of the night, but a bit of comfort and kindness thrown into the main business. A nice young lady of easy virtue was what he had an appetite for and that is what I gave him. He was neither very handsome nor very rich, but he was good-humoured and respected me and I liked him for that. And while I regarded all of my gentlemen as work, with Lord A it was a pleasant kind of work, for he would talk about his other life, about his home in the country and his house in the town, his business, his wife and his nephew who lived with them, for he had no children of his own, and diverse subjects as were preoccupying his thoughts.

"Bring me a drink, Doll," he would say as he pulled off his boots. "I am come to unbend myself." And although it was all about him, I think with Lord A I was more nearly myself than I was with anyone but Janey. Sometimes we would dally and talk only, if he was tired, but mostly he would have his way, and I would squeal and shriek and make out he was the wickedest man alive – that was his pleasure.

Janey too had a favourite, though hers was a more intense affair for she talked about her William so much I feared she was actually falling for him. He was the son of a duke, but a younger son, which is never a good sign, as they generally have no hopes of inheriting anything worth having, and consequently little care is taken with their education and little notice taken of how they spend their time (as so little is expected of them), and in consequence they tend to be a light, unreliable and rather spoilt breed of boys. I do not say William was a bad lot, as he was gentle and nice in his manners and seemed smitten with Janey, but there was something about him that was insubstantial, and I feared she invested too much feeling in a weak and unworthy vessel. But Janey could become mightily vexed when I spoke against her William so I learned to keep my own counsel on this score.

30

e did not tarry always at Clerkenwell, except on certain nights when we expected company, and often went abroad. I remained no stranger to Covent Garden, and also frequented the Exchange, but my preferred place of assignation was the playhouse, and we generally set forth two or three together, not only because there was a certain safety in numbers, but because it made us less subject to abuse. Modest women of course never ventured to the playhouse singly, so going two or three together avoided attracting the wrong kind of attention, and though we were painted and masked, so, to a lesser degree, were many ladies of fashion, and by these means we attracted only the gentlemen who were seeking the kind of entertainment we offered.

I had a particular fondness for the playhouse not only for the plays but for the playhouse itself, which from my first experience of it had shown itself to be full as entertaining as the action on the stage. In the first place, much of the *haut ton* barely noticed the play at all, and certainly did not pay the performance the attention they do today; there was a constant traffic of young idle people coming in and going out, often catching one act at one house and another act at the other. To see and to be seen was the reason for going for a multitude of the audience. The most outlandish fashions might get their first outing at the playhouse, as it seemed in a sense a privileged arena, and the most fashionable ladies could succeed in a get-up in the rarefied atmosphere of the playhouse that they would not be so bold as to wear in broad daylight, in Pall Mall or the Strand. I have seen a duchess in the playhouse with the front of her gown so low that her very nipples (which were painted scarlet) peeped out as if they too were trying to watch the play.

At the playhouse, as nowhere else, ordinary Londoners might see the King in the company of his wife or mistresses, and many other fine and titled people, and behaving one to another quite naturally and with unusual freedom. Sometimes the King showed his favour to one or another lady, and once the Queen walked out when an actress the whole town knew to be one of the King's mistresses came on to dance a jig. I think it was one of the reasons the King was so popular, that he allowed himself to be seen often by the people at the theatre, which his father had not. And it also made the playhouse perhaps the only place in the country where a King and any poor fellow who could raise the price of a bench in the pit, could sit in the same place, and look on each other, and enjoy the same entertainment.

And as well as rich and poor laughing at the same jests, men and women mixed there with more freedom than I think anywhere else but at a masked ball. For some reason, behaviour seemed accepted at the playhouse that would be frowned on elsewhere. A lady might sit in her male companion's lap, and much courting was conducted in the playhouse. Parliament men and prostitutes, duchesses and apprentices, shared in the same comedies and tragedies, laughed together and, on occasion, wept together.

More to the point, as regards the interests of women of our profession, the mere presence of men in the playhouse guaranteed that here was a concentrated number of them with money to spend and the leisure in which to spend it: the hours we passed there were rarely wasted; it was indeed unusual to walk out of the door without having secured a companion.

One night, Kat, Janey and I had gone to the Duke's Playhouse, and the play proving dull, we fell to amusing ourselves. It was a kind of sport to us to detect among the spectators that new breed of whore, the Miss, so resented by Mother Cresswell and Pris Fotherington. Kat nudged us and nodded towards a box where a rather beautiful lady in a pale blue silk gown was conducting some kind of communication with a young man in the pit, mainly with her fan.

"She's a whore, though she'll neither drink nor swear," said Kat. "She's a whore for all her fine clothes and right jewels. I'll warrant she lives in a great house in Pall Mall. She'll have a velvet bed, stores of plate and handsome attendants, yet she's a whore and an arrant one." I was rather surprised at the assurance with which Kat said this, and wondered how she could be certain, but she was, as it turned out, quite correct, for when I looked again both the lady in blue and the gentleman in the pit had vanished. I looked at Janey to see whether she had observed this, but she had caught sight of her William and was mouthing and signalling him to meet her afterwards.

We then turned our attention to the play (which I think was *Mustapha*) and at least the spectacle of the moving scenes kept our interest, if the actors did not. The costumes had abundance of richly coloured silks and great feathers about them, and the Sultan even had a little African attendant, who you could see was really black, and not a white child painted. And as I looked on this handsome and exotic scene, a strange sensation gripped me, starting at the pit of my stomach and rising to my ribs so I could barely breathe, as my gaze kept being drawn back to this little servant, whom I became increasingly certain I knew. I tried to tell myself that just because it was a black boy did not mean it was Joe, and Joe was almost certainly dead. And then I began to wonder if I was in a manner being haunted by the memory of Joe, because I had not protected him and his sister as I had promised Aunt Madge I would, and this was why they came to me in dreams. But this did not have the quality of a dream. I could barely concentrate on the action on the stage and debated going behind the scenes after the play to satisfy myself that it was not him.

After the play was over, Janey bade me and Kat go with William and his friends, but I made an excuse and said I had business of my own to attend to, so off they went and I made my way to the door by the stage. No one seemed to mind me, but I could not see the boy, so asked one of the actresses what was the name of the little black boy from the play, and she said, "Sooty? What do you want with him?" and as I was about to reply, the boy came along. "Lady here asking after you, Sooty," said the actress. "Don't run off, now," she added before going into the tiring room.

"Yes, mistress?" said the boy.

I felt sure now that it was Joe but I had to find a way of ascertaining this without revealing my identity to him. I was quite sure he did not recognise me, painted, masked and dolled up as it were. So I said, "Is your name Joe?"

The child looked frightened, which pained me, and twitched, in a manner drawing his chin to his right shoulder momentarily. I had not noticed this when he was on the stage. Joe certainly did not use to do it.

"They call me Sooty here. Who's asking?" he said.

"A friend," I said. "An old friend of the family."

"I have no family," he said, and there was the twitch again. "What do you want? Who are you?"

"Joe, I need to be sure you are who I think you are before I tell you who I am."

"Sooty!" called a man's voice. "Gentleman here's got something for you."

This provoked a double twitch.

"I haven't got time for riddles, lady," said the boy, then gave a little bow and turned and walked briskly away. And then I heard myself saying,

"Fair stood the wind for France

When we our sails advance,
Nor now to prove our chance,
Longer will tarry… "

And as I spoke I saw the boy slow his step, then stop and slowly turn back. He said,

"But putting to the main,
At Caux, the mouth of Seine,
With all his martial train,
Landed King Harry."

And I took off my mask and said, "Don't you know me, Joe?"

And he cried "Miss H!" and ran to me and we embraced. Over his shoulder I saw a man coming calling him so I whispered, "Say nothing to anyone. Meet me outside at the same time tomorrow," and then I let him go and put on my mask again. And I stood and watched as he walked off with the man, who held him tight by the shoulder.

31

he next evening, I learnt from Joe that both Sal and Cook had died of the plague, but he was one of the lucky ones who recovered for reasons no one comprehended and was eventually freed from the plague hospital. He told me all this with his eyes fixed firmly on some point in the distance (when he did not twitch) and I guessed that he must have seen some terrible things. He did not dare return to the house at Cheapside, Roger's behaviour having perfectly terrified him, and he had been obliged, like me, to live on the streets and, as I had sadly suspected by the manner of the man in the playhouse, had been obliged to earn his bread the same way as I.

The man, whom we shall call Mr Fricker, was a minor player, fallen on hard times, as he told Joe. Fricker, I later found out from my playhouse friends, had once been a very beautiful actor, but had somehow crossed his mistress (a lady of my own profession, by all accounts), who had, in an argument, thrown acid in his face. The deformity he now bore had put paid to his life on the stage but also deformed his heart: though the manager kept him on to help about the playhouse, his bitterness lost him the few friends he had had, and he had begun to look about for other beauties he might exploit. To cut a long story short, he had in a manner adopted Joe, when he had found him on a street corner dancing for pennies. (Joe and Sal had both loved to dance, and Joe was yet small for his eleven years and a pretty fellow and it was an easy matter to see what a quaint and appealing sight this would have made.) Joe had been grateful for a roof over his head and a protector, and Fricker brought him to the playhouse, where he was often used to add a little colour and interest to a scene, and also sent him off with gentlemen, and, I ascertained, kept the money rendered for both these services, keeping Joe merely in good clothes and food.

I had to break to Joe the fact of Evelyn's death and told him how I too had been turned out of the house and that I thought both Roger and Sylvia must be dead and he should return to Cheapside, where Aunt Madge must have returned, and where he would be loved and looked after, as I was determined to get him out of the hands of Fricker, who, before I even learned his history, I recognised to be an unscrupulous and cruel keeper.

"But you thought *I* must be dead," he said, "and I'm not." He twitched three times before he was able to say: "What if Master Roger is still there?"

This was a fair point, I thought, and we pondered how we might discover how things stood at Cheapside. I promised Joe I would think of something, and he was to look for me outside the playhouse a week hence.

The next day I took the risk of going to Cheapside to see what I could learn from appearances. I decided to walk past (I was painted and masked of course) one way, busy myself at a stall and then pass back the other way, thus getting two opportunities to have a good look. I too was for some reason terrified of seeing Roger, or indeed my aunt, for although Doll had great face and a seeming confidence, there was nothing underneath.

In fact I passed and re-passed the house three times without being able to read anything from it and I was on the point of giving up when a boy ran to the door with a letter and knocked. I looked to see who would answer it and bless me if it wasn't dear Reg Potter! I almost cried out with the shock and relief of seeing so familiar a face. I walked away quickly, trying to control my feelings and wondering how to use this information to Joe's benefit.

I needed a go-between, someone who could speak to Reg and find out what the situation was at Aunt Madge's, and whether it was safe for Joe to return. But who? And could I get Joe away in the meantime to Clerkenwell where he would be safe? Although Mother Cresswell did some business with young gentlemen of our profession, she would not deal in boys, and though some of her girls were very young, they were not children, for there, to be fair to her, she drew the line. I quickly rejected this line of thought as, should we be followed or any connection be made with me, we should bring trouble on Mother Cresswell's house, and I would be turned out, and then where would I be, and what use to Joe?

As to the go-between, I needed someone I could trust and who seemed respectable. I immediately hit on Kat, as she was naturally elegant and ladylike and, though we never discussed our respective histories, I sensed she had fallen from a great height, as she was refined in her manners even when there was no custom about. I found an opportunity to speak to her alone and asked if she could do me a great favour, and I offered her a guinea for doing it. I told her that there was a child I wished very much to see reunited with his friends, but that I could in no way be seen to be personally connected with the business, and needed her to go in my stead and establish whether it would be safe for him to return, principally by enquiring after Roger. She was to go to the kitchen door and ask for Reg or Ted and discuss the matter with no one else. After I had assured her that there was no danger involved, and that she was free to take flight at any moment should she sense there might be, she accepted. She could not go till Friday, which was the day I had arranged to see Joe again, so she agreed to come straight from Cheapside to meet us at a coffee-house in Drury Lane.

32

at was on time and looked pleased. She said she had seen both Reg and Ted and that as soon as she mentioned Joe, Ted made an excuse to leave and when he returned it was with a lady, and she described an older, sadder, thinner Aunt Madge. At this point Kat threatened to leave as she said she was in no way empowered to deal with anyone but the Potters, but that as soon as the lady had wept and had made it clear she earnestly wished to have Joe back, she had been obliged to trust her too. Aunt Madge had then spent a long time writing a letter which Kat was to give Joe, which Kat now presented to me and which, after encouragement from Joe, I read aloud to them both. It ran:

My dear Joe,
I cannot tell you how happy I am to learn you are alive and well and urge you to come home at once, my dear, dear boy. Your friend tells me that you are anxious to know whether your return here would be welcome and I assure you that nothing would make me happier.

When I returned from the country last November I found no one but the Potters here, who had returned only days before me. The rest of our dear friends and family, apart from Frederick, whom it pleased God to spare, are alas gone and the only remembrance I have of any of them is a certificate of Roger's death and a letter he wrote shortly before he died. In the letter he states that he behaved very wrongly towards you and your sister and towards my two nieces, and that he believed none of you were like to have survived and that dear Evelyn was certainly taken, for he witnessed this himself. He also states that, he knows not how she got away, but Sylvia abandoned him as soon as he showed tokens of the plague. (I have reason to believe that she made use of a certificate of health provided by Mr Fluke, who tells me he furnished my nieces with four, and on my return here I found only two, one of which was made out in your dear name.) Roger ended his letter "May God forgive me" and I am sorry to say that he then took his own life.

I hope you can rest assured on that score: Roger can hurt you no more. I should add that, learning some weeks later of Roger's death, Sylvia had the temerity to return here and claim his fortune as his widow. To cut a long story short I came to a legal arrangement with her and she too will trouble us no more.

Let these reassurances bring you home, dear Joe. All these shocks and misfortunes have greatly afflicted me and it would make my heart glad to have you with me again, my dear boy.

Finally, whatever you may have done, or have been forced to do, while you have been away, will not make you seem any less in my eyes. These have been hard times and we have none of us escaped unscathed.

Your loving aunt,
Margaret.

Joe and I were just recovering from the emotion we felt on reading these words, when Kat threw a purse on the table.

"There you are. We get the rest when we deliver him."

For a moment I was speechless. A chill ran through me.

"Kat! You didn't ask for money!"

"Of course I did!" said Kat. "What do you take me for?"

"But Kat! We're not *selling* him! We're *rescuing* him. You should never have asked for money!"

"Come, come, Doll, people expect it. She could afford it. What's the matter with you? She gets her boy back, we get ten guineas each: everybody's happy."

"Kat! We're not criminals!"

"Oh yes we are, Doll," said Kat. "Or do you work in a hat shop?"

"We must give it back," I said, feeling sick to the stomach.

Kat snatched up the purse and counted out five coins, which she put in her pocket, and then threw the purse back on the table.

"Give yours back," she said, "since your conscience is so tender on that score," and walked out. And as my eyes followed her out I saw, sitting in the corner, watching us, the unpleasing sight of Fricker.

It was unreasonable to suppose that Fricker was about to let me merely walk off with his little goldmine, so I unwillingly bade Joe good-bye and watched him go into the playhouse as one of his tasks was to sweep the stage each night and collect up the properties. As if he did not trust me, Fricker followed Joe, throwing a most filthy look in my direction. I dawdled outside the playhouse for a while, undecided as to whether to go straight back to Clerkenwell or look about for a little business first, as these out-of-doors opportunities were ways of making extra money which one could avoid declaring to Mother Cresswell, if one were discreet about it. I soon noticed a gentleman standing a little way away from me who also seemed to be waiting for a stranger.

I don't know how it was, but those of our trade could easily recognise our opposite numbers in the male sex (though they were of course much fewer in number than ourselves) and this was most definitely a brother. He had a very beautiful face, and though there was nothing womanish about him, he was very pleasing to look upon, and moved with graceful assurance, and dressed with a little more attention to studied carelessness than most men bothered with. He caught me looking at him and smiled and tipped his hat and turned slightly away, to show he was demonstrating his manners rather than his interest, and that, combined with the fact that I noticed that, though a gentleman, he did not wear a sword, confirmed my suspicion.

In the normal course of events I should have moved on, but something about him struck me as familiar, yet I did not recall ever seeing him at Mother Cresswell's, though she did sometimes recruit casual bum-labour, like the citizens' wives, when required. It is strange that when you recognise someone but cannot place the memory, sometimes a part of that memory comes with something associated with the face that recalls it – sometimes a place, sometimes other company that was there, sometimes the emotion you were feeling at the time. This face trawled up a feeling of great excitement and pleasure, and I had a flash that it was associated with the theatre. Yet I felt sure I had not seen him in the playhouse, and that this was a memory from a different field, and out of doors somehow. The more I tried to fathom out the rest of the memory, the more specific it became, and I recalled it having something particularly to do with something *associated* with the stage – properties or perhaps costume. I looked at him harder, as if to will his identity to the front of my mind, and as I did so, as though affected by the power of my thoughts, he fell over.

I ran over to assist him and discovered he had fainted. I did not know what to do and had seen salt of hartshorn administered on like occasions but all I had was a little bottle of perfume which I wafted under his nose and which seemed to do the trick.

"Thank you, sister," he said, and the minute I heard that voice I knew him. This was Katharina! From *The Taming of the Shrew*! At the fair all those years ago!

33

ome rural personages may criticise my narrative as casting doubt on its own veracity by the occurrence of coincidental meetings and reunions such as these, but I must point out to my provincial reader that London (so I have read) is a city of about half a million people, in a country of only five million all told, so it is quite probable that if you are going to cross the path of anyone you know outside the place you first knew them, it is likely to be in London, though I willingly concede that meeting two people from one's past in a matter of days in the same vicinity is going some. Still, it did happen, and I should be telling a lie otherwise, and real life is never as neat and reasonable as fiction. Real life is in fact downright untidy, and you do not even know which is the beginning, the middle, and the end, until it is all far too late.

I took Katharina (who was really called by the most un-Katharina-like name of Godfrey) to a nearby ordinary, for it turned out he had fainted of hunger, and when he came to himself he was delighted to know I had remembered him after all this time (which he calculated, to my shock, was only two years ago) and he said he thought he did recall a little girl with an odd name, and I reminded him that he had said one day he might see me upon the London stage, and we both laughed heartily at where fortune had brought us.

We got along very well, and had one of the best meals I had had for a long time, not because the food was special, but, I later thought, because it was a long time since I had eaten, or spent any time, with a man who was a companion with no complications, and attended by no underlying anxiety of business to be accomplished or effort of games to be played.

In any case, Godfrey, as I must call him now, was still an actor, though not at this time working. He had hopes of a part in a new play at one or other of the theatres but at the moment was penniless. All this was on account, he said, of having been disappointed in a most promising situation. The promising position, it transpired, was that of lover to a duchess I may not name, but whose identity may be easily guessed at, who so famously fell in love with his 'Alexander' that she most shamelessly took him up and showered him with sweet promises, rich gifts and hard cash. Having been selected as a fit instrument for her abandoned pleasure he had become so happy in his circumstances that he had acted only at intervals (and this is not of course to mention the private performances he gave exclusively for my lady) and finally, in his pride (he admitted), had fallen out with the theatre management over certain issues, and quit the house with much ill feeling on all sides. Still, he had no longer needed the money, having become, thanks to the duchess, a gentleman of leisure.

Unfortunately the duchess in time tired of her conquest, and the river of endearments, presents and coin ran dry. Now Godfrey had a household (the house itself had been leased by the duchess for him) he could not afford to run, he had paid off and dismissed his servants, and rattled around a vast, richly furnished property in Lincoln's Inn Fields, the rent on which was paid until the end of the year, but had not a crust to put in his mouth.

"Did you make no savings?" I asked Godfrey, but it transpired he had never hit truly hard times before so did not have my instinct for hoarding up treasures for future uncertainty, and had run up vast bills (as I perceived any young man with money did) at his tailor's and vintner's, not to mention other creditors, but at least he had calculated he could discharge these debts by selling almost everything in his house (the duchess had furnished it most elegantly), which he was in the process of doing. So he was to be free of debt but, as he put it, destitute and prostitute.

Having learnt how matters stood with me he wondered whether I might be able to put in a good word with him at Mother Cresswell's for when she had occasion for a gentleman of his talents, and I said I certainly would, and thought inwardly that Mother would think him something of a catch, on account of his great beauty, nice manner and good clothes. As we parted, with many friendly adjurations to meet again soon, he told me his address at Lincoln's Inn Fields and I told him mine at Clerkenwell, and slipped one of the guineas Kat had so wrongly acquired (which I intended to replace and return) into his hand, which he received with a wordless expression of the utmost gratitude, and we went our separate ways having assured each other of the pleasure we took in our reacquaintance, and I know not how he went home but I fairly skipped all the way.

34

ver the next few days it became clear that Fricker had an idea I had designs on his little slave, as he did not let Joe out of his sight except to go off with a gentleman. And this gave me the idea of enlisting the assistance of my new-found old friend Godfrey. I had already enquired of Mother Cresswell whether she would like to make his acquaintance so I intended to kill two birds with one stone and made my way to his house, which was indeed a most handsome one, but when Godfrey answered the door to me I saw for myself that though it was indeed most richly furnished, he kept no servants, and the fact that there was a fire going in one room, was, he said, thanks to a part of my guinea. While Godfrey went to put on clothes he thought suitable for the interview I looked about me and imagined what it must be like to have so much money that you could rent a great place like this and not even use it.

He came down the staircase looking splendid and I believe, though I could not swear to it, that he had made a little use of black paint round his eyes, and I felt rather proud to be accompanying so handsome and fine-looking a fellow through the town, as heads turned in his direction wherever he went. And though people's attention was caught by Godfrey's beauty, they then inspected me with some interest.

"They are all wondering what a fine-looking gentleman like you is doing with a little slut like me," I whispered to him.

"Not at all," he whispered, smiling and bowing to a lady who was ogling him most boldly. "We make a fine couple," he said, and as I caught sight of us both in a shop window, I could see his point. I continued to take great pains with my dress, which I now used to emphasise my figure (for this had improved as I had grown a little fatter) rather than to attract attention by garish colours. I also toned down the paint in the daytime and this made me look less alarming to the ordinary eye. A whore is a whore down to her very bones and has learned to look for profit in everything and I was no different, so as I considered this handsome-looking pair in the window, I began to wonder how I could turn this new discovery to my advantage.

As it turned out, Mother Cresswell seemed to have the same idea, as she said we were as fine-seeming a pair as any at court and might do very well for the gentlemen who like, as she put it, "a bit of both". We left it that she would send me to fetch Godfrey when she had occasion to need either him, or us both, and after I had intimated to her his great present want she very delicately slipped him a sovereign as an advance. Before we left, I went to my room and counted out some coins from my money box. Ten guineas were to be returned to Aunt Madge with Joe and I purposed to give another to Godfrey in return for luring Joe away from Fricker, plus five shillings which I reckoned to be the very most Fricker would demand for Joe's services, and another five shillings for any emergency.

We then set off for the playhouse and hatched our plot. Godfrey would solicit Joe's services and once he had got him away from Fricker, would bring him to me at the Cock and Bottle in Fleet Street, and I would then deliver him to Cheapside.

I was beginning to get anxious that something had gone amiss when Godfrey and Joe finally arrived, out of breath, having run a lot of the way so as to get far away from Fricker as quickly as possible so that we should not cross him on our way. I thanked Godfrey and set off with Joe at once, with a thrilling feeling that I was accomplishing a very good deed which would make both Aunt Madge and Joe very happy, and compensate in some deal for the miseries they had passed.

The roads were unusually crowded on account of a bad fire further south, and we had to stand aside on one occasion to let a number of soldiers sent to put it out through. A sad number of people whose homes had been burned were to be seen with their households piled on carts, and one assembly struck me with great poignancy as the children of the family walked behind the cart, a small girl weeping and carrying her cat.

When we reached the west end of Cheapside I pulled Joe into an alley and sat him on a barrel to hear the lecture I had prepared. First I told him my address in Clerkenwell but said this was only for the direst emergency and he was on no account to tell it to anyone, nor to come visiting.

"Now, Joe," I continued, "I will not see you after today, and you must not, *absolutely must not*, tell Aunt Madge that you have seen me since the night you left her house."

"But why?" asked Joe, twitching unmercifully. "And why must I not see you again?" And as his eyes filled with tears, I had to work hard to control my own feelings.

"Now, Joe," I continued, "you must be a brave boy. I cannot explain why, save to say that I can never go back to Aunt Madge, for I would bring her only shame and dishonour, and we love Aunt Madge too much to wish unhappiness on her, do we not?"

He nodded.

"So promise me, Joe, that you will not mention you have seen me."

"I promise," he said.

"All you know is that you told your story to a kind gentleman who brought you home."

"Godfrey?" asked Joe.

"No, you must not say his name either. Say you don't know

his name. And give this to Aunt Madge," and I gave him the purse with the ten guineas, "and just say the gentleman said it was not needed."

"I told my story to a kind gentleman who brought me home and gave me this because he said it was not needed. I do not know his name and I haven't seen Miss H."

"Good boy," I said, "but you must not mention me at all. Now think of this as a new life. When you walk through that door you must forget everything that has happened and begin again. Be a good boy and always be kind to Aunt Madge, for she loves you." I was now almost in tears myself, so said, "Kiss me now and I will take you home."

Joe kissed me and hugged me so long and tight I had in the end to disengage his little arms and lead him back into the street. As we arrived opposite Aunt Madge's house I found a shop window which gave me a good view, by reflection, of the door to the house.

"Go now, Joe," I said, "and don't look back."

Joe hesitated before running across the road and up the steps. I watched in the window until the door opened and then quickly turned and began walking away, but heard Reg's cry of delight when he saw Joe, and then when I was safely out of Cheapside, I stepped into a doorway and wept very hard.

35

On my way back to Clerkenwell I found I was in the train of many people leaving the city and it reminded me a little of the great exodus during the plague the year before, except that on that occasion it had been the rich who left, but here people of all walks of life were herding their families through the streets and the extent of the possessions of some was quite pitiful. One family carried all their possessions in a wheelbarrow; others carried nothing but little bundles. When I got to Mother Cresswell's I heard many conflicting reports of the seriousness of the fire, Mother herself being of the opinion that the Lord Mayor should be hanged, drawn and quartered and it was the incompetence of the authorities which made decent people like herself wonder why they should pay their taxes.

She told me that I had a gentleman waiting (who turned out to be my sea captain, back from his travels), but that if he hoped for satisfaction the next day also I should arrange to see him early as she had an engagement for Godfrey and myself later in the evening. She had evidently not been slow to put out word of her new acquisition and I must say you could never fault Mother Cresswell for her business acumen.

I satisfied the captain, and then another gentleman I did not know, and was glad finally to have my bed to myself, as the events of the day had been exhausting. I had difficulty sleeping that night, however, due to the noise all night of people coming out of the city and setting up camp in the fields behind our house. At one point I rose and looked out of the window, and could easily see the light in the sky from the great fire, though it was so far away, and thanked God I was safe in my little room. I imagined Joe safe in his bed and pictured Aunt Madge smiling in her sleep and with these thoughts finally slipped into sleep myself.

We were not very busy the next day due to the disruption caused by the fire, so Mother had us make soup and take it out to some of the people in the fields and this kept us busy enough. It was pitiful to see them huddled together, for it was cold, and I heard a number of older people had died in the night, due to the shock and the cold combined. Alarming reports of the spread of the fire arrived all day, and I began to feel concerned about my family in Cheapside, but was assured by others that it was far enough away, and that the authorities were making fire breaks and it should soon be out.

In the afternoon I went to fetch Godfrey and he told me that he had been to Drury Lane and deliberately put himself in the way of Fricker, who had asked him what he had done with his boy. Godfrey said he gave one of his best performances, stating that Sooty had left him at such and such a time, and affecting great indignation that Fricker should accuse him of doing anything with his boy. Fricker immediately backed down, but asked if Godfrey had seen where he went and whether he met a little slut, and described me. Godfrey said he had seen no one but assured Fricker he would be the first to know should he see Sooty anywhere. Fricker seemed greatly cast down at the loss of his apprentice, but to accept Godfrey's version of events. We agreed that we had better not be seen in each other's company round Drury Lane as Fricker would easily put two and two together.

Then as we went on our way, Godfrey asked me what I knew of our assignment for the evening and I suddenly remembered the sea captain was coming early and we had better hurry. The truth was, I was feeling rather apprehensive about our joint appointment and what we would be required to perform. I had dealt with more than one gentleman in the past, but they had been customers merely and Godfrey was my friend and I was distinctly ill at ease, which I believe Godfrey sensed, for he said, "Are you worried about anything, Doll?"

I started to say I was thinking about the fire and whether it would spread to Cheapside, and he let the matter drop and talked of other things as he knew I loved to hear stories of the playhouse, and he told me one which he said was true, of the days soon after the Restoration when women had not yet been trained for the stage and they were still using boys for the women's parts. On this particular day the King had arrived at the theatre a little early, so everyone was running about to get ready, as you did not keep the King waiting, and when His Majesty enquired as to the reason of the delay, the manager had to come out and explain that he was sorry but that the Queen was still shaving.

"He meant the actor who played a queen in the play," said Godfrey, as I did not react at the end of his tale. "Well, I thought it would amuse you."

"I'm sorry, Godfrey," I said, stopping him and taking his hands in mine. "The truth is I am not sure what to expect this evening."

He looked baffled for a moment and then laughed and gave me a little hug and took my arm and walked on, saying, "You are a comical baggage, Dollie." And then he laughed again.

"Why do you keep laughing?" I asked, not a little put out.

"Because you are such an intrepid little thing, and yet you are afeared of some old fool who can't make up his mind whether he likes boys or girls."

I thought about this and agreed that it did seem foolish, but he could see my anxieties were not allayed.

"Look, Dollie," he said, "it's just a game. It's all just a great game. Just make it up as you go along. And anyway, I'll be there, so you needn't worry."

There seemed no merit in admitting that that was precisely the nature of my worry, so I resolved to grin and bear it.

36

disposed of the sea captain in about half an hour, while Godfrey took tea with some of the girls, and then I set my room straight, washed and treated myself to clean linen, and changed into my handsomest dress, and repaired my paint, all the while telling myself this was nothing whatsoever to do with Godfrey. When I went into the parlour he was clearly already a great favourite with the sisters.

"Ah, Dollie! I say, you do look a treat," he said.

"*I* shouldn't mind doing a double with your Godfrey," whispered Janey (as far as Janey was capable of whispering; it was in truth more of a husky shout), which immediately revived all my queasiness on the subject.

Then Mother came in and made the girls bustle about tidying the saloon, for it was here Godfrey and I were to entertain, and then shooed them out.

"Now my dears," she said, "your guests are here..."

Guests? I wondered. I had been under the impression there would be just the one gentleman.

Mother dropped her voice, "They are paying *very well* so do not disappoint. I'll send in some wine and then you'll be on your own." She bustled to the door, where she turned and added, "Oh, and they like to watch." With a wink she was gone.

I was still taking this in when she showed in a fine-looking gentleman and an equally fine-looking lady and for a moment I considered there must have been a mistake and these people had perhaps come to the wrong house. The gentleman introduced himself and his wife as Mr and Mrs Smith, and Godfrey introduced us as ourselves, as I seemed to have lost the power of speech momentarily, then Mother Cresswell poured us all wine and left us to it.

It was not, you will understand, that I minded another woman being part of our entertainment, for various combinations of the girls often worked together when occasion warranted, but that the focus of attention was evidently to be on Godfrey and myself. I took a great draught of wine and Godfrey immediately filled my glass again. Mr and Mrs Smith settled themselves on one of the couches and Mr Smith said, "Please, begin when you are ready," and they sat there expectantly.

Godfrey put out some candles and moved others so that a soft light illuminated one side of the room, while the other, where the couple waited, was in almost darkness, and I took the opportunity of a lull in proceedings to sink another glass of wine. Moving swiftly, he adjusted the position of the other couch and rearranged the cushions. There was a screen in the corner of the room which he also moved, considered, and moved again, and I realised that, playing to his theatrical strength, he was creating a stage, and that we were to be players upon it.

Then Godfrey beckoned to me and took me behind the screen and whispered, "I will lead the way, all you need to do is follow. But you have to help me."

"Of course," I said, feeling a little more equal to the challenge now the wine was taking hold.

Godfrey looked as if he expected something to happen and I didn't know what it was, but felt I was required to do something.

"Come here," he said, and slipped his arms round my waist and surprised me by kissing me most tenderly, and then more passionately, and then ran his hands over my breasts, and, then, seeing I still did not understand what was required, took my hand and placed it on his prick. At last I understood. It is not that I was particularly dense in such matters, for now I got along famously, but that my gentlemen usually required little encouragement, and I had, until that point, felt a little reserved because it was Godfrey. Anyhow, when he was ready to go, he led me out from behind the screen and we started all over again, and I began really to enjoy myself, for Godfrey did indeed do all the work and sometimes prompted me with a whisper to do this or that to help matters along.

The various positions in which we consummated our passion were unusual (though not, on the whole, unknown to me) and largely uncomfortable in themselves. This, Godfrey later explained, was because we were not performing for our own pleasure, but for theirs, and they had to be able to see everything; therefore we had to adopt poses which set off our actions to greater advantage for the spectator. He illustrated this point, by giving the example of how actors often face the audience when they are in fact addressing each other, because what they say is more for the audience's benefit than the actors' (who know what they are saying anyway).

After a short while I became aware of some movement and sound in the darkness, and though I could see into the gloom only indistinctly, realised that Mr and Mrs Smith were about the same business as we were, and yet continued to watch us all the while.

My gentlemen usually liked me to make a deal of noise to prove how much they were pleasuring me (although Hole-In-The-Sheet insisted on absolute silence) and Godfrey had a repertoire of exclamations, such as, "Oh you gipsy! You witch! You jade!" which certainly added spice and variety, and I may add that when it came to the point where I would act most of all, I did not have to act at all, but cried out in genuine and thrilling ecstasy, which just shows what a pleasure it can be to work with a consummate professional.

Our guests arrived at the same point only moments after ourselves, and we went behind the screen again and dressed while they did the same. Godfrey planted a great smacker on my lips and said "good work" and I said "you too" and we felt fairly pleased with ourselves, and as with every new thing I did, I felt relief that it would not in future be a problem to me, as I knew now what was expected and found I could work quite happily with Godfrey. It was late by the time our visitors politely took their leave of us and Mother Cresswell came in and said we had done well and they would in all probability be back or she was no judge.

She paid Godfrey his portion on the spot, and it was indeed a handsome sum, even taking into account her deductions, and then suggested Godfrey stay with us the night as the roads were so clogged up that even a walk of fifteen minutes took an hour and with her habitual delicacy offered him a room that was empty although the bed was not made up. Considering the extent of our intimacy during the evening (and the fact that I was unaccountably weary and could not face fetching sheets and so on) I suggested that Godfrey could sleep with me and he said that would more than suffice if Mother Cresswell would permit this for he should not like to bring dishonour on her house (he was full of nice touches like this which Mother lapped up, as he had a knack of being witty in a way which made the other person feel that they were just as witty by virtue of sharing and understanding the jest), and we bade her goodnight and retired.

Godfrey undressed down to his shirt and got into bed and then made a great business of not looking as I got undressed which made us both laugh. I, too, got into bed and before I had time to consider how one should comport oneself towards a bedfellow in these circumstances, Godfrey wrapped his arms round me, kissed me on the cheek, wished me goodnight and using my shoulder as a pillow went to sleep almost immediately.

I do not know if I was asleep or only nearly so, but I suddenly heard Godfrey exclaim "H!"

"What?" said I, sitting up in a panic, thinking the house was on fire.

"H! That was it! I was trying to think of the curious name of the little girl at the fair. It was H!"

I was assailed by most mixed feelings at this.

"But why H?" he asked. "Doll is short for what? Dorothy? What has H to do with anything?"

"It's a long story," I sighed.

"But you'll tell me one day, eh? H?" he persisted.

"Please don't call me that," I said.

"And you'll tell me all about what little Joe was to you? And all your history?"

I didn't answer. Godfrey sat up and looked at me most thoughtfully and then cupped my face in his hands so I had no choice but to return his earnest gaze.

"You know we could do very well together. Like this evening. But even in acting there has to be truth. We can be whoever we like to the world, but we would do well to be very true and honest one to another, as we are to ourselves." He considered me a little longer, then kissed me lightly on the forehead, as one would kiss a child goodnight, and laid us both down and settled to sleep. But I did not sleep for a while, for though it was most comfortable to be in Godfrey's arms, it was most unpleasing to think of being entirely true and honest to Godfrey and even worse to think of being entirely true and honest to myself.

37

he next morning I awoke to find Godfrey beside me already awake and reading one of my playbooks. He looked over at me and smiled.

"Sleep well?" he asked.

"Yes," I yawned, "thank you."

"Dollie… " he began, as though he were going to ask something I might not like. "You know what we said last night about always continuing very honest one to another?"

"Yes," I said, dreading what he was going to say.

"Well… " he said. "Dollie, I have to tell you, dear girl, you ain't no oil painting in the mornings."

I jumped out of bed and snatched up my hand mirror and saw a smudged bleary-eyed visage which looked like my own face if it had been left out in the rain for some time.

"Well, if truth be told, you ain't no bowl of fruit yourself!" I retorted, and threw a pillow at him.

Then I admitted my head ached terribly and we dressed and went down to breakfast. We had no sooner finished than, to our astonishment, Joe was shown into the room.

"Joe!" said I, standing up and preparing to be very angry.

But he threw himself on me saying, "I'm sorry to come but you must come! Everyone is being sent out of Cheapside and Auntie won't leave the house!"

As it was an emergency Godfrey went to find a coach, and I

ran upstairs and slapped on some paint and got my mask, as if I were to go anywhere near Aunt Madge I must be disguised, and snatched up some money from my box. Godfrey's task was of course fruitless, as there was not a coach to be had in all London over those few days, every wheeled object being in full employment ferrying people and their belongings out of the city; however he had an idea that if we walked to Lincoln's Inn Fields, where he had his house, we should have better luck, as the Fields were being used as a depository for people's possessions, which meant that if full vehicles arrived, empty ones must leave, and this proved to be the case.

When we arrived at the Fields, Godfrey set off to find transport while Joe (and Tobypuss, who was delighted at seeing Joe again and had insisted on accompanying us) and I waited. It was only now that I began to realise the true scale of the calamity. Many hundreds, perhaps thousands, of people were gathered here, wandering about as if in a daze, their furniture lying in piles about them. It struck me that these were mainly persons of quality, most unfit for any kind of hardship, which seemed to make it worse. Because whereas the plague had mainly done its deadly work amongst the poor of the city, the fire was not so nice in its choice of victims, and the fire had moved so swiftly and indiscriminately that the rich had not had any more chance of fleeing than the poor and, of course, had far more to lose. The vast majority of citizens could easily carry their valuables, if they had any, whereas the wealthy were overburdened with property. Never having had to fend for themselves before, they had brought impractical things and left behind those of less value but more use. Though they were surrounded by riches, many had not a blanket to lay over themselves.

"Going the wrong way, ain't you?" said the carter, as we hopped up behind him.

"We've got to fetch someone from Cheapside," said Godfrey, "an old lady."

"Well I can't bring you back," said the carter. "I've got a

queue of households waiting for me to bring them out. Gold dust, this cart is," he said with some satisfaction.

"I have money," I said to Godfrey.

I have never seen the city in more chaos than during the fire. The streets were jammed with carts, coaches and barrows piled high, often too high, so that they spilt over and blocked the way, and worsened the congestion, as well as many people on foot. As we approached St Paul's we became caught in a jam and decided it would be quicker to walk the rest of the way, so I paid the carter and we jumped down. I asked Godfrey to carry Tobypuss as I was afraid he might get crushed in the traffic, and kept Joe close by my side.

Although we could not see the fire, we could hear it, see and smell its smoke and feel its heat most wonderfully. As we made our way to my aunt's house, I began to think how we were going to get her out without betraying my identity. I would have to be Doll, that much was certain, but we would make Godfrey the main player, he being the kind gentleman who had sent Joe home in the first place and to whom Joe had now appealed for help once more. Yes, that made sense.

I could see as we approached that our aunt's coach was at the door, which was a blessing, though Reg had his hands full fending off a desperate offer by a gentleman and his family to buy it outright on the spot, and we easily gained admission as the front door was wide open. Most of the furniture seemed to have gone ahead, which made the house seem strange, but there was no time to dwell on my feelings at being back at home now. I tied Tobypuss up in the hall, as his reappearance would only confuse matters, and we followed the sounds of voices to the library on the first floor where Ted was pleading with Aunt Madge, who had evidently been coaxed as far as the doorway, but had now jammed herself to it, her hands clasping the frame either side, her knuckles white. It was shocking to see how she had aged and how small and frail and confused she now seemed.

I hung back at the top of the staircase and watched as Joe

went forward and introduced Godfrey, who he said was a good friend and had come to bring Aunt Madge away. Aunt Madge then said something in a most distressed voice, which I could not hear. Godfrey and Joe coaxed and cajoled but Aunt Madge was absolutely resolved not to budge. I caught her voice as it rose, imploring Ted and the others to go on without her. She would stay and make sure the house was safe. This went on for some time and then a series of explosions frighted us all and shook the house. We then heard a great cry from the street and running footsteps and Reg shouted up the stairs that the east end of Cheapside was alight and we had to leave at once.

Godfrey and Joe came back to me and Godfrey said, "She won't move. She insists that the last time she left the house she lost her family and everyone she loved, except for Frederick. Who's Frederick? No matter now. I think we are going to be obliged to carry her away by force."

The mention of Frederick gave me an idea and I sent Joe downstairs and told him what to do. I had heard that when someone is somewhat out of their mind, as it were, a complete change of scene or tone can cut through their delirium and bring them a little to their senses. I now walked purposefully up the landing and dropped a curtsey before my aunt.

"Madam," Doll said, and continued in a most businesslike manner, "Master Frederick has sent me to bring you away. You are to come at once. Your coach is waiting below. Come along now," and I proferred my arm.

"Frederick?" queried my aunt, moving to take my arm, and then checking herself. "No, I can't go. I cannot, under any circumstances, quit the house. What about little Joe? I cannot leave him. Roger will throw him out."

"Joe is ready to go with you and waits below," I continued resolutely. "Everything is packed, but you must come now. Master Frederick's orders, madam." She dithered and a further explosion made me play my last card immediately. "Look madam, little Puss is waiting for you. Puss?" At this Tobypuss dutifully barked and I indicated she look over the banister, which she did, absently taking Ted's proffered arm, and coming out of her room to do so.

"Puss?" she queried. "Is it dear old Puss?"

His evident delight at seeing his old mistress did the trick and assisted by Ted and Godfrey, she hastened, as far as she was able to hasten, down the stairs, but according to my instruction Joe was ahead of her and, untying Tobypuss, led him slowly out of the house and into the coach, while Aunt Madge followed as meekly as a lamb.

My work here was done and having ascertained from Godfrey that Ted and Reg had no idea where to go, as their original destinations, the homes first of Dr Rookham and next of Mr Fluke (who I was glad to learn incidentally were both yet living) had been either consumed by the fire or yet lay in its path, and the Potters feared Aunt Madge was unequal to undertaking the journey into her estate in Gloucestershire, we resolved Godfrey would take them all to his house at Lincoln's Inn Fields in the meantime. I decided the less Aunt Madge and the Potters saw of me the better, so set off on foot, while the coach rolled away.

38

 headed back in the direction of Clerkenwell, but was obliged to make many diversions. In some places roads were blocked, and in others militia men were forcing evacuations so they could blow up houses with gunpowder to make fire breaks. The atmosphere in the city was turning most ugly as people looked for someone to blame for the disaster. Rumours had abounded for the past two days that the fire had been deliberately started by the Dutch (which at least made sense because of the war), or the French, or Republicans, but most people were happy to blame the Catholics, as when a dog is to be beaten, any stick will serve. As a consequence there had been most unhappy scenes of violence, and I believe more people were killed in these outbreaks of general hysteria than died in the fire itself.

I kept being thrown back in the direction of the fire and in some places got far closer to it than was comfortable and heard the incredible news that at least two thirds of the city had already been consumed, including the entire length of the north bank of the river within the city walls, and a third of the houses on my beloved bridge. I did not realise how late it was becoming, as the brightness of the fire prevented darkness falling, casting a diabolical light on the unnatural scenes about me.

The fire itself had the noise of a whirlwind in it which,

combined with the wails and cries of the people, seemed the sound of Hell itself. Everywhere there were people weeping, wringing their hands, smiting their breasts, cursing themselves for their powerlessness and appealing to Heaven to help them. To see mothers carrying their children, men their wives from child-bed, and the young bearing away the elderly, out of their houses with only the clothes they stood up in, was a most sorrowful sight, and all were most frighted and having nowhere to go added confusion to terror and everyone went about with desperate faces. In other places the lack of activity was more alarming than the panic. People stood about, as if turned to stone by grief, making no attempt to fight the fire or save their belongings, but simply looking on as their houses and shops were consumed.

When I finally reached the house at Clerkenwell I learned that Frenchie had got into some trouble and Mother Cresswell had been gone all day in pursuit of her, and that Winnie had had her baby, who was a dear little girl, to be called Rose, and all the girls were besides themselves with excitement, having assisted Janey in the delivery, and one would have thought from their accounts that each one was uniquely responsible for the child's survival and that it had, by one token or another, identified each of them as its particular favourite aunt. It was perhaps not the best time to break to Janey, who was tired after the day's travails, that I had been obliged to part with Tobypuss. She was mightily vexed, and though I tried to explain that Tobypuss in truth belonged to neither of us but had gone to his original owner who was an old lady on her own and needed him, she continued mightily out of order and reproaching.

All evening Janey was dinging about the house like a Fury, and even snapped at Winnie, so I kept out of her way as far as was possible, and was frequently summoned to admire Rose, and was told that she was the first baby to thrive in the house for many years, and then Kat and I wept a while together, for we had both lost babies in our time at Mother Cresswell's.

Later that night, when Janey had calmed down somewhat, and stopped shouting so, and was reduced merely to the odd "Pfffff!" it transpired that she was particularly out of sorts because she had lent money to her William, which he had failed to repay. This struck me as most serious and the most fatal proof that she was indeed in love with him, for a whore gives love for money and the moment the transaction is reversed and she starts giving money for love it is only a matter of time before she is utterly undone. She made me swear to tell no one and said she forgave me about Tobypuss though she would miss the little toad for he had been a good companion to her in a hard time, but I knew she was only diverting my attention and appeasing me for I was angry with her for what she had done.

Mother Cresswell and Frenchie arrived home very late, and in horrible distress. Frenchie's clothes were all torn and dirty and she had evidently received most harsh treatment. It transpired that she had gone to see her sister who lived with a family (she was a seamstress), and she had been helping her sister evacuate the livestock from the yard behind the house, when they had been recognised as foreigners and set upon by an angry crowd. The extent of the madness of the crowd can be imagined, for as Frenchie's sister was running, carrying a dozen or so chicks in her apron to deposit them in a box in a cart at the end of the road, she was accused by some over-zealous patriot of carrying fireballs to throw into people's houses, and once the cry had gone up that here was a Catholic arsonist, people who were quite strangers to her began to chase her. Frenchie had gone to her assistance, but could not get to her, and saw the crowd fall on her and then to save her own skin began to run away, but because she uttered some French exclamation, herself became the subject of the crowd's wrath and had to run for her life, suffering many blows on the way.

"They did not know me!" Frenchie kept crying. Mother Cresswell had set off in pursuit of Frenchie as soon as she had learnt of the trouble against foreigners, to give her safe passage home, and had passed on her way the mob who had moved on to attack a Dutch bookseller, and arrived to discover Frenchie by her dead sister's body, which had been horribly disfigured, namely by having had her breasts cut off. She was surrounded by the crushed remains of the chicks, some of which, in her shocked state of mind, Frenchie had scooped up and put in her pockets. I relieved her of this sorry stuff while Mother Cresswell raged against the treatment Frenchie's sister had received.

"Now, I ask you, where," demanded Mother Cresswell, "was the need for that?"

It seemed to me extraordinary that even in the face of a common calamity such as a great fire, people could turn on each other in this manner, but then I recalled how cruel the plague had made people to each other, and was obliged to concede that there is no disaster which can befall humanity, that we will not fail to make worse by our own hands, for it is fear that makes us cruel.

"Ignorance!" exclaimed Mother Cresswell. "She can't help being French can she? It's not her fault. I confess sometimes I am ashamed to be an Englishwoman, so I am, to see how a nation that could not even keep its own King's head on should be so jealous and angry at a poor little foreigner. She speaks English as nice as what I do, don't she?"

The next day I met Godfrey by appointment to learn how all went at his house. Aunt Madge, he declared, was a proper old fashioned darling, and it was clear to me from his account that, though she had for a period mislaid her wits, she had lost none of her old charm, and that Godfrey was mere putty in her hands. If I had thought I might have any hand in the management of her it quickly became clear that she and Godfrey had already made plans. She had immediately become apprised of his pecuniary embarrassment, he said, and had most delicately assumed control and responsibility for the household finances. Reg and Ted had already recruited a cook and two maids from the quantity of homeless humanity that flowed past their door, and Aunt Madge had affected to notice that some of the rooms were bereft of furniture only in so far as it might not inconvenience dear Godfrey if she had her own furniture sent here, which was currently Lord knows where, in a field no doubt, and the sooner it was got indoors the better. While Reg and Ted were gone about finding the furniture she asked dear Godfrey if he would mind very much if they stayed for a month perhaps, until she had sorted her affairs in town and could remove permanently to the country, which she did not relish on account of her natural aversion to mud, draughts, cows, stupidity, and other features of the countryside, but which she feared had to be faced sooner or later.

Godfrey had of course naturally assured her that she was at liberty to remain for as long as was convenient, that he only rattled around this great house on his own in any case, and he was delighted to be of service. He added (to me) that Aunt Madge confessed to being bewildered by the appearance of "the little painted lady" at Frederick's request, and how Puss had come there, though she had written to Frederick at Oxford for enlightenment and so as he should know where to find her when he came to town.

Whether by the efforts of the militia and citizens, aided by the King and the Duke of York themselves, or by the east wind mercifully dropping, the great fire eventually ceased its relentless despoil of the city, leaving, so it has been calculated, only one in six buildings standing within London's walls. I easily recall this figure, as it chimed in a kind of contrary tune with the plague toll, which had killed one sixth of Londoners.

39

hen I went to see the devastation in the days immediately following the fire, I could not have found the location of Cheapside, nor any other landmark, had I tried, for blackened ruins and wasteland stretched from the river in the south to Cripplegate in the north, and from Fleet Street in the west to the Tower in the east so that not even streets could be identified. And though an end was made to the disaster, the memory of those few days in September will not be erased from the city until its last witness passes into the hereafter, so swift, shocking and devastating was its impact.

Its population shrunk by plague, and the city itself all but laid waste by fire, yet London carried on: men wandered in this vast grey desert, taking measurements and making plans. And so did we.

Life in Clerkenwell altered radically in the weeks and months that followed. A number of the refugees who had flooded into the quarter showed no signs of moving, indeed had nowhere to move to, and it became very crowded and uncomfortable with the result that much of our usual clientele found it too inconvenient to visit us. In addition to this our usual places of resort and assignation in the city were all gone, so that more whores thronged in what remained of the West End of town than could ever have been concentrated in one place in history, and pickings were slim. Mother Cresswell decided we should have to swallow our pride (such as it was) and open our doors to the more modest sort of patron, namely drawn from a new class of customer, comprised of the great number of craftsmen drawn into London in order to build the city up again. This class arrived with extraordinary haste; it seemed no sooner was London gone, than it was to be made again, but better.

So it was out with the sons of earls and lords, the clergymen and the sea captains (although, to give my own gentlemen their due, they mostly continued to come to me, or arranged to meet me elsewhere, though for others of my sisters, who had not been so diligent in cultivating a regular clientele, it was all change) and in with the surveyors and architects, then the bricklayers, plasterers, carpenters and painters. I did not object to our new patrons, but they had shallower pockets and consequently the girls were obliged to work more, and there was more coming and going, and the house took on an improvised, transient air that I found unsettling. I began to think again of casting about for an easier way of life. As it happened, Janey's fortunes took a change of direction at this time which was to have an unforeseen influence on my future.

She burst in one evening, flushed and excited.

"William's putting me on the stage," she hollered. "What do you think of that?"

"What does Mother say?" asked Kat.

"Pfff! She says it's alright by her, as it's good to have playhouse contacts, and provided I send business her way she don't see no harm in it."

The other girls congratulated Janey, but Winnie frowned.

"You want to be careful, Janey," she warned. "Remember Cherry? She was picked up by a gentleman what bred her up for the theatre, learned her to talk, and move, and made her proud; give her clothes, plate, jewels and things, and she ran mad at the extremity of the alteration till he couldn't stand her airs no more, and by the time he left her to ill luck and she lost her place in the playhouse, she was so unfit for any other way of life the last I heard she was drinking herself to death in a garret, without so much as a pot to piss in."

"Janey's no Cherry, though," averred Kat. "She has a head on her shoulders and I believe she may well succeed. The men fawn upon the actresses so behind the scenes, and the tiring rooms always throng with admirers. Once her face is famous, even if she loses her William she can soon pick up another champion. What spark would not wish to walk abroad with an object of every man of the town's desire on his arm? Everyone loves an actress."

Mother Cresswell entered the room at this point, demonstrating an uncanny knack she had for knowing what had been said on a particular subject before she came in: "You need not fear for Janey on that score. She is as well quantified to be an actress as any, and more than most. I know not why Janey may not do as well as others, and she may be an example to the commonality that a girl may rise through this profession to the very precipice of society."

"Besides, a player is but a whore writ large," said Kat. "It is all games and dreams and gratifying the customer. We are all players, are we not?" And this brought back, with an immediacy that almost took my breath away and made my heart beat hard, as any memory of my past life tended to do, Sylvia's friend Melissa saying "*All* women are actresses, are they not?"

"You won't like the pay, Janey," said Bessie. "Even Mrs Butler only gets thirty shillings a week and the men get twice that. At least in this game there is equality."

"What have they offered you, Janey?" I asked, rather meanly, for I guessed the answer.

Here Janey looked a little abashed.

"Well, they don't pay nothing to begin with, it's like I'm an apprentice, learning the craft."

At this the girls began to express doubts, and I felt sorry for pouring cold water on Janey's news.

"Now, now, girls, let us have a little *esprit de corpse*,"

admonished Mother. "Never mind the money, for there is more than one way to swing a cat. Janey will still have a roof over her head here and may earn her keep by throwing custom in our way. We must cultivate our connections in these hard times. I view Janey as our ambassador in town."

We could all, in truth, see the sense in this.

"But what about your good name, Janey?" teased Winnie. "Everyone knows what actresses are."

"When it comes to women, fame and infamy are the same thing," asserted Mother with her usual unquestionable authority. "Die a maid or marry to be poor if you want a quiet life. If you want a slice of the cake you must pay for it with your name. And what is a name good for after all? It neither puts bread in your mouth nor clothes on your back."

No one could dispute the veracity of this.

"In any case, why did the good Lord bless our Janey with such a powerful pair of lungs if she was not meant for the stage?" demanded Mother, to which again no one had an answer. "It is the girl's destiny; it is her *fate accompli*."

I said nothing more to all this. I considered William putting Janey on the stage was his way of discharging his debt to her, and a cheap way at that for he had exerted only influence and she was still out of pocket. I also considered he must be as madly and blindly in love with her as she was with him if he believed she could make a living on the stage, for this, I suspected, was a deal harder than it seemed, and demanded much more than a pretty face and a bold tongue, which were Janey's principal assets. So I determined to keep my own counsel on the matter unless Janey asked me, which I knew she would not, for she guessed it.

Yet life is constantly surprising, and as it turned out, Mother Cresswell was right and Janey did far better than I had expected. She only had small parts to begin with, but she began to be paid, ten shillings a week. More importantly, her employment in the playhouse paid dividends to her sisters in Clerkenwell, and to me in particular, as she came home one day with the offer of unusual extra work for me. The King's Playhouse, to which Janey was attached, had lost its women's dresser and needed someone urgently. I did not see that I was any more fit for this job than anyone else, and did not greatly fancy it, although I thought it might be entertaining to be among the playhouse people, but Janey explained there was more to the job than that.

"They need a dresser what reads, to learn the actresses their lines."

This made all the difference to me. I already taught Janey, who didn't read, her lines, and the opportunity of this kind of work was more than I could resist. To be paid to read plays! It seemed such easy money.

"What would Mother say," I said, "what with you gone to the playhouse already?"

"Pffff!" exclaimed Janey. "One step at a time. See if Mr Killigrew gives you the job first. But I've put in a good word and you're to come tomorrow to meet him."

So I said nothing to Mother the next day about where I was going except that I was on an errand, and made my way to the playhouse. The boy on the door sent for Janey and when she took me in it was most surprising to see how different the house looked when there was no audience and no candles lit, cold and hollow and a little shabby. Janey bade me walk about on the stage, which I did, and it was a mighty strange and pleasant feeling.

To go behind the scenes was most interesting and to see the quantity of cables for moving the scenes that they employ old sailors to work, so handy are they with ropes, and Janey, who was you may understand quite the old hand, said you must never whistle on the stage for they use a code of whistles to communicate, as they are used to at sea, and if you whistle on the stage you are like to get a scene dropped on your head and be killed. I was careful to remember this, and also, she said, to suffer no abuse at the hands of the sparks who came behind the scenes between the acts, for some of them thought any woman employed in the playhouse fair game, though if I chose to have ado with them this was my business of course and she laid a finger to the side of her nose and said Mother need be none the wiser on this score.

And then she let me wander among the properties, which were much finer than those Godfrey had shown me at the fair at Harlow, but it was strange to see so many all mixed up. A wooden leg lay next to a sword, a crown next to a head, and all manner of food made of paste, and I had a similar unpleasing sensation as before: it was not so nice to see how poor they looked, close to in daylight, when they seemed so fine on the stage, by candle-light. And the costumes too were quite dirty and worn close to and looked rather like sad old ghosts without people in them.

Janey took me up some stairs into an untidy room full of papers and playscripts and introduced me to Mr Killigrew. I was a little afraid as he was not only the theatre manager but a famous playwright – and a wit. He looked up briefly from his writing, reached across the table and threw a bundle of papers at me. I was not expecting this but Janey was, as she caught it easily, untied the ribbon and handed the script to me.

"Go on then," said Mr Killigrew. "Read."

"Which part?" I asked.

"Any part," he said, sighing.

Janey picked out a page.

"Shall I read the names of the characters and the directions or just the words the players say?"

"It doesn't matter!" he cried. "Just read!"

So I read:

"Celadon: Provided always, that whatever liberties we take with other people, we continue very honest to one another.

Florimel: As far as will consist with a pleasant life.

Celadon: Lastly, whereas the names of Husband and Wife hold forth nothing but clashing and cloying, and dullness and faintness in their signification, they shall be abolished for ever betwixt us.

Florimel: And instead of those, we will be married by the more agreeable names of Mistress and Gallant."

"That will do," said Mr Killigrew. "Come at noon each day to teach the women their cues, then stay to help them dress for the performance and remain for any costume changes. I pay ten shillings a week." And he resumed his writing.

I was a little disappointed, for I had heard a good deal about Mr Killigrew's repartee. As Janey shut the door behind us I said, "I thought Mr Killigrew was a great wit."

"Great shit, more like," said Janey.

"I heard that!" came a roar from behind the door, and Janey giggled and put her arm through mine and we ran downstairs.

Then Janey took me into the tiring room where I met Mistress Gwyn who was mighty pretty, just as when I had first seen her in *Thomaso*, and also very witty and warm.

"How much is the old skinflint paying you, darling?" she asked.

"Ten shillings," I answered.

"Well, you can make a lot more besides, if you've a mind; neat little piece like you," she said and winked at me, which I was surprised to find made me blush – something I hadn't done for a very long time – as I was feeling this was almost a respectable job and had almost forgot my true calling. "Don't blush, sweetheart," she said, "there ain't no crime but poverty." And then she gave me some fruit and a gentleman took her away.

Janey told me Mistress Gwyn had not been back in the playhouse long, a lord, no less, having taken her off the stage and given her one hundred pounds a year, but this had all cooled and Mistress Gwyn had come back to work, at which all of London rejoiced as she was such a favourite, and men being what they are the lord now spoke scurrilously of her, and said she had had all she could get of him. It is pretty to observe how many a man willingly gives a woman money only to despise her for taking it.

40

did not relish my coming interview with Mother as I guessed she might not approve this scheme and as I went home I debated not telling her at all, as I could be out several hours a day with no questions asked, as long as I brought a respectable amount of coin home with me, but decided too much risk was attached to that course. I would have to face it out.

Bessie told me Mother was in her chamber and though I knocked on the door, she was somewhat deaf and didn't answer me, so I opened the door. She had her back to me and was locking a large cupboard set in the wall I had never noticed before, and immediately realised that this was because a picture usually hung in front of it – this picture, of a child playing with some ill-proportioned dogs, now stood on the floor, leaning against the wall. I quietly withdrew from the room at once. The girls had often wondered where Mother kept her fortune, and now I knew. The devious old bird often made a point of saying that she kept no large sums in the house, presumably to deter house-thieves – or us. I knew instinctively I had better not let on I had discovered her at her treasure, as if anything ever went missing I should be suspected. She once lost a locket and made no bones about turning all our rooms upside down and there was a mighty unpleasing feeling in the house until she recalled she had sent it to have the clasp mended.

I knocked again, louder, and called and this time she answered, "One minute!" and when she came out, slipping the great key into her bodice, through the open door I saw the picture was back in its place. She listened to my proposal carefully and asked several pertinent questions.

"Tell me why I should agree to this, Doll," she said finally. "I already have Janey in the playhouse and do not require another agent. Why am I to lose you for half the day? What, in fine, is in it for me?" She smiled sweetly, disarmingly.

"I will give you a quarter of my wages," I said.

"Half," she said.

"Or I could move out," I continued. "I could keep myself on my playhouse money and trade on my own account."

We both knew this was my trump card. Mother sucked her lips thoughtfully.

"I should be sorry to lose as good and honest a girl as you, Doll," she said.

"I should be sorry to go," I said.

We both allowed a little time to elapse while we pretended to consider our positions.

"Yet there's many a poor young whore would be glad of a place in a respectable house such as this," she sighed.

"Not all of them good and honest girls, I fear, Mother," I said.

More moments of feigned deliberation passed.

"Very well," she said eventually. "Due to the high regard I have for you, Doll, you may assist the player women and I will accept a third of your playhouse wages, but on two conditions."

"Yes, Mother?"

"As far as the girls are concerned, you're paying me half."

"Of course, Mother."

"And if the playhouse takes up more of your time than I think is warranted, these terms is void."

"Agreed," I said, and we both went about our respective business, each warm in the knowledge that she had never had any intention of allowing me to leave, and I had never had any intention of going.

No one was more delighted with the arrangement than dear Janey who went round the house hollering the news to our sisters, for Janey was beginning to want to get out of Clerkenwell as much as I, and now we both had a foothold in the playhouse, she talked of us setting up home together independently of Mother Cresswell, and maybe one day getting out of the game altogether. (She, like me, had her little hopeful box of savings.) The thought of turning honest greatly appealed to me, but I knew it would be a hard life for we would never earn enough legitimately as single women to live comfortably, and both Janey and I had seen all we wanted of hardship. Also, as Janey herself had observed, every whore talks of turning respectable, but few enough succeed.

My days spent at the King's Playhouse were to be some of the happiest of my life, and not merely because Janey and I saw more of each other. Apart from the presence of Fricker, who always seemed to be in a corner somewhere conducting some dark business, and never failed to save a sneer for me whenever our paths crossed, the playhouse people were all very familiar with each other and with me, and Mistress Gwyn and I were soon Nellie and Dollie. It was easy to forget that we were of an age, both now about seventeen, as Nell had had a hard early life which had given her wisdom well beyond her years, and though she now had a measure of security and fame, she always had an eye to the main thing – I mean the money – for none dread poverty so much as those who have known it. She used often to tell me that I must look to myself and my own good before anything else, for no one else would, and I must not account this selfishness, but self-preservation, and that she had raised her own stock in the world by never undervaluing herself.

We were playing *Secret Love* at that time (the play Mr

Killigrew had had me read from) which was a very funny play but there was something in it that made me indefinably sad, because it took as read that marriage could never really be happy, and the solution the couple in the story hit on could never really happen, nor would be tolerated in society. It was like a kind of dream of how marriage could be, as if our wishing for something could be a balm against the reality. Indeed Nell said that was what theatre – or comedy anyway – was for: that it let us imagine that there were solutions to life's problems. "Everybody loves a happy ending," she would say, "for it may be only a made-up story, but the happiness it makes us feel is real enough." The more I saw of plays and playing, the more I came to see that the theatre is indeed a house of hopes and fears, where people come to dream.

She told me a hundred other interesting things when I was dressing her, or when she was painting, and we often laughed too for she was very quick and full of quips, having begun her career in the playhouse as an orange-woman, and they were famous for their brisk repartee – their only defence against the importunate sparks in the pit who sought riper fruits. I soon learnt that my responsibilities included controlling who went into the tiring rooms, as many gentlemen seemed to believe the price of a seat in the playhouse included a sight of the actresses in their deshabille. Janey put me right on this score: I was to accept no less than half a crown for granting this privilege, and while I split this revenue with the player women, this money, along with other fees I was given for carrying messages, tokens and gifts to the actress half the men of the town were in love with, all added to my growing stock of capital. I did not declare them to Mother Cresswell nor to anyone else.

41

ometimes life seems to be merely a series of shocks and surprises: the next disconcerting revelation was that Janey proved an exceptionally fine actress. One day, having finished my work and thinking to pick up a little trade, I donned my mask and ventured into the pit and watched the play, and I may truly say that when Janey did her soliloquy she had the house in her hand, as I found I almost believed she was who she pretended to be, and was in the predicament that character found herself in. There were very few actresses who could cry real tears when called upon to play some tragic scene, but Janey did something better, for she acted attempting *not* to cry: you could hear the strain in her voice, and see her lip quiver, and her eyes shone with tears unshed. It was sadder than unchecked emotion, it was sorrow controlled and suppressed, and this seemed somehow infinitely more upsetting. I looked about me and saw that the whole house was silent, watching, almost not breathing, and then when she had finished, erupting into applause. But much as I admired Janey's performance, it made me uneasy on another score. If I trusted anyone in this world, it was Janey. I now realised that she could lie more convincingly than anyone I had ever known. I should have to be careful.

As she turned to leave the stage I observed that Janey was, as Mother Cresswell would have said, "sick of a two-legged tympani", that is to say, she was expecting a child. I wondered that I had not noticed before, but I suppose I generally saw Janey close to, but here, as I saw her from a distance in profile, more objectively, as it were, I saw her swollen bust, and her belly just beginning to show; the signs were unmistakeable to one who knew her shape as well as I. I wondered that she had not told me, and then unconsciously looked about the pit for William, but could not see him, and realised I had not seen him about for some little while. However, another gentleman had caught my eye, so I lacked the opportunity to speak to her until we were both back at Clerkenwell that evening.

When we had dispatched our various customers, Janey and I found ourselves alone in Mother Cresswell's saloon. She busied herself mending her stockings and I had a book in my hand, but was reading and re-reading the same passage over and over, and wishing she would confide in me.

"Your performance today was the most convincing I ever saw," I said eventually.

"Pffff!" said Janey. "I love the sad parts. It's all I'm good at. You should see me in comedy! Now *that's* a bleeding tragedy!"

"I heard Mr Killigrew say you had great promise," I said, which was true.

"We'll see," sighed Janey.

"But your performance these last few weeks has been just as convincing." I could not help saying it, and realised with a pang that her secrecy had hurt me.

"I don't know to what you're referring, I'm sure," she said, her voice recovering its penetrating timbre.

"Oh leave off, Janey," I cried. "You know you are in a condition! Why did you not tell me? How long did you think you could keep up this pretence?"

Janey looked at me, and seemed to consider keeping up the charade, but gave up and her face crumpled into tears.

"Oh Doll, I don't know what to do! It's William's and he don't want to know!"

I leapt up and comforted her.

"There, there, Janey. How can you possibly know it's William's?"

"I just know it is," she sobbed. "I want it to be, anyway." She reached into her bodice, as I thought, for a handkerchief, but withdrew a crumpled piece of paper. "He sent me this."

"Well, what does it say?" I asked.

"I don't bloody know, do I?" shouted Janey. "I was too ashamed to ask you to read it, and I couldn't ask anyone else, could I?"

"Come on," I said, and took the letter and read it to her, which was very hard indeed.

My dear Janey,
I have been called into the country by my family and may be sent abroad on business so shall not be in town for a – oh, sweet Janey, I cannot lie to you: I am to be married. It is not of my choosing, but I am to obey my father or be turned into the world without a penny. I trust you will manage your unhappy situation as you see fit. I can never see you again. I have been a fool.
Please do not hate me, your ever-loving William.

"Oh Janey," I said – she was now in floods of tears.

"Why can he not marry her and keep me?" she wailed.

"He can," I said. "He chooses not to. He's not worth it, Janey. Come, now."

But Janey was not to be appeased.

"But he said he loved me! He promised he would look after me! I gave him everything! He took everything! Oh, God help me!"

"What did you give him, Janey?" I asked, dread creeping through me. But she was now incoherent with grief.

I ran to her room and pulled out her money box. It was completely empty. She had given that unworthy boy every last penny of her life savings.

I comforted Janey for the rest of the evening.

"Them bleeding herbs!" she wailed.

This was a reference to her efforts to avoid falling pregnant. The wenches at Mother Cresswell's had many means of preventing becoming mothers which of course was a hazard they ran as much as any married woman, and though I did not need to be concerned about this, I took an interest as it was a subject of some debate about which was best. I early on learnt that Frenchie put little hats on her gentlemen (made of the intestine of some animal, I believe), which were knotted at one end and tied on the root of his tarse with a ribbon at the other. She maintained these inhibited inception and the pox, which made both her and her cullies the easier and indeed she never did breed nor get a clap all the time I knew her, and I also resorted to them to keep clear of the dreaded disease, and whether it was these or luck I know not but I also never was ill. The drawback was that they were quite dear but you cannot put a price on your health can you, and besides I never had time off work as other girls did because I never was sick, so I looked upon them as an investment. To avoid getting with child the others used washes and salves and pessaries and potions of varying efficacy. Some used these concoctions every day, while others made use of them only if they feared they were a-breeding. Bessie swore by the juice of the herb savin – which from my childhood in the country I knew as covershame, and never knew why it was so-called till this time – and Kat used a wash of camphor, castor oil and rue, while Janey herself used a mixture of marjoram, thyme, parsley, lavender and fern. Though she always smelt lovely and sweet like a herb garden she had been got with child just the same.

When Janey had calmed down I gave her a lecture about in future thinking only of herself, and never ever letting her feelings get the better of her judgement, and she said she knew she had been a fool and I was to look after her money from now on as she feared if she but saw her dear rascally boy again she should give him even the clothes off her back if he asked for them, so I could see there was no real reasoning with her, not yet, and assured her that time would heal all, and put her to bed, and read to her until she went to sleep.

I lay awake thinking how much of a step backwards this was for Janey. She would lose her place in the playhouse, that was certain, and before long would not be able to work for Mother Cresswell, so would fall into debt to her, which would take her a while to work her way out of after the baby came before she could begin to think of starting to build up her little hoard again. I decided I would take her at her word, and look after her money in the future; that was one thing I could control for her as she had no mastery over herself. But our little hopeful dream of leaving and setting up home together receded even further with the loss of her money.

42

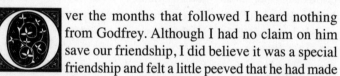ver the months that followed I heard nothing from Godfrey. Although I had no claim on him save our friendship, I did believe it was a special friendship and felt a little peeved that he had made no effort to see me since just after the fire. Of course he could not come to me at the playhouse, for fear Fricker should see us together and guess our complicity in kidnapping Joe; neither could I go to him at his house, and risk recognition by the Potters or Aunt Madge herself. However he could have come to Clerkenwell and I wondered why he did not. When these thoughts entered my head I pushed them away by reasoning that Aunt Madge very probably kept him busy, although a less happy explanation lay in the possibility that he meant rather more to me than I did to him. In any case I was pleased when Mother Cresswell sent for him as Mr Smith had sent word he and Mrs Smith desired our company again.

I was as vexed as Mother when he sent the message back that he regretted he could not come on the day appointed, nor any day soon. She voiced the opinion that though she had hoped he was of a different stamp to most thespians, it was well known that player folk were fickle and flighty characters and she shouldn't be surprised if this were "not *au revoir* but *bon voyage*". I was mightily out of order, and angry with myself for being so, and after much debating I decided to write to him, pretending to myself that I did so merely to enquire how Aunt Madge did. His reply came the same evening.

My dearest H (for so I must now call you),
I am so sorry I have not sent word before but there has been much to do in order to make my lady comfortable. You may rest assured that she is in good spirits and in tolerable health, and not so confused as she was.

Also, as the weeks have turned into months since we last met it seemed a harder thing to write, although I made many beginnings. Anyway, here I am, alive and well, and often *thinking* of you, my dear girl, if not *writing* to you.

We have had a visitor! Your cousin (for you will see that I now know all your history) Frederick came as soon as your aunt (as my suspicion is now confirmed she is) sent him word of her new address and I may say I find him a most capital fellow and a most loving son. His presence has been a great comfort to your aunt and he plans to remain until he has her affairs tolerably in order. There have been many difficulties about the property in Cheapside, and the rights to rebuild on the site, all further complicated by the fact that the deeds burned with the house and at one moment it seemed your aunt might lose the land, but Frederick has taken it all in hand most wonderfully and though I do not pretend to understand it all he seems to be making fine progress at last. He has decided to suspend his studies and remain with your aunt as her advocate and adviser until all these matters are satisfactorily resolved.

After the first surprise of hearing my lady speak of her niece "H", little by little, from conversations between Frederick and herself, I have been able to piece together your relationship to them and I must tell you, my dear H, and this may be a shock, that they believe you to be dead. Both evidently harboured the most tender affection for you and it is strange to hear them speak of you as though you are no longer living.

Dearest H, you may be sure that I have said nothing to them about you, and would not do so without your consent. However this situation cannot obtain indefinitely. I beg you to share with me all your history and let us see if there is not some way in which you and your family could be reconciled, or at the least let them know that you are yet alive and well. Frederick questioned young Joe and me most thoroughly about "the little painted lady" your aunt believed he had sent to bring her out of Cheapside, and both are puzzled at how this same young lady had custody of Puss. (Puss thrives and is naughty; Joe thrives and is good.)

Please send word when we can meet.

Your loving friend and obliging servant in all things,
Godfrey

However good and kind Aunt Madge and Frederick were, I could not imagine them happily re-admitting a common prostitute to the family fold, even if I proved able to face relating how I had lived since Evelyn's death. I knew I could not tell my aunt the cause, as to learn what Roger did to me would surely break her heart and yet do no good. As for her dead grandsons, I could barely think on that subject, let alone imagine speaking of it. The lasting unhappiness and shame my story would bring her, I knew, would outweigh any brief joy occasioned by my reappearance. As far as Aunt Madge and Frederick were concerned, it was imperative that H remain in the plague pit with Evelyn.

Godfrey, however, was another matter. He had discovered too much to be fobbed off with a tale and I dreaded the explanation which I now felt I owed him. H and Doll were drawing uncomfortably close already; telling Godfrey my whole history would close the gap. It was time to think of becoming someone else.

43

ome weeks later, I was awoken in the middle of night by Janey telling me the baby was coming and I must say I believe I was almost as excited as she was. I roused Mother Cresswell and she made up her own bed for Janey while I comforted the mother-that-was-to-be. I knew that Janey had been pregnant before, more than once, but she told me little about it and I sensed I shouldn't enquire too much as the subject seemed to give her pain and all I gathered was that there had been no babies in the event. She had remained convinced that she carried her sweet William's child and his abandonment of her made the child dearer, if anything, to her. She knew better than to talk of William to me anymore but I still sensed her weakness for him and dreaded his reappearance, for both our sakes.

"For a girl what's helped so many children into this wicked world you don't half put up a fuss, Janey!" said Mother, for indeed Janey had woken everyone in the house with her shrieks and curses when the baby was well on its way. But after Frenchie had filled the basin in Mother's closet with warm water, she and the other girls were excluded, as Janey was mighty proud for a girl of our profession and did not want them all "seeing everything".

"It's different when it's your own!" shouted Janey. "And it ain't that bad – " here she paused to give vent to an almighty yell, then subsided into weeping, " – making a noise just makes me feel better."

"Almost there now," said Mother Cresswell. "Come on Janey, push! Think that you're shitting a melon!"

This made Janey laugh through her tears, and then she squeezed my hand so tight I too howled and in a few moments the baby came out. It was a bawling girl, and while Mother took her into her closet, soothing her, I kissed Janey and told her she had done well.

I don't know what made me go into the closet, but the baby had stopped crying, and I went to the doorway and saw Mother standing very still with her hands in the basin, and I looked down and saw water on the carpet, and was suddenly back in the home of my childhood. What was I doing there? I was bathing Tibbs's kittens of course. Till they were clean enough. Till they were dead enough.

I leapt forward and snatched the child out of the basin, pushing Mother backwards. The child was motionless and so pale it seemed blue. I patted its back. There was no change. I turned it upside down, hanging it by its heels with one hand and patting its back with the other. Finally, she made a choking noise and expelled some water before she finally took a great gasping breath and began to cry again, most angrily.

"I was only bathing it!" Mother protested, but her face, white with fear, told me everything.

"Get out!" I hissed.

"I was only bathing it!" Mother repeated, but she backed away towards the door. "I'll go and tell the girls the good news," she said, and went.

My hands shook as I wrapped the baby up. I took her in to Janey, who was too preoccupied with her little darling to notice the state I was in.

"Don't let her out of your sight," I said, and just managed to quit the room before I vomited.

I retched and shivered all that night, and each time I drifted into exhausted sleep, woke with a jolt of horror, recalling what

I had seen. For hours I kept at bay the longer, darker story behind the night's events, pushing away the remembered words of the girls, words which, though spoken in innocence, now told me what I half knew. Janey's disbelief at the loss of both my babies. No thriving babies born at Mother Cresswell's for ever so long. Until Winnie had Rose. And Rose was born during the fire, on the day of the riots against foreigners. And Mother had been out of the house, looking for Frenchie. My little boys...

It won't seem it now, she had said, afterwards. *But it's for the best.*

44

I needed time to consider what to do and took refuge in sickness, though perhaps I really was ill. I refused to come out of my room, in case I infected the baby, I said, and at that time there was still sufficient fear of plague for the girls to respect my wishes. They left food and drink at the door, and asked how I fared, and told me how Mary, Janey's child, did, and otherwise left me alone.

Little Mary was doing well, and I did not now fear for her safety, as, I reasoned, Rose had survived. Mother Cresswell's strategy had been to strike early, before the child drew breath, if possible, when malice would be least suspected, and when such sad events were not uncommon. In any case she would not dare do anything, I judged, now that I had discovered her crime. She had not been near me except once, the morning after Mary was born, to say (through the door) that she and I should have a little talk. I had not answered her, and she had gone away.

As long as I knew her secret, she could not consider herself safe, as if I told the girls what had been going on, they would surely tear her to pieces at worst, or at best turn her in to the magistrates. But equally, my knowledge put me at risk, for what lengths would she not go to to prevent the truth coming out? These were my rational thoughts. My instinct, which I fought every minute at first, was to kill her, and I am not ashamed to admit that I gave this serious consideration, and only the thought of ending up on the gallows myself prevented me taking this course. Whatever I did, I knew I had to act quickly. I began to formulate a plan.

I wanted to get away from Clerkenwell, and to take Janey and Mary with me, but Janey was yet too weak and uncomfortable to bear such an upheaval, so our departure needs must be delayed until she was up and about. I also felt it was cowardly to merely clear out, without doing something to prevent Mother Cresswell making away with more babies, or without warning our sisters about her. But my plan depended on giving her no hint that I planned to leave. It was a problem. Finally, I hit on a solution, but it depended on Mother Cresswell being out of the way. I would put everything in place, and then bide my time, ready to make my move when the moment of opportunity presented itself.

Knowing I had to tarry in Clerkenwell a little longer, I decided I had to come to an understanding with Mother Cresswell, for I could not avoid her for ever. I went to her door, but as I was about to knock, heard voices. I put my ear to the door. She had Pris Fotherington with her. Mother Cresswell's growing deafness meant that she and her companion were obliged to converse quite loudly, and Mother's stage whisper was perfectly audible.

"Whatever I done," the old bitch was saying, "I done in my girls' best interests. This is no life for a mother, Pris, and no place for a child, neither."

"They wouldn't have fell for them in the first place, if they had a choice," Pris said. "They often enough try to get rid of 'em themselves in the beginning."

"Just so, my dear. I makes it easy for 'em, that's all."

"You do what has to be done," said Pris. "You've nothing to reproach yourself for."

"I ain't proud of it!" continued Mother Cresswell, "And I don't say as how I like it. But there it is. It's for the best."

"So what about Doll? What will you do? I can take her into my house if it suits. Till she cools off and sees sense."

"No need," Mother Cresswell assured her. "Coin will serve. It's what makes her tick."

I came away from the door, shocked at her opinion of me. Then, on reflection, I saw that it was true. Money was all my interest, winning it and keeping it. But to believe that I would collude in her crime for base profit! Yet, I reasoned, on the other hand, if she believed she could buy my silence, I would be safe at Clerkenwell a while longer. I made a point of going back to see her that afternoon.

"I'm glad you've come, my dear," she said. "We need to have words."

And she ushered me in and offered me a glass of sack, which I took.

"Are you feeling better, Doll?" she asked. "You still look a bit pale."

"I'm much better, thank you, Mother," I said. "But to tell the truth I don't remember much, after Janey had her baby. I think I may have been overcome. By emotion. I think I may have been... mistaken. In some way. I seem to recall I was worried you might drop the baby."

Mother Cresswell considered me.

"Good girl," she said at last. She drew a purse from her pocket. "I want to give you a little bonus, Doll. No, don't refuse, now, I insist." She pressed the shining guineas into my hand. "There now. We understand each other, do we not?"

"Yes, Mother," I said, and bobbed a curtsey and moved to leave.

"Haven't you forgotten something Dollie?" she said. I knew what was coming and braced myself for it. "What about a kiss for your old mum?"

I made myself kiss her, though at the moment my lips touched her cheek I had to check an almost irresistible urge to bite her savagely. The effort to control myself had been such that when I left Mother Cresswell I ran straight out of the house, and kept running, to a place where I was not known, and gave the guineas away to any poor people I met, and when they were all gone I went to the nearest pump and washed and washed my hands and cheeks and lips till they were sore.

45

"I don't fancy the game no more," bawled Janey one day shortly after this episode. "I look at her little face and I wonder how I'm ever going to tell her how I kept her fed. And what are the chances of her – raised in a bawdy house – going the same way? I don't wish this life on her, Doll. I want out." Her expression, as she bent over her little daughter, was a heart-rending blend of the earnestness of her wish and the acknowledgment of the futility of wishing.

I was glad Janey was ready to move on but not ready to tell her my strategy, for she had a habit of blurting things out at inopportune moments or before inappropriate company. It wouldn't have been so bad if she weren't such an incorrigible loud-mouth, but when Janey said the wrong thing, the whole world knew about it. So all I said was, "Don't fret, Janey. Something will turn up. Look at Kat. Who'd have thought she'd find a kind keeper?"

As it had turned out, we were not the only ones thinking of moving on, as Kat had informed us she was being taken up by a gentleman who was going to keep her in a house in King Street; she was to have servants and a carriage, and he was even settling a portion on her.

All her sisters were very happy for her, as drudging for one man is infinitely preferable to drudging for all-comers if the money is the same, and she should have leisure and clothes and servants besides – everything, in fact, a young bride might expect from a good marriage, saving of course, the miseries attendant on the station of wife. (That was the theory, in any case.) The cause of her good fortune was the recent marriage of her inamorato, Gerald, to an heiress. He had not been able to afford to reserve Kat for his exclusive attentions previously, but now the writings were drawn up and signed, Gerald's young wife had his ring and his name, and he had her considerable fortune at his disposal. We all wished Kat great joy of her news and not a few of us envied her.

"There's many a slip 'twixt cup and lip," Kat said. "You never know, I may be back some day."

It was because Kat was such a level-headed girl and because I needed an accomplice to carry out my plan that I decided to share with her alone that I had discovered Mother Cresswell had been doing away with our babies. I made sure we were both away from the house when I told her, as I feared her immediate reaction might undo my plans. To my surprise she accepted my revelation calmly and said she had suspected something of the kind. Still, the confirmation of her suspicions had turned her very pale and we took a glass or two together to steady ourselves before returning to Clerkenwell. In that time she agreed to assist me by whatever means she could in accomplishing my design. Though I found Kat reliable and trustworthy, she was icy round the heart; she was never my bosom friend, but she was – perhaps even as a result of her coolness, for what is a flaw of character in one situation may often prove a strength in another – the most dependable instrument at hand. Her new situation also gave me the idea of how to achieve my own independence. I decided I too would become a kept woman.

As I intended entirely to abandon my life as Doll, I gave notice at the playhouse. Mr Killigrew was angry and Nell was sorry, but Janey was plainly baffled.

"I thought you liked it here! I thought we were getting out of the game together!"

"We will. It's not that I'm not happy here," I said.

"What is it then? You're not a-breeding are you?"

"No, nothing like that. I've been taken up by a gentleman, that's all."

For a rare moment Janey seemed struck dumb.

"I know I should have told you," I said.

"Well I can say nothing to that." And she coloured slightly, as we both remembered how long it had taken her to tell me she was with child. "You are a dark horse, Doll. Well, you're wasted here, in truth. An appealing little phiz like yours, and a tidy shape too. I can't say I'm surprised. Anyone I know?"

"No," I replied.

"What are your terms?" she enquired.

"A coach and six, liveries of my choosing, four servants besides and three hundred pounds a year," I said.

Janey's mouth fell open.

"Fuck me, Dollie! What you got then, a duke?"

I laughed and said I didn't know what he was, but that he had a good deal of money and that was the main thing.

"I just thought… " Janey swallowed hard. "I hoped… "

"Janey, listen," I said. "This isn't the end of our plans. It's the beginning. You'll see. Just trust me. And when I send for you, just come."

46

odfrey and I had arranged to meet at a coffee-house in Holborn, as he had no wish to get an earful from Mother Cresswell about his unreliability. I had asked Godfrey to dress up, although to be fair he always looked most handsome, and he had done me proud, appearing quite the wealthy gallant, in a pale blue brocade coat and waistcoat, velvet breeches, and silver buckles on his shoes. As a finishing touch his hat was trimmed with great pale blue feathers.

"Very fine," I said, curtseying to him.

"I wore it in *The Wild Gallant*." He bowed. "You don't think the hat is too much?"

"The hat is perfect," I said. If anything was too much, it was the silver-topped cane, fluttering with blue ribbons, but he had gone to such trouble I did not like to mention it.

"You're very pretty yourself," he said. "Pink suits you." I too had pulled out all the stops and was in a gown of my own making, shell-pink silk trimmed with cream lace. "Who are we today?"

"We are husband and wife. That is to say, we are to *appear* husband and wife, but in fact we are lovers. We are looking for rooms in which you are to install me."

"I am to be a keeper! That is a part I have never played. Am I a kind keeper?"

"Very kind. You can't do enough for me. Why are you staring at me so?"

"I am in my character. I am looking at you admiringly."

I took a carriage for the day as we had a deal of ground to cover, and we set off for the first of three addresses I had found. I had thought to go out of town, as I had a fancy to live in the country, but the first house, in Hammersmith, was too large even for my ambitions, and the second, in Chelsea, was dark and ill-appointed. The last was in a pleasant part of town by St James's Park. The landlady, a Mrs Snags, showed us up to a set of rooms on the first floor.

"It's only been built five years," she told us, "and has every comfort." She was eyeing Godfrey most unashamedly and I left them together while I explored. The rooms were large and bright and in excellent order, and all connected by large double doors.

"Don't you want to look with your wife, sir?" I heard Mrs Snags ask.

"Oh she has an eye for these things. She wears the breeches, isn't that so, H?"

"If you say so dearest," I called.

"H," repeated Mrs Snags. "That's an odd name. What does it stand for?"

There was the briefest of pauses.

"Halcyon," Godfrey decided.

Damn him, I thought. Now I was lumbered with Halcyon.

"Pretty," said Mrs Snags.

On one side the rooms looked into the street, but those on the other overlooked a small garden and then the park, so one had the impression of being in the town on one side and being in the country on the other. I liked it immensely. I completed a second tour of the rooms before returning to Godfrey and Mrs Snags.

"I fear Mrs Snags has discovered our little secret, my dear," Godfrey informed me.

"I merely said he allowed his wife such liberties, my dear,

234

that he spoke of her rather as one who pays court than one...
shall we say... joined at the church door." Mrs Snags smiled.

"Oh Mrs Snags you will not betray us?" I moved urgently
towards her and took her hand, looking appealingly into her
face.

"Oh my dear, there's many a young couple sits down to
dinner before grace is said, you'd be surprised." She winked.
"Come," she said conspiratorially and beckoned us to follow
her to the window overlooking the park. "Look down there,"
she said softly, as though to emphasise her discretion. "See
that alley that runs along the bottom of the gardens? And see
the gate in the garden wall? Your young gentleman may come
and go entirely unobserved."

"Mrs Snags, you are an angel!" exclaimed Godfrey.

"We'll take it!" I decided. "Godfrey – talk terms with
Mrs Snags."

"You see Mrs Snags? I am a mere slave to Mistress Halcyon."

Godfrey paid the knowing Mrs Snags six months' rent in
advance from the purse I had previously given him and we
spent the rest of the afternoon ordering and buying furniture
and I explained my plan to Godfrey, of how I was to set myself
up as a kept woman. He did not at first comprehend why
I did not merely set up as an independent Miss, and why I
insisted on the pretence of having a keeper, but I had an idea
my gentlemen – who were to be a select, well-paying few –
would be more easily governable with the shadowy figure of
an absent protector in the background.

"And if they misbehave I could rush in and fright them!"
He demonstrated a swordly flourish with the cane that was a
little too much.

"There'll be no need for that," I said. "In any case, you are
my keeper for today only. They need never see my gentleman.
It's better that way."

I had thought it all through, you understand. No woman
could have real independence (except, of course, the wealthy
widow, and I was saving her for my old age), so I sought

liberty under the cover of a fictional protector. As it proved in the event, the existence of my fabled friend was to add spice to many of my encounters, for some like an element of danger to their love-making.

Godfrey also expressed concern at the amount of money I was laying out and indeed the cost of the rent and the furniture had sadly depleted my store, reducing it to a mere ten pounds. Still, as I had a plot to restore my fortune, I treated us both to a fine dinner at the Bear at Bridgefoot. Although Godfrey protested he was tired and Southwark was entirely out of our way, he relented to humour me, knowing the pleasure I took in crossing the bridge. Besides, we had the coach, I reasoned, and it would take us home too. As for the money, I told him not to worry about it – as with the rest of my future, I had a plan.

Over dinner came the moment I had been dreading.

"Well, Mistress Halcyon," said Godfrey, smiling. "I have played your game all day, and you have promised in return to tell me all your history, about you and your aunt and your cousins. I want the whole tale, nothing omitted." Seeing my expression of anxiety he took my hand in his and said, gently, "Dearest Doll – or H – or whatever name you go by today – nothing you can say will shock me, or make me think less of you. But you have entrusted your aunt to my care, and besides you have a place in my heart, and I must know how it came about that you ever left her household and why you cannot return or even let her know you live and breathe."

Even within this private place, we had our own booth, so I knew I could unburden my tale away from the curious gaze of strangers. I both dreaded telling my story and desired the relief of sharing it, and indeed shed many tears of all kinds in the telling. I need not tell you, patient reader, my story so far, for you know it. Godfrey was silent throughout my tale and did not speak immediately when I had done. Eventually he said, "I can say nothing to what that evil woman Cresswell has done to you – she should be hanged for it. I see that you have passed through terrible times, H, and I am sorry for it. But I also think you see too much blame in yourself for these events. You cannot be the sole cause of your sister's misadventures, or your father's death."

"Oh but I was!" I exclaimed. "I whined to go to the fair; I insisted on seeing the play; don't you see?"

Godfrey stared at me.

"You were a mere *child*, H. And I do not think you can blame yourself for your cousin's abuse of you. His was a wicked, selfish and cruel crime. You were a victim merely. You did not comprehend the warning signs, you said so yourself. And in all probability you could not have saved the children and the cook."

Here I fell to weeping again and protesting that in dallying and worrying who to save I had saved no one, and no one could be blamed for that but myself.

Godfrey sighed and took my hands in his again.

"Listen to me. You do not see the good that is in you."

"What good could be in me?" I sobbed. "I am a common prostitute. I may wear a brave face, but I know what I have sunk to. And I have brought it on myself, and hurt others on the way."

"The good that is in you is what makes you feel responsible for all these things. Yes, your heart aches, but with pity for others, not for yourself. You care – even for your despicable cousin, you care. And when it has been in your power to take the right action, you have: you saved Joe. You saved your aunt from the fire, when no one else could move her. You mean to help Janey. The foolish, selfish little trollop you describe would not do these things. I think you have had bad luck, that is all." And then, as if he suddenly remembered, he added with a laugh, "You even saved me! When I – a perfect stranger – fainted in the street for hunger, you helped me, and fed me, and gave me a guinea. Don't you remember?"

"Yes," I admitted. "But I wanted… a friend."

"And you have a friend! A friend who loves you even though you have been such a thoroughly wicked creature!" And he smiled and kissed me and wiped my eyes and told me my paint had all run.

"Now, what about your Aunt Madge?" asked Godfrey. "I agree your history and Roger's part in it would come as a terrible shock to her, and I can also understand that she could not take you back into the household, for though she may forgive you, the world will not, and will turn its back upon her as well as you. I know that as surely as you do. But it does seem cruel that she believes you dead. She believes herself responsible, you see. She feels she should never have left London without you and your sister. Anyone can see she is racked with guilt whenever either of you is mentioned or remembered."

It had never occurred to me that Aunt Madge might reproach herself for this and indeed I wished I could alleviate her suffering on that score.

"Does she truly think about us so often?" I asked.

"Oh yes! She and Frederick. Almost every day, I'd say. But Frederick is such a capital fellow he always reassures her that she could not have foreseen how things would turn out. Although, between us, he too blames himself."

"But he was not there!"

"I know. He has spoken to me of the circumstances. He thought of coming back to London, but when the court turned up in Oxford was persuaded it was sheer folly to return. He has never forgiven himself, for he knew his brother's character."

Were it possible to let them know – and indirectly the rest of my family – that I was yet alive and well, it would indeed seem a kindness both to them and to myself to know they were not suffering. But I knew that they would be bound then to make efforts to find me, and that I could not allow to happen.

"Would you not consider," suggested Godfrey, "reinventing your past somehow – some harmless fiction – to explain your absence?"

I had thought about this more times than I could count. Had I been a boy it would have been simple. I could have been pressed into the navy and disappeared for years on end. But females don't just disappear – not to reappear later, anyhow. I had heard stories of people who, having taken a knock on the

238

head, or having a terrible shock, could forget who they were and become lost for a time, and had toyed with this idea. But in any event, I did not think I could lie every day to people I loved and remember the lies too. Godfrey looked wide-eyed at this, saying I had lived a lie ever since the day I became Doll, which hurt me a little, though I knew the truth of it. The question remained unresolved.

The carriage took Godfrey to Lincoln's Inn Fields and I travelled on alone to Clerkenwell, alighting a few streets away from home, as I did not want to arouse Mother Cresswell's suspicions. As I walked the rest of the way I hugged my secret future life to myself. My new home was ready and waiting; Mrs Snags would supervise the delivery of the furniture, so when I arrived with Janey and little Mary in tow everything would be ready. All I had to do before making my final move was to inform the gentlemen I wished to keep on of my great good fortune.

Suddenly I was grabbed from behind and dragged into an alleyway, the man who had hold of me slamming me against the wall.

"Keep your trap shut or I'll knife you, you thieving little bitch!"

I tried to protest nonetheless but the man's knuckle was pressed so hard on my throat I could only whimper.

"Shut it!" he said, and smacked me across the face with his free hand. As he turned, the light caught both the blade he held and his face. The unnatural whiteness of his scarred cheek declared my assailant was Fricker. He must have seen me with Godfrey.

"I know you've got him," he snarled. "I saw you with him, and him with your backgammoner friend. Now you get him back to me or I'll slit you from hole to hole. I won't be bettered by a fucking whore and a Mary-Ann. I'll be at the Bleeding Heart at Long Acre at this hour one week today and you'd better be there with my little monkey, or I do assure you, you will be sorry." He let go of me and easily cut my purse from my belt. "That's for loss of earnings." He began to walk away down the alley, turning to call, "And I know where you live, so don't try to be clever, you fucking slut, or I'll burn you."

I made my way home, trying to calm myself by being thankful that I had only a small amount of coin in my purse, as I had been waylaid before, and ever since had carried any large sum in a privy pocket in my shift. At Clerkenwell I found Kat, pulled her into my room and told her what had happened.

"At least it's clear Fricker doesn't know where Joe is," I added. "He merely put two and two together when he saw me with Godfrey."

"But what happens when you don't produce the boy?" asked Kat.

I didn't have an answer. Kat looked at the floor for a long time, then at the ceiling for longer, and then at me.

"You won't be free of Fricker while he is alive," she said finally.

My throat tightened.

"What do you mean?"

"We have to get rid of him," said Kat. She was perfectly calm.

"What do you mean?" I said again. "You don't mean—"

"There are people," said Kat. "Soon, if all goes well, you will have money. You can pay them."

"Kat!"

She grabbed my wrists.

"What do you think he will do to you if you don't produce Joe? Or maybe he'll give you another warning. He's seen you with Godfrey. He saw you with *me*. He must have worked out we were both involved in getting the boy home. Don't you see? We're at risk too."

It was all horrifying.

"As you say, we will have money soon," I stammered. "I will pay him to go away, to leave us all alone."

Kat shook her head.

"He'll keep coming back for more. Why should he not? You must make an end of him."

47

I had a few days to decide what to do about Fricker and for the time being was grateful to have to devote my attention to the gentlemen I hoped would support me in my new venture. I had decided to keep, if I could, my city merchant, who I reminded of his first sweetheart; Sir Robert; my member of parliament, who liked to keep a check on the status of my depravity; Lord A, of course, of whom I was most fond; and young Jasper. I expected to attract more wealthy admirers once I was established, but these would do to be going on with. The first three were straightforward enough, and once they had been assured that my keeper would give me warning of his visits, agreed without question to substantially higher fees for longer sojourns in the greater comfort my new premises had to offer. Each of them, of course, believed himself the sole recipient of this, my special favour. I gave them the address and assigned a day of the week to each and advised them of when this new arrangement was to commence and forbade them to breathe a word of my design to anyone, especially Mother Cresswell.

Lord A and Jasper reacted somewhat unexpectedly. I had enough respect for Lord A not to affect that he was the only one of my gentlemen to whom I was extending this invitation. When he understood me, Lord A asked me if I were sure I wanted to place myself under the protection of this man, and asked me many questions about his character, and once he was satisfied that I had not rushed into this agreement thoughtlessly, wished me good luck but regretted he could no longer pay me visits as, while he did not condemn me for wishing to entertain gentlemen other than my keeper he could not, in all conscience, be party to such a deception. This surprised me, as it is well known that a Miss set up in a fair way by one lover often supplements her income by allowing the attentions of one or more others, and as long as she exercises some discretion, this is tolerated. But I could see that Lord A was a man of principle and would not be moved in his decision. It was only then that I decided I could trust him, and him alone of all my gentlemen, with the true state of affairs.

I asked him whether he would feel differently if there were, in fact, no gentleman supporting me; if I had invented one just to keep my other gentlemen in order? At this he looked at first astonished, then he laughed and said I was a rare one and the most cunning jade he ever knew. Then he stopped and said, "You are telling me the truth, Doll? You are not saying this just to make me easier? For I will not trespass on another man's property. I have my good name to think of. And a conscience besides."

"I know that," I said, "and I also know that for a whore to tell truth is as unlikely a discovery as cat's eggs, but I swear this is the truth of the matter. My keeper is a phantom, a mere shadow. It is all my gentlemen who are my keepers. And I should like to lose you least of all."

Lord A took me in his arms and said, "I do not scruple to say, Doll, that I should sorely miss our time together. I believe you, and I swear to keep your secret, for the sake of what Madam Cresswell calls our little *tit-à-tits*." We parted on good terms, Lord A pleased that my new address was much nearer his own, as he was finding the journey to Clerkenwell more troublesome as the town became more crowded, as it had done noticeably since the great fire.

Jasper was altogether a different matter. He listened with an expression of growing incredulity as I explained my new fortunate circumstances and then exclaimed: "Damn it all Dollie, *I* would have kept you if you'd only said!"

This surprised me a great deal.

"Well, why didn't you say so?" I asked.

He looked a little abashed.

"Damn it all, a fellow doesn't like to... I mean to say, if you'd said *no*... I would have felt a proper fool." I suddenly felt very sorry for him. I knew he cared for me but had not realised quite how deep it went. "Truth is, Dollie old girl, a word from you could smash a fellow into a thousand pieces." I saw he was very nearly in tears. I put my arms round him and laughed and kissed him and told him he was a dear.

"I should have liked to have you all to myself," he mumbled, blushing somewhat. "I don't see any other young ladies, you know," he said. "You know, like I see you."

"I know," I said, and sat on his lap and hugged him.

"I don't say I haven't tried," he added. "It just ain't the same."

I enumerated the advantages to him of the new arrangement and he was a little mollified, but added that he hoped he shouldn't meet my protector, for he had pipped him at the post and he should very strongly like to knock his block off. I promised him that should I ever tire of my gentleman, Jasper would be first in line for promotion, and to see the effect this hope had on him was most pathetic. Still, he left me with the look of one who has learned his sweetheart is to be married and the memory of his crestfallen expression trailed around after me all day.

That night I stayed in Clerkenwell. It was the night of my appointment with Fricker, which I of course did not intend to keep, as I did not intend to produce Joe. I had avoided Kat and thus any decision about Fricker and wondered what his next move would be. I had been careful not to go out alone since he had jumped me, but this was merely delaying things.

I did not have to wait long to find out, for I was woken the next morning by a blood-curdling scream. I scrambled out of bed and ran down the stairs to find Janey sitting on the floor by the open front door cradling the baby, as I thought, in her lap, and weeping. Full of terror that something had happened to little Mary, I cried, "What is it Janey? What's the matter?"

She opened her arms to reveal not Mary, but Tobypuss. He was dead.

"I found him on the step," she sobbed. "Someone's cut his little throat. Why would anyone do that?"

Fricker could not have put his message more eloquently in words. He was telling me he knew where Joe lived, and had got close enough to take Tobypuss. He was telling me that if I didn't produce Joe, he would not hesitate to do to me what he had done to the dog. He was telling me he meant business.

The other girls gathered, summoned by Janey's wails, and as she and I held each other and cried over dear Tobypuss, I felt a hand on my shoulder and turned to see Kat.

"Now do you see?" she said quietly.

I nodded. I did see. I hated Fricker with all my heart and had resolved, as soon as I had the means, to free myself of him, somehow.

We buried Tobypuss in the yard and Bessie composed a poem for the occasion, and inked it on a piece of wood which we set as a head-stone. It read:

> *Here lies a dog both small and white*
> *Who did not growl and did not bite;*
> *Well loved on Earth, he's gone ahead*
> *And now sleeps by the good Lord's bed.*

She had wished to add a further couplet:

May misfortunes pile of many types
On him who cut his little pipes.

But Mother Cresswell declared it "*de trop*" and admonished us all with the words: "*Toujours l'amour*, my sweets, *toujours l'amour.*"

Though I did not pray these days, on this occasion I did say a few words commending Tobypuss to Heaven and was inwardly thankful that the day of my own deliverance, of a kind, was at hand. I was ready to make my move.

48

My younger readers will not recall the Shrove Tuesday riots which occurred regularly at this time, but as the next part of my narrative concerns them I should perhaps explain the circumstances and character of these annual events a little. I had been but dimly aware of the riots prior to my attachment to Mother Cresswell's house, noticing only that the traditional festivities were generally taken too far by over-zealous apprentices whose revelry spilled over into violence against the city's places of entertainment, namely the theatres and brothels. I do not know when this tradition began, but believe there were cases long before the civil wars where apprentices would, with the tools of their respective trades, dismantle whole playhouses, breaking up the benches and smashing the place indiscriminately to pieces. Bawdy houses were given similar treatment and were so despoiled that in some cases the buildings were entirely pulled down.

During my first Easter at Clerkenwell, Mother Cresswell ordered me, along with the other girls, to clear out of the place, having first assisted her in nailing boards over the windows and otherwise making the house secure. In fact, we usually got off lightly as Clerkenwell was too far out of town to receive much attention, but Mother Cresswell said you couldn't be too careful and you never knew.

I must confess to having been a deal baffled by these occurrences. Why should the apprentices, who frequented the bawdy houses and playhouses as much as anyone else, vent their rage on them on this day of the year?

"It is a day off work for roaring boys inflamed by drink," Mother Cresswell explained, as I helped her nail the back door fast. "What else can they vent their rage on? Not Whitehall, nor the courts of law, nor the churches, for the soldiers would defend them. But who will stand up for the poor whores and players? Your government men choose to look the other way, for they are grateful that it is us and not them getting the brunt of it." She sighed. "You would think, to hear great and learned men talk, that we was the only folks what took money for favours. This world is, and ever was, a great brothel," she said.

I still did not understand it, but then I had never understood why the same young men who spent money at our house one night would come another night, drunk and penniless, and break our windows. Mother Cresswell would shrug and say, "Men," and that was all the answer I received.

Shrove Tuesday, then, generally represented distraction, disorder and upheaval, which was why I had selected this particular day to make my move and part with Mother Cresswell for good. As usual, the girls decamped, although Janey thought to stay home, or to go and leave the baby with Mother, but we persuaded her to go and take Mary. As the weather was fine, the girls had elected to spend the day in the country at Islington, and were to overnight at an inn there owned by an aunt of Winnie's, returning the next day. Also as usual Mother Cresswell elected to remain immured in the house for she had a positive aversion to ever leaving it empty – to protect her hoard, as I supposed. Kat and I volunteered to remain with her to finish making it secure, promising to catch up with the girls later on, at the inn. This of course was all part of our plan.

I had wanted to use no violence on Mother Cresswell to achieve my ends as I feared that once I started I might not be able to stop. All my aim was to get the key on the lilac ribbon which hung about her neck. I had talked to Kat of drugging her, but Kat said that was only for plays and stories – it was difficult to get the dose right and we might kill the old cow by mistake and then where should we be. We would have to tie her up, Kat said, but this proved to be much easier said than done.

Kat and Mother Cresswell were talking in the saloon when I entered holding the necessary rope behind me. Mother had her back to me, which made it easier, and Kat's steady expression gave her no hint I had come in. But at the very moment I went to loop the rope over Mother's shoulders, she turned suddenly, and seeing me jumped back. The rope slipped down only round her neck, and though I did not mean to strangle her, I did not mean her to escape either, so I pulled it tight. Kat stood rooted to the spot until I cried "Hold her arms!" for Mother's arms were flailing wildly, scratching and clutching at me and at the rope round her neck, and I could not get out of her reach without letting go the rope. Kat grabbed at Mother's arms from behind, allowing me to slide the rope down over her shoulders and make a knot, but neither of us had appreciated how strong she was, and she wrested herself out of Kat's grasp and kicked me so hard that I let go the rope and fell backwards onto the floor. Then, when she might have escaped, she instead fell to kicking me, and abusing me, though I could not understand her words as she was still gasping from being nearly strangled, and I could not understand why Kat did not help me, as I feared Mother Cresswell meant to kick me to death, so hard did her blows rain on my head, my stomach and my back. Then she lifted up her foot to stamp on my head, as I thought. I instinctively shut my eyes and though I heard a horrible crack, felt nothing. I opened my eyes in time to see Mother Cresswell fall to the floor, revealing Kat standing behind her with the poker in her hand.

Kat helped me up and we both looked at Mother Cresswell

and then at each other. She seemed to be breathing, though very shallowly, in a red pool that was growing at an alarming rate.

"Who would have thought the old girl had so much blood in her?" said Kat, who seemed almost transfixed by the gory sight.

I snatched the ribbon with the key from Mother's neck and pushed Kat into Mother's room. I took down the picture and opened the concealed cupboard. We began to empty bags of coin and rolls of notes into a small trunk, but soon realised that the cupboard was much larger than I had at first assumed. Although the door was perhaps eighteen inches square, the alcove itself was perhaps four foot wide, and full of plate and jewellery as well as money. It was clear that here there were not hundreds but thousands of pounds. We emptied another small trunk of clothes and filled that too. Then we lugged them outside and Kat sat on them while I fetched our own luggage. I could hear Mother Cresswell moaning and while I was relieved she was not dead I was concerned she might crawl into the street and raise the alarm before we were clear of Clerkenwell, so as a precaution we nailed up the front door. We knew the girls would free her when they arrived the next morning, by which time we would be far away. When we had finished I remarked to Kat that it reminded me of the plague houses being shut up.

"It is a plague house," said Kat.

Now it was my turn to sit on the trunks while Kat went for a coach, and we were soon on our way out of Clerkenwell for ever. Kat and I looked at each other and smiled. Mother Cresswell's fortune was greater by far than either of us had imagined in our wildest dreams.

49

s we got further into town we began to understand
that the apprentices were setting about their task
with greater vigour than ever before. We had
already learned from the coachman that they
had been pulling down bawdy houses in Moorfields and the
court had been sufficiently alarmed at the anger of the mobs
rampaging through the city to deploy troops throughout not
only the city but Westminster. We had to pull aside to allow one
such detachment to pass, drums beating and trumpets blaring.

"You'd have thought the French were coming," shouted
the driver, with some satisfaction. Later we had to pull aside
again as a gang of malefactors was being escorted to the new
prison at Clerkenwell. Bystanders on the street, learning they
were being arrested for pulling down bawdy houses, cheered
them rather as heroes, as Londoners are wont to side with
anyone the authorities have taken against, unless he is plainly
the worst kind of villain. It was pretty to see the unease of
the militia, vastly outnumbered by the crowd that harangued
them. We had no idea, at this time, how ugly the scene would
turn, and that the mobs of apprentices who moved through
the crowds in tidal waves would later break open the prison
and free their fellows. Still, it was a deal alarming and both
Kat and I were glad to be safe in our carriage and not on the

streets, where whores were like to be roughed up and abused at the least.

At last we got to St James's where Mrs Snags was discomposed to see my condition (as Mother Cresswell had made quite a meal of me) and Kat, with her easy gentility, explained we had unfortunately got into a rough crowd and got caught up with the apprentices, who had not minded us as they should, and that what her dear sister (that is, myself) would most appreciate would be a dish of tea. Mrs Snags bustled off to effect this, most apologetic that I should have received such treatment, as though she considered herself entirely responsible for my well-being, now that I was living in her house. The coachman summoned a pair of urchins to help him get the trunks upstairs and complained that they were so heavy they might contain bodies, but was appeased by the judicious deployment of an extra half a crown and Kat's wry explanation that they were merely the bodies of our husbands.

And so Kat and I found ourselves in my new rooms, already furnished, and more conveniently and pleasingly so than I could have imagined. After the extraordinary and violent events of the day we had passed, it may seem strange to you, dear reader, that I felt so calm and untroubled, but I was relieved and content to be at last in a place of my own and mistress of my own destiny. Yet Kat and I were not so secure that we did not share a bed that night, and kept our newly acquired fortune about us, and once woke together at the same moment and checked ourselves and blessed ourselves and knew we were really safe.

The next morning we set about assessing and dividing the part of our fortune that was in note and coin. I had determined, when I first secured Kat's assistance, that whatever Mother Cresswell's fortune consisted of, it should be divided in six parts, one for each of the regular girls at Mother Cresswell's. But Kat insisted that it should be entailed in eight parts, of which she and I were entitled to two each, for the danger and trouble we had passed in securing it. Kat would not be gainsaid in this matter, and when I demurred on my own part she said, besides, I had lost two children, and that counted for more. I did not argue with her, recalling the trouble our differences of opinion about money had caused over Joe, and when I saw the extent of the money, which could set each and every one of us up more than comfortably in an independent existence, reflected that none of the others could or would complain at the bountifulness of their windfall. So I went along with it, considering also what dear Nell had told me about thinking of myself and my own interest.

We had decided it would cause too much trouble to explain to the girls our plan in advance, and would merely present them with the outcome. The second part of Kat's involvement in the plan was to make contact with each girl and present her with the facts of what Mother Cresswell had been doing with our children, and their fortune at the same time, enabling them to make a clean break. I left this – and a complicated matter it was too, if we were to avoid Mother Cresswell's attentions – to Kat, as I had Janey to deal with.

I had taken the precaution of leaving, at Winnie's aunt's inn, a letter for Janey, which contained my address and two pictures: Janey's carpet bag and a face with a finger to its lips. As she did not read I hoped she would understand that she was to show the address to someone who could bring her here. And so it turned out. I had it all worked out in my head and had rehearsed in my mind the moment I would bring her home many times. She would arrive at my fine new lodgings and say, or rather shout – although to be fair, she had got better at adjusting the volume of her conversation since the baby had been born, as we said it should not get enough sleep if its mother were shouting her head off the whole time, though as it turned out, little Mary must have got used to her mother's voice in the womb, as she slept through the night, Janey's hollering not withstanding, from six weeks of age which is a thing almost unheard of – but I digress, and as I say, I imagined Janey arriving at our new home and marvelling at its beauty and richness – although it was not gaudy or in any sense showy, as I knew the most successful Misses gave to all intents and purposes an outward show of being respectable, so Mother Cresswell's cerise velvets and turquoise rugs should not do here; here all was muted, mustards, creams, watercress greens, cool and unexceptional, but smart, fashionable, pretty and clean – so as I say, I imagined Janey coming in and being overwhelmed by the beauty and respectability of her new surroundings. Then she would shout: "But how have you paid for all this?" And then I would explain how it was all a cover for our new venture. And then she would look sad but would not say that she wished to get out of the game altogether for Mary's sake. And then I would guess her feelings and say, "But that is the beauty of it Janey! You need be a whore no longer! I can earn enough to keep us both and I shall need a maid, and you and Mary can live here happily, and we will divide my income, and she can grow up a respectable girl and we shall send her to school, and she shall have a respectable mother, et cetera, et cetera." And we should hug each other and kiss each other and kiss and bless Mary and know that tomorrow brought only profit and respectability, outwardly at least. It was a moment I had played in my head so many times, I could not imagine taking real pleasure in my new state until I shared it with Janey.

But, as so often is the case with the best laid plans, this was not how it turned out. When any of us made plans, Frenchie was wont to say, "*L'homme propose; le Dieu dispose*", and when I asked her what it meant, while she struggled for a translation, Kat supplied her own: "We make plans, while God laughs."

50

As soon as Janey arrived it was clear that something was terribly amiss. She was white as a sheet.

"Oh Doll you are safe! And Kat!" She fell on us and kissed us. "You will never guess what has happened! Mother Cresswell is dead! I thought you might be dead too!"

Kat and I exchanged glances but maintained our composure. This was a blow indeed. But Janey's next statement was even more surprising.

"Our house is gone! Burned to the ground! Poor Mother couldn't get out – well you know how it was all shut up, a mouse couldn't have got out – she was burned in it!"

I asked Janey whether she had seen the evidence of this herself, wondering whether this was wild hearsay, as reports of the apprentices' excesses were sometimes exaggerated, but she said she had and that when they had all returned to Clerkenwell that morning the house was reduced to a pile of smouldering timbers and Mother Cresswell's remains had already been taken away.

"At first we thought it was the apprentices what done it – for they broke open the prison you know – but the neighbours saw a man on his own running away and gave chase and apprehended him and were like to tear him to pieces for you know we were not unpopular with the neighbours and Mother

Cresswell was always charitable but the watch arrived in time to take him but the fire could not be put out and it all went up like a tinderbox. And you will never guess who it was! That little toad from the playhouse – what's his name? The one with the scar. He should swing for this or there is no justice!"

"Fricker!" I exclaimed. Fricker who would not be bested by a whore; Fricker who said he would burn me if I did not produce Joe; Fricker who had slit poor Tobypuss's throat; Fricker who had meant to kill not Mother Cresswell but Doll.

"Supposing we had all been at home?" Janey cried. "Or if I had left the baby with Mother?" She fell to sobbing loudly, which made the baby cry too, and Kat and I comforted them as well as we could and then after a while Janey said she could murder a dish of tea, and anyway what was this place and how came we here, as the neighbours said they saw us moving out, and what, in short, was it all about?

It took some time to make Janey understand our new situation and she was shocked in the extreme when I told her what Mother Cresswell had been doing with our babies and at first refused to believe it so that I was obliged to tell her that it was only because I happened to walk in at a particular moment that Mary had not been drowned too. This revelation, on top of all the strange events of the last day, was too much for Janey and we had to put her to bed, as she began shivering like a person who has sustained a bad shock and the baby became inconsolable. Kat and I were also extremely shaken at the thought of what would have happened had we all been at home that night. It was not, in short, the happy homecoming I had so fondly dreamt of.

Janey had told us that the girls, having nowhere else to go, had returned to Winnie's aunt's inn, and having lost all their belongings in the fire were reduced to the utmost extremity and had not the faintest idea how to shift for themselves. Kat and I accordingly revised our plans, sent some money to the inn to relieve their immediate want and to buy mourning garments, enclosing a message directing them to tarry there until Mother Cresswell's funeral when we would all be together and discuss the future.

We then spent the next two days converting Mother Cresswell's hoard into hard cash, making it both easier to divide and more portable. Besides, we had no idea what the jewellery was worth. Kat was vastly knowledgeable about jewellers, as she was in the habit of immediately selling any gifts she got, for she had a widowed sister with many children and a sick mother in the country to support, and she managed this side of things. I looked after Janey and the baby meanwhile, and we began to become quite the little family.

Finally, the whole fortune was encashed and one night we counted it all out, and then counted it a second and third time to check we had not made a mistake, for the total sum seemed an incredible fortune.

51

here was no wind the day of Mother Cresswell's funeral, and the London smoke thickened the air, veiling the city in a grubby grey. On hearing of her friend's death, Pris Fotherington had assumed charge of the management and cost of the funeral, which was to be held in Clerkenwell, for although Mother Cresswell's parents were buried in Cornhill, bawds and whores (like hangmen, actors and others on the margins of the world which wants their services but does not want to admit them as full members) cannot of course be buried within the city walls, so she was not to be laid alongside her family, but alongside her neighbours. However, such niceties over margins seemed not to trouble those who had known Mother Cresswell and who now paid their respects. It was quite astonishing to see how many people, and of what quality, attended, or sent their coaches. You could read the heraldry of half the great families, old and new, of our nation, Kat said, on the doors of the carriages which followed Mother Cresswell to the church. All the neighbourhood also seemed to have turned out to watch the procession pass, even the tanners pausing in their bloody work to stand hatless and silent as we passed. Mother Cresswell, it must be said, was well known for her charity in the locality.

For our part, the girls from Mother Cresswell's house did

the old bawd proud. The Clerkenwell sisterhood, swelled by former members, whom Janey, Kat and myself joined at the church, took up two pews at the very front, and behind us sat Pris Fotherington's girls, and then whores of the other great London houses. I recognised Damaris Page, the great bawd of the seamen, who kept two houses, one for officers and one for the lowly sailor, accompanied by her cattle of both degrees. Mother Bennet, Mother Ross and Mother Temple were all there, their girls tricked and trimmed for the occasion, and sailing behind them, the most famous whores in London: Sue Lemming, Betty Lawrence and Jenny Cromwell, in all their rigging. All in all, there must have been more than a hundred whores present, and to see so many, in full paint, ornament and mourning garb, gathered together in one place made, though I say it myself, a most magnificent sight. Quantities of jet had been procured from somewhere, and as well as gloves, Janey and I had given each of the Clerkenwell girls pearl ear-rings as a kind of advance against the fortunes they as yet knew not were to make them so happy, so we all gleamed and glistened in the gloom like diamonds in a mine. The yards of black stuff in our mourning veils had surely left bare every draper's shelf in London, and there could not have been an ostrich in all Arabia who did not run about bald of his black feathers that day. Mother Cresswell would have been, as we all remarked afterwards, most gratified.

There was something in the ritual that followed, in the extravagance of it and the strangeness of it, which made it feel as though we were not merely marking the passing of one infamous bawd, but that this was a memorial in a sense of all those poor whores who had passed, and would yet pass, unremembered into unmarked graves; the painted faces who were there one day and gone the next; those we had known, those we did not know, those we had yet to know, and of course, ourselves.

On a day of such wonders, I was not surprised to recognise the presiding clergyman as Hole-In-The-Sheet, who I am sure did not recognise me, for he had made a point of never looking me in the face. Today of all days, and for the first time in the whole of our acquaintance, he made me laugh. After he had read the story of the Woman Taken In Adultery, and we had all been admonished not to cast the first stone unless we were without sin – which met, unexpectedly, with a sustained round of applause – he said some prayers before he delivered his homily, and we were all most interested to see how he would manage this.

"Many years ago," he began, "Mrs Cresswell made me promise that, when the time came, I should deliver the oration at her funeral. She asked most particularly that I should speak only well of her. This, of course, has caused me no little difficulty."

This provoked a titter, which, gaining confidence, grew into great laughter, which ran round the church. Hole-In-The-Sheet's face gave nothing away. He waited until the noise had died down before continuing:

"However, I can truly say that our dear departed sister was born well, lived well and died well."

At this there was a little amused consternation as we wondered how he could justify this.

"That is to say," he continued, "she was born *Cresswell*, lived some time in *Bridewell*, and died in *Clerkenwell*."

As this sunk in, applause and some cheers broke out, which grew and were sustained for some time. Then we sang Psalm 139, which I discovered, to my surprise, I largely had by heart. As we began, the words reminded me most painfully of home, and they seemed to speak not of God, but of my father: my all-knowing, all-seeing, all-judging father.

"O Lord, thou hast searched me, and known me.

Thou knowest my downsitting and mine uprising, thou understandest my thought afar off.

Thou compassest my path and my lying down, and art acquainted with all my ways.

For there is not a word in my tongue, but, lo, O Lord, thou knowest it altogether.

Thou hast beset me behind and before, and laid thine hand upon me."

And I remembered how Father had laid his hand upon Evelyn, when she had begged him not to turn our sister Grace away.

"Such knowledge is too wonderful for me; it is high, I cannot attain unto it."

And I fully attended for the first time to these words as we sang them: "Whither shall I go from thy spirit? Or whither shall I flee from thy presence? If I ascend up into Heaven, thou art there: if I make my bed in Hell, behold, thou art there." And I began to understand that in setting myself apart from my old world, my family and home in Hertfordshire, my aunt and home in Cheapside, I had unwittingly set myself apart from God too, believing that just as my family could never love what I had become, neither could He.

I continued to listen as I sang: "If I take the wings of the morning, and dwell in the uttermost parts of the sea; even there shall thy hand lead me, and thy right hand shall hold me." And though I reasoned that I had not felt Him holding me in the plague year, or when I had tried to do away with myself, I had, in fact, survived, and perhaps His hand had indeed led me, although I had not known it. I continued to sing as if in a trance, as if a light were breaking not upon me, but within me, and at the end of the psalm I was reminded of what Godfrey had said, that I did not see the good that was in me.

"Search me, O God, and know my heart: try me, and know my thoughts: and see if there be any wicked way in me, and lead me in the way everlasting."

It was something of a revelation to admit to myself the possibility that I was not quite perhaps the hopeless case I had tended to believe, for if there was good in me, might this not mean that I had not been abandoned? And if God loved even Mother Cresswell, as Hole-In-The-Sheet assured us He did, might He not also love me? These thoughts were consoling. I had not been in a church, I realised, for years now, and I wondered whether chance had brought me here at just the right moment, in time, at least, to set little Mary on the right path. I decided that we must have her baptised and I would be her godmother, if Janey did not object.

I put these thoughts aside as we followed the coffin out to the churchyard where we saw Mother Cresswell into the ground. I do not think I have ever been to a merrier or more strangely affecting funeral, and the generosity of those who attended was also something to behold, for everyone knew Mother Cresswell's daughters were now homeless and penniless, and they were showered with many kind gifts as parting tokens.

Frenchie and Bessie had sobbed extravagantly throughout the proceedings, and even Winnie had lost her *joy de vie*, and I realised that though Mother Cresswell had done terrible and wicked things, in other ways she had indeed been like a mother to these girls, and she had, as I had reflected more than once, taken me in when I was at my lowest ebb and least useful to her. I was even prepared to admit that she might have truly believed that the wicked deeds she had performed were "for the best". But while I allowed that God might forgive her, I myself could not, despite the holy thoughts I had been entertaining, for she had deprived me of the only children I would ever have; I could not think on her memory without anger and bitterness, and any tears I may have shed that day were not for her but for myself.

There was, of course, a horrible beauty in the way she had met her end. The two surviving arch-villains in my story had destroyed each other. If Fricker did not swing for setting the fire, he would be transported, that much seemed certain, and a great weight of anxiety was lifted from me. I began to feel what real freedom was like and found it most agreeable.

Pris Fotherington had arranged the averil to be held at our local inn, the Cock in Hand, and there the generous supply of funeral biscuits proved not enough to soak up the quantities of strong waters that were being consumed, and Janey, Kat and I prevailed upon Winnie, Bessie and Frenchie to come away with us before Pris Fotherington's girls began dancing on the tables.

I need not repeat here the information we then imparted to them, and the disbelief and tears with which they received their unexpected fortunes of eight hundred pounds each you may easily imagine yourself. Suffice it to say that that evening as we bid farewell to each other at Islington it would have been difficult to find a gathering of six happier young women in all England. As Janey and I prepared to quit for St James's and Kat was about to set off for her new life under the care of her kind keeper, Winnie, Bessie and Frenchie still struggled to believe that, though that same morning they had all been homeless paupers they were this evening free of their old lives and mistresses of their own destinies. It was hard leaving, and we kept singing another song, and proposing another toast, and embracing each other for the last time again, but finally Janey and I tore ourselves away.

As our carriage rolled out of Islington I looked out of the window at the Moon which that night appeared unusually lovely.

"Janey," I said. "Do you think there is a God? I mean, do you really believe in Him?"

"Pfffffff!" said Janey. "I always believed in 'im. But I'm beginning to think now that He believes in me and all."

And we hugged each other and travelled home in silence, looking at the beautiful Moon.

PART THREE

'HALCYON'

52

I may truly say that my time as a Miss was the happiest part of my life. My lovers – as they now considered themselves to be – visited me on their appointed day of the week and I otherwise led a life of leisure. Janey was the happiest I ever saw her, and my recollections at that time are of her going about her domestic duties fairly singing her head off. When I had a visitor she played the maid to a fault: all deference and discretion before "the mistress" and her guest. Little Mary grew fat and bonny, and the most pleasurable part of the day was the morning, when Janey would bring her into my bed while she dressed, and I would play with her and make her chuckle, which was the prettiest and merriest sound I think I ever heard.

Sunday was the best day of the week, being our day off, and began with church for me and Mary. Janey did not object to Mary going, as she had not objected to her being baptised, but drew the line at attending church herself.

"He knows where I am if He needs me," she would say, and that was that. After church, if the weather was fine we would go for a walk or a drive and dine at The Bear, purely for the pleasure of crossing the bridge to do so. Sunday afternoons were reserved for visits by Godfrey, whom we had persuaded to stand godfather to Mary, and she loved him extremely, and we would play games and read and he would tell me how things went at Lincoln's Inn Fields – for my aunt never did move out – and life was, in fine, most sweet.

Godfrey had quickly become both devoted and indispensable to my aunt, who soon began to fret at the unconventional, not to say rackety, appearance to the world of their combined household (or *ménage*, as she described it, in a kind of scandalised whisper, according to Godfrey). Concerns for 'appearances' had been thrown to the wind in the social chaos immediately following the fire; however the old world was soon nailed back into place. A widow and a single gentleman (for Aunt Madge never doubted Godfrey was a gentleman, and of course, in every aspect excepting the vital detail that he was not born one, he was; I think we have all known true-born gentlemen whose real actions did nothing to deserve that description) could not live under the same roof without expecting to excite comment of the most unpleasant sort, sooner or later. Yet she soon found she could not do without Godfrey, who calmly, gently and authoritatively managed every problem which arose, which, had she been left to her own devices, would have sadly perplexed my dear aunt. Frederick, blessed dear cousin Frederick, provided the solution.

Godfrey, he observed, already fulfilled all the functions of a professional secretary to his mother, and therefore should be properly invested with that title. This also conveniently dealt with the small matter that, once the Duchess's lease expired, Godfrey was not contributing in any form to the household exchequer, a point which made him most uncomfortable. The more I heard of Frederick, the more I yearned to see my cousin again, and merely enjoy his company, yet I acknowledged the sad impossibility of this. In any case, my aunt's problem was resolved, and Godfrey continued as a member – the most exalted member – of the household staff, while continuing to be my aunt's best friend, closest confidant and comfort. Frederick, according to Godfrey, prompted by my curious questions, in no sense resented this, but loved Godfrey almost as a brother. This I could well believe, as Godfrey was, I believed, utterly loveable, and Frederick had always shown all the best qualities (that is to say, the best qualities in my eyes) which could be expected of his sex and background. Frederick was a gentleman by any standard.

I had reordered my life too. Since Godfrey now called me H or Halcyon, despite my entreaties, so did Janey, and as soon as I divined that they did this purely because it annoyed me, I stopped complaining, in the hope that they would tire of it. They did not. (Janey, who actually called me 'Haitch', which was even more irritating, in fact spent an entire day musing aloud on what 'Haitch' might stand for, and made Godfrey laugh until his sides ached by deciding, in the end, that it stood for 'Hore'.) And so I stopped complaining about being H or Halcyon, and in fact it suited me to break with common Doll, for I was now a woman of quality.

At first my week was exclusively devoted to my superior regulars from Clerkenwell and ran thus: Monday – Lord A (my favourite); Tuesday – Sir Robert; Wednesday – parliament man; Thursday – city merchant; Friday – Jasper. Saturdays I used to keep clear, and would go out, often to the playhouse, and cultivate potential admirers. I often met up with Kat for this purpose, for respectable women, as we now appeared to be, do not go to any place of resort singly if they wish to remain respectable. By these means when I lost a lover I had a ready replacement. Thus, when my city merchant went to India, and my member of parliament died suddenly, and Sir Robert was forbidden any excitement by his physician, I allowed the attentions of another panting cully in their stead. Of course, my new gentlemen had not known me in my previous life, and thus conducted themselves towards me somewhat differently: as a mistress – professing love, sometimes promising marriage at some distant date and in some never-to-be-realised circumstance. They liked to be seen about town with me and to show me off before their companions. While all this had the merit of being more entertaining than simply the main business, it was all emptiness and show, and I sometimes found it tedious and always tiring.

Neither did my new breed of gentleman care to deal in cash, for it soothes a man's sense of himself that he does not pay to have knowledge of a woman, but merely lies with her and gives her gifts. Such gifts, though often worth more than I would have bargained for, were full inconvenient to translate into money, and besides, my cullies often wished to see me wearing the jewellery they had bestowed on the lovely Mistress Halcyon. Though they must have known they were not the sole recipients of my favours, this fiction was maintained on both sides, and should I meet one of them at the playhouse, or at the pleasure gardens, or walking in the park, while I was in the company of another, it was something we never spoke of when we were alone together on our appointed day.

I made each new gentleman seduce me from the path of virtue afresh, first scattering in his path many objections and obstacles, as I always delayed the moment of first consummating his passion for as long as possible. This assured him I was a lady. During this period he would grow hotter and hotter, and use all his powers of persuasion. He would ask to see me alone – this I naturally declined, being chary of my reputation, but in such a way as began to suggest I longed that it were possible. Eventually he would persuade me into agreeing to a meeting in some quiet place, and he would believe he was now gaining ground, especially when I allowed him some familiarity, and to kiss me finally. We would then reach an impasse, where he was satisfied of the strength of my ardour and most dissatisfied at the strength of my virtue, for I would not grant him the last favour.

At last I would give him to understand that he should have all he desired if he would but give me the freedom of his purse.

53

The day that Kat and I went to Tyburn to see Fricker hang drew a line finally under the awful events which had brought our life at Clerkenwell to a close. We did not even tell Janey where we were going, for though all the girls knew we had taken Mother Cresswell's fortune, we had told no one of the hand we suspected we had had in her death. As I have already described Fricker's end in detail, I shall not rehearse it here, but suffice it to say that knowing Fricker was out of the picture brought us both a great sense of relief.

However there remained a particular bond between me and Kat, which could not be dissolved, and though on the night that we had divided Mother Cresswell's fortune between her girls we had all agreed to meet up on that date once a year, I knew I would continue to see Kat in the interim. Unlike our Clerkenwell sisters, neither she nor I had seen fit to quit the profession, though we were both now well provided for financially. I was determined not to touch my capital which I had pooled with Janey's, and she was happy to entrust me with all money matters. We lived well, though without ostentation, on the money I earned, and we even put a little of that aside each week. We were happy enough just to carry on as we were, but Kat's plans had not worked out so straightforwardly.

Her keeper Gerald's new wife had not proven the goldmine Kat had been led to believe. That she was indeed an heiress to a substantial fortune was in no doubt, but her father still lived, and while he had paid a hefty dowry, much of it was tied up in property, and worse, in Kat's eyes, the parents of the bride had gone to the unusual trouble of settling on their daughter money to which Gerald could lay no claim while she lived.

"It is an outrage!" Kat complained. "What is the world coming to when a wife may keep her own money? If this fashion takes, it will be the death of keeping."

"Is it such an awful thing?" asked Godfrey. (For Kat had come to pass a Sunday with us.) "Perhaps if wives could keep their own money their husbands would treat them better."

"What is that to me?" exclaimed Kat. "You know, I am beginning to see that a Miss has full as painful a life as a wife in any case. Gerald comes home, with his friends, at all hours of the night, expecting I will keep open house at their convenience – and spare them a kind word and an easy face. He drinks, games and whores like any husband. It is insupportable! In fact, I'm in no small danger of getting the foul disease by his lewdness."

At this Godfrey, Janey and I could not help laughing, but Kat was in no mood to join in our mirth.

"I tolerated that easy fool for months in expectations of him snaring a rich wife whose fortune I was to lavish! But now I discover things go not forwards with me, but backwards! I find I am paying my own bills! Were it left to him my coach would have vanished, my servants gone, and I should be running about in last year's gowns! The mere thought of it is enough to give one a fever." Kat shuddered. "I was to have a settlement and twenty guineas a week. What did he give me this week? *Forty shillings*! He should be put in the stocks for so deluding me. I, who gave him my virginity—"

"Kat!" Janey exclaimed.

"Oh he doesn't know any different," continued Kat. "I told him that *all* his wife's fortune was never worth the jewel

I offered up to him. I may one day get my money, but my name is lost for ever." And here Kat pretended to weep most theatrically and pathetically, until even Mary clapped her little hands in appreciation.

"So what you going to do?" demanded Janey.

"I've taken another gentleman of course," said Kat, "and I've another in my sights. Now I believe I am with child and I shall fleece all three for its upkeep as well as my own."

"Kat!" Janey exclaimed again.

"Come, come, Janey," said Kat irritably. "Where would you be now if you had had to depend solely on your William? Has he given you a penny for the child?"

Janey blushed, which I guessed had a deeper meaning, for I had reason to believe that William was back on the scene again, much to my unease.

"No, he has not," Kat continued. "How many times must you be told to consider only your own interest? No one else will, you may be assured of that, a man least of all."

"But to make a man believe a child is his own – it ain't right, Kat," maintained Janey.

"It ain't right?" Kat repeated in disbelief. "It ain't *right*? When did right ever come into it? The *worst* of us are not so bad as the *best* of them! Learn this of me: they that first debauch us do it for their own pleasure, without any consideration of our ruin, so we that are debauched ought to value no merit equal to our own interest. Yes, we may cheat and lie and lay traps, for all legitimate ways are shut to us. And besides, we were deceived before. It would not be so painful, I will admit, did men not have such high conceits of their sex: they say theirs is the stronger sex, and the wiser sex, and the wittier sex, and such a sex – well, they may be a notable sex among themselves, but, compared with us…! It is a foolish woman indeed who will not outdo them in their own ways when she has the opportunity: out-lie them, out-flatter them, out-dissemble them. But don't bleat to me of what is right. It was all wrong from the beginning. It was all wrong from the

271

moment some hot gallant poured treacle in your ear, while sliding his—"

"Kat!" exclaimed Godfrey, clapping his hands over Mary's ears, which, startling her, made her howl.

While Godfrey mollified Mary, I suggested a bottle of Canary and a game of cards, which altered the tone of conversation for the better, and soon we were all at ease again.

Later, when Mary and Janey had lain down for a rest and Godfrey was reading and dozing, and Kat and I were sitting contentedly warming our stockinged toes by the fire, I suggested to Kat that since she now had her own fortune she might be better to cast off Gerald altogether and retire.

"I have thought of it," she said. "But somehow I can't trust even that. Life has betrayed me too many times. As long as I can make money, I shall. It's the only thing I can depend upon. You of all people should understand that."

I did, indeed, understand that.

"But you can at least afford to turn off Gerald and cast about for a better prospect. After all," I observed, "one wealthy keeper is infinitely less troublesome than three of indifferent and uncertain fortune."

"Like yours?" she said and winked.

"Not quite like mine," I said, and winked.

She sighed.

"I have considered it. There are one or two I could work on easily. But it seems this one's wife, the poor bitch, is sickly and like to die. And a bird in the hand is worth two in the bush."

We both fixed our gaze on the sea-coal burning in the hearth and I could not pretend to guess at Kat's thoughts, but I considered how strange it was that the unhappy demise of one young woman would inevitably produce a wonderful transformation in the fortunes of another, without either of them having ever known or even seen the other.

"Then again," Kat said, "it may not be true. He may just be flamming me off with high hopes."

54

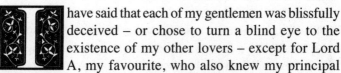have said that each of my gentlemen was blissfully deceived – or chose to turn a blind eye to the existence of my other lovers – except for Lord A, my favourite, who also knew my principal keeper was a mere fiction. He was a plain dealer: he treated me right and did not tell untruths. He would never say he would marry me, nor say he would advance my prospects, nor hint he would introduce me into Court, nor make promises of future riches, and such nonsense, as others were wont to. Now a whore must lie to live, but it was a mark of my respect for Lord A that I returned the compliment, and never lied to him – at the least, not in great matters.

He never dressed up the transaction between us in gifts as other men did, but always paid me hard cash. Lord A did not deceive himself in this and besides he knew that at first I needed, and now I valued, the money. When he left I would always find two sovereigns on the table, never more, never less. And even if he were unable to keep the appointment, which admittedly, was a rare event, he still sent the money. So, in his own way, he kept me, if only a fifth of me.

On the day I am to tell you about, where this part of my story begins, as he was dressing I noticed he had left double the usual amount.

"Are we to have another bout, fubbs?" I asked. "You know you need not pay twice."

"It's not for me," he said. "I need to talk to you."

This was a bad sign. When a man begins to pass his Miss about amongst his friends it is an invariable omen he is about to cast her off. And it was not merely that Lord A was a steady source of income, but I must admit my pride was piqued that he would do such a thing.

"This is not like you," I said, careful not to sound as peeved as I felt, for many Misses make the mistake of being angry with their gentlemen, forgetting that their gentlemen can get that at home, and why pay for a Miss who is as much trouble as a wife?

But his explanation was not what I feared. He hoped to save the family's fortunes by making a good marriage for his nephew. (When his brother died, Lord A had inherited not only his brother's considerable debts but also his son.) Lord A had found a widow, rich as Croesus, young and not ill-favoured, and persuaded her into a match with his nephew. Her fortune would be more than enough to keep her and his nephew in great comfort and her dowry would considerably relieve Lord A's financial difficulties. As matters stood, Lord A had mortgaged himself to the hilt to send the boy to the university at Cambridge, which, whatever they say, is never cheap, and could now barely afford to get him a suit of new clothes, let alone a living.

This was all most interesting, but still I did not understand the extra sovereigns, unless they were by way of sharing his anticipated good fortune.

"Charles is a good boy," he explained, "honest, well-mannered, obedient and loyal. He has consented to the match as much out of a sense of indebtedness to me as for affection for the young lady – if not more. But he is innocent as snow."

Aha, thought I.

"You are very dear to me, H, and a good friend. I ask you a favour: to show him what is required of a husband."

"Are you sure he does not know?" I asked. Sometimes this world seemed one great bawdy house to me where the merest child knew what went on between the sheets. "Was he not brought up in the country? Has he not seen the animals?"

Lord A laughed.

"I am sure he has an idea of what goes where," he said.

"And is his bride not a widow? She will hardly prove your blushing virgin."

"You will barely believe it, but her first husband fell ill on the very day they were wed. He died within a week. The marriage was never consummated."

By the expression on my face I could not check, Lord A understood that I thought this a likely tale.

"I have made enquiries. I assure you it is the case. Listen, H." The manner in which he took my face in his hands confirmed the seriousness of the matter. "This marriage must not fail. Even your fortunes are tied to its success. Charles must not make a hash of things straight off." He could perhaps read from my expression that I did not follow his reasoning. He said, with a little, bitter, laugh, "You don't know about women at all, do you, H? She will exploit any weakness, do you see? He must start as he means to go on. In control. In charge." He let go of me and sighed. "Of course, you may refuse."

"Well," said I. "I will help the poor boy. After all, it is a terrible onerous thing for a man to be a virgin on his wedding night."

We smiled and drank to our compact and Lord A went off whistling, which was always a good sign. I rather dreaded the coming encounter, but resolved to keep up my spirits and think on the money.

55

was looking forward to making the acquaintance of Lord A's nephew with all the anticipated pleasure one might expect from bedding a country booby. He would not be the first I had initiated, but was certainly the first by such an invitation and so well paid. While not relishing the job, I had resolved to do my best by the boy for dear Lord A's sake. I only hoped he was tolerably clean in his habits and, though by Lord A's account I suspected he might not be the sharpest young man, I hoped he was not a mere idiot. I have serviced idiots in my time and the best that can be said of them is that, like very elderly gentlemen, and old soldiers with parts missing, they are grateful. I should have guessed something was amiss by Janey's saucy wink as she put her head round the door and announced, "Gentleman to see you, Mistress."

I supposed I had a minute or so before he climbed the stairs and checked the glass quickly. I intended not to frighten the poor child, so was dressed simply, demurely even, and wore no paint. I did not aim to play the coy virgin, however, but to seem respectable yet approachable. I had selected a pale pink gown, modest yet most becoming. And easy to remove. I had intended to arrange myself prettily on the sofa, but the gentleman was already at the door as I turned from the glass and you cannot imagine my great surprise.

Far from the grinning bumpkin I expected, here was an exceptionally well-made young man, dressed smartly but without affectation, with much curly brown hair, the face of an angel and the most killing blue eyes framed by long curling eye-lashes like a girl's. Yet this was no proof he was all there in the head. He bowed stiffly and said, in an uncertain voice, "Madam? I understood... my uncle said... you were expecting me?"

I realised my mouth had dropped open and shut it quick.

"Of course," I said. "Please sit down." I had got to the couch with indecent haste and was patting the cushion beside me rather hard.

He looked at the dust rising from the cushion and then at me and finally came and sat down.

"May I offer you some wine?" I asked, rising and going to the decanter on the table.

"Thank you, no," he said and appeared to study the pattern on the carpet.

"You need not be shy, sir," I said gently. "I know why you are here. I mean to help you."

He raised the killing eyes to mine with a strange uncomprehending expression. His face was so open I felt I might fall in.

"I mean to be your friend," I said, sitting down again.

"Why... thank you," he said, and returned his attention to the floor, his face almost as red as the rug.

Suddenly an awful thought struck me. The old devil had not told him!

"You do know why Lord A sent you to see me, I hope?" I asked.

"No. It is all most mysterious. I hoped you would enlighten me," he said.

Damn the old bugger! This was going to be twice as difficult as I thought. I took the young man's hand gently in mine. I felt he instinctively wished to snatch it back, but courtesy prevented him. He withdrew it carefully, saying, also carefully, "Madam, you should know I am to be married soon."

Now it was my turn to blush – I! I who had been one of the most shameless sluts in the city!

"I know that. Your uncle told me. It is why he sent you here." His face told me he was utterly ignorant of my intention. There was nothing for it but to jump in with both feet or I should never be done with it. "Your uncle thinks that before you are married, for your own sake and your wife's… " but I found I could not say it! This boy's innocence was a stranger to me. I did not know how to begin to explain.

"Yes?" he said.

I got up and poured myself a glass of wine.

"Have you ever had ado with a lady?"

I knocked the wine back in one draught.

"Ado? What lady?"

"Have you ever been to bed with a woman?"

He looked thunderstruck. I poured a second glass and passed it to him. He held it for a long time before he drank it.

"I do not mean to offend you, madam," he addressed the Persian rug, "but am I to understand that my uncle sent me to you to… to… "

"Yes!" I cried. "I am to put you on the right road. I am to show you the way. I am to be your friend."

"Good God," he said and put his head in his hand.

After a long moment he stood up. He placed the glass on the table. He took my hand and kissed it.

"Thank you," he said. "But that will not be necessary."

And he was gone. No sooner did I hear the front door shut than I heard Janey running up the stairs.

"Blind me, that was quick," she said. "First time and all that I suppose. What's the matter with you? You want to shut your trap before something flies in."

"Nothing," I said.

"Lovely-looking lad, or what?" she said and collected the glasses and took them downstairs.

I was aggrieved. Damn Lord A!

Now I should have to return the money.

56

"he bridegroom's back," said Janey. "Shall I let him come up?"

"Yes," said I, though dressed, not entirely awake, having had a rowdy boozy night with Jasper and a number of his hangers-on. I could not think who the bridegroom was until he appeared at the door.

It was Lord A's nephew. My heart gave a jolt such as it was not used to, though I covered it to him, and to myself. Memory, for once, had played no tricks. He was a fine figure of a young man. His eyes, if anything, looked bluer and more lashy. He stood in the doorway apparently trying not to smile.

"Madam," he said and gave that endearing bow, a little less stiff than before. "I wish to apologise. May I come in?"

I gestured to the sofa, remembering to keep my jaws closed, and made a business of tidying the table. Of course he would not sit until I did, but I took a chair across from him, I know not why.

"My conduct, last time we met, was most discourteous. I am sorry for that. I trust you might find it in your heart to forgive me."

Though this was a statement, he seemed to wait for my assent. I nodded slightly and, as I thought, graciously.

"I was merely taken utterly by surprise. I meant no insult

to your person… " He hesitated somewhat. "Nor to your profession."

Though he could not have been plainer nor kinder I could not find one word with which to answer him.

"Moreover, I have given the matter some thought," he said, colouring and once more addressing his Persian friend on the floor. He had evidently rehearsed his opening address but was having some trouble with the meat of his message. "My uncle knows… I have led a very sheltered life… If I am to be married… My bride is young and innocent… "

"You should hate to make a pig's ear of it," said I.

"Exactly!" He was so relieved it was almost pitiful. "My uncle has been most kind to me. He has been a good judge and a kind friend – almost a father. Even though I had misgivings… I am inclined to trust his advice and follow his direction. If he thinks it a matter of such import… That is, if your generous offer still stands… to be my friend."

"To set you on the right road?"

"To show me the way." With a trembling lip in which shyness and boldness competed for mastery came a smile that would tempt a saint. It was all I needed to swing into step.

"Very well. You are Charles, are you not? What do your friends call you?"

"Charlie."

"Then I shall call you Charlie. And my friends call me Halcyon, or H. Whatever you prefer. But no more madam."

"I am your humble servant in all things," he said, and we allowed ourselves a little smile.

"Now, Charlie, how about a drink? I find it oils the wheels of – " and I was about to say 'business', but substituted "conversation."

"Alas, I have an appointment," he said. "I had hoped to arrange a meeting with you – at your convenience, of course."

Of course. An appointment. Of course.

"By all means," said I, smoothly. "This evening?"

He was visibly taken aback. Evidently he had expected to

have more time to prepare himself for the awful ordeal. Soft, soft, I told myself. Not too fast.

"Very well," he said, swallowing.

I rose and held out my hand.

"Until tonight then. About the hour of nine?"

"Nine! Nine it is!" He kissed my hand without emotion and did his dear little bow again.

"Charlie," I said, as he went to go out of the door.

"Madam? I mean, H?"

"Don't worry."

He blushed. His lip trembled. He was gone.

"Blind me!" said Janey moments later, eyeing the untouched glasses. "Haven't you slowed him down any yet?"

57

s the clock of St Margaret's struck nine, Janey announced the arrival of the bridegroom. I was ready for him. We had put candles all around the room, but not lit the chandelier, to create an agreeable effect of rosy gloom. I instantly offered him a drink. He accepted. I sat him on the couch and said, in a low voice, "You must submit to being my pupil."

He drank deeply, but calmly, I thought, and said, "I place myself entirely under your tutelage," in a way which made me think it was not the first drink that had passed his lips that night.

"In the normal run of things," I said, making so bold as to take his hand and place it on my waist, "I would show you simply what has to be done to make a baby." I touched his cheek, stroked it. He flinched slightly, but did not pull away. "But I am going to show you how to please a woman. I am going to show you how to make love to a wife, and keep her." I kissed his ear.

"Thank you," he said, in a way that almost made me want to weep. He was such an open, honest darling.

I had been determined – indeed made many resolutions – to do nothing merely to please him; I was after all to strike a blow in favour of his wife's pleasure, but I needed to set him at his ease, so unloosed his shirt from his breeches and began gently exploring his body, while planting gentle kisses on his face.

"Imagine this is a rehearsal for your wedding night," I said. "Your wife may be afraid. You need to reassure her. Begin your love-making by kissing her face and holding her body close." I waited.

"Sorry," he said, and put his arms around me and planted dry kisses on my cheek.

"Sweetheart," I said, "Charlie," I implored, "kiss me. Just kiss me as if you love me. As if you had wanted to kiss me for months and now was your chance."

I ran my finger down his spine, then placed his hand on my breast. I could tell by the swelling in his breeches he was up for it. Good. My job was half done. His kisses became more real, his breaths more uneven, he began to run his hands at least over my back and hips.

"Now you must tell her you love her."

"I love her," he dutifully said.

"Tell her what you love about her," I said.

"I love her eyes," he said and kissed my eyelids with such tenderness they were soon wet. "I love her lips," he said and kissed my lips from end to end. "I love her ears," he said and kissed my ears with the most deafening smackers.

"Charlie," I breathed in his ear, "you can do anything you like with me. Do anything you like with me."

At this he unloosed my shift with surprising haste and stared at my breasts.

"Touch them," I said. "Kiss them."

He did. So softly and sweetly that again I almost wanted to cry.

Unbidden, he returned his mouth to mine. I peeked my tongue between his lips and felt his surprise, then his pleasure. Both his hands were on my breasts, which responded gratefully. Already I was as hot as an ox on a spit, but had to control myself. His tongue then ventured into my mouth and I bit and sucked him gently, not like I would with a general customer. I eased him out of his breeches, at which I felt

283

him trembling, and again said, "Don't worry Charlie. I will show you the way. I will be your friend." I led him into my bedchamber, kissing and stroking him all the time, but he was now returning my kisses and caresses.

I lay down on the bed; he sat on the edge. I said, "Now, Charlie, there is no point going at it hammer and tongs without a thought for your wife. You must make her want you before you go inside her. There is a secret part of a woman, here… " and I took his hand and guided him. He looked like a good schoolboy determined to get it right as he allowed me to take his hand. He explored a little, with my hand holding his, then I took a candle and held it closer so he could see the seat of women's pleasure.

"It's so little," he said. "How can I possibly find it in the dark?" Well, this made me laugh, and then he laughed, and we tumbled on the bed and fell to giggling and tickling and then I said, "Darling, Charlie, we must carry on our lesson."

"Lead on," said he.

"You must touch and kiss and lick and suck until I beg you to come inside me."

He dutifully began. A little uncertainly at first, but I taught him how.

"How long must I go on?" he asked.

"Until your tongue aches," I declared, with an inward smile for the strike I was making for all womankind.

The consequence was that I was fairly on fire before I said, "Now, sweetheart, now." And then I don't know what happened. For a moment sheer desire seized me. I pulled him onto me and told him he had to put his – and then I couldn't find a word for it that I thought he would know – but he knew alright, and before I could say knife he was inside me.

Of course, he delivered his burden almost immediately. As he lay on top of me gasping for breath I was sufficiently composed to tell him that he had done well, for a first attempt.

And as he lay there in my arms, I unnecessarily kissed his ears and smelt his hair and stroked him and, to tell truth, began to love him.

58

In vain did I try to turn my thoughts away from Charlie in the days that followed, as they continually ran in that direction. Every time his voice, his skin, his scent, invaded my thoughts, I told myself I was a fool, and that I had not come this far in my profession by allowing myself the luxury of such feelings. Besides, he was a mere boy. Besides, he was to be married. Besides, he was Lord A's nephew. Besides, I would never see him again. This was a silly passing attachment, borne of having too much time on my hands. I walked, I read, I played with Mary. Yet as I walked, I knew I looked for Charlie. And I began to see him everywhere, and to follow strangers, until I had satisfied myself they were not he.

I returned from one such fruitless outing to find Janey's old flame William had been renewing his suit. I was aware they had happened to meet in the playhouse a few weeks before, and though Janey assured me she would not make the same mistake again, I knew she had a fatal soft spot for him, and I stood on pins waiting for him to become irresistible to her once more, dreading all the trouble which would follow when he needed money, as he inevitably would. As I say, I came home in time to pass William's footman leaving the kitchen. This meant only one thing: that messages were passing between them, for of course Janey could neither read nor send a note.

I am sorry to say that I flew into a perfect rage and said some harsh and unforgivable things to Janey, who was most upset and hotly denied my accusations. And I think it was because I feared the same weakness in myself that I was so angry, for what is anger but a response to fear, and what was I, in the end, but fearful? She finally flung out of the house with Mary, saying she would return when I had recovered my senses and that if I hoped for any dinner I had better recover them before then.

I stamped about the house for a while and then took up a book Nell had given me as a parting gift, and threw myself on my bed, and tried to read. The story was by one of my favourite writers, Mrs Behn, who was a friend of Nell's. As though some star – lucky or ill, I know not – knew exactly my preoccupations, I found myself reading these lines: "She found not in her heart that cruel constancy she thought there so well established. She felt pains and inquietude, shed tears, made wishes; and, in fine, discovered that she loved." Like a young enamoured fool who seeks out sad music to lend charm to his own agony, I read these lines over and over, wondering at the thrilling pain they produced. I threw the book across the room. I picked it up. I threw it out of the window. I ran downstairs and retrieved it from the garden. I threw it into the fire. I picked it out with tongs. I sat down on the hearth and hugged the book to myself and wept. Charlie had a damned hank upon my heart, and I did not know what could dissolve the charm.

59

few nights later, I was dreaming that Charlie had come to see me, to ask me to be his wife, if you please, and to run away together. Although I could hear him ringing the bell at the street door, I found all the handles had gone from the doors, and I could not open them to get out and answer him, and was afraid he would go away again. Suddenly I was awoken by the doorbell in fact being rung most insistently. As I got out of bed I heard Janey throw up the window to see who it was, and she called that it was Godfrey, and that he had someone with him. She ran down to admit him while I threw on a manteau and lit the withdrawing room. It seemed to take them a long time to come up the stairs, and when they came in I understood why. Godfrey was half-supporting, half-carrying, a woman.

Where her cloak fell open I observed that underneath she was dressed only in her shift, and had somehow lost one of her slippers. Blood stained her clothes and her face was bruised, with one eye closed completely.

"Here, now you are safe," said Godfrey, and helped her limp to the sofa and gently set her down. While Janey went to heat some water to bathe her wounds I knelt beside the poor creature and tried to comfort her.

She was trying to speak to me but it was difficult to understand her, as her lips were so bruised and she seemed to have lost a tooth or two. Then I realised she was repeating "H" and then she lisped "Is it really you?"

"Yes, it's me, H," I said. "How do you know me?"

And she looked up at me with her one good eye and said, "It's Diana. I'm Diana. Oh, H. We thought you were dead."

Diana? What Diana did I know? I searched my mind if there had ever been Dianas at Clerkenwell and could think of none.

She clasped me to her most tightly, saying, "Oh, my dear sister," over and over, and I began to feel the ground shaking and quaking under me, and then I realised like a thunderclap that this poor wretch was my own true blood sister. This was a most awful shock. I kissed and held her while she wept and assured her she was quite safe now. But, as usual, I had my own interest at the forefront of my mind. Janey returned with the necessaries to make our visitor more comfortable and I took the opportunity to pull Godfrey into the next room.

"What are you thinking of, bringing her here?" I hissed, for I was most angry with him.

"I have not had time to send to you, but your aunt is very ill," he said. "Your sister woke the Potters an hour ago in this state, begging for sanctuary from the brute that is her husband. I could not risk disturbing your aunt, for fear of the shock. I couldn't just turn the poor woman away. What was I to do?"

I could see there was no remedy and acknowledged Godfrey had had no choice, but was most aggravated as I began to see that it was all up with me, that my past and present lives could no longer keep the separation I had so carefully maintained.

"Why did you not tell me my sister was in London?" I asked.

"I didn't know until tonight. They have removed here quite recently I think. From the little I could understand from Diana, she had hoped for a reformation in her husband's character, but he has continued to beat her and tonight half-killed her, so she ran away to the only address in town she knew."

"Now she will know everything," I sighed. "And soon they

will all know everything. And poor Aunt Madge, who is sick as well!" And I could not help but begin to weep at thinking of the effect on the poor dear lady.

"Come, come, H," said Godfrey. "This seems a respectable enough household, does it not? Your sister cannot guess what you are, nor what you have been, if you are but careful."

But I continued to sob, for Diana, for myself, for Aunt Madge, until I was as exhausted as my sister, so we bade Godfrey goodnight, put Diana to bed, and promised to talk everything over in the morning.

Diana stayed in bed late the next day, giving me time to work up a story explaining why none of the family had heard of me since the plague year. I had of course pondered this question many times and had never come up with an entirely satisfactory tale. In the end I settled for the following: After being turned out of Cheapside I had fallen ill but had been one of the lucky few who survived catching the plague, but I had been ill for many months afterwards and lay like one dead in a charity hospital, largely unconscious, but even when awake incapable of lucidity. (This took care of why my family had not been traced and informed.) I had been put into a poorhouse in a state of imbecility and by the time I had recovered my health and my wits the only home to which I could lay claim had been burned to the ground. (This was the weakest link in my story, as it covered a period of well over a year, and after the fire the whole of London was of course covered with signs and notices redirecting people to new addresses, but I reckoned to a newcomer to London, it might pass.) Unable to find my aunt, I had made a happy alliance with a well-to-do mercer who had married me and conveniently died soon afterwards, leaving me reasonably well set. It was nonsense, but was all I had to hand.

I was well aware of the great gaping holes in my story, and that it would not pass muster to a close inspection, but in Diana's agitated and self-interested state, it seemed to satisfy her. And besides, she had much to tell me of herself. Mr

Pincher, for she still referred to her husband as 'Mr Pincher' throughout our interview, had, according to her, beaten her more or less regularly throughout their marriage. As a child I well remember Diana running home to us soon after she was married. Our father had sent her straight back, with injunctions to be more obedient and give her husband no cause to berate her, and warned that should she venture to come home again she could expect nothing but another drubbing from our father. After that, the advent of children, Diana said, had prevented her from leaving. Seeing the comfort she found in them, Mr Pincher had sent all three boys away to school from an early age.

I had been too young, when Diana was first married, to know or understand the cause of the trouble between them, but she now told me that her husband had begun to find fault with Diana on their wedding night, when she had responded with too much ardour to his embraces. He had slapped her and admonished her to lie still and make no sound, otherwise he should think her a whore.

"Well, he should know," Diana continued bitterly, "for he has a whore he keeps in London, who gives him all the flame and rapture he wants when business brings him to town, while he expects his wife to prove her modesty by living quietly in the country and remaining cold as stone in bed. Both my company and my conversation he finds tedious. Well! What do I have to say? My life holds no gaiety, no chat, no discourse but of the cares of this world and its inconveniences; if I ever venture an opinion on any subject he laughs and tells me to hold my peace, for I only make a fool of myself by showing my ignorance."

Miserable Diana had formed a friendship with one of her husband's clerks, to whom she poured out her troubles, and while nothing had occurred which went beyond the bounds of the strictest propriety (she said), Mr Pincher had sensed a kindness between them and had hauled Diana off to London where, he said, he could keep his eye on her, for she was not to be any more trusted to behave herself than a bitch on heat. It was only when she came to town that Diana discovered that her husband kept a mistress, and that their removal here had been as much to do with that as anything.

While Diana was neither allowed visitors nor to pay visits, was kept short of money, and her wardrobe was curtailed to the barest essentials, she said, she had found bills of sale from milliners and manteau-makers which suggested that her husband's whore lived in a far finer style than his wife. One day she had made so bold as to follow her husband to see where he went, and saw this *bona-roba*, this lady of delight, and was astonished to find that her coach, dress and equipage far exceeded her own. But worse than this, she said, far worse, was to see how happy Mr Pincher was to see this fine piece of dirt, how civilly he conducted himself towards her, how solicitous he was to her comfort, how interested he seemed in her conversation, and how gaily he laughed at her pleasantries. Worse than the fact that he lavished such vast sums of money on his concubine, he was also generous with his mirth, his humour, his smiles and his kisses, spending them all freely on *her*, when he never even had a kind word to spare for his wife.

It was when Diana had felt emboldened to complain to Mr Pincher of her competitor for his affections that he had given her the last and most severe beating which had sent her running out of the house in the middle of the night, fearing for her life.

Although Diana's appearance was like to expose my whereabouts to my family, which was most unwelcome, she did bring me news of my sisters, for which I hungered. Clarissa continued high and mighty, as was to be expected, and delighted in her husband's elevation to town mayor.

"Oh, God, should Clarissa but get a sniff of the things my husband accuses me of, she will not scruple to cut me off as she did Grace! I cannot bear to think of it."

"Poor Grace," I said.

"Disgrace, more like. Clarissa says she lives most infamously."

"Grace lives?" I exclaimed. The last time I had seen Grace was coming out of the workhouse just before I had tried to make an end of myself on London Bridge. Having seen her state then I had thought it unlikely she yet lived. But Diana had learnt from Clarissa that Grace not only thrived, but, wonder of wonders, dwelt in *London*, and even greater wonder of even greater wonders, was supported by our other sister Frances – presumably now discharged from the army!

This was all wonderful and surprising news, and I immediately expressed a desire to see Frances and Grace, but Diana threw up her hands in horror at this, and said Frances was no better than Grace, that she was in a sad and disreputable condition, and ran an ale house by the river, which was known to be little better than a brothel. This clearly made an end to the matter as far as Diana was concerned, and I was about to remonstrate when I realised that this would not sit well with my supposedly respectable state as the widow of a well-to-do mercer, so I swallowed down this unexpected joy and, with a placid smile, covered my resolve to somehow get the address out of her and later make my own enquiries after my other dear sisters.

60

found myself in the unpleasing position of wishing to give my sister refuge, but being unable to conduct my normal business while she was resident in my house. I was anxious to keep her away from Lincoln's Inn Fields, as not only my existence but my whereabouts would then be known to my aunt, and all should then come out, but fortunately Diana was, having found me, equally anxious to avoid our aunt if possible and to keep her unhappy story between only us two. I sent to the usual visitors I expected over the next few days to say I was unwell and could not see them, but this situation could not last, and I had no idea how long Diana planned to remain with me. She had no other friends in London, and I certainly did not want to make her feel unwelcome when her only option was to return to her husband.

I also did not know what to do with her. She and Clarissa had been my least favourite sisters so we had no stock of friendship on which to build. More problematic was the fact that I had never acquired the art of doing nothing, which she, in common with all respectable women of her class, was used to. She did not read nor draw, and she had no desire to be seen about while she was so bruised and marked. The feeling inside the house was also affected, as Janey and I could not be so familiar or natural with each other as we were wont. Diana showed a polite interest in Mary but clearly disapproved of her spending so much time with me, but most of all of me harbouring an unmarried woman servant with a child. (I had not had time to invent a dead husband for Janey.) She could not understand, now that she had apprised me of Aunt Madge's whereabouts, why I was not anxious to see her, although Godfrey was good enough to remind us both that she could receive absolutely no visitors. She also puzzled how her aunt's secretary knew where to find me, though my aunt had never let the family know that she knew my whereabouts. I gave such flim-flam answers to these queries that she would have been a fool not to suspect all was not what it appeared.

Janey put up with Diana's rudeness towards her and kept Mary with her as far as possible, but I knew she too was aching for Diana to be gone, and a return to easy normality. Between us we fitted Diana out with clothes, but though Diana was much nearer Janey's shape than my own, she was reluctant to wear Janey's clothes, though they were nice, new and clean and, though simple, not unfashionable. Janey bore all this with a good grace but I missed hearing her singing about the place, an activity curtailed by Diana begging her to "stop making that abominable noise".

Even so, everything could have passed off without too much difficulty, had everyone stuck to the rules, but things began to fall apart when, quite unexpectedly, Charlie turned up. I had heard the doorbell and assumed Janey would send whoever it was away, but he apparently bounded up the stairs past her before she had a chance to prevent him and fairly burst into the room where I was sitting with my sister. A more experienced lover would not of course have done this, fearing to find me with another man, which would not have been obliging to anyone concerned. But Charlie did not know the score.

My heart turned over twice: once at the sight of Charlie, who was no less appealing than in my fantasies, and once again at the immediate difficulty of explaining him to my sister. Evidently not expecting to find me in company, he nevertheless kept his composure and made a low bow to us both.

I introduced him to my sister, who I was surprised to notice, blushed and giggled like a green girl at meeting so pretty a young man, and I was thinking how to get rid of him when he announced, to my horror, "I am come for another lesson, madam!"

"Another lesson?" asked Diana, pleasantly intrigued. "What's this, H?"

"Mr Carroll is… my… dancing master! He is come to give me my dancing lesson! I had almost forgot!"

"Oh how thrilling!" Diana clapped her hands. "May I watch?"

I managed to turn my back to Diana while facing Charlie so I could look at him most meaningfully as I said, "I am so sorry Mr Carroll, but you cannot give me my lesson today, for my sister has come to visit *unexpectedly*."

"Oh, don't mind me!" exclaimed Diana. "It will be diverting, I am sure. Please, H, I insist. I have put you out too much already."

I gave Charlie an agonised look, and he seemed suddenly to understand, but proved most naughty, as he said, with a winning smile, "Well if your sister doesn't mind… your movement does require some attention, madam. Now, what shall we begin with? How about 'Fain I Would'? Or 'Lady Lie Near Me'?"

I was appalled and glared at him.

"But we have no music!" I protested. "The musician must have forgot too! We will have to *leave it*, I am afraid, Mr Carroll."

"Oh, I can play!" offered Diana, and fairly ran across the room to the spinet and began riffling through the music. She sat down. "Now, what shall we begin with? Oh, look, here is 'On The Cold Ground'! Oh you have all the latest things, H."

And so it came about that Charlie gave me a dancing lesson, while my sister played, and to see Janey's expression when she put her head round the door made the prettiest picture I had seen for a long time.

It was as well that Diana faced the wall as she played, for whenever Charlie came close to me as we danced, he took the opportunity to kiss me, whispering "I love your eyes, I love your lips, I love your ears," and though I fought to withstand the onslaught I fairly wilted in his arms.

"Stop it, Charlie!" I hissed. "Why did you come back? You were not supposed to come back."

"I want another lesson," he repeated.

"You don't need another lesson," I said.

"I did not say I needed one. I said I wanted one," and he clasped me by the waist and pulled me close against him as we twirled and turned and I could tell that he did indeed want one.

"Oh, Charlie!" I meant to exclaim, but half-sighed.

"I am to be married next Friday. I will never see you again afterwards. So how can you refuse me now?"

I confess I couldn't think of one good reason why I should refuse him now, excepting the presence of Diana.

"Think of it, H. In only a few days I am to be locked into a loveless marriage, until death do us part. I may never know happiness again. If I were a soldier, going off to war, you would grant me that favour, would you not? Well it is as good as the same thing. I beg just one night with you, and then I swear you will never see me again."

I became aware that Diana had stopped playing and was watching us.

"Will you have a lesson, Diana?" I asked, a little too gaily, breaking away from Charlie.

"Well… I shouldn't object to learn a new step or two," said Diana, blushing again.

"Very well. Show her, Mr Carroll. I must send Janey to the post with a letter."

"Oh, but you can't leave us!" exclaimed Diana in genuine panic, as I headed out of the room. It took me a moment to gather her meaning, so out of the habit was I of conventional social intercourse.

"You will be quite safe!" I assured Diana. "Mr Carroll is a most gentlemanly gentleman. Here, I will leave the door open. I will only be in the next room."

I left Diana standing open-mouthed and went next door to write a note to Charlie telling him I would leave word at The Black Dog when he could see me, as I was now as determined as he to have my night of bliss.

Diana was exceedingly flushed when I returned and did I not know Charlie better I might have begun to wonder whether he had been practising on her. She laughed and chattered in a flustered way, hiding her poor missing teeth behind a fan she had begged from me, and though Charlie was charming to her, I felt she noticed as keenly as a rival might that his eyes followed my every move.

It was with the greatest difficulty that I persuaded him to leave, pressing the note in his hand as I did so. When he had gone, Diana was unusually quiet and remained so for the rest of the evening and went to bed betimes saying her head ached from all the dancing business. I sat up chatting quietly with Janey while we mended some stockings (for though I dressed well, I was ever frugal in my habits), and I hoped she would not quiz me about Charlie and I refrained from doing the same about William.

61

quickly calculated that the following Monday would be the earliest I could see Charlie, and that it would have to be a daytime assignation, Monday night being sacred to his uncle, whom I could not put off. I knew I could get him safely away long before Lord A made his customary visit. (I guessed from the way Charlie spoke of his uncle that he had not the slightest inkling of the nature of the liaison between Lord A and myself.) I was just returning from the coffee-house, where I had left a note for Charlie, when I met Godfrey coming to my door. He carried a letter for Diana which had been sent to her at my aunt's house. I hoped it might offer some path to a solution to her troubles, as I needed her out of the way by the time Charlie came on Monday.

"I'll wager it is from that beast of a husband, begging her to come back," said Godfrey. My aunt, he added, was much better, though still weak from her illness, which cheered us both.

We found Diana in the parlour, and she went white when the letter was produced and seemed to fear its contents too much to read it herself so asked me to do so.

"'Dear Mrs Pincher,'" I began reading. "'I would apologise for expressing myself rather too forcibly during our interview last week, were it not for your disgraceful and dishonourable reaction: to quit your home, your husband, and, most unnaturally, your children.'"

"My children are safe at school!" exclaimed Diana. "I should never have deserted them!" and commenced weeping at the mere thought of this dereliction of maternal duty being ascribed to her. "This is his way!" she sobbed. "He says it, or writes it and therefore it is true! He is a lawyer down to the very bone."

"'In view of your shameful conduct,'" I continued, "'and the sin which I choose not to name, for which reason we removed to London, in hopes of a reformation of your conduct... '"

"*My* conduct!" she cried. "It was *he* who promised to reform! A fresh start, he said."

"'... I consider it in your interests, more than anybody's, that you return home immediately, before I am obliged to retail the details of your infamous behaviour to your family and friends.'"

"Oh, God! God help me!" cried Diana, her face in her hands.

"'Yours faithfully,' – he has underlined 'faithfully'."

Diana was quiet for a long time, rocking slightly, her head still in her hands. I put my arm around her shoulder and said, "Will you send a reply?"

"What is the use?" she moaned. "This is blackmail. I shall have to go back."

"No, madam!" exclaimed Godfrey. "You cannot, under any circumstances, go back to that brute! Look what he has done to you! And he will do it again, you know that as well as I."

"I have no choice! You don't understand, do you? You are a man, and H is a widow: you may both do as you like. But I am a married woman. Mr Pincher can turn my name to dirt. Besides, I have no money. How can I live?"

"I have money!" I cried. "I will look after you."

"I will never see my children... "

This gave me pause for thought.

"We will get a lawyer – another one – one who will expose his lies, and get him to settle an annuity on you, and put it in writing that the children may live with you, or at least let you see them."

Diana looked at me with real anger in her eyes.

"What fairyland do you think such lawyers live in, H? They all stick together. Half the women in the country would leave their husbands if it were that simple! He has already threatened me with the madhouse, and has a doctor – whom, needless to add, I have never met – waiting ready to put his name to a paper to say I am out of my mind. He will stop at nothing to get me back, or silence me for ever."

I continued to remonstrate with my sister and at least succeeded in eliciting a promise from her to do nothing hasty, to remain with me a few days longer at least, in the hopes that during that time I could persuade her not to return to her tormentor and think of how to set her up in independence and in safety. Although I was most anxious to be rid of her, I was not yet so selfish I would sacrifice her happiness to my convenience.

62

he next day I was enjoying an hour of reading in peace (as Diana claimed she was bored when I read) as Janey was accompanying my sister for a turn about the park, and Mary was having her rest. It was a beautiful day and after a while I laid my book aside and went to the back window and watched the people enjoying the sunshine in the park. As I increasingly found myself doing, I realised I looked out for Charlie. I watched a little boy trundling his hoop with gathering expertise across the grass, until his path crossed that of an unwelcomely familiar figure. It was Jasper, carrying a great basket of flowers, and he was headed for the little alley that ran behind the garden. I fairly shot down to the back door to head him off. I opened the door just as he was about to knock.

"Well, if it ain't—"

"Yes, it is Miss Dollie, for you know perfectly well this is where Miss Dollie lives, and in any case I wish you would call me Halcyon, or H, or anything, and I also wish you had not come as it is most inconvenient and not according to our understanding."

"Sorry Dollie," said Jasper, looking nothing of the sort, "but I am about urgent business. I bear tidings of great import!" He hovered, and then presented me with the flowers.

"I suppose you will not go until you have told me, so do so and be gone."

Taking this as an invitation to come in, he did so, and ran up the stairs, two at a time. I hurried after him and followed him into the drawing room. He pulled off his hat and turned it in his hands, evidently brimming with emotion.

"Ring the bells and send for the sexton! The old man is dead," he announced.

I thought at first this was another of Jasper's impenetrable expressions which in actuality meant nothing.

"And your news?" I asked.

"My father is dead," he explained.

"Oh, I am very sorry to hear it. Truly, I am sorry, Jasper. But you cannot stay here. Please go."

"You do not understand, Dollie. My *father* is *dead*."

"I understand you perfectly Jasper. I perceive you are upset and I am sorry for it. However—"

"You see before you the Earl of Tewkesbury. I am my own master: master of my own fortune, master of my own destiny."

"Congratulations, my lord. Now, go, and come and see me another day."

"By Jupiter, I love you, Dollie!" he declared.

"Love me?" I cried, knowing that a declaration of this kind – from Jasper, at any rate – had to be dealt with swiftly and harshly. "Love me? What if you do? How far will that go at the Exchange for new shoes? Will the grocer take it for current coin? I can neither feed nor clothe myself with words! If you must express your feelings, do so with your purse. That is a language I understand and value."

"What is the reason that you use me so inhumanly, Dollie? You must know that I am consumedly in love." He had grasped my hands between his and was now squeezing them unmercifully. "I am furiously in love. Up to the ears. I stand on thorns."

"Jasper, stop this nonsense at once!" I confess he had my bones rattling. Apart from feeling most uncomfortable

302

at Jasper's outburst of ardour, I was afraid my sister would return at any moment.

"No! By Hector, it is you who must stop!" he almost shouted, then seeming to collect himself, laid his finger gently to my lips, and added in a softer tone, "Prithee hold your peace a little till I have done." Shocked and surprised into submission, I allowed myself to be led to the couch and sat down. Jasper knelt beside me. "The first glance you cast upon this poor soul, your servant, leapt straight into my heart with a... " Here he stopped and seemed to search for the word. "... with a tickling kind of pain. That little kind of scurvy pain has remained there ever since. Nothing will make me happy my dear sweet Dollie until you agree to be mine, mine exclusively, only mine. And now I have my fortune and can do as I please, I want to reserve and keep you all to myself."

"I see," I said thinking fast. "I will have to have time, Jasper, to think about this. You know I already have a keeper." And already my mind was racing ahead, calculating whether I could make Jasper become my keeper – or at least let him think that he was – and how much I could get of him, and how long it might take to persuade him to settle an independent income on me, indentured for life, and how long I would have to put up with him before I could jump ship, and when, perhaps, I could finally retire. And so my mind ran on...

"Stone the crows and shoot the ravens, Dollie! I don't mean to *keep* you, dear heart! I mean to *marry* you!"

For a moment I was dumbstruck, and then my throat emitted a sharp sound, somewhere between a shout of laughter and a scream.

"Have you been in the sun without your hat?" I eventually asked, searching Jasper's face for signs of insanity. He looked excited and rather flushed, but not, so far as I could tell, deranged.

"I know what you are thinking. You are thinking that I will attract the scorn of society by marrying a... lady of your calling. You may be right. I have examined my heart on this

303

score and have discovered the amazing truth: I don't care. I honestly, truly, do not care what the world thinks. You may be the arrantest whore that ever wore a petticoat, but I'm dying of love for you, and I would have you for my wife."

"I... I... I... " I could not find the words to express my astonishment and I realised I was trembling.

Jasper reached into his pocket and I prayed he would not produce a ring on the spot. "Here's the best softener of a woman's heart!" he said, and emptied a purse of gold coins into my lap. "Two hundred pieces, and plenty more to come! Come, kiss me Dollie, and seal the bargain." And he proceeded to smother me in kisses, pushing me backwards on the couch.

At that moment Janey came in, and quickly taking in the scene, tried to prevent Diana following her through the door, but it was too late.

To my sister, in common with most modest women, appearances are everything, and certainly more to be trusted to, in the long view, than mere facts. Despite the unusual circumstance that she had come into the room on one of the rare occasions that a quite legitimate act was taking place – that is to say, that Jasper was proposing marriage to me – the presence of gold tumbling from my lap and the familiarity which my suitor took with my person all added to the doubts she had begun to entertain as to the character of my household, and confirmed beyond question that I was a woman of the lowest and loosest kind. As soon as Janey had succeeded in bundling Jasper out of the house, Diana opened her attack.

Her angry reaction was driven in the first place by fear: fear of her association with me, and what the world, and especially her husband, would make of it. Were he to discover that she had been residing in a house of wickedness, she declared, his power over her would be boundless: he would hold her reputation in his hands and could damn her to social Purgatory at the moment of his choosing. Her emotions ran back and forth between angry recriminations and expressions of self-pity: my thoughtless actions had made it impossible for her to remain under my roof – her *one place of safety* – and she should have to return to her husband immediately. She repeated the old saw, which I began to find most tiresome, though true, that once a woman's character is stained not all the water in the Thames will wash it clean, and I did not argue with her, except to beg her not to go back to Mr Pincher, who had shown her such unconscionable cruelty, but instead to take refuge with Aunt Madge, whom Godfrey had said was improving, but this suggestion brought forth a most unexpected tirade.

"Aunt Madge," she sneered, "I suspect is no better than she should be."

"Diana!" I exclaimed, horrified at where this madness was leading.

"Why did she not inform us you were alive and well? Why did she not apprise us of your whereabouts? Because she *knew*! She knows not only *where* you are, but *what* you are!"

"This is not true, Diana! She does not know! Aunt Madge is innocent of any wrong!"

"Ho! You must think me an easy fool, H. Her *secretary* – if indeed that is what he is, for I begin to form a nasty sneaking suspicion as to his true position in her retinue – *he* knew! He brought me straight here!"

"It does not follow that Aunt Madge knows! Godfrey is my... my... special friend."

The sneer this statement drew from my sister was indescribably horrible.

"Your special *playhouse* friend! Don't think I don't know about you and your *dancing lessons*! I know what you are!"

I did not know what to say. What could I say?

"I am going to pack," said Diana, and swept out haughtily, only to return a few moments later, looking a little foolish, for of course she had nothing to pack. "Good-bye," she said with a stiffness that precluded any kind of embrace or token of affection passing between us, "and may God have mercy on you, for the world will not."

"Diana!" I caught hold of her hand as she turned to go.

"Don't tell your husband you have been here. He cannot find it out himself. Say you have been with Aunt Madge – he believes you there, or he would not have sent the letter. I swear she is beyond reproach."

"You live a life of falsehood and now you would draw me in and have me lie too?" asked Diana.

"It is only for your own good," I said. "I am truly sorry Diana."

"So am I," she said, and was gone.

I went into the kitchen to look for some comfort from Janey, but was most displeased to find William's footman there again, and Janey flushed with pleasure and guilty-seeming. I had neither the energy nor appetite for a confrontation, and went out again feeling worse than ever. My life was unravelling from both ends.

I lay on my bed considering what could be done and was a little cheered in the remembrance that tomorrow was Sunday, and Kat as well as Godfrey were coming to eat dinner with us. They would be full of good counsel.

63

n the event, no one was interested in Diana. Janey and Godfrey had pitied but not liked her, and Kat, who only knew her by repute, declared that if she valued her good name above her health and happiness, that was entirely her concern and I should not trouble myself about it. As to my infamy being carried to the rest of my siblings, they did not comprehend why I cared. Was it not years since I had seen them? And was it likely I would ever see them again? What did their opinion matter? I thought carefully on this. I realised that my craving for Clarissa and Diana's good opinion was childish, but still the mere thought of Clarissa and Reverend Grimwade's chilly, damning gaze made me shiver. But I should certainly have liked to see Grace and Frances again, and had every intention of doing so, now that I had an idea where they lived.

There again, Kat pointed out, if Grace and Frances had sunk so low in Diana's estimation, would they judge *me* so harshly? I pondered this and agreed that no, they possibly would not, as I would not judge them. Godfrey then observed that he knew I valued Aunt Madge's ignorance of my condition of life, but he believed she would rather know I lived at any rate, and in any case the rest of my family never saw her. "But you have not told them the most important thing!" said Janey.

"What most important thing?" I asked.

"The Earl!" she prompted.

"What owl?" asked Godfrey, mystified.

"Earl, cloth-ears! Her faithful servant, the Viscount Jasper," Janey announced, "is come into his earldom and wants to marry her!"

There was an astonished silence round the table.

"Fuck me, H!" said Godfrey at last.

"Godfrey!" chided Janey, for Mary was playing with her doll under the table.

Kat raised her glass and laughed slightly hysterically.

"May I wish you good cheer of your most amazing good fortune, H! You deserve it."

"Fuck me," said Godfrey again, under his breath, and they all drank to me.

"Hold, hold! Not so fast!" I exclaimed. "I have not agreed."

Kat looked utterly confounded and Godfrey choked on his wine.

"Incredible ain't it?" Janey said to them. "Madam don't know whether she *wants* to marry an earl, if you please."

Kat and Godfrey stared at me as though I had gone stark staring mad.

"Well! To be obliged to live with such a fool!" I objected. "With his 'slit me breeches!' and his 'kiss me bollocks!' Imagine waking up every morning to hear the idiot lying next to me shout: 'Damn me if it ain't Miss Dollie!' What thought or fancy could make my hours supportable with such a bafflegab?"

"Why, a thousand acres and ten thousand pounds a year, H!" cried Janey. "Take hold of that and then of what you will!"

"Besides, he might die, and leave you rich, and then do as you please!" added Kat hopefully.

"Money isn't everything!" I caught myself saying. They all stared at me again.

"I begin to think we should carry you to Bedlam and chain you up until you come back to your senses," sighed Janey.

"I cannot credit this, H," said Godfrey. "What possible

objection could you have to such an offer? He behaves well towards you, does he not? He does not abuse you?"

"Oh, he dotes on her," Janey averred. "He always has. They'd live like doves."

"So what is it, H?" demanded Godfrey.

"Can you see me as a silly, pretty household thing?" I asked. "Paying and receiving visits from ladies? Passing the endless hours of leisure with trivialities? Occupying my time in the assassination of characters and the murdering of reputations?"

"Not all ladies are such arrant bitches," insisted Kat. "You may find a friend. Perhaps even a gentleman friend, who may help your hours pass more tolerably."

"Oh, I couldn't do that to Jasper," I said.

They all stared at me agape again.

"Not if we were married," I added.

"Pfffff!" said Janey, standing up to clear the plates away. "I don't know what's got into you, I don't. This is your chance to get out of the game, to be rich, to be happy. You'll never get a better offer. So what you waiting for?"

What *was* I waiting for? All I knew was that Charlie's face inconveniently invaded my thoughts whenever I did not work hard enough on banishing it.

"Would you really see me a wife?" I found myself pleading. "Yes, now Jasper makes me his queen, his mistress, but soon enough I'd be his slave. We know – of all people we know – what men truly think of their wives. They swear at the altar they will be kind to none beside their bride, and soon enough they are kind to everyone *but* her. What do I offer up to gain all his acres? I sell my liberty, my freedom, my very self."

"To speak plainly, H, what else do you sell, nightly, but yourself?" inquired Godfrey. "What's the difference – except that this is a safer, more enduring bargain?"

"My freedom!" I cried.

"Your freedom to do what, may I ask?" chimed in Janey.

"Your freedom to open your legs to anyone who can pay your price?"

"Yes, if it comes to that! My freedom to say yes and no, where and when. My liberty to come and go when I please; to answer to no one."

"And when you grow old?" asked Kat, staring darkly into her glass. "What then?"

"Then I shall have my little fortune. And Janey, and little Mary, to comfort me."

Here I detected Janey squirm in her seat a little.

"A mistress is a name that implies command," I declared. "Why should I choose to be a slave?"

Godfrey sighed.

"Your friends would choose to see you settled, H; that is all. This remarkable, unlooked-for offer would remove all your cares at a stroke. And think on your precious family: what a prize this marriage would be to your sisters!"

"Ho, yes!" exclaimed Janey. "To see dear Diana's face would be a prize itself! Oh, H, think of it: you an earless—"

"Countess," Kat corrected her.

"—a countess! And your rotten sisters spitting nails!"

"Do it," said Godfrey, taking my hands in his, and looking as earnest as I think I ever saw him. "Marry Jasper."

"You realise," I said, "it would be the end of us. Just as I am not a fit wife for an earl, you are not suitable companions for a countess."

A silence fell on the table.

"Oh, I don't know but Jasper's a good sort," said Janey at last, "one of your Dear Hearts. He mightn't object to H seeing her old friends once in a while."

"No, Janey," sighed Godfrey. "H is right, in this at least. She would have to let us go. It wouldn't be fair."

"Never!" I declared.

"Then it might be up to us," said Kat standing up, "to let you go. For your own good."

"You know she's talking sense," said Janey gently. "If it

was me what had an offer – and he wouldn't have to be an earl or be rich – but if I had someone what loved me and wanted to make an honest woman of me and give Mary a name and make me happy, you'd let me go, wouldn't you?" I guessed this was not merely a device of reasoning, but that William had something to do with the way her mind was working, and I think she sensed this. "I'm only saying," she added.

The party then broke up, somewhat to my relief, as I sorely wanted my bed. One advantage of Diana's sudden departure and Jasper's proposition had been to crowd out Charlie from exclusively occupying my thoughts, but as I lay in bed, he took his accustomed place, removing other cares. I looked forward with mixed sensations to the next day, for Charlie was coming to claim his 'lesson' and it would be our last meeting.

64

hen Charlie arrived late the next morning, we fairly fell upon each other the moment he came through the door, leaving a trail of clothes, as Janey later disapprovingly remarked, leading to my chamber. Charlie's love-making was intense as it was fast, but I did not mind this as he was up for several repeat performances. My emotions were in a tumult, as were his, and we laughed and wept by turns, like deranged people. We talked, loved, drank, loved, mused, loved, compressing whatever future we might have had, in some other life, into a few short hours. Neither of us wanted the day to end, so after we were exhausted to the point of being sore, we took a bath together, again to much huffing and puffing from Janey, who grumbled that she had better things to do than heat and carry water when it wasn't even Saturday (our usual bath night), and that she hoped he was paying well, but I didn't care, for I was with my Charlie, and nothing else mattered.

We both fell to smiling and weeping again in the bath, though this may have been the effects of the wine we had been taking copiously, at the thought that it should be the first and last we should take together, for I think in his own way Charlie was as smitten with me as I was with him, the difference being that I had discovered the real folly and enduring pain in such an attachment, and believed I should go to my grave in love with someone I could never have, whereas for him it was merely his first romantic adventure.

Out of the respect he had for the sanctity of marriage he did not even suggest pursuing our friendship after his wedding, and I should not have agreed in any case, knowing how important the marriage was to everyone, including myself, for we were bound through Lord A in a chain of financial dependence, to a greater or lesser degree. So there was not the faintest hope of this being anything but a farewell, and as is always the case with such bittersweet assignations, the hands raced almost visibly round the clock on the mantelpiece.

After our bath we went back to bed and lay in each others' arms, and I remember to this moment how exquisitely our bodies seemed to fit together, not as in the passionate act of fucking, which is a different kind of congress, but in soft and sweet embraces and divine encirclings, as if we had been made originally from one piece of flesh and only happened to be divided into two people, and had at last found our original fellow half. When one of us moved, the other moved after, so that we were always in some way connected. I think I have never experienced a sensation so close to complete and perfect contentment, nor so deep an appreciation of the power of human intimacy, and I wished we could stay there, entwined for ever. I guessed the feeling approached what it was like to be married to a husband you really loved, and who really loved you back, and that you could have this bliss every night, just as a matter of course, so that you even might take it for granted. As Charlie drifted into sleep beside me I let fall tears of gratitude to God for affording a sinner such as myself this insight into pure and true happiness.

But the evening which began almost as a beautiful dream turned in an instant to a living nightmare, for when I awoke it was dark, Janey was shrieking my name in shrill panic and Lord A stood over the bed, having ripped off the bedclothes, waking Charlie and myself in confusion. I do not know how I had forgot my appointment with Lord A, as in the morning I had remembered it, but then Charlie and the wine... I had not intended to sleep for so long, and now I awoke to an utterly horrible reality.

"What is this?" shouted Lord A, whom I had never seen so angry; he was perfectly incandescent with rage. "What are you doing here?" he demanded of Charlie, who could not yet work out where he was or what was happening. "What is he doing here?" he demanded of me.

"I... we... he wanted another lesson," I said feebly.

"What are *you* doing here, Uncle?" stammered Charlie.

"Get dressed!" he commanded Charlie, who scrambled out of bed and began to look for his things, which Janey had helpfully gathered together and now thrust in his direction. "Wait for me in the next room!" Charlie obeyed. "Now you silly little slut," Lord A said to me, with unaccustomed rudeness and taking me roughly by the arm, "what game are you playing? He was supposed to come once only. Do you mean to make a fool of me?"

"No!" I cried, "I... he... "

"This is the first time I ever knew you lost for words, Miss! I demand an explanation! He who pays the piper calls the tune, does he not? So? Give me your song, Miss!"

"You do not pay, sir," I said.

"If he pays, I pay! It is all the same!"

"No one pays," I said quietly.

"I say," said Charlie, who had returned, alarmed, at the raised voices, "should I... should I have... offered something, Halcyon?"

"So... " Understanding dawned on Lord A's face. "*Halcyon*, is it?" He laughed, a short, bitter laugh. "So this is an affair of the heart, am I to understand? How touching. A whore in love! This is rare! This is rich indeed!"

"Prithee, Uncle, you mustn't talk to her like that," entreated Charlie. "She is my friend! She has shown me the way! Just like you said!"

"Silence, boy! This is no business of yours," snapped Lord A.

I was weeping by this time. I did not dare to appeal to Lord A's better nature, for old time's sake, as I doubted how much Charlie knew of my friendship with his uncle, as we had never spoken of it, or even how much he understood of my profession. I was at a loss at what to do or say for the best, for I entertained a healthy respect for other people's lies.

"Will I put the kettle on, madam?" asked Janey, desperately, who had been standing by all the time.

"Damn the kettle! Get out!" shouted Lord A.

"Please don't cry, Halcyon," said Charlie, brimming up himself. "I don't understand all this, but... please don't cry."

"Prithee be not so blind to think her true for weeping," said Lord A scornfully, "for sighs and tears are the whore's ammunition, the tools and implements of their damned profession."

"Why do you use me so cruelly?" I implored Lord A, but again dared not appeal to our history, for fear of what Charlie did not know.

"A whore?!" cried Charlie. "How can you call her that?"

"What do you think she is, you fool?" demanded Lord A.

"But she is a lady, Uncle!" protested Charlie. "Look at her!" I stood before them, dear reader, as naked as the day I was born, and Charlie quickly realised my appearance did nothing to serve his argument. "Look at her house!" he appealed. "Consider her clothes!" he added pathetically, "When she is wearing them."

"That's no rule, child, for whores wear as good linen as honest women. Be assured, fine clothes and good linen are the working tools of their trade."

"I love her, sir! I will marry as you wish, and I will never see her again, but I protest and declare and you must know that I love her! And she loves me!" Charlie seemed desperate – uncomprehending and utterly desperate.

"Trust not to that, you poor animal," said Lord A with a

pitying look at him, and then a hard look for me, "for women of her profession love men but as far as their money goes. She knows you are making a good marriage and would have a part of the spoils, that is all. Do not make the mistake of considering the principles of a mistress beyond those of a good companion. They are both the instruments of pleasure for a time, and can be trusted to nothing beyond that meeting."

A terrible expression came over Charlie's features and I knew with the most heavy sinking feeling that the truth – the truth I had not considered he did not know – was gradually revealing itself horribly to him.

"Uncle, am I to understand that you... you and Halcyon... "

"Me and half a dozen others, yes! Your 'sweetheart' doles her private favours to all mankind alike for profit."

"Not *all* mankind... " I ventured, stupidly, thinking that such a distinction had any meaning to Charlie.

"Any beast with money, to be sure!" asserted Lord A. "Your true jilt shall cope with any brute for profit, with two legs or with four, take that for Gospel," he added bitterly.

"That will do, sir!" shrieked Janey, who was wielding a broomstick. "Out, both of you, out! Out!"

"Don't concern yourself; we are leaving," said Lord A, throwing me the most baleful look. "You may consider our association at an end. And the direst consequences will attend any attempt by you to trouble either of us again." As he turned to go, gathering Charlie to him, he seemed to hesitate a moment, and then, still facing away from me, added: "What a fool I've been. I thought you were different, H."

"I thought you were different too," I said, though perhaps too quietly to be heard, as they went down the stairs.

When they had gone Janey approached me with a most concerned expression.

"How do you do, sweetheart?" she asked.

"Very bad, Janey," I said. "Most wretched, in fact," and I fell on my bed, too tired and too troubled with inexpressible grief even to cry. (For you know, I was, and remain, a foolish thing given overmuch to weeping.) And Janey, bless her dear heart, lay by me all night, murmuring reassurance, though I was inconsolable.

The days that followed passed as if in a bad dream. Whenever I gained a sane moment, a moment of tranquility, perhaps, with little Mary, or found some peace looking into the fire, with Janey beside me (for she never quit my side throughout my great trouble and unhappiness), the awful happenings of that night pounced upon me, making my heart leap and race till I felt sick and even began to fear for my sanity. I thought interminably of Charlie's range of expressions, however hard I tried not to, that expressed the death of our connection that night, and also suffered a more complex pain, underlying everything, attending how my friendship with Lord A had unravelled, and how it had obviously been such a slight and expendable thing to him, a fact I had never considered. His words that damningly confirmed my true status, that I was an "instrument of pleasure for a time, and could be trusted to nothing beyond that meeting" shocked me repeatedly, with the palpable sting of a slap in the face every time I thought of them. I had been in a fool's paradise, I realised, to think there was any such thing as honour or decency in my transactions, and as a consequence, I found I could not face any of my other lovers, and accordingly sent word that I could not receive them.

I do not think I went really mad, as I was able sometimes to laugh at myself, albeit in a bitter, hard way, but I will admit to having had strange thoughts. I believed myself a bad and worse than useless creature, and vexed myself and puzzled over what H stood for, as though this not having a proper name meant something, or H itself meant something. It could not be Hope or Happiness, so was it Hell or Hate? Janey clearly feared for me, was happy to carry my messages of cancellation, and sought a hundred ways to cheer me and bring me out of my melancholies and obsessions. She insisted I walked for an hour every day, just to "get about", as she said, and to "be among real people" as I think she knew how unreal people, or rather memories and impressions of real people, crowded my fancy. And this is why what I saw a few days later was so troubling. I was walking through Covent Garden and suddenly saw Charlie. This was not unusual, for I had been in the habit for some time of suddenly seeing Charlie everywhere. However, this really was Charlie, as I thought, helping a lady out of a carriage, who might have been his aunt, and then helping another lady out, who by her age I judged to be his fiancée, Miss Sophia Phipps, and then standing by respectfully as Lord A got out, which confirmed I was not dreaming.

But most distressing of all was the fact that I recognised Miss Phipps. No change of wig, no powder or patching, no passage of time could disguise the awful truth that Charlie's heiress was none other than... I searched my brain, tried to get a hold on my sense of reality, told myself I must be dreaming, or even having a waking nightmare (which Janey, due to my propensity towards them, and the range of anxieties they played out to dreadful ends, had named a "*might*mare")... but to cut a long diversion short, the woman whom Charlie gallantly guided out of the carriage – the woman to whom he was to be married – I knew with awful certainty to be none other than Sylvia.

65

ll I had known from Lord A of the woman Charlie was to marry was that she was an heiress, a widow and a virgin, to boot. The only part of this I knew to be true of the woman I had seen was that Sylvia was indeed my cousin Roger's widow (though they had parted before his death in circumstances most unflattering to the idea of marital duty, as he lay dying of the awful visitation) and that she was at that time definitely with child, so hardly your blushing virgin. Where she had been in the time since her escape from Cheapside in the plague year, after she had turned me into the street with nothing but the clothes on my back, I had no idea, but I knew she now represented herself to Lord A's family as something quite other than what she really was. Worse, Charlie was marrying her with the sole idea that she was heiress to a substantial fortune, which would save his uncle's estate, and unless I did something to disabuse them she would latch herself on to him, and could be nothing but the worst kind of burden to him, and to Lord A and the family, adding to, rather than relieving, their troubles.

When I got home I told Janey immediately. She was all for my leaving my discovery alone and letting events run their course. It was not my affair, she said, and could do me no good to involve myself. Besides, had not Lord A treated me most shamefully? Why should I trouble myself about what happened to him and his kin? But even in these objections, I knew Janey was merely humouring me. It is a most sad aspect of an affliction of the mind, which Janey now believed I laboured under, that one is not believed even when one has lucid moments of clarity and sanity, and I detected Janey doubted I had a true grasp on reality. Had I really seen Sylvia? Had I even seen Charlie? Was my mind not, in its great turmoil, mixing up all my past troubles and producing one new one? These, I knew, were her unspoken doubts.

I discovered the extent of her concern when Godfrey called not on a Sunday, and I could immediately detect in his line of conversation that Janey had primed him with accounts of my madness.

"I hear you think you have seen Sylvia," he began.

I confess, dear reader, that I walked clean out of the room and locked the door to my bedchamber behind me. My poor head was in such a mithering tangle I simply had not the patience to go over everything with Godfrey again. They did not understand. No one understood.

But Godfrey, bless his dear tender kind heart, stood at my door pleading with me for what must have been most of an afternoon, and remained even when I did not answer, declaring he had no intention of leaving until he saw me with his own eyes. It was only when, as a last resort, he threatened to send for Jasper that I opened the door.

He eyed me suspiciously.

"How do you do, H?" he asked.

"Ask the frog how the mouse does," I said in an agonised voice. "Ask the bat how does the owl! They do not know!" and I howled like a banshee and grabbed him by the elbows and danced round the room with him until I eventually decided to grant him mercy and said, "Ha! I had you there, I think!" and he perceived I had been fooling with him all the time (for I could at times smile at myself) and burst out laughing in relief.

"Come now, H, though," he said at last. "What's going on? What's all this about the dreaded Sylvia?"

He knew of course from my revelations at The Bear the fullest version of what had passed between us. I told him simply the little I had recently discovered.

"And you have a special affection for the young man concerned?" he asked in the kindest possible manner. "And a professional attachment to his uncle?" Damn dear Janey; she had clearly told all.

I sighed.

"Not anymore. That is all in the past. I have no axe to grind, none at all. I simply see a great wrong looming to those that were my friends, and remain good people, and would prevent it, but lack the means to do so."

Now it was Godfrey's turn to sigh.

"Let it go, H. Marry Jasper and forget everything else. Get out, while you have the chance. Look about you: unhappy things happen every day. See the beggars in Covent Garden, the poor skinny whores by Hatton Wall, the sad relics without number that are pulled from the river. You cannot save them all. It is not your calling. Your responsibility is to look after H."

I did not answer, for I knew the truth in what he said.

"What's the worst that can happen?" he continued. "Your lover boy marries a harridan. Happens every day. But consider the other side. What is Sylvia but a survivor, like you? Perhaps she will subside into a good respectable wife. You have no way of knowing."

Godfrey of course could not feel as keenly as I did – in fact I surprised myself by the strength of the feelings that rushed through my being the minute I clapped eyes on her again – about the woman who had shown me and my sister such cruelty. It was not, if I am honest, only that I wished to prevent her hurting those I believed to be good people; my personal pride was also piqued. If I could not have Charlie it seemed most unkind that the one who should have him was the only surviving author of my misfortune, indeed could be charged with setting me on the road which had dumped me down to this hidden economy, which prevented my dealing with respectable people on the square, and thus prohibited me from ever being considered in her place. And besides all that, if I were entirely and truly honest with myself, to think on Sylvia enjoying the benefit of the many bedroom tricks I had taught Charlie quite choked me.

I began to tell Godfrey of an idea I had worked out. I had seen in a play, and had heard of true cases besides, how a priest could be substituted with another person (say, an actor), thus producing a marriage that was in fact invalid, giving those who had reason to doubt the character of one or other of the parties time to produce their evidence, *or* giving the unworthy party to the marriage time to expose their devious ends. And would he be willing to help me out in such an endeavour?

"You are always about some plot or other, H!" exclaimed Godfrey with unusual fervour. "No more of your damned projects! Damn your stratagems! If you must play games do not drag in your friends. To rescue little Joe was fair enough, indeed an admirable and worthy enterprise I am proud to have undertaken, but this… this is an old score and you would do well to leave it unsettled. I will not help you. And there it is."

And he took his leave of me, and I cannot blame him for it.

66

can now see, of course, how unrealistic my plan must have seemed, but – and I freely acknowledge that I may yet have laboured under an illness of the mind – I found I could not leave it alone, as my friends had advised. The next day, which was the day before the proposed wedding, I took myself to Lord A's house. Janey had flatly refused to carry the message in my place and clearly considered the whole enterprise great folly. I had never approached his home before and had no wish to embarrass him but made it as plain to the footman as possible that I would not quit the step until his master came down to speak to me.

Lord A eventually emerged, vastly irate, and not at all pleased to see me.

"It is outrageous that you visit me here," he said, "and a clear abridgement of our bond."

"I thought you had dissolved our bond," I could not help saying, "but in any case, the warning I bring you does not enrich me. I come merely for your own good."

"What warning?" he asked.

"Miss Phipps is a charlatan. She is not an heiress. She was married to my cousin and is a most wicked woman. She will bring your family not a penny – nothing, in fact, but misery."

Although Lord A looked surprised, it was immediately

clear to me that he did not believe a word of it. I detected a woman's voice call him from within.

"I see that you have conceived a most inappropriate affection for Charlie," he said in a low and very angry voice, "and I believe you now wish to wreck this marriage by any means. I wish I had never set eyes on you. Go away, and do not bother us again or I will not hesitate to set the watch on you." He moved to close the door.

"If you do not abandon the marriage, I shall be there; I shall prevent it," I said.

Lord A looked horrified. The woman's voice called again.

"Do nothing," he said. "I will come to you." And he closed the door.

And indeed he did, only an hour or so later. Janey received him with a surly face, for she was both angry at the harsh way he had used me last time he was under our roof, and embarrassed at the trouble I was causing. I knew she would be listening at the door to our conversation, for she monitored what she perceived to be my madness like any nurse.

"I understand you think you have reason to raise an objection to my nephew's marriage tomorrow," he said patiently. "Please enlighten me."

And then I told him all I knew of Sylvia's character. He heard me out, and then declared that this person could not possibly be Sophia Phipps. I asked him on what authority he had formed his opinion of her character and background. Letters, he said. This he could see I scorned.

"And have you seen any records? Of her marriage? Of her fortune?"

"In common with many people, as you must know, all her records were lost in the great fire. As for proof of her fortune, I am gentleman enough to take the word of a lady."

"Do you not see it, sir?" I cried. "She could be anybody!"

"Even assuming your fairytale were true, why on earth would this woman wish to marry Charlie?" he demanded.

"I would guess that you have rather over-represented your

own fortune in this case," I said, not unkindly, and Lord A had the decency to blush a little, "and that she looks merely for an easy husband, a comfortable life and, in the long view, a title and a fortune. It is not such a strange ambition for a young woman."

"And what about you, H? Do you not want the same things? Is not all this nonsense prompted by you wanting to snare my nephew?"

"Now there I have the moral advantage," I replied, smiling a little sadly. "I appear to be the only one that knows there is no fortune, on either side. I never intended to see Charlie again, certainly not after his marriage. But I do love him; I cannot deny it and I cannot help it, and I cannot bear to see him enter into a marriage that will make his life a misery. I want him to be happy. That is all."

Lord A seemed to think for a while. Finally he said, "I do not now think you mean us harm, H, or that you are moved by vengeful reasons. But I think you are mistaken. However, you have warned me of what you believe to be a real threat to us. You have discharged what you perceive as your duty. Now please let the matter rest."

This, I recognised, meant he intended to do nothing to prevent the marriage.

"Allow me to offer one final solution," I said. "You sought this marriage purely for financial reasons, did you not? To save your estate?" He nodded ruefully. "What does she bring, then? Twenty, thirty thousand pounds?"

Lord A laughed.

"I wish it were so! Six, I believe, all told."

"I will give you the money," I said. This was my trump card.

Lord A said nothing for a moment as a strange expression came over his face, of having discovered a terrible truth.

"Dear God," he said huskily, and I perceived tears welled in his eyes. "You do love him. And it has made you mad." And he left without another word.

67

had deliberately remained calm during my last interview with Lord A as I did not want him to suspect that I still fully intended to stop the wedding if he did not stop it himself. If he were on the lookout for me I could find myself ejected from the church – perhaps even carried forcibly to a madhouse – before I had had the chance to act. Janey was also keeping a close eye on me, so I tried to appear normal, though I was extremely apprehensive at the thought of what I intended to do. Though even dear Nell had once suggested I might make an actress, because of my seeming confidence, I had been so shaken by the whole affair with Charlie that I pondered whether I would be able to stand up in church and speak in front of everybody. I had lost so much belief in myself that I began to wonder whether I really was insane, or at least a little unbalanced. The face I saw in my looking glass seemed a stranger to me, and bore a relation to myself that was at once distant and familiar, like a sister I had never met.

I set forth early in the morning so as to give Janey the slip. I walked for a long time before the city was properly awake, and it reminded me how the city had seemed during the plague year, with few people about, except that London now lacked the neglected, closed appearance it had then had. Also, in the early-risers, the milkmaids carrying their pails into the city and the carters bringing in their produce, there was the promise of the bustle, activity and business of the day ahead, which I had missed in the dead days of plague. This gave me courage, for it brought home to me how things could transform themselves, how my life had at other times seemed hopeless or miserable, but how fortune's wheel had turned again for me, and I now had a home, and money and a little family of sorts in Janey and Mary. Still, every time I rehearsed the speech I was to make, I shuddered, and felt quite ill with nervousness, and at those moments would have exchanged places with someone going to have a tooth pulled. I watched the sun rising over the river and consoled myself with the thought, as Evelyn had taught me to do when I was indeed once going to have a tooth pulled, that before it was high in the sky my ordeal would be over and I could get on.

Charlie had mentioned the name of the church and I knew the wedding was due to happen at ten o'clock, so I installed myself in an ordinary over the road, took a table in the window where I had a clear view, and ordered up a fine breakfast, for which I had a good appetite after my walk, which was spoiled only by some disagreeable coffee which tasted of soot and cinders.

The wedding party arrived just on the stroke of ten. I had decided to wait until the ceremony had begun before going into the church, thinking that if I went in quietly, they would be too engrossed in the service to notice me, and besides would have their backs to me. And so it proved. I was surprised there were not more people there – no one, of course, on Sylvia's side, but a rather portly maid of honour who stood beside her – and only Lord A, his wife and two elderly relations, as I supposed them, on Charlie's.

They had clearly got off to a late start, for the priest only now began with "Dearly beloved, we are gathered together here in the sight of God" and all that, words I had heard my father intone countless times. Lady A suddenly turned round, searching in a little bag and then drawing out a handkerchief. I noted what a sweet face she had, and Lord A had indeed said she had a most kindly and affectionate disposition, though she had a strong dislike for anything carnal, which was why he visited me, and it suddenly struck me that the revelation about Sylvia I was about to make would inevitably lead to other revelations. This sweet-faced lady would doubtless learn that for several years her husband had been regularly visiting a prostitute, otherwise what was my connection to the family? And even if he managed to muddy the waters concerning this... But I had no time to think, for the priest was already at the third cause of marriage, and after that... Before I could think what to do I heard the words: "Therefore if any man can show any just cause, why they may not lawfully be joined together, let him now speak, or else hereafter for ever hold his peace." I was shaking from head to toe and discovered I could not stand. The silence extended, as though giving me time to pull myself together. In my anxiety I dropped my prayer book. Only Sylvia turned round to see whence the noise came, and quickly turned back, and then the vicar began speaking again. No matter, I knew there was a second opportunity, despite the business of holding my peace for ever if I did not speak now. There was definitely a second opportunity, I felt sure I remembered.

But seeing her face had given me further pause for thought. This was not the angry selfish face I remembered, that had told me not to wrap my dead sister in one of the best sheets. This was the face of a hopeful young bride. Do not mistake me, it was definitely Sylvia, but it was a different Sylvia. Was Godfrey right? Was she merely making her way in the world, as I was? What right did I have to get in her way? To be brutally honest, as I now was with myself, I was not even sure that my evidence constituted a 'just impediment'. Usually a just impediment meant a pre-existing spouse. My 'just impediment' was that Sylvia represented herself as other than she was. But was it a crime to claim to be a virgin, when one had had a child? (And where was that child? I wondered.)

Was it a crime to change one's name, as she was about to do, anyway? Was it a crime to claim to be an heiress to a great fortune, when one was no such thing? The truth was, I did not know. I now trembled from head to toe, felt a fool, and was in a parlous state when the second, and final, opportunity for intervention occurred.

"I require and charge you both," intoned the priest, "as ye will answer at the dreadful day of judgement when the secrets of all hearts shall be disclosed, that if either of you know any impediment, why ye may not be lawfully joined together in Matrimony, ye do now confess it. For be ye well assured, that so many as are coupled together otherwise than God's Word doth allow are not joined together by God; neither is their Matrimony lawful."

I saw Charlie turn to Sylvia, and his dear profile opposed to her most hated one redoubled my strength. I dragged myself, with an immeasurable effort, to my feet. "At which day of Marriage," the priest continued, speeding up now, as this was so much dross to be got through, "if any man do allege and declare any impediment, why they may not be coupled together in Matrimony, by God's law, or the laws of this Realm; and will be bound, and sufficient sureties with him, to the parties." My head now spun as if I were drunk, and I tried to speak, but merely gaped like a fish out of water, and nothing came out but a squeak, and Lord A spun round with a most murderous expression, and I think recognised me, though I was right at the back of the church. "Or else put in a caution, to the full value of such charges as the persons to be married do thereby sustain, to prove his allegation: then the solemnisation must be deferred, until such time as the truth be tried." The priest finished and turned the page. I think I must have fainted, for I languished in my pew gasping for air when the most astonishing intervention occurred.

The door that I had opened so quietly was now flung open with a crash. I, and everyone else, turned to see, most astonishingly, Godfrey and another man burst into the church and march down the aisle. The other man I quickly recognised, though I had not seen him for several years, as my cousin Frederick.

"Hold!" he called, and I think the sound of his dear voice almost made me faint again. Was I dreaming? Sylvia turned white, and drooped like a dead white flower, for of course, I had at least sense enough to realise, Frederick was the spit of her dead abandoned husband.

"Hold!" he said again.

He made his way to the front of the wedding party and took a good look at the swooning bride.

"This woman is not Miss Sophia Phipps. This woman is Mrs Sylvia Hardcastle, widow of my late brother. Learn this of me as truth: she is a liar, a cheat, and as good as a murderer for her infamous conduct in our family. She is no heiress that I know of, or if she is, why has she sunk so low as to beg money from my mother, her mother-in-law, who has given her, out of human pity, an annuity merely to leave her in peace?"

I was too transfixed by this shock to take this moment to leave, as I should have done. Frederick handed Charlie a piece of paper. "Come and see me," he said, "and I will lay all the evidence before you." Then they both stormed back up the aisle. Frederick threw me a casual glance, and did not seem to recognise me, but Godfrey raised his eyebrows at me, before following my cousin out.

I left the church in a daze, while Lord A's family attempted simultaneously to revive, question and berate Sylvia, and was overtaken only by her maid of honour, who fairly fell over me in her haste to get away, and who I now recognised as Melissa, somewhat fatter.

68

felt very tired coming home and my nerves still jangled, for I had been in a state of anxiety for some days, and though the cause of the anxiety was now removed, I still felt ragged round the edges and jumpy. I wondered whether Janey would make me a bath, even though it was not Saturday, and thought she would, as she went out of her way to make me comfortable in what she considered to be my derangement. She would be as glad as I that the cause of all my disquiet was now resolved. But when I climbed the stairs to our rooms I found no sign of her. I went down again to Mrs Snags, who seemed always to be in a state of cheerful untidiness.

"Where's Janey?" I asked, after exchanging the usual pleasantries.

"I don't know, dear. She left you a message. She got me to write it down for you. Now where did I put it? Where did silly Mrs Snags put it, Mary?"

I saw that Mary was sitting in the corner playing with Mrs Snags's peg bag. "She has left Mary?"

"She just asked me to take care of her until you came back. I must say she looked a picture. We've had our dinner, haven't we, Mary?"

"How long will she be gone?" I asked, panic rising in me.

"She didn't say, but she took a trunk with her. That footman that's always in and out – he came for her."

William's footman! She had gone off with William! I left Mrs Snags rummaging for the note and bounded back up the stairs. Janey's best dress and bonnet were gone, but her trunk was still in her room. It did not make sense. Feeling sick to the very stomach I ran to my own room. I sank to my knees before the open cupboard door. The trunk containing our fortune had vanished.

I heard Mrs Snags calling up the stairs and made my way unsteadily down to her.

"Found it. Here we are." She carried the note to the window and read: "'Dear H, You are always saying as how I should think of myself and do what is best for me in my eyes and I have. Janey.' And then she said you were to look after the little one, but I didn't write that down." She looked up. "Oh dear, you do look queer. Sit down and I'll make you some tea. Oh look, here's another letter for you. It came last night. I had quite forgot. Silly Mrs Snags."

I gathered up Mary and carried her and the letter wearily upstairs. I was still in a state of shock, I think, at the extent of Janey's treachery. Had she taken her share of our hoard and gone without a word, it would have been a terrible blow, but to leave me without a penny! It was incredible. My misery was compounded by recognising my own foolishness in not anticipating this event. Had not Janey given me a hundred hints that she was considering leaving me for William? I should have debarred that servant of his from the house as soon as I realised what was afoot. And had I not, as she reminded me, told her over and over to put herself first and consider no one and nothing greater than her own interest? I was the author of my own misfortune, and this was the most galling of all. My throat actually ached from grief, from suppressing the sobs that I knew I could not express, for fear of never being able to stem the flow. How was Janey capable of such a thing? I asked myself repeatedly. How *could* she? And then

I remembered with a frisson how I had once cautioned myself never to entirely trust her, when I had seen her on the stage at the King's Playhouse, and realised what a consummate actress she really was.

My mind continued to race. It puzzled me why she had left Mary behind, though I was glad she had, for to lose both of them would have been a loss I do not think I could have recovered from. But as well as a blessing Mary was a burden, for how could I work and look after her? Janey had left us both to starve together, I thought bitterly. Thank God, I suddenly thought, for Jasper. Now I should have to marry him, and perhaps being a countess wouldn't be so bad as I thought. This made me smile, and then laugh, until I was crying at last.

Mary was as tired as I, and I lay down with her on the couch and must have slept for a while, for when I came to, it was getting dark. The recollection of Janey's desertion hit me as hard as ever, and I carried Mary to her own little bed and then realised I was hungry, for I had not eaten since my breakfast at the chop house. How very long ago that now seemed! And how far and how violently had fortune's wheel turned in that time!

As I lit the lamps in the kitchen, I was surprised to hear the front door opening, and footsteps running up the stairs. I could not face a visitor of any kind and considered remaining quietly in the kitchen and hoping whoever it was would go away. To my utter astonishment, Janey sailed into the kitchen, in her best dress and bonnet, grinning from ear to ear.

"Give me great joy, H," she shouted, "for you see before you a married woman!"

"Janey!" I gasped. "What are you doing here?"

"Where's Mary?" she asked, taking off her bonnet and slinging it across the table.

"Asleep," I said, still taken aback and mystified. "What made you come back?"

"I live here, don't I?" she said. "Now don't frighten me, H, by going completely off your head. What about some dinner?

We should celebrate." She took a bottle from the shelf and set about opening it.

"Janey, stop a minute! What's going on? Where's our trunk?"

"Oh, Thomas is bringing it up," she said. "I may say, I hoped you wouldn't miss it."

Thomas was William's footman. Why was he bringing it up? Why didn't she think I'd miss it?

"Janey, I don't understand any of this. I demand an explanation. You have married William, that much I understand—"

"William!" shrieked Janey. "Pffffffff! Not *William*! *Thomas*!"

And at that moment, Thomas dragged the trunk into the kitchen. He took his hat off and stood in front of me looking somewhat abashed.

"Are we forgiven, mistress?" he asked at last.

I was lost for words. I pointed dumbly at the trunk.

"Now, you mustn't mind, H, but I thought it the safest thing," said Janey. "I heard you offering to give it all away to stop your darling Charlie marrying that woman. Now, I couldn't risk that, could I? You haven't been quite right in the head, have you? Now, no, don't take on so, H. No tears now, please. This should be a happy day, shouldn't it?"

"Oh, yes!" I cried and embraced them both. "A most happy day!"

69

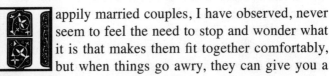appily married couples, I have observed, never seem to feel the need to stop and wonder what it is that makes them fit together comfortably, but when things go awry, they can give you a dozen reasons why. Happiness, perhaps, does not bear close examination. Evelyn once told me about the centipede who was asked how she walked: as soon as she thought about it she fell over. I believe happiness is the same. It is simply the state of things not going wrong.

The morning after the wedding that wasn't, and the wedding that was, I awoke with the intensest feelings of happiness because of things that hadn't happened, rather than because of things that had. Most of all, Janey had not betrayed and abandoned me. I decided there and then, as I drank my tea in bed, with Mary babbling away, that I would stop chasing after some future imagined happiness, and stop believing that I knew, better than other people, what would make them happy, and from now on would enjoy the very real happiness I had not valued, until I believed I had lost it. As Janey had said: what was I waiting for?

There was one thing I had decided upon, however, which I knew, without a shadow of a doubt, would make everyone who loved me happy, and that was to marry Jasper. The fact that Janey, who was as dear as a sister to me, had married without telling me made me realise how tyrannical my love had become. I knew she and Thomas and Mary would stay with me, but I had to set her free, free to make a proper home and perhaps have more children, and she would not see me live alone. Also Godfrey could stop worrying about me, as I knew he did. (Jasper of course, would be, as he had said, the happiest man alive.) My adventure with Charlie, I now saw, was the clearest warning that I had to get out of the old game; that I simply didn't have the right kind of heart for it anymore.

As I dressed I decided to write at once to my remaining lovers and regretfully inform them of my coming marriage, and also to Jasper to accept his proposal. I wondered for a moment whether I should write to him first, and be assured he really did intend to go through with it, before I burned my boats, and it was as I was thus deliberating that I felt in my pocket the letter Mrs Snags had given me the day before. In all my grief at believing Janey gone, and then my joy at discovering her not gone, I had completely forgot it. I had not even noticed it was in Godfrey's hand.

My dearest H,
I write in haste to beg you not to interfere in any way with your friend's wedding tomorrow.

Of course, I reasoned, Mrs Snags had said the letter arrived the night before yesterday and I had gone out so early in the morning she could not give it to me.

I do not have time to explain fully now but I have been so concerned about you and what you might do that I told Frederick about Sylvia's reappearance and he immediately declared his intention of putting the facts concerning her before your friend's family. However I need to know your friend's address, or failing that, when and where the marriage is to take place, so please send this information at once.

This explained why they had arrived at the church as if in a play, quite at the eleventh hour, having presumably had to find these things out themselves.

I would come in person, but I am sorry to say that your aunt has suffered a relapse and seems to be sinking fast. I entreat and beg you to consider coming to see her as soon as you can, as it may be, I fear, your last chance.

Etc. etc.,

Godfrey.

Poor Aunt Madge. I wished desperately to see her, and comfort her, yet also wished desperately for her not to see me. At last I understood the expression on Godfrey's face that had puzzled me as he left the church the day before – it had seemed a kind of questioning look, meaning: would I go? What flim-flam he had told Frederick in order to explain how he knew about Sylvia's relationship to our family, I could not begin to imagine, but guessed with a sinking feeling that he must have mentioned my existence and involvement somewhere along the line as even I could not think of a good enough lie to cover that one.

"What's the matter?" asked Janey, seeing my face as she scooped up Mary, "Someone nicked your trunk?" This was a tart reference to some rather uncomfortable exchanges the evening before when it dawned on Janey that I had suspected her of making off with our money.

"Don't Janey. My aunt is dying. Godfrey thinks I should go to her."

Janey put her free arm around me and Mary put her little arm round my neck, and laid her head on my shoulder and said "aunt". Janey and I looked at each other in astonishment and then laughed (and as usual I wept a little). It was her very first word.

70

s the carriage turned into the street where my aunt and Godfrey lived, I realised how very ill she must be, for the road outside had been laid with rushes, to dull the noise of traffic for her comfort. By the time I was standing on the doorstep I was trembling from head to toe. The door opened to reveal Reg Potter, who asked my name, before his face lit up with surprise and delight.

"Miss H! Come in, come in! Mr Godfrey hoped you might come. Well I can barely credit it, after all these years! What a fine-looking lady you've grown into. If you don't mind me saying," he added hastily. And we stood staring at each other for a moment, and then he said, "It is so very good to see you again, Miss, albeit on such a sad occasion. Or is it missus now?" And then Ted appeared and we greeted each other all over again.

"You'll want to see Mr Godfrey first, I suppose," said Ted, and they took me into a great room, where Godfrey sat at a desk and a dark young man stood beside him.

"H!" Godfrey jumped up and embraced me. "Be good fellows and fetch some tea would you?" he said to the Potters, who disappeared.

"Joe!" I exclaimed, suddenly recognising him. His prettiness not quite gone, he promised to be a very handsome young man.

He recited, smiling, in a clear strong voice:

"Fair stood the wind for France

When we our sails advance,

Nor now to prove our chance,

Longer will tarry."

"Well remembered, Joe! My, how you have grown. Shouldn't you be at school... or something?"

Joe kissed me, smiling bashfully.

"Joe and school didn't quite agree," said Godfrey, and I remembered he never was a very apt pupil. "Freddie has been tutoring him at home."

"Ah, yes, Frederick," I said, all my discomfort returning. "What have you told him? And Aunt Madge? What does she know?"

"H, it is a long story and I fear we do not have much time. Go up and see her, and we will talk over tea after. She knows nothing and is not expecting you, as I could not be sure you would come, at the last."

Godfrey led me up the magnificent staircase that I remembered admiring the last time I was there, when Godfrey had been so poor he had been selling his furniture to feed himself. He led me along a broad corridor, opened the door at the end of it, and bade me go in. He remained outside. The room was quite dark, though I could see Aunt Madge lying in bed, apparently asleep, looking much smaller than I remembered her, and Frederick sitting beside her. Seeing me, he got up. He looked older, sadder than I had noticed at the church.

"H!" he exclaimed, but quietly. "This is a surprise indeed," though he did not look surprised. "She will be so glad to see you," he said to me, but his own face expressed no gladness. "You need to speak up, as she is quite deaf." He beckoned me to sit by the bed, and then had gone out before I realised I had not said anything to him at all.

I did not wish to wake her, so sat reading her dear face

for a time, revelling in every old detail and noting every new. Eventually she stirred, and I took her small hand in my own.

"Aunt Madge?" I said.

"Who's there?" she asked in a small quavering voice. "Who's there?"

"It is H," I said. "Your niece, H?"

"Who?" she asked.

I repeated what I had said, louder.

"Good girl," she smiled, a beatific smile, but her eyes remained closed. "You have been gone a long time. Did you get the message?"

I had no idea what the message might be.

"The message? What about, Aunt?"

"The ribbon."

"The ribbon?"

"For Evelyn's bonnet," she chuckled. "She should have pink, not green. Pink is more gay."

"Yes," I said, and unsuccessfully fought back tears.

She must have heard me snivelling, for she said softly: "Don't cry, H. It will all be the same in a hundred years."

"I love you, Aunt," I said and kissed her hands.

"Good girl," she said, though her voice was getting weaker. "It is good to love."

She slipped back into sleep, and once I had satisfied myself that her breaths were regular, I made my way back downstairs.

I found Godfrey and Joe in the drawing room.

"She is asleep," I said.

"Did she know you?" asked Godfrey.

"I think so, but she was not making sense. She seemed comforted, anyway."

Godfrey sighed and poured me a dish of tea.

"It is increasingly the way. I think it is the draught the doctor gives her, for the pain. She rambles in her thoughts, but sometimes she is quite lucid." He cleared his throat. "It will not be long now, H. Will you stay, to the end?"

71

immediately sent word to Janey not to expect me back, perhaps for a few days. Besides making myself useful here, I considered the newlyweds might be grateful to pass their honeymoon without me playing the gooseberry. Frederick had gone out on a business matter, giving us an opportunity to speak freely and I begged Godfrey to tell me what Frederick and the Potters knew of my history since I had left Cheapside, so I should not put my foot in it.

"I do not know what the Potters guess," said Godfrey, "but I have only recently told them that you and I are old friends, that you have had a very unhappy time since you left the family and that you did not like to talk about it. They were amazed to learn that you were the little painted lady who got Aunt Madge out of the house during the fire, and then both affected to have guessed as much, of course. They were outraged to hear of Sylvia's tricks and delighted we were able to prevent her entrapping an innocent young man. She had made quite a nuisance of herself to your aunt some while back, as I think you know; in fact, that was the beginning of her ill health. So, as I say, I do not know what they surmise, but they have only ever spoken well of you. From what I know of them they are clever enough to come to their own conclusions, and good enough not to trouble themselves about it, above being most glad to learn you were alive and well."

This was a relief, for though the Potters were merely servants in the greater scheme of things, they had been good friends to me and Evelyn, indeed, had been the last to abandon us at Cheapside, and were devoted to my aunt, and their opinion mattered very much to me.

"And Frederick?" I asked, dreading this answer far more. "What does he know?"

Godfrey and Joe looked at each other.

"Well, H, you know I vowed I would never tell Frederick all your story," began Godfrey, "and was only forced to admit to your existence and to our friendship when I had to warn him about Sylvia's skulduggery, as it was clear I had no independent way of knowing of her previous connection to your other cousin. At that time I simply told him I was bound by a solemn promise not to give him any further details of you, or your whereabouts."

"And you have not told him since?" I asked.

"No," said Godfrey.

I did not feel as glad to hear this news as I had expected. I think I had half-hoped that Godfrey would have at least prepared the ground for me in some way, although this would have meant him breaking his word to me.

"So am I to understand he knows nothing?" I asked.

Godfrey and Joe looked at each other again.

"He knows everything, H," said Godfrey.

"But you said you had not told him!" I exclaimed.

"I did not tell him!" insisted Godfrey.

"I told him," said Joe, quietly.

I stared at Joe.

"Why? And what… "

"I saw the awful difficulty Godfrey was in, because of his promise to you, and Frederick was becoming angry and fearful of what had happened to you, and wanted very much to find you again. He could tell I knew something, and saw

I refused to tell, but then he said Godfrey was bound by his word of honour as a gentleman, but I was bound by the greater ties of kinship, for I was in fact Aunt Madge's stepson, for my father and his mother were married, and that made us brothers. And even if we weren't brothers by blood, you were cousin to us both, and he begged me as I loved you, and as I loved him, to tell him everything. And so I did."

I looked at Godfrey as if to ask whether 'everything' actually meant '*everything*', and he shrugged and nodded, as if it probably did, and looked at me, pursing his lips. We all fell quiet for a while, considering the new state of things.

"How did he take it?" I asked, at last.

Godfrey and Joe looked at each other again; their tacit alliance was beginning to irritate me and I felt excluded.

"He has not spoken of it since," said Joe uncomfortably.

"There has been very little time," Godfrey said kindly. "We were trying to find out where this accursed wedding was occurring, and Aunt Madge has been so ill… "

"He does not wish to speak of it," I said. "And I cannot blame him." I sighed. "And neither do I blame you, Joe. I had put you both in a hard place. The chickens have finally come home to roost."

I sipped my tea and found it had gone cold.

72

rederick seemed to avoid my company as far as possible over the next three days and barely spoke to me. The four of us took turns to sit by Aunt Madge so she was never alone, and when it was neither my shift nor his, he always found some business to occupy himself, whether it was tutoring Joe or tending to some domestic or legal matter. Though Godfrey said he had hardly got a word out of him either, and that Frederick's spirits were greatly depressed by his mother's condition, I felt Godfrey was finding excuses. I saw this was Frederick's way of dealing with me, and respected it.

I was cheered by a letter from home, that is to say when I had eventually deciphered it, for it was clearly penned by Thomas, whose grasp of the written word proved only slightly stronger than Janey's.

DEAR H.
All is well here Mary has had a cold and asks for her ant that is to say yr. self. Missus snaggs says what cheer.

The owl has been and frets for an anser we have not told him of yr. werabouts he is mity cast down but Jany thinks he wil live.

Hoping yr. sad trail will soon be over and yr. ant
will RIP.
Love from yr. friends Jany Thomas Mary xxx

Old Dr Rookham attended my aunt daily, prescribing ever
greater doses of tincture of opium, and though he greeted me
most courteously he never asked me any questions, which
made me think he had been primed not to. I learned from
Godfrey that Mr Fluke still lived and had been to say his good-
bye to his dear old dinner companion Aunt Madge.

Aunt Madge drifted in and out of consciousness and
usually confined her conversation with me to urgent millinery
matters, to be conveyed to Evelyn; but on the last day, when
she was weaker, yet more clear in her mind than I had seen
her, she spoke of her dead husbands.

"I have often wondered," she said thoughtfully, her eyes
closed as usual, so I had just believed her asleep, "which of
my husbands will be my husband in the life after this."

"That's a good question," I said. "But I do not know that
you should worry yourself about it now."

"Oh, I'm not worrying. Just wondering."

I was about to ask whether she had a preference but stopped
myself just in time.

"I should like to see my parents again," she said. "But will
I be a child? They were younger than I am now when they
died. How will it all work?"

"I don't know, Aunt," I said, feeling most unequal to the
theological turn her thoughts had taken.

"Will Roger be there?" she asked.

Roger. At one time the name would have made me shudder.
Now all that mattered was that Aunt Madge was not troubled,
if it could be helped.

"I should think so," I said lightly. "Leading them all a
merry dance, I expect."

She chuckled softly.

"And Evelyn," I said.

"No, not Evelyn," she chided me. "She is just gone out to buy lace." She fell silent for a while. "You never knew my first husband, did you, my dear?"

I said I thought he had died when I was young, if not before I was born.

"Cecil. A good man. He really wanted to marry your mother, but our father said as I was the eldest, it had to be me or neither of us. He did not want to be left with an old maid on the shelf, he said. I was nineteen years of age! Old maid indeed. But he settled for me and was a good enough husband. He gave me my dear boys. He died in the wars of course, poor Cecil. But Harry! He was a husband and a half!" she chuckled again, in a way which for a moment recalled clear as day the old, unbuttoned Aunt Madge, who would hoik up her skirts before the fire to warm her legs, or sit with her feet on the mantelpiece, unbending herself with me and my sister after some play, or dinner.

"Would you fetch me a book from the library, dear?" she asked suddenly.

"Of course, Aunt," I said, surprised for I had not yet seen her open her eyes, let alone attempt to read. But strange fancies sometimes took her, and we humoured them to soothe her. "Which book?"

"No matter," she sighed, seeming to change her mind, as she often did.

I picked up my sewing again.

"Why do you not fetch it, H?" she asked.

"Sorry Aunt. I thought you said it did not matter."

She smiled slightly.

"I meant it does not matter which book you bring. Mind it is an old one, though."

I returned a few moments later with a well-worn book of poetry I remembered from Cheapside. She took it in her hands and, still not opening her eyes, held it to her face, opened it, and inhaled deeply. She repeated this several times and appeared to derive great satisfaction from so doing.

"It's almost gone. But it's still there," she said weakly. "It smells of him."

She let the book fall out of her hands onto the counterpane. I took her hand in one of mine and the book in the other and sniffed it experimentally. Very faintly I detected the once familiar scent of cinnamon and cloves. When I looked up again, I saw those glittering clear grey eyes looking at me. I felt I should call the others at once, as I sensed the end was nigh, but was torn as I did not wish her to pass away alone, while I was gone. Should I stay or should I go? Should I call to them, or would that alarm her? Death seemed as mercilessly full of dilemmas as life. Finally, I managed to stretch out to reach the bell-pull without letting go her hand.

"I'm so glad you came, my dear," she said very softly. "But I am afraid I must be going." Frederick, Godfrey and Joe came in quietly and stood by me as her breathing slowed until it stopped and then with a great emotionless sigh her life was over. We all shed tears, but Joe wept most bitterly of all, repeating "She was so good to me," and it was most touching to observe how Frederick comforted him, like a true brother.

73

e made a sad table at dinner. The four of us had not eaten together in all the time I had been there, and now none of us had any appetite. The Potters and the maids were all upset too and there were many red eyes round the house. Godfrey and Frederick began to discuss the funeral arrangements. My sisters were to be informed at Frederick's insistence, as apart from those present these were my aunt's only surviving relations. He did not look at me while he spoke of them. My brother-in-law Reverend Grimwade would, he guessed, assume control of the service.

"Dr Rookham and Mr Fluke will of course want to come. Do you have anyone you should like to bring, H?" asked Frederick, for once looking me straight in the eye. "For moral support perhaps?" I could not detect whether there was an edge to the moral part, for he was cold with grief.

"I... I... I had not thought to go myself... " I began.

"Oh, but you must!" exclaimed Godfrey.

"Yes, H, please," implored Joe. "For us."

"H must do as she sees fit, of course," said Frederick, returning his attention to his plate. "But if she prefers not to come alone, that is quite understandable." I could not tell whether this was an attempt at kindness, so I could represent myself to my family as a respectable married woman, perhaps, or a hint that I should.

"Thank you," I said at last. "I will think on it."

In my room at Lincoln's Inn Fields that night I thought on it to the point of not being able to sleep. In the end I got up and decided to go home. I was going in the morning anyway and tossing and turning here all night was only so much time wasted. I wanted my own bed and my little family about me. I had only brought a small bag with me, so quickly packed, and then crept along to Godfrey's room to see whether he was awake. Under the door I saw that a light burned within, so I opened the door as quietly as I could and you may imagine my surprise to find not one sleeping figure, but two in Godfrey's bed. Intrigued (or spying, as Evelyn would doubtless have observed), I moved closer to see who his bedfellow was.

You may imagine my astonishment when I realised that it was Frederick! And this was no convenient bunking together of companions for the night, either. For a start, Frederick had his own perfectly serviceable room, and for a finish, the way Godfrey's arms encircled him, his leg casually thrown over Frederick's – and the pair of them as naked as the day they were born – this was love! I made my way back to my room as quietly as I could and found myself wiping tears from my face. I was happy that Godfrey had a special friend and Frederick had a special friend, and then of course many things Godfrey had said fell into place. Frederick was such a capital fellow from the beginning in his book, and it explained why, though Frederick had always been very kind and affectionate to myself and Evelyn, I recalled there had been a strictly brotherly quality to his dealings with all women of whom he was fond, and I never saw him flirt. Even Godfrey flirted. But then, I reflected, Godfrey was another kettle of fish. And I confess my tears were mixed, as I finally admitted a little part of me had once been hoping one day to be something more than I was to Godfrey. I had a little picture in my mind of a day in the park when he and I had been playing with our god-daughter and Godfrey had looked at me in a tender way that seemed to say that we could, in another life perhaps, have been a real family. I admitted to feeling a sharp bright pang of what must have been jealousy.

I scolded myself for my self-pity, and quickly scribbled a note to Godfrey. It only told him I had gone home and I awaited advice as to the funeral details, and I had thought mischievously of adding 'aha!' or some such foolery to show I had found him out, but I decided leaving the note on the table beside his bed would be quite mischief enough.

I found a carriage easily and realised my happiness about my discovery was now unmixed. I slipped into the house at St James's without waking anyone and crept to my bed feeling most surprisingly contented, considering that my aunt had died that day. I fell asleep comforted by the warmth entwining Godfrey and Frederick, and hoping my aunt had found her second husband in Heaven and that they both now lay together as newlyweds in a fragrant bed of mixed spices.

74

spent the next few days looking after Mary as much as possible, to enable Janey and Thomas to have something of a holiday. I had decided I would go to Aunt Madge's funeral, and I would go alone. I knew I could have taken Jasper, and would have been protected by the cloak of wealth and status his presence would afford, but my new resolve was strengthened by having been reconciled with Aunt Madge, which had made me realise that, in the end – at the end of life, that is to say – none of the things I had worried about her worrying about really mattered. It is said that good timing is everything, and though I had happened to come home at the time that reconciliation with my aunt was easiest, it had in a sense buoyed me up, as I felt I was on a tide of change. And if I cared about what people thought of my actions, I simply had to take that on the chin. I had done my best, in the circumstances, and though I may have lived a wicked life longer than I needed to, I had begun my wicked ways as an alternative to starving to death, and was now barely qualified to lead any other. Please understand that I do not mean I in any sense walked in pride – quite the reverse – but I was prepared to bear any humiliation my family felt entitled to pile upon me. I am what I am, I thought, as they are what they are. We were all only trying to do our best. The only difference, in my case, was that I had done my best with an eye to the watchman on the corner, as they say.

On the appointed day, needless to say, all this confidence deserted me, and I lay in bed for as long as possible, until Janey shouted at me to get up, for she and Thomas were intent on coming with me for "immoral support", and Janey never liked to be late. (It might be fashionable to be late, she maintained, but it was still late.) Though I intended to wear a plain black dress, Janey laid out my new black silk and a beautiful black lace mantilla I had never worn and indeed had forgot I had, and said if I was going to do this, I was going to do it in style, with my lady's maid and my footman in attendance. So we left Mary with Mrs Snags, who approvingly remarked that we looked like a regular household for once, and put our best feet forward.

As it turned out, we were late anyway, as our coach lost a wheel about a quarter-mile from the church, giving us all a horrid jolt, and Thomas decided it would be quicker to walk the rest of the way, and took a shortcut he knew which turned out to be a shortcut to getting entirely lost, and it was only when we ended up exactly where the coach had broken down that he finally capitulated to Janey's repeated entreaties to merely ask of someone the right road.

The service was already well underway by the time we arrived at the church, and the sight of my brother-in-law in the pulpit made me instantly queasy and I found myself trembling. It might as well have been my dead father standing there, as nothing about Reverend Grimwade's chilly exterior suggested that something so vulnerable as a human heart might beat beneath. How Frederick had been persuaded to accept this arrangement, I had no idea. I saw Reg and Ted Potter behind everyone else, and we took our seats with them. Then I began to look about me and recognised the family members I had not seen for so long. Clarissa must have arrived early to ensure they would occupy the front pew, as she was ever careful to make everyone aware of her vast importance in the world.

Next to her I saw Diana and Mr Pincher, the wife-beater. Behind them was a woman I judged might be Grace – dear long-lost Grace – who had a small child with her, and next to her a gentleman I did not know.

On the other side of the aisle, and directly in front of me, I could only see the backs of a number of gentlemen, among whom I knew must be Frederick, Godfrey, Joe and Mr Fluke. As I was trying to identify others I knew, I recognised the unforgettable nape of a neck I had kissed many times and my heart lurched as I knew it to belong to Charlie. Looking more carefully I saw that Lord A sat beside him. And beside him was that great dunderhead Jasper! Why on earth were they here? And I was sorry that I could not see my sister Frances anywhere.

Janey had been strictly prohibited from speaking, a precaution amply justified by the fact that her whispered remark that my sister Clarissa (who had turned round to see who was there) had "a face like a slapped arse" was perfectly audible even to my brother-in-law in the pulpit. I scowled at her and Thomas pinched her so hard she squeaked, but she was silent for the rest of the service, except for exclaiming, "Blind me, not another bleeding hymn!" before 'All Praise To God Who Reigns Above'. But fortunately, this blasphemy was largely covered by the noise of the congregation scrambling to its feet.

It was only when Dr Rookham got up to deliver the eulogy that the atmosphere was truly imbued with the memory of Aunt Madge, for he spoke with great warmth of her kindness, her hospitality, and her humour, and it was most affecting to see Joe's shoulders shaking, and Frederick put his arm round him, and Godfrey put his arm round Frederick.

When it was time to follow the coffin out to the churchyard, Clarissa again assumed precedence over her sisters, fairly pushing Diana and her husband out of the pew, so that she was only behind Frederick at the head of the file of mourners. We, of course, would be last to leave, being at the back, and my sisters seemed to know me as they passed me, though I was glad I was veiled, for I hardly knew what face to wear. Diana had clearly given no good account of me, for Clarissa threw me a haughty look of disgust, while Diana herself treated me to a baleful glare. Grace and her friend were obscured from view by Godfrey and Joe; then came the elderly gentlemen, followed by Lord A, Charlie and Jasper, each of whom honoured me with a slight bow as they passed. I still could not fathom what, or who, had brought them there.

It began to rain as Reverend Grimwade finished the ashes to ashes etc. and after the last amens had been said, Frederick addressed the assembly, entreating everyone to cross the road to the Lamb and Flag, where we would partake of custard tarts and claret, two of his mother's favourite things, and hear the will read. I gained the opportunity to snatch Godfrey aside and quiz him about this as we made our way thither, as I had not thought of the will, and he said it was going to be done next week, but Clarissa had asked if it could be done today, to save them all the trouble of coming back into town again.

"Pfffff!" said Janey. "No wonder it was such a good turnout."

75

hen we had all filed into a large and pleasant upper room in the Lamb and Flag there was a brief hiatus as everyone stood around not quite knowing what to do, as it was for Frederick to set the tone and he and Godfrey and Joe with the aid of the Potters were involved in a complex negotiation with the landlord about an insufficiency of chairs. Grace and her man friend had gone into another room, presumably to see to the child, and I took the opportunity to remove my veil. I was suddenly aware that every pair of eyes in the room was trained upon me.

"Well," declared Lord A, who was the sort of man likely to have an easy pleasantry for every occasion, "bless me if we are not all got here like characters at the end of a play!"

"Well said, sir!" said Jasper. "And if it were a comedy, it should by rights end in a wedding!" he offered amiably, looking rather meaningfully at me, and seeing no help there, grinning round the company.

"*If* it were a comedy," Clarissa's husband intoned disapprovingly, as though he were still in the pulpit, "and not a funeral."

Jasper looked suitably abashed, and Clarissa and Diana tut-tutted like a pair of hens. The uncomfortable silence descended once more. I had decided I would not make the first move towards any of my family, for fear of embarrassing

355

them, but would be receptive to any approach, and of course most earnestly hoped for this. Everyone seemed to be looking at me again, except for Clarissa and Diana, who had their heads together most ominously.

For once in her life, perhaps in recognition of the awesome atmosphere, Janey only muttered: "Who do you have to fuck to get a drink round here?" and in one elegant movement Thomas stood on her foot, while drawing out a chair for me, saying:

"Will you have a seat, mistress?"

This prompted the other gentlemen to see the ladies seated and after a brief murmuring and scraping of chairs everyone fell again into a merciless silence.

At that moment Grace and her gentleman came in, and Grace, bless her, fairly fell upon me, showering me with endearments and greetings, and we kissed and wept a little, and then I was not a little surprised to be most familiarly embraced by her friend, and seeing I was somewhat taken aback, Grace said: "It's Frankie, you silly! Your sister Frances!"

And indeed it was. The boy who had walked away from our house in Hunsdon to go for a soldier had come to London a man! Not that she was in any actual sense a man, of course, but she wore man's clothes and carried herself like a man.

"Blind me!" everyone heard Janey whisper to Thomas, "And I thought *my* family were a rum lot!" In all the tumult, Grace's little boy began to cry. "Give it here," said Janey, taking the child easily from Grace. "Talk to your sister. We'll be downstairs," and Thomas obediently followed her out.

"Well, what are you doing now?" I asked Frankie.

"I keep a little inn at Wapping," she said. "The Mermaid."

I knew it well from the old days. It was in Damaris Page's stamping ground and a favourite resort of the faithful old sea captain I had entertained at Mother Cresswell's.

"Well, it's no life at sea for a woman," she continued, as it turned out she had been to sea many times as a soldier, "but I know what sailors want when they come ashore – grog and home comforts." Then she lowered her voice and added, for my ears only, "I give 'em the grog, and Gracie takes care of the home comforts, one way and another."

I wondered briefly whether she was well acquainted with my old sea captain but decided this was neither the time nor place to ask.

"Well, it's so good to see you Frankie," I said, "and you, Grace. And what a dear little child you have."

"Oh we both dote on him, don't we Grace? He's down to inherit The Mermaid. Well, there ain't no father to be certain of and we don't want him going for a sailor, that's for sure," said Frankie, who I realised was oblivious to the prevailing sense of decorum, or perhaps, was above or below it, for although Diana and Clarissa had done their best to encourage a babble of light conversation to obscure our proceedings, one could almost see ears bending towards our corner.

"I guess you've had no easy journey either," Grace said quietly to me. "I was very sorry to hear about Evelyn. It must have been very hard for you, you and her being so close. And then you having to fend for yourself, as it were." At this she squeezed my hand.

Very touched by their delicate acknowledgment of my history, I thanked them and then Frankie rejoined, confidentially, "Listen H, Grace and I aren't really wanted here," and though I began to protest she continued. "No, H. We only came to pay our respects to Auntie and in the hopes of seeing you. Why don't we wait below and see you after? Catch up a bit? If you've a mind?"

I said that I very much had a mind, as I had a thousand questions, and Frankie asked me to give their very earnest condolences to Frederick before latching Grace's arm on to her own, and with a polite nod and a slight bow towards Clarissa and Diana in turn, they were gone. Clarissa and Diana both looked mightily affronted by being acknowledged publicly by such disreputable specimens as these two sisters, and more than ever seemed to me nothing more than a pair of silly chickens clucking in disapproval. The overall effect had been to make me care less than ever for their opinion. Frankie and Grace had shown me more affection in a single minute than they had deigned to dispense so far. My heart was hardened enough to bear anything from them now, or so I thought.

"Thank God they are gone," I heard Clarissa say to Diana's husband.

"Monstrous," he agreed.

76

ortunately, Frederick and Godfrey now returned, Frederick apologising for the delay. And with the arrival of the host, and the circulation of the claret, the conversation became easier. My heart sank as I saw Frederick, with Godfrey in tow, approach Clarissa – now the poison would start to flow in earnest. After an exchange of introductions and condolences I heard Frederick ask, quite loudly, as though to ensure everyone heard the conversation: "Will you not greet your sister, Clarissa?"

"There is no sister of mine present but Diana," said Clarissa, delighted at the opportunity to show her quality. Godfrey looked as though he would say something, but bit his lip.

"But surely you have seen your sister, H, is here?" Frederick pressed on, mercilessly, affecting puzzlement.

"I do not recognise her," said Clarissa.

"She is dead to us," added Diana, wishing to be in at the kill. Godfrey could hold his tongue no longer.

"How can you be so heartless? If you were a man I should knock you down!" he exclaimed, furious.

"If *you* were a man I should let you!" rejoined Diana's husband.

"Well, I suppose it would save *you* the trouble, you brute!" snarled Godfrey.

All conversation had ceased. It was too quiet even for me to make my exit, as I now dearly wished to, before matters could get any worse. But a hand on my arm detained me.

"What a long time it's been, Miss H!" said Dr Rookham kindly, and shook me warmly by the hand. "Mr Fluke is keen to see you too."

"I fear my being here is an embarrassment to everyone," I said quietly.

"Nonsense, dear girl," he replied, but Clarissa and Diana continued to look as though there was a bad smell in the room, such as a dead rat under the floorboards (which in a way, of course, there was). By contrast Diana's husband, Lord A, Charlie and Jasper were engaged in an animated and friendly conversation – "I had only gone to borrow a book!" exclaimed Mr Pincher, to much laughter – when Clarissa, learning that there were titles in the room fairly fell over Diana in her haste to get to them first. She clasped hold of her brother-in-law as though he were a very large unruly puppy and bade him effect the introductions.

She then asked Lord A whether he knew Lords X and Y, who were "very dear friends", but dropped him like a hot coal when she realised Jasper outranked him and was soon all over him like a swarm of bees.

"'Tis a plaguey day, a most unlucky day," sighed Jasper.

"Did you know dear Aunt Margaret long, my lord?" Clarissa fluttered.

"Never met the old girl, sorry to say. Sounds a proper peach, though."

"So, may I ask your lordship," asked Clarissa's husband, "why you have honoured us with your presence today?"

"Me? Oh, friend of H," said Jasper simply.

"Friend of H?" Clarissa exclaimed. "H?"

"But I must pay my compliments to that lady," said Jasper, indicating Diana, sitting with only a large plate of custard tarts for company.

"So must I," added Charlie hastily, and they abandoned the

astonished couple. Diana regarded their approach with horror, and looked about to see where her husband was.

"Madam, I feel sure we have met before – " began Jasper.

"No, no, I am quite sure I have never seen either of you gentlemen before," she said, looking quite terrified.

"But surely you recall our dancing lesson?" asked Charlie.

"No, I assure you!" Diana insisted. Then, seeing her husband approach, she hissed: "I have never been at H's house. Please do not talk to me."

Somewhat baffled, Jasper and Charlie retired to recharge their glasses.

"Bit of a puzzle, what?" mused Jasper. "She don't know H, she don't know us. Do you think she lacks it up here, poor girl?" he tapped his forehead.

At that moment Godfrey appeared with a drink for me and I took the opportunity to ask him why Lord A, Charlie and Jasper were present.

"Frederick asked them," he said.

"Why?" I asked, wondering what further humiliation Frederick had in store for me.

"Lord A came to see Frederick the day after the intervention in the wedding. He was extremely grateful for it. He has since been making enquiries about Sylvia and has discovered everything he had told him was true. Moreover, she has vanished, and there is no more clue as to whither she has gone, than to whence she came, compounding her guilt. He asked whether there was anything he could do for Frederick in return for helping his family make such a narrow escape from that witch, and Frederick said it was all your doing, and any thanks were due to you, and if he wanted to help you, he and Charlie should come here today and support you. So here they are."

"But why should Frederick care about me?" I asked.

"H! You are his cousin! He knew you feared the family would give you a rough ride and he wanted you to have friends here. So I asked Jasper as well."

I still did not understand.

"But if all this is true, why does Frederick try to humiliate me? Why did he so publicly invite Clarissa to address me, knowing that she wouldn't?"

"He didn't know she wouldn't, I'd guess," said Godfrey. "I think he hoped he could press her into it, by asking her publicly. In his eyes I believe her refusal humiliated no one but herself."

"But he has been so cold towards me ever since I came to Lincoln's Inn! I confess I cannot credit this change of heart." I could not puzzle it out at all. Then, just as suddenly as this little flame of hope that Frederick did not hate me had ignited, it was extinguished as an awful explanation dawned on me. "It is because he knows I know," I said.

"It is because he knows you know what?" sighed Godfrey, not a little exasperated.

"About you and him!" I said.

Godfrey laughed.

"Ah, yes, your little goodbye note. That was very naughty of you, H."

"So that is why he has changed his tune and now is kind to me. He thinks I am so low as to raise a fuss – to blackmail him, even."

"Hold, hold!" said Godfrey, and it was one of the few times I ever saw him angry with me. "You do him wrong. He does not know you know. I got rid of the note before he saw it. He would not know it would make no difference to your opinion of him. His mother had just died. I didn't want to add to his cares. I will tell him by and by." At that moment Joe came and kissed me and said the will was about to be read and I asked him to summon those who had gone below. Seeing I was alone at last, Jasper pounced.

"Stand and deliver!" he exclaimed, pointing two invisible pistols at me. "I demand the price of one broken heart, madam, payable immediately! Well if it ain't… Miss H!" he remembered himself just in time, dropping a low bow.

"Thank you for coming, Jasper," I said, surprised at how touched I was to see his smiling stupid self.

"Oh the pleasure's all mine – anything to be of service. Gadzooks! You don't look half bad when you're done up a bit, H! You should wear black more – suits your shape – doesn't make your arse look half so big." And with such endearments Jasper led me to a seat as the family assembled before Mr Fluke, the lawyer. Janey and Thomas returned and told us that Grace and Frankie had gone home for the child's sake, but that we were welcome to join them at The Mermaid afterwards, and bring what friends we liked and they would treat us to a dinner.

s expected, the bulk of Aunt Madge's fortune passed directly to Frederick, but she also left ten guineas to each of her sister's children, that is to say, me and my sisters. From Clarissa's expression I divined that the cost of the trip to London had been more than worthwhile. Then came a great surprise in three separate legacies, each of five thousand pounds, to Godfrey, to Joe, and, to my utmost amazement, to myself, should I be found yet living. What touched me more than the money itself (though I freely confess money always touched me), was the idea that for all those years Aunt Madge had never given up hope that I might yet have survived. This seemed to me as great a demonstration of the power of love, in the face of such overwhelming odds, as any.

Clarissa and company were in disarray. They would have been quite happy with their ten guineas, I knew, had not, in their eyes, far greater riches gone to such dubious beneficiaries. Joe they had treated all day as a servant, despite being informed he was Aunt Madge's ward; Godfrey they had mocked and sneered at; and myself they had done their best to shun and humiliate. Why them and not us? I could see them thinking.

Diana's husband rose to his feet, and I do not pretend to recall the legal terms he used but, in short, he contested the will. Rather than feel in any sense inhibited, he seemed provoked by the immediate flurry of gasps around the room.

"Who, exactly, are these people? I should like very much to know." Mr Pincher had adopted the tone of the courtroom advocate. "It is my deep suspicion that this blackamoor, this so-called secretary, and this… what shall we call her before ladies? … inveigled their way into Mrs Hardcastle's affections when she was incapacitated both in body and in mind."

This brought cries of support and protestation on all sides.

"Gad, now my blood's up, I am a dangerous person!" exclaimed Jasper, leaping to his feet and laying his hand on his sword. I was aware of a banging sound, and as everyone else became aware of it, I saw that it was Dr Rookham, precariously balancing on one stick while he rapped repeatedly on the table with the other. One by one they all fell silent.

"If there is to be debate," he began, "and I, for one, intend to contribute to it, then let it be conducted through the good offices of Mr Fluke."

Mr Fluke, who I think had never seen such a reaction to the reading of a will, seemed flummoxed, and reluctantly agreed to act as chair as long as it was generally understood that the proceedings had no legal weight.

"Then, Mr Fluke, may I speak?" asked Dr Rookham.

Mr Fluke nodded.

"You all know I was the dear departed lady's family doctor and, I may say, honoured also to count myself her friend." Dr Rookham paused and cleared his throat. "What I have to say concerns young Joseph." Then he looked across at Frederick and asked: "Do I have your permission, sir?"

"Of course," said Frederick. This vastly intrigued everyone, although I knew what was coming.

"Joseph has loyally served Mrs Hardcastle from early childhood. Long before she was ill she declared her intention of making generous provision for his future. And if these proofs of love and devotion are not enough to satisfy you, I and Mr Fluke himself can attest that Joseph is the natural son of her late husband."

Diana squeaked in shock. Clarissa stuffed her handkerchief into her mouth in horror. Her reverend husband turned as white as Joseph was black.

"Ods bodikins, this is better than a play!" I heard Jasper say to Charlie. The pair were sitting directly in front of me and appeared to be becoming fast friends.

"I'll say!" agreed Charlie, and Lord A told them to be quiet.

"May we consider the matter of this young man's right to his inheritance closed?" asked Mr Fluke.

A nervous voice piped up from the back of the room.

"Mr Fluke, me and my brother should like to speak in favour of Mr Godfrey." It was Ted Potter, standing awkwardly, with his brother Reg, equally uncomfortable, beside him. "We were Mrs Hardcastle's footmen, Mr Fluke."

"Servants should be seen and not heard," declared Mr Pincher.

"Begging your pardon, sir," said Ted and promptly sat down. Reg pulled him to his feet again.

"We want to say, your worship," he began, even more nervous than his brother, "that we have seen with our own eyes, if it please your honour, the excellent service Mr Godfrey gave to our mistress. Your lordship could not find a better servant nor a truer friend than she had in him."

"As I said, he took advantage of a witless old woman! He is a filcher, a cadger, a jack-in-the-box, a Captain Sharp!" interrupted Mr Pincher, to cries of "hear, hear" from his faction.

"Sit down Mr Pincher!" ordered Mr Fluke. Diana gasped, I sensed half-admiringly.

"Mr Godfrey gave our mistress a home – gave me and my brother a home – when she lost hers in the great fire," continued Reg.

"All part of his plot! It's plain as day, he had her in his sights, and gained her trust only to gain her money! This man's a fool," cried Mr Pincher.

"Take that back, sir!" cried Ted, surprising everyone, including himself.

"Sit down, Mr Pincher!" shouted Janey, but then had the goodness to blush when all heads turned towards her.

Reg continued: "He showed the same kindness as Mrs Hardcastle herself, God rest her." He turned his gaze on Clarissa and Diana and their husbands as he added, "And I would take this opportunity to add that that good lady would feel ashamed – most bitterly ashamed – to be part of a family that can demonstrate such meanness of spirit as some of them have shown today." He was almost in tears by the time he sat down, to most touching applause.

"Outrageous!" spluttered Mr Pincher.

"May we move on?" asked Mr Fluke. "Before we do so, I should caution everyone here that to impugn the good name of a lady is a most serious matter and should not be lightly entered into."

I knew that no one could give such a good account of me as had been given to defend my friends, and that everything was now bound to come out. Accordingly, I stood up, and though Clarissa's and Diana's husbands pointedly remained in their chairs, all the other gentlemen rose.

"Please be seated gentlemen," I said in a voice that sounded far more assured than I felt. "To save the feelings of my family and friends," I began, "I am quite prepared to renounce my claim on my inheritance and have the sum divided between my sisters."

Above the murmurs of surprise which ensued, Mr Pincher's voice rose triumphantly. "There! That is legal!" he cried. "She has said it before witnesses!" Diana stopped clapping her hands in glee the instant she realised she was doing it, and Clarissa stuffed her handkerchief into her mouth once again in excitement. By his expression of supreme concentration, I guessed Clarissa's husband was calculating five thousand pounds divided by four.

"Mr Fluke!" Frederick was on his feet. What on earth was

he going to say? I prayed and prayed he would sit down and gestured to Godfrey to make him. But Godfrey chose not to see me. "I would not have my dear mother's wishes, as expressed in her will – which was made, incidentally, as Mr Fluke here will attest, when she was perfectly sound in mind and body, so let's have no more of those scurrilous imputations – as I say, I would not have her wishes over-ruled by anyone, for any reason." General applause broke out to the dismay of Clarissa and company. "Moreover, I would not have my cousin bullied out of what is rightfully hers for fear of what might be said about her character." Stop now, I thought. Please stop now. But he continued. "I should like us all to take a minute or so to examine our feelings and consciences."

"Yes, let us do that," said Mr Fluke. My sisters and their husbands conferred most earnestly in a huddle.

"How do you think it will end?" Charlie whispered to Jasper.

"Like all good tragedies, in a pile of dead bodies if anyone says anything about H," Jasper said ominously. I laid my hand on his shoulder and he looked at me with a rueful look which I hoped meant he understood I strictly forbade him killing anyone.

The conference broke up, and by the looks on their faces I guessed the prosecution was to continue.

"We are not at all sure, Mr Fluke," Mr Pincher said, and I sensed a courtroom flourish approaching, "whether that woman actually *is* our sister H!" In the uproar that followed, in which even Dr Rookham rose to his feet protesting, I detected that Mr Pincher had pursued a line of argument not altogether approved by his clients. Defeated, he gave way to Reverend Grimwade, and the furore died down.

"The question to which we should all like an answer," Reverend Grimwade intoned, as though invested with the authority of an invisible pulpit around him, "is: where has our sister been, and how has she supported herself, since she left our aunt's house in Cheapside in the plague summer?"

As Janey later observed, you could have heard a mouse

fart in the silence that followed this question; the question I had been dreading since I first sold myself to Pinky in a room above a coffee-house. I shut my eyes and gathered my strength and was about to rise to speak when I heard Frederick's voice.

"Because an explanation is demanded, it does not follow that one should be given," he began. "However, it is meet that the truth be known. Mr Pincher has been an admirable representative for the prosecution, and I now appoint myself counsel for the defence." You would have thought that Frederick had studied for the bar, rather than the clergy, as he now addressed the assembly with the ease of the practiced lawyer. He turned to me: "With your permission, of course, cousin."

I realised I was gaping like everyone else, and nodded in submission and resigned myself to my fate.

"The facts I lay before you I have learned over a period of time from eye-witnesses whom I wholly trust. As a result of inhuman treatment by my late brother and infamous sister-in-law, and in the absence of her protector, my aunt, my cousin here was turned out of the home she had made in Cheapside. Friendless and penniless, alone in the plague-ridden city, what was she to do?" He paused, allowing this to sink in. "What indeed *could* she do?" He allowed it to sink in even more.

"Is it better to die with a blameless reputation or to survive at any rate? Is a good reputation worth starving for?" He fixed his gaze on Mr Pincher: "Is a good name worth half-killing your wife?" Then on Diana: "Is a good name worth being beaten half to death?" Then on Clarissa: "Is the good opinion of the neighbours worth abandoning a sister to the workhouse?" (He referred, of course, to Grace.) "Is the good opinion of the world worth abandoning that sister's defenceless child to the parish?" Then to Clarissa's husband: "What is a good name worth when it is purchased on such terms? When you arrive at St Peter's gates, do you think he will ask you whether you have kept a good name? Or will you be asked whether you treated your brothers and sisters on Earth with kindness and compassion? And do you think God would have wished H to die of starvation when her life had barely begun, rather than preserve the life that He gave her, and go on to do the best she could?"

"How dare you speak to me of God!" growled Reverend Grimwade, his face now almost purple with rage.

"Over-ruled," barked Mr Fluke, forgetting he was not a real judge in a real court, and as entranced as everyone else by Frederick's performance.

"Had H starved to death, as some of you would presumably have preferred, to keep her precious good name, Joe here might yet remain in the miserable condition she found him, a slave to a villainous brute. Mr Godfrey is here today because she did not die, but lived to find him, fainted away in the street for pure hunger, and helped him. My dear mother should have died before this, in the great fire, had H not saved her. Weigh a good name in the balance against these actions, and which will be the lighter, do you think?"

Here Jasper went to put his hand up like a good schoolboy who knows the answer, but Charlie gently restrained him. Lord A rose to his feet.

"I should like to add that Miss H did my own family a great service, for which we will always be in her debt," he said, and turned and bowed to me before resuming his seat.

Jasper then got up and said, "And I want to say... Damn and blast it all, she won't say she'll marry me—"

"And he's an *owl*!" chipped in Janey.

"That's right, Janey," rejoined Jasper. "And I'd say that makes her standards pretty high! I haven't the faintest idea why you've all got it in for H, but I'm sure she don't deserve it. That's all." And he sat down.

"And, your honour," Janey piped up again, "she saved my baby's life." Thankfully she did not go into further details.

Clarissa's party saw that they risked being vanquished

from the moral high ground and now could barely even look each other in the eye, let alone face the rest of the company.

"Well," said Mr Fluke after a few moments. "Am I to understand that this will is *not* now to be contested?"

"I have not done, sir." Reverend Grimwade rose to his feet again. "The Church," he intoned, "is not to be dishonoured thus with talk of weights and balances. You, sir, are no St Peter. It is not for you to judge."

"I do not judge," rejoined Frederick. "I merely ask that others also refrain from judging."

"I perceive you are an honest man, cousin," said the vicar, "for I may call you that, may I not?"

"We are closer, sir. Brothers, in God's eyes," said Frederick.

"Indeed. And Cain and Abel were brothers, were they not?" and here for the first time I discerned my brother-in-law's vanity, as I saw – only momentarily and fleetingly – that he looked to the rest of his cabal for approval of the effect he hoped to produce. At that second I began not to be afraid of him. He was a man, like other men. And other men was a subject on which I was comprehensively well-versed. "These testimonials regarding our sister's charitable actions are touching indeed. But they do not address the main question. Are you, an honest man, giving us to understand that our sister was never..." and here he paused for what he must have presumed to be dramatic effect, "... an *actress*?"

Here the cabal gasped, as though the very word could contaminate. Frederick looked as astonished as I felt.

"An *actress*?" he repeated.

"Playhouse trash. The sweepings of the stage. A player. Call it what you will, it is all the same. We have heard the rumours."

Frederick looked at me, nonplussed. I decided to speak for myself.

"Brother, I may honestly say I have never been upon the stage, since it matters so much to you. But I am proud to have known players and counted them my friends. I think there are far worse things than being an actress." I sat down.

"I think there are not," said Reverend Grimwade. And that was that. He sat down, somewhat deflated.

"Is that all?" asked Mr Fluke. "Am I *now* to understand that this will is *not* to be contested?"

"Yes, you are, Mr Fluke," said Frederick firmly, and no one raised a murmur against him.

"Good. Then I bid you all good day."

78

larissa, Diana, and their husbands were the first to leave the Lamb and Flag and we doubted we should see them at The Mermaid. We all followed them downstairs where Lord A's coach was waiting at the door.

"I did you wrong, H," he said as we parted, "and I am truly sorry for it."

"Oh, all water under the bridge, I assure you," I said.

He embraced me, and as he did so, whispered in my ear: "Marry Jasper."

It seemed my friends had been talking. Then he stepped into the carriage and waited for Charlie, who had been deep in conversation with Jasper.

"Dear H," said Charlie, taking my hands in his. "How can I thank you? For everything?"

"Dear Charlie," I said. "Just be happy."

"May I kiss you?" he asked.

"I think better not," I said. And with his dear little bow he was into the coach and away.

Jasper appeared.

"Well if it ain't... I say, H, you ain't crying are you old girl? Come, come, now, or your paint will run."

"I'm not wearing paint!" I said, taking his proffered handkerchief.

"Well, you should. Your nose has gone red and your eyes are sort of... piggish," he decided. "Come inside," and he led me back into the tap room, where I said my farewells to Mr Fluke and Dr Rookham, and finally fell into a chair by the fire. I felt utterly exhausted. All who remained, I considered, were those very dearest to me: Janey and Thomas, Godfrey and Frederick, Joe and, after today, Jasper finished up the list.

"I propose," said Godfrey, filling us each a glass, "a toast to dear Aunt Madge followed by dinner at The Mermaid."

We all agreed. And after we had toasted Aunt Madge, Jasper toasted me, then I toasted all my friends, and we poured ourselves into a coach (though the newlyweds chose to ride atop, for the sun had come out) and made a very merry party down to Wapping.

"Have you given up your campaign to make H marry you, Jasper?" teased Frederick, a little drunk by now.

"Hang a wife!" exclaimed Jasper, at least as drunk as Frederick. "What is she, but a lawful kind of manslayer? Every little hug in bed is a degree of murder."

We all stared at him.

"Jasper!" Godfrey exclaimed.

"It's the claret talking," said Frederick, amused.

"Actually, it's Mr Dryden," said Joe. "It's in a play."

"Yes, sir," said Jasper. "Mr Dryden has it all worked out. Marriage is poor folks' pleasure, that cannot go to the cost of variety, that's what he says. Damned clever fellow."

"And do you really mean it, Jasper?" asked Joe.

Jasper looked out of the window.

"Not a word of it, dear heart. But it consoles a fellow."

"Oh, poor Jasper!" I said and kissed him on the cheek, and the others laughed, but not unkindly.

"You know, H, if you wanted to be married, but did not want a husband, you could marry one of us," said Godfrey, meaning him or Frederick. Frederick blushed deeply.

"I don't know that Fred is so keen on the idea," I said.

"Oh no, I just... actually... that's a rather good idea Godfrey. We could all live together... "

"... And it would look well in the eyes of the world... " added Godfrey.

"Damn and blast the eyes of the world!" said Jasper. "And what about me?"

"You could visit!" I said. "We could revive Aunt Madge's monthly dinners."

"Weekly," said Jasper. "Daily. What do you think, Joe?"

"I think I would like us all to be together better than anything in the world," said Joe, looking steadily out of the window, "and I think Aunt Madge would too." And I realised he did not jerk as he used to, and then recollected that I had not seen him twitch for some time. Perhaps everything was mending now.

79

ur party was given the warmest possible reception at The Mermaid, and Grace placed us at a table at a large window affording a fine prospect of the Thames. To tell you all Grace and Frankie's adventures since we last met, and how they had found each other at the last, would make a whole book in itself, and moreover one that only they could write, but suffice it to say that they had built a fine business together and it was easy to see had gained the respect and affection of their salty customers, who regarded their special visitors with open and bemused curiosity.

I cannot say whether I was surprised to see my old friend the sea captain enjoying a pipe with his jug of ale, as I had known he frequented the inn, but I was certainly pleased. Being a man of surprisingly delicate sensibilities, seeing I was with friends, and gentlemen among them, he did not immediately approach me, but when I went to him he greeted me warmly and was delighted to learn that Frankie and Grace were my sisters and said they were mighty fine women and he would do anything in the world for them. He then fell easily into conversation with Jasper and Joe. I used to feel a deal uncomfortable when customers of mine got their heads together but realised that I no longer thought of either Jasper or the captain in that way, which perhaps meant I had ceased to think of myself in that way. In my mind I had quit the game already, it seemed. But I did not have time to dwell on this now as I had much to catch up with my long-lost sisters.

When we had eaten, and everyone was most affable, and I saw my friends were in conference in the corner with the captain about something, I took the opportunity to put a question I had been burning to ask to Grace and Frankie.

"I do not wish to revisit all the past," said I, "but satisfy me on one point. Do you have any idea what my real name was? I mean my full name? The name that H stood for?"

Frankie laughed.

"Don't you know?" she said. "No, of course you don't, you're the youngest, how could you?"

I was still none the wiser and indicated as much.

"Who taught you your alphabet?" asked Frankie.

"Evelyn, I think," I said.

"And how did she teach it?" asked Frankie. "D'you recall?"

This seemed an extraordinary odd question until I began to consider the answer. It was a sort of a rhyme which began with the names of our brother and sister who had died before I was born and then ran through ours.

"A is for Abraham," I began, remembering, "B is for Belinda,

C is for Clarissa, D is for Diana,
E is for Evelyn, F is for Frances,
G is for Grace and H is for *me*,
then I, J, K, L, M, N, O, and *P*,
Q is a question, the answers it's *said*
R: S, T, U, V, W, X, Y, and Z.

But I still don't understand. 'H is for me.' What does it mean?"

"Father was nothing if not methodical," said Frankie. "We were named alphabetically, and when they got to H, Mother and Father could not agree. Father wanted Hannah and Mother wanted Harriet, or Mother chose Hermione and Father chose Hephzibah, I can't recall now, but they never could agree. Probably for the only time in her life, Mother refused to back down for some reason – remember she was dying – and so, due to their combined stubbornness, you remained 'H'."

There it was. I was, after all, really H, merely H; it was my name. It didn't stand for anything else, it was itself. I really was uniquely, completely, H. And after all this time, considering this name had served me well enough, I wondered whether I really needed to add another to it.

"Godfrey," I called. "Guess what – my name is really H, nothing else, just H."

"Does this mean your Halcyon days are over?" quipped Godfrey.

"When you were green in judgement?" chipped in Frederick.

"Green as a gooseberry," I answered, considering the pair of them.

But before either had a chance to respond to my teasing, the captain, who had been talking quietly with Grace, and seemed to have gained her approval, approached me and said, "As this is a rare visit to my neck of the woods, I wonder whether you would honour me by a tour of my vessel?" This odd offer was made more curious by the looks passing between Janey, Jasper, Frederick and Godfrey, evidently meaningful to them, but inscrutable to me.

"What are you up to?" I asked, somewhat suspicious.

"Oh do say yes, H," said Joe. "I should love to go on a ship."

"Humour me, my dear. For old time's sake. She's just alongside," said the captain, taking my arm, and leading me and my entourage out onto the quay. Now I do not pretend to know much about ships, and the *Now Or Never* looked much like any other, but I allowed the dear old captain to lead me onto the deck, where he stood expectantly. What he was expecting I did not know, so I said it was a very nice ship. Turning back to the quayside I saw that all the sailors were turning out of The Mermaid and joining my friends and family gazing towards me and the captain. I wondered whether there was something behind us they were looking at, but looked and saw there was nothing out of the ordinary.

"Am I missing something, sir?" I asked the captain.

"I must confess I have got you here under false pretences," he said. And I thought he said, "I mean to marry you." My head spun, and the slight movement of the ship combined with the wine I had drunk was making me feel powerful queasy now. Had I heard aright? Was he mad? Was he going to cut us adrift and carry me off to foreign parts? Or was it all this talk of marriage in the coach that had confused my poor mithered brains?

"But I don't want to marry you," I murmured.

I must have staggered as the captain caught me by the arm and supported me. "Oh not to me, my heart. To him." And I felt a strong arm round me, and saw Jasper had caught me. The captain seemed to drift away.

Jasper held me by the waist with his unmerciful grip and cried, "Alone at last! Marry me, H! Just say it! Just say it now! You can learn to love me later!"

"Jasper!" I exclaimed, coming to my senses, highly embarrassed, turning away from the gaze of the crowd of sailors which seemed to be growing horribly, as they recruited their friends to observe the spectacle.

"What are you waiting for, H?" shouted Janey.

"Yes, what are you waiting for, H?" asked Jasper, pulling me close to him and kissing me powerful hard. "Am I not," and I saw his lip tremble, "yet good enough for you?" I felt a great rush of warmth for Jasper at that moment, and suspected to my considerable discomfort that I had begun learning to love him already.

"Oh Jasper," I cried, turning away, and happening to look upriver to my beloved bridge. "If I married you," I found myself saying, "could we live in a house on the bridge?" What had possessed me? I knew not.

Jasper sounded as though he would explode with joy.

"If you married me, we could live on the Moon for all I care!" he said, and as he gripped me even harder I felt that he was trembling and saw that there were tears in his dear eyes. "I would be the best husband, H. I promise. I will try to deserve you. Damn it all, H, say yes."

"And could I keep my own money?"

"Of course. Mine too."

"You know I can't have children," I added.

"We shall get a little dog," said Jasper. "Like the one you used to have."

And then I saw that there was no other remedy, for him or for me.

"Then yes!" I heard myself cry.

"Yes!" he shouted, throwing his hat in the air. "She said yes!" Then he danced me in a most undignified jig around the deck and the sailors all cheered and even the old captain wiped his eyes, before stepping forward and gesturing for quiet.

"Who gives this woman away?" he asked.

"We do," called Frederick, as he, Godfrey and Joe scrambled aboard, with somewhat indecent haste to be rid of me, as I later pretended to protest.

"But we cannot be married now!" I cried. "Not here! We must have a priest, and a church!"

"On a long voyage, where there is no priest, the captain is sometimes obliged – and authorised, I may say – to act in his place," said the cunning old sea dog. "Have you not been, as I am given to understand by your friends, on a long journey?" he asked, with a twinkle in his eye. "And am I not a captain? And is this not a ship? And are you not willing?" He winked conspiratorially at Jasper. And I realised that for once in my life I had been utterly outmanoeuvred.

And so Jasper and I were wed on the *Now Or Never*, and I became the Countess of Tewkesbury. As I write, he has been far more than a good enough husband, and I have come to discover that happiness may be more than merely the state of things not going wrong, and that, as Aunt Madge said, it is good to love.

And though we could not have children of our own, Grace was later kind enough to give us the care of one of hers. So there is a little Jasper to inherit the title, and Grace has recently intimated she may be kind enough to supply another. We strongly suspect we may grow to be quite a large family on the basis of Grace's well-known kindness. And I do not yet know whether that is the end of my story, for the truth is, as I have before observed, that real life, unlike fiction, is untidy, and you do not know what is the beginning, or the middle, or the end, until it is all far too late.

ACKNOWLEDGMENTS

Thanks to Sarah Hosking and the Hosking Houses Trust, who gave me space and time to write, and Jacky Bratton, without whom the book would probably never have been written at all. Thanks to the book's champions and author's supporters, Matthew Burton, Midge Gillies, Kate Penning, Jem Poster, Ian Shircore, Leslie Stewart, everyone at Legend Press and, last but not least, my wonderful agent, Eli Keren.